Bound by Passion, Divided by Desire...

Wendy and Sarah and Charlotte—three special women, so different on the surface, so similar beneath the facades they showed to the world. Each of them hoped going to Adams College would be a chance for a new beginning, a place to escape their pasts. But prejudice and snobbery soon shattered their young girls' dreams. Brought together by pride and pain, Wendy the rich girl, Sarah the rebel, and Charlotte the outcast formed their own sorority, thumbing their noses at fate. Then from a dangerous summer in Mexico when each must come to terms with desire, to the years of marriage and new and destructive passions, *Sorority* is the story of their friendship and their lives...the odysseys of three extraordinary women you will never forget.

Sorority

Also by Sheila Schwartz

LIKE MOTHER, LIKE ME
THE SOLID GOLD CIRCLE

ATTENTION: SCHOOLS AND CORPORATIONS

POPULAR LIBRARY books are available at quantity discounts with bulk purchase for educational, business, or sales promotional use. For information, please write to SPECIAL SALES DEPARTMENT, POPULAR LIBRARY, 666 FIFTH AVENUE, NEW YORK, N Y 10103

**ARE THERE POPULAR LIBRARY BOOKS
YOU WANT BUT CANNOT FIND IN YOUR LOCAL STORES?**

You can get any POPULAR LIBRARY title in print. Simply send title and retail price, plus 50¢ per order and 50¢ per copy to cover mailing and handling costs for each book desired. New York State and California residents add applicable sales tax. Enclose check or money order only, no cash please, to POPULAR LIBRARY, P. O. BOX 690, NEW YORK, N Y 10019

Sorority

Sheila Schwartz

POPULAR LIBRARY

An Imprint of Warner Books, Inc.

A Warner Communications Company

For my agent, Harvey Klinger,
my editor, Bernard Shir-Cliff, and
my daughter, Elizabeth Schwartz

POPULAR LIBRARY EDITION

Copyright © 1987 by Sheila Schwartz
All rights reserved.

Popular Library® is a registered trademark of Warner Books, Inc.

The author wishes to acknowledge with thanks permission to use excerpts from the following works: "Ku Klux," by Langston Hughes. Copyright 1942 by Alfred A. Knopf, Inc. Reprinted from *Selected Poems of Langston Hughes*, by permission of Alfred A. Knopf, Inc.
Invisible Man, by Ralph Ellison. Copyright 1952 by Ralph Ellison. Reprinted by permission of Random House, Inc.
I Have a Dream, by Martin Luther King, Jr. Copyright 1963 by Martin Luther King, Jr. Reprinted by permission of Joan Daves, 59 East 54th St., New York, N.Y. 10022

Cover photograph by Bob Wolfson

Popular Library books are published by
Warner Books, Inc.
666 Fifth Avenue
New York, N.Y. 10103

A Warner Communications Company

Printed in the United States of America

First Printing: February, 1987

10 9 8 7 6 5 4 3 2 1

CONTENTS

PART ONE:	The Sorority	1
PART TWO:	Careers	171
PART THREE:	Coming Apart	273
PART FOUR:	The Survivors	377

PART ONE

The Sorority

CHAPTER
One

For the rest of her life, Wendy da Gama was to remember the enchantment of her sister's coming-out party, held on her seventeenth birthday. Her mother, Edita, had worked for over a year with the staff of their hotel, the Virgin Isles da Gama, to make certain that every detail was perfect. Tables with snow-white linens and magnificent orchid centerpieces had been set up around the banyan tree in the central courtyard of the majestic hotel, and the lush tropical foliage had been draped with hundreds of little lights, making it look like fairyland. Even the weather that night was perfect. A soft balmy breeze blew across the courtyard, and a full moon lit up the breathtaking expanse of beach and ocean.

It was 1938. In Europe, Hitler's armies were on the march, and most of the United States had still not struggled out of the Depression, but the world's problems were remote and rarely discussed within the confines of this grand old hotel. Here was only wealth, beauty, and privilege. The very best people came to the hotel, year after year. New guests were accepted only on the recommendation of one of the regular guests.

Edita always said that her guests were her friends. On this special night, their friends had come from the mainland enclaves of the rich to celebrate the event. William Randolph Hearst and Marion Davies were there. A contingent of Hollywood people including Norma Shearer and Irving Thalberg, Darryl F. Zanuck, James Kevin McGuinness, Anita Loos, and Zoe Akins had arrived earlier that afternoon.

Balenciaga and Coco Chanel, who made all of Edita's clothes, were there, as was Elsa Schaparelli, who made Edita's hats. The guest list was a copy of the social register. Everyone was rich, everyone was successful, and everyone was happy. The diamonds worn by the women reflected the twinkling lights that surrounded them.

Francisco da Gama looked at his family with pride. Edita was still the most beautiful woman on the island, and he loved her as devotedly as on the day of their marriage. And his daughters were equally beautiful. What an extraordinary picture they made sitting at the head table together. All three had lustrous, thick raven-black hair, well-formed heads that they held regally high, straight, perfect noses, flashing smiles, and flawless, creamy white complexions. Their eyes were dancing, long-lashed, fringed violet pools, and their long-legged, supple bodies in white lace Balenciaga gowns were as beautiful as their faces.

"A superb evening, my darling," Francisco whispered to Edita, as Paula blew out the seventeen candles on her cake and the guests burst into a joyous chorus of "Happy birthday to you."

"Isn't this absolutely the most marvelous night of your life?" Wendy asked, excitedly squeezing her sister's hand. Paula turned to look at her, and Wendy looked back in amazement. Paula's eyes were filled with tears.

Francisco, looked with pride at his daughters. Just what women should be! he thought. Chaste and innocent, and yet they were modern American girls, speaking neither Edita's native Russian nor the Spanish of his ancestors. The nuns had taught them well. They shone with inner light, like rare and precious gems, and were as modest as they were beautiful. He would marry them to royalty! No one remembered that Edita was Jewish. She'd converted many years before. Perhaps there had been marranos among *his* Spanish ancestors. What matter? He'd heard that even the Mountbattens had a strain of Jewish blood. It would not hurt his daughters. With their beauty and breeding and his vast holdings on the island, he anticipated no obstacles to his plan. They would have the best for the rest of their lives.

He smiled at Paula. "Are you happy, my darling? Is it possible that I see tears in your eyes?"

"Tears of happiness," she murmured. "I hope this evening will not tire you, Papa."

He reached out and gently caressed her glorious hair.

"There is no need to worry, my daughter. God watches over me. He has given me two fine daughters, a kind and beautiful wife, good friends, a good reputation, and vast wealth. God smiles on me. He does not intend to take me yet."

Edita turned toward her husband with tender concern on her face. She had not forgotten his heart attack, which he now passed off as a simple bout of indigestion. "But you do look tired. You must go up to bed as soon as possible."

"Very well."

Then he rose, still every inch the proud Spanish grandee although he had aged since the attack, and thanked his guests once more for coming. The party was over.

The moment they were freed, the two girls raced toward their suite on the third floor of the hotel, dropped the constricting dresses on the floor, and quickly pulled on simple shorts and cotton blouses. Wendy looked longingly at the stack of gifts piled beside Paula's bed, but Paula said, "Not now. I have to talk to you where nobody can hear. Let's go down to the beach."

"A secret! How exciting!" Usually Paula told everything to their mother, but now she had a secret for Wendy. It made her feel so grown-up. But before they could escape, their nurse Carmen came waddling in. Sighing in disapproval, she bent to pick up the expensive dresses from the floor. "Where you two off to this time of night?"

Paula's voice was as sweet and guileless as usual. "Just going for a little walk, Carmen dear."

"Remember your papa don't want you fooling around with no guests."

"We'll remember, Carmen."

Each of them dropped a kiss on the smooth, plump cheek of their nurse, then ran down the stone steps to the beach. Without speaking, they walked until the lights of the hotel were far behind them. Then Paula dropped to the sand hugging her knees to her forehead and resting her face on them. "Let's sit here."

"At last!" Wendy dropped beside her. "I can't wait another minute. I bet I know what it is. You're in love again."

For a few moments, Paula said nothing, and then, shockingly, she exploded into noisy sobs. Wendy looked at her in astonishment. "Paula darling! What's wrong? Did somebody hurt your feelings? The boys were all fighting over you. And so many presents! What is it, darling?"

The torrent of weeping continued until Paula had regained some control. Then, in a voice filled with horror, she whispered, "I'm pregnant."

Wendy trembled in shock. "Pregnant? But that's not possible. How can it be possible?"

"How do you think? Don't be a little idiot. You know the facts of life." Despite their parochial school education, life at the hotel had made them both sophisticated beyond their years.

"But who? Where?"

"Where is right here. On the beach! At this very spot. And 'who' is someone you don't know."

"You mean a guest?"

"No. I mean the thin boy who plays the steel drum."

"Oh, I've seen him. But Paula. How can that be? He's black!"

"That's the point," Paula said. She wrapped her arms around her knees again and began to keen and moan.

"Oh, don't cry, Paula dear. I love you. I don't want you to be unhappy." She fluttered frantically, floundering for wisdom that was far beyond her. "Tell me about it. Please."

"I never meant for it to happen," Paula sobbed. "It was just by accident, unexpected. I was walking along here one night and I saw him. Just sitting here, looking out to sea, under a bright, full moon. I recognized him right away from the band. He looked so handsome, burnished wood like an African sculpture. It was the way he held his head, I think. His chin pointed up so I could see the cords of his neck, and his eyes looking far out to sea. When he first caught sight of me he looked frightened, as if I would scold him for being here. But then I smiled and nodded to reassure him. He knew who I was, of course, so he smiled that kind of remote token smile, you know the way they sometimes do, just expecting me to walk on past.

"At first that was exactly what I was going to do. But then, all of a sudden I wanted to talk to him, get to know him. I was filled with curiosity. What did he do when he wasn't playing at the hotel? What did he think about? What did he feel? I thought to myself that I had never really in all my life had a conversation with a black person who wasn't a servant.

"It was such a beautiful night. Winds from heaven! So I sat down, and for a while he was uneasy, and it was hard to make conversation until he said, 'Hey, listen to this song. A new one from Jamaica.' Then he began to sing, such a sweet, clear tenor. It rang out across the waves, the stars were whirling, and then, suddenly, just like that, I was on fire. Yes, on fire. It wasn't that I wanted to make love. I wanted to touch him. Just touch him, kiss him, feel his skin touching mine, lie there in his arms with the sound of the waves breaking and the stars spinning around us.

"Everything about him filled me with a sense of beauty. I think black people are more beautiful than white people. I guess I've always thought so in my heart."

Her words were revelatory to Wendy. I guess I've always thought so too, she suddenly realized.

"The breeze was like velvet fingers," Paula continued, "and I could smell the sea and hear the waves pounding in my ears. It got stronger and stronger. I felt as if I'd break apart if I couldn't touch him.

"When he finished his song, he looked at me, and then he looked away. I reached out and ran my hand across his smooth cheek, and pulled his lips to mine. The next thing I knew we were making love. His lips tasted fresh and sweet, his skin was firm and smooth as polished ebony, and his body was so graceful, like a limbo dancer's. We stayed together for about half an hour, and then we parted without a word. We both knew that it could never happen again. Somehow, I never thought I would get pregnant."

"Oh, Paula! Maybe you're not! Have you been to the doctor?"

"The doctor? Of course not. In one hour, everybody on the island would know."

"Then how can you be sure? Maybe you're wrong. People miss periods, don't they?"

"But I've missed four. I've been starving myself to stay thin so nobody would suspect. Even you and Carmen haven't noticed. But feel this, Wendy." She took Wendy's hand and held it against her stomach. "Now tell me if I'm wrong."

Wendy held her hand there, silently praying that nothing would happen. And then it came, a slight movement, something moving; a little outward push. She pulled her hand away, as if it had touched a flame, and shivered.

"I don't know, Paula. Maybe you're right but I'm not sure. I think I did feel something." She threw her arms around her sister. "But maybe I'm wrong. I make mistakes lots of times." She sat there hugging her fiercely, loving her so achingly much that it hurt, and wanting desperately to help. She felt so useless.

"What are we going to do, Paula?"

Panic flared in Paula's beautiful eyes. "I don't know. I just don't know. I've been going crazy worrying about it. I think it's too late for an abortion even if there were somewhere to get one. Do you have any ideas?"

Wendy wrung her hands in distress. "Of course not. You have to tell Mama. Right away! She'll understand! You know she will. She understands everything."

Edita had the same sophisticated attitude toward sex that she had toward most things. As hostess for a romantic hotel that catered to guests who were rich enough to do exactly as they pleased, she had to be tolerant.

"I don't know if she'll be so understanding about this, Wendy. But it's not Mama I'm worried about. I'm mostly worried about Papa. You know she'd tell him. She tells him everything, and I'm afraid this would give him another heart attack and kill him." She started to sob again. "Did you see how proud he was tonight? I never wanted to disappoint them. I love them both so much. I just can't tell them."

"We could run away."

"Don't be stupid. This is an island. And even if we got to the mainland, where could we go? Florida? And then give birth in some cracker hospital to a black baby? And then what? Sooner or later everybody would find out. We'd never live down the scandal. Maybe people would even stop coming to the hotel." Wendy gasped. They had been trained to view the hotel as a sacred trust.

The Sorority (9)

"Let's tell Carmen, Paula. She'll give you a voodoo charm."

"No! She'd go right to Mama. I guess I just have to think about this some more myself. Don't tell anyone, please."

"Of course I won't. Not if they tear out my fingernails or boil me in oil."

Paula looked at her tenderly. "There's not much chance of that. Let's go home Wendy. I think I know what to do."

"I love you, Paula. I wish that I was smarter for you."

"I love you, too. Tomorrow, you can go through all of my gifts and take anything you like. Anything!"

Wendy lay awake for a long time that night, worrying about Paula. If only there were something she could do to help. She finally dozed off and then, toward dawn, was awakened by the sound of Paula moving about in her adjoining bedroom. When she heard the door to the hall open, she quickly threw on shorts and a blouse and followed, wanting to be there if Paula needed her but anxious not to intrude if she wanted to be alone. It was light enough for her to see that Paula was wearing a bathing suit. So that was it! She was going for a swim. Edita had always forbidden them to swim when there was no lifeguard, but Paula was a wonderful swimmer. And Wendy would keep an eye on her from a distance.

Paula walked along the beach for half an hour until she reached the base of the high cliff from which native boys dove for pennies thrown by guests on cruise boats, and immediately she began to climb. Wendy hated the spot, hated the very idea of boys' risking their lives for pennies and the amusement of indifferent people. She always closed her eyes each time a boy jumped, terrified at the possibility of disaster.

She watched from the base while Paula climbed. Many times they'd climbed up there together, shrieked and clutched each other in safe fear, then turned and clambered down again. But neither of them had ever gone up there alone before.

She hovered around in indecision. Should she climb up there to be with Paula or would Paula be annoyed at her intrusion? She couldn't decide so she sat down and waited until she saw Paula appear at the top, sit down cross-legged, and look out to sea.

Paula sat immobile for a long time. What was she doing? Perhaps Carmen had given her a charm to get rid of the baby, and it might spoil the charm if she interrupted. Edita always said that voodoo was just superstitious nonsense, but Paula might be trying it out of desperation. As a last resort! There was nothing to do but wait. The charm was bound to fail and after that Paula would have to tell her mother.

Still, Paula sat there, motionlessly contemplating the sea, probably waiting for the charm to work. Wendy lay down on her stomach and continued to watch. But the air was soft and balmy, and the roar of the waves gradually lulled her into a state halfway between wakefulness and sleep. Suddenly shocked awake, she sat up and looked at Paula. What was she doing now?

The sun was coming up, illuminating Paula's head and body with fire. She stood up, walked to the edge, and looked down at the sea. Wendy scrambled to her feet, intending to start up the cliff.

And then, suddenly, before her horrified eyes, Paula jumped off the cliff, head first, without spreading her arms for protection, as if she wanted to land on her head and die.

"No," Wendy screamed as her sister's body descended, "no, no, no." Then Paula was gone, and Wendy's screams were carried out to sea by the wind.

Still screaming, she ran to the water and plunged in. She swam around and around in desperation, until, exhausted, she crawled out onto the beach, gasping until she could breathe again. Then, weeping hysterically, she ran back to the hotel for help.

Gasping for air, dripping sea water, blood from a cut streaming down her face, she ran to the hotel, dashed across the lobby past the curious servants who were just beginning to set up for breakfast, and up the lushly carpeted stairs to Edita's suite. "Mama, Mama," she screamed, banging on the door. "Mama, Mama."

Edita flung open her door, took one look at the hysterical girl and instantly knew that something was very, very wrong.

She threw her arms around her and tried to keep her voice from quavering. "What is it? What is it?"

"It's Paula, Mama. Paula! She drowned! She drowned! She drowned!"

"Oh, my God. It can't be. No, it can't be. You must be mistaken. She's a wonderful swimmer."

She quickly threw on a robe. "Hurry, but be quiet. Let's not upset your father needlessly." They tiptoed past his suite, and then, swift as a whirlwind, Edita ran through the lobby, gathering up waiters, busboys, and Mario the night clerk, her husband's youngest brother. "Quickly show us where," Edita said, and they ran behind Wendy to the beach.

Deliberately turning left instead of right, she led them to a different stretch of beach. "Here," she said. "She was swimming here."

The runners stopped in confusion and looked about them. There was nothing to be seen except for eternal nature: sea, waves, rocks, and gulls. The breeze caressed them with mocking gentleness as another perfect island day began.

Edita, struggling for composure, turned to Wendy. "Think darling. Think. Are you absolutely sure that this was the spot?"

"Absolutely, Mama."

"But how can you be sure?"

"I just am."

Edita looked at her in perplexity, as if dimly sensing holes in her story and yet not quite able to come to grips with her vague and unformulated suspicions. Then she lit on something. "How come you're wet, but you're not wearing a bathing suit?"

"I didn't feel like swimming, Mama, but I ran in when Paula didn't come out. I looked for her, really I did." She began to sob heartbrokenly. On the verge of collapse herself, Edita held the girl tightly in her arms.

"I know you did your best. Carmen, take her home. We'll keep searching. Perhaps she's in her room by now."

Carmen grasped her firmly by the hand. "You bad girls," she wept as they walked. "Playing tricks. Sneaking away from Carmen. But she all right. Her not drowned. Not that Paula. Her swim like fish." Tears continued to flow down her face as she led Wendy back to her room, washed and bandaged her cut, and put her to bed.

"Stay with me, Carmen."

"Don't me always?" the nurse wept. "And for what? For this." She sat in the rocker beside Wendy's bed and wept and rocked and prayed. Wendy clutched at the lifeline of Carmen's hand until she fell into a deep sleep that was like a swoon of death. She awakened screaming in an hour and screamed for the rest of the day and through the night seeing, over and over again, Paula's body hurtling off the cliff and disappearing into the water far below.

They searched for Paula's body for a week before Francisco, reluctantly accepting her death, held a memorial service in their own chapel that had been built by his grandfather on the hotel grounds. Running a high fever, incoherent with grief, Wendy sat between her distraught parents at the service, irrationally consumed with guilt. She should have saved Paula. Why had she moved so slowly? Wouldn't it be better to have had the baby than to commit suicide and be consigned to the eternal flames of hell? Would good, kind, generous Paula go to hell? No. God couldn't be so mean. Probably there was no such thing anyway. That's what Paula had said. No hell and no heaven and no God! There was only guilt and sadness and loss.

If there were a God, how could He have let this happen? There could not really be a God, for any God worth worshipping would not have let this happen to Paula, would not have left Wendy in loneliness and perpetual torment, compelled to be the guardian of a terrible secret, the perpetrator of a lie, a would-be rescuer who had been unable to rescue, an outsider, a pariah, alone for the rest of her life, isolated in horrible grief that she could never share with anyone.

She held tightly to her father, but he was locked in numbness. Shrunken into himself, he looked more like eighty than sixty. His sobs rocked the chapel. "God has punished me," he wept. "Pride goeth before a fall." Edita, aware that she must be strong for all of them, held his hand and tried to comfort him. Her other hand held Wendy's throughout the service.

As Wendy listened to the priest, a bitter wind of loneliness swept through her. She knew that she was saying good-bye to more than Paula. She had been expelled from paradise. The old life was over. Nothing would ever be the same. *She* would never be the same. She had lost her innocence. All of her past values and beliefs, hopes and dreams had washed out to sea with Paula. Numbly, she leaned her head against Edita's perfumed shoulder, aching for sleep.

After the funeral, she stayed in bed for six months with a fever loosely diagnosed as mononucleosis. Time passed in a dream, and when she finally returned to life, unsteady on long, coltish legs, she was five feet eight, ravishingly beautiful, but curiously hollow inside. At the hotel, life went on as before, but for her the island was no longer Eden. It was tainted, spoiled, haunted by her memories of Paula. She could not return to the convent school and walk around each day pretending to believe in God. She could never again go to confession.

Edita hired a private tutor for her, but she was a poor student. Only music comforted her. She would sit for hours listening to records by Bix Beiderbecke, Sidney Bechet, Billie Holiday, Bessie Smith, and Louis Armstrong—wonderful jazz that friends brought from the mainland. She ached to escape from the island, to get away to where she would never again hear the pounding of the sea or smell the lush tropical blending of gardenias and eucalyptus. She dreamed of cities! She had made up her mind. She would never take over the hotel. The island would not be her future home.

Francisco never recovered from Paula's death. Overnight he became an old man, indifferent to the hotel, spending long hours on his knees at the chapel or sitting on the balcony with binoculars, gazing endlessly out to sea for his lost child. Edita, who up until then had not been involved in the business aspects of the hotel, immediately took over, maintaining the same high standards of service as before. For the guests, nothing had changed.

Edita continued to greet their guests with the same serenity and warmth, Pepe continued to run their superb kitchen and vegetable gardens, the housekeeping staff kept the rooms as immaculate as before, gardeners tended the same magnificent tropical gardens, and the same gay limbo music filled the air. Everything seemed the same. Only Paula was gone.

Their socialite guests came and went, and most of them never mentioned Paula. Occasionally one would murmur, "So sorry," to which Edita would briskly reply, "Thank you," and then immediately change the subject. Guests didn't like sadness, gloom, morbidity. They invested in expensive vacations in order to be happy, and Edita understood that very well. All traces of Paula were erased from hotel life as completely as they had been on the beach. But the walls of Edita's and Francisco's suites were filled with photographs of her, and each night, in the privacy of her own chambers, Edita permitted herself to weep.

Paula's room had remained untouched. But as soon as Wendy seemed restored to health, Edita insisted that she unlock the connecting door, go into Paula's room, unwrap the gifts, take what she wanted, and pack the rest for charity.

"I don't think that I can do it, Mama." Wendy shivered.

"I know it's hard, darling, but it has to be done. Do it today. Get it over with. I can't help you because we're expecting a cruise ship this afternoon, but I'll send Uncle Mario to help you." She sighed and shook her head. "Perhaps he can do at least that much right."

Uncle Mario, her father's youngest brother, was twenty years younger than he, about Edita's age. He lived alone in a small cottage on the hotel grounds and was not very bright, but he loved the hotel. It was his home, where he had grown up. It was his life. He was like an eager puppy when anyone asked him to help.

Francisco had tried him at a variety of jobs and finally put him on as night clerk where he could do the least amount of damage. Plump, round shouldered and homely, and so nearsighted that he even slept in his glasses, he had a kind nature and was totally devoid of malice. "I'll be glad to help you after lunch," he said. "I have nothing else to do."

He stood in the hallway while she unlocked the door that connected her room to Paula's. Before turning the key, she squeezed her eyes shut and prayed, let her be in there. Let all of this have been a dream. Let her be in there and I'll believe in you again. Then she flung the door open, but Paula's bed was still empty. Neatly stacked on the floor beside it were all of her gaily wrapped gifts, still waiting for the girl to whom they belonged. The sight of those waiting gifts and the memory of vanished happiness filled Wendy with such aching and yearning that she could feel her heart cracking all over again. Weeping, she flung herself onto the bed, pressing her cheek against Paula's pillow.

Mario pulled a chair up beside the bed and gently patted her heaving shoulders. She turned over on her back and looked at him. "How can a person just disappear from the earth, Uncle Mario? Where did she go?"

"Maybe," he said simply, "she went back to where she was before she was born. Back to the mind of God."

"I want to see her," she wept. "I want to be there with her. I miss her so terribly much."

Unaccustomed to dealing with emotions of any depth, he looked at her in dismay. He knew of only one solution.

"I'll be right back." He scurried from the room and returned almost immediately with two glasses and a bottle of brandy.

"This will help," he said. "It always makes me feel better. Drink up. At first it feels like fire in your belly. Then it starts to warm your soul."

She drank, coughed, and feared she'd throw up, but then, as he had promised, a delightful, healing warmth began to spread through her body. For the first time since Paula's death a feeling of calm descended on her. "More," she said. "More."

They sat on Paula's bed companionably, talking and drinking, and gradually her agony seemed to diminish. She had never before spoken more than a sentence to her uncle, dismissing him with the same contempt for his incompetence that her parents always had.

"How come you never married, Uncle Mario?"

"You really don't know?"

"No. I never even thought about it before." It was true that he was stupid and ugly, but he *was* a da Gama, and any member of their family was aristocracy on the island and could marry quite easily.

"Well, I'll tell you. The only woman I ever loved was your mother. I'll never forget the first time I saw her. It was around 1920 when she came here all alone from some little Russian village, got off the boat, and walked in here to ask for work. I was at the desk when she walked in. The most beautiful girl I'd ever seen. A vision! Proud, erect, beautiful, looking very much like you do now. When I asked her why she had come here, she told me in broken English that she was searching for a place where it was always warm. She was eighteen and I was twenty and I immediately fell head over heels in love with her. But she never even noticed me after she met your father. It didn't matter that he was twenty years older. It was love at first sight for them both. His first wife had died in childbirth, and he had been grieving for ten years. Every woman who came here threw herself at him, but he was waiting to fall in love again. They're still deeply in love with each other. Don't you worry. They'll get through this thing with Paula because they have each other."

She was a little drunk, so she was able to speak without weeping. "They have each other," she said sadly, "but Paula was my best friend. Now I have nobody."

"But, honey, that's not true. Not true at all. Your mama loves you. Your papa loves you. Now even more than before because you are all he has left. Everybody loves you. I have no children. Pepe has three ugly boys, but you are our only girl. Everybody loves you."

"Thank you," she said, putting her arms around his neck. They were so drunk that they fell back on the bed. He patted her beautiful hair, stroked her back, and kissed her lovely face. It felt lovely lying there that way; floating, drifting, for the moment not agonizing over Paula. She liked the way he smelled; a mixture of rum and good Cuban cigars.

And after awhile, not knowing how it happened or how he could have done such a thing, he found his hand moving across her perfect thighs and between her legs to her clitoris. Then gently, slowly, he began to stroke and stroke, and she arched her body against him, feeling new and indescribable comfort from his touch. "There, there," he said as he stroked. "There, there, my beautiful girl."

She felt herself sinking into pleasure. And after awhile she felt her thighs parting. She could feel his fingers gently pushing against her, slowly, slowly, slowly entering her. It hurt. She could dimly feel that through the brandy. But she didn't mind. This, or something like it, must have been what Paula felt on the beach that night. She liked the feeling of his fingers, stroking her clitoris and then moving inside her, back and forth, deeper and deeper. In a dream, she felt him move on top of her, spread her legs with his knees, and open his fly.

Passion and the brandy had made them so self-absorbed that they were aware of nothing outside of themselves. They did not hear Edita open the door, run to the gun room and return. They did not hear her until she screamed from the doorway, "Son of a bitch. This is the last straw." Raising the gun and taking careful aim, she fired it into the wall above Mario's head. He let out a scream of fear, like a cornered animal, and Wendy lay there drunk and cowering, her hands over her ears.

"I want you off this island in fifteen minutes, you bastard," Edita screamed, "or I'll blow your balls off. Just be glad that Francisco didn't find you."

Mario began to wail. "Forgive me, please. I didn't mean anything. Where will I go?"

"You should have thought of that before. I don't care where you go, but go. Fifteen minutes."

He stood there immobile, paralyzed, weeping and shaking and begging for forgiveness until she raised the gun and fired another shot over his head. He let out a scream of terror and scrambled out of the room like a frightened animal.

As soon as he had gone, Edita fell to her knees beside the bed and began to weep. "Oh, my poor darling. First Paula and now this. Forgive me, darling. It's all my fault. I sent him to help you. But I never guessed that he could do such a thing. To get you drunk and take you. Come, darling. Let's go to my bedroom."

She supported the staggering, bewildered girl to her bedroom, ran a hot oil bath in her onyx bathtub, lowered her into it, and tenderly washed her as if she were a little baby. Then she helped her out, gently dried and powdered her, dressed her in one of her best satin nightgowns, and lay down beside her in her large double bed.

"Your father must never know," she said. "After Paula, this would kill him."

"I won't tell, Mama. I'm good at keeping secrets. But won't he wonder where Uncle Mario is?"

"I'll think of something. I have to worry about you and your father. I cannot worry about Mario." She buried her face in her hands for a moment. "I always thought I was doing such a good job of protecting both of you, that my daughters would never know the sadness, fear, and poverty I knew as a girl in the shtetl. But everything was in vain! There is no protection from anything. Listen to me, my darling. You must forget all about this. Promise me no more sex until you're grown up and know what you're doing."

"I promise, Mama." It would be easy to keep that promise. For a long time sex would be inextricably linked in her mind to fear; the explosion of a gun, the bullet holes in the wall, and Paula's terrible suicide on the beach. "Please don't be sad about this, Mama. Please stop crying."

"All right, my darling. We'll both try to forget about this. We must try to be happy together in the few years we have before you go to college."

"I don't want to go to college, Mama. I'm not a good student and I hate school. I want to go to New York, to nightclubs and theaters and movies and museums. I want to hear lots and lots of jazz. Could you get me an apartment there instead of sending me to college?"

"You must go to college. I never had the opportunity."

"Oh, Mama. You're beautiful and elegant and smart. Nobody would ever guess you hadn't gone. Nobody cares."

"I care. I want you to have an education. I'll make a bargain with you, darling. You can have an apartment in New York City if you'll go to college at the same time. I heard one of our guests talking about Adams, a small girls' college on Long Island. It's elegant and private, rather like a finishing school, and all of the girls commute from the city. Perhaps you'd like that. But you have three years to decide. You might change your mind."

"I won't change my mind, Mama. That's excatly what I want. To live in New York City. I'll go to that school if you like."

Lying there in her mother's arms, still mellow from the brandy, she dared to ask a question she'd wanted to ask since Paula's death. "Did you love Paula more than me? Do you think the wrong daughter died?"

Edita tenderly kissed her cheek. "Oh, my darling, neither one of you should have died. Given the choice, I would gladly have died for Paula, but I was never given the choice. And I would die for you, too. So you must never think of that again.

"Life must go on. We will always grieve for Paula, but we will go on. The pain of that will fade for you and the memory of today will too. And you will go on and have a wonderful life. Now sleep, my darling." They fell asleep with their arms twined around each other.

Francisco never recovered. He died, a broken man, the year before Wendy left the island forever.

CHAPTER Two

On a beautiful spring day in 1937, thirteen-year-old Sarah Stern sat cross-legged on her brother's bed, watching him pack. From the window she could see the familiar, reassuring sights of Central Park, people playing ball at Sheep Meadow, riders cantering along the bridle path, the first yellow patches of forsythia. Spring was so beautiful in New York, but her soul felt the chill of winter. If only he would stay.

"Don't go," she begged him. "Please don't go to Spain. You'll get hurt. You'll get killed. Daddy will be angry. He'll blame Mom. He'll scream. Please, please Jimmy, don't go."

His packing done, he sat down beside her and took her hand. "I have to go."

"Why? Why do you have to go? What does Spain have to do with us? What do we have to do with Spain? You're the smartest boy at Townsend Harris. Everybody says so. And what about Columbia in September? Daddy already paid the tuition. He'll have a fit. Oh, why must you go away? You're my best friend. The only person I have to talk to."

She looked at him, her heart breaking with love. They were so much alike. They even looked alike. Both of them were small, dark-eyed and olive-skinned, with brown curly hair like her mother's. Their older brother, Claude, was tall and broad and fair like her father. They were both lousy reactionaries. You couldn't hold a logical conversation with them.

But she worshipped Jimmy. She and he had their own private world, and she guarded that secret. He had explained to her long ago that his political ideas and activities must be hidden completely from their father, the reactionary, autocratic Judge Stern.

He told her about the Oakies, the sharecroppers, about lynchings, the miners of Harlan County, the Wobblies, the Chicago Steel Massacre, and the Triangle Shirtwaist Fire. Sometimes when he talked about all of the injustice in the world his voice would crack and he would cry for all of the beaten and abused, for all of those he couldn't help.

Jimmy knew more than politics. He knew about everything: art, music, theater, literature. And he taught her everything. No other eighteen-year-old brother paid so much attention to a thirteen-year-old kid sister, and he didn't treat her like a kid. They were friends. He dragged her all over New York: to the Apollo Movie Theater on Forty-second Street to see foreign films, to plays, concerts, meetings, hootenannies, rallies, protests, sit-ins, classes at the Jefferson School. He was always talking, teaching, and explaining. He had helped her to understand their divided family.

"It's the political spectrum in microcosm. Dad and Claude are so anxious to be all-right-nik Jews that they're to the right of Tom Dewey. You and I are left. And in the middle, there's mom, a liberal. Know what a liberal is, Sarah? A liberal is a person who runs scared. They're even worse than people on the right because you think they're sympathetic. They say all the right words, but at every time of crisis they sell you out. Summer soldiers and sunshine patriots."

"Don't be hard on mom, Jimmy. She's just beaten down from a lifetime of his tantrums."

"I believe in free will. She has nothing to lose but her chains. She's a coward! If she ever once stood up to him, she'd start to live. What would he do? Kill her? Divorce her? Not a chance. Judge Stern would never do anything to damage his public image. Can you believe how much the world admires him? Nobody would believe what a thorough stinker he is."

Many times, her father had stood above poor, naked Jimmy, beating him endlessly with a heavy leather belt for some infraction or other, while she screamed and wept and begged him to stop. Even when she was only five years old she remembered begging her mother, "Stop him, Mommy. Please stop him. Please help Jimmy." But her mother never had. She couldn't help her children. She was too timid to even help herself.

To Sarah, Jimmy was a kind of miracle. A lifetime of beatings had not turned him into a beater but only made him more determined to protect those who were beaten. Despite his awareness of the cruelty and suffering of the world, he had a kind of divine innocence about him. Young as she was, she understood that he was a superior kind of human being.

She continued to plead. "If you really go, Jimmy, I think you should at least say good-bye to Mom. She'll be so upset when she finds you've gone. Maybe she is a coward, but she really loves you. Don't you love her at all?"

"Of course I love her. She's my mother. I love her and I pity her. But I sure as hell don't respect her. She's made us fight all her battles against him. She's a coward, and I don't want to be a coward like her. That's why I have to go. I just can't sit by and watch that lousy fascist Franco overturn a legally elected government with the help of Hitler and Mussolini. Roosevelt won't commit us to back the Spanish government and curb fascism, so people like me have to do it on our own. Spain's the right place to be now. Hemingway is there, and John Dos Passos and George Orwell and André Malraux. That's the place to stop Hitler. I want to be part of that fight. All our lives we've had this comfort and wealth and privilege, and we never did anything to earn it. I want to earn it. I don't think we were put on earth to have a free ride."

"Oh, Jimmy, Jimmy," she wept. "Please don't go."

"I have to go and you know it. Come on, Sarah. Would La Pasionaria cry? No. She said, 'It is better to die on your feet than to live on your knees. No pasaran.' That's the only way that I can live. But please don't worry. Nothing's going to happen to me. I'm too ornery to kill. My ship sails tonight and they'll get my letter the day after. For the sake of peace, just pretend you knew nothing about it."

He died in Spain. She never saw him again, but from that time on she looked for a man just like Jimmy to marry. Even though she seemed on the surface to be a happy, cheerful girl, she was always lonely for him. Her father, denouncing Jimmy for having caused his own death, forbade all mention of him in their home. Her mother retreated into herself and cried all the time, never understanding that Sarah's grief and loss might be as terrible as her own.

In the five years that followed, she went through the motions of ordinary daily life: private school, dinners at the club, summer camp in the Poconos, and dozens of public functions every year at which her father received some kind of legal, religious, or political award. She hated them all.

The big confrontation between Sarah and her father, which had been brewing for years, took place the night before Claude shipped out to the Pacific. They had argued many times before, of course, especially when he started to pick on her mother or made some dumb reactionary political statement, but she had always been careful not to push him too far, and he had never before hit her. That night he was especially on edge about Claude's departure, and any excuse would have been enough to set him off. She knew that something was wrong from the moment she sat down to dinner.

He glared angrily at her throughout the meal but waited to explode until after Mattie had finished serving coffee in the library. As soon as she had shut the door behind her, he reached into his desk, pulled out a copy of the *Daily Worker*, violently ripped it in half, and threw it into the fireplace.

Then looking as powerful and omnipotent as Jehovah, he turned to her in a fury, towering over the tiny, trembling, girl. "Now you listen here to me, young lady. While you live in my home and while I pay your bills, you are never again to bring home a copy of the *Daily Worker*."

She clenched her hands into little fists. "How dare you go into my room."

Claude, handsome in his first lieutenant's uniform, tried to make peace on his last night at home. "Don't let her upset you, Dad. She's just trying on poses like a little idiot. Jimmy filled her head with all kinds of nonsense, so she thinks it's romantic to be a radical. She doesn't even know what she's talking about. Ignore her! Let's not fight on my last night at home. She'll change as soon as she gets married."

"I will not change. I'll marry somebody like Jimmy, not like either one of you two dumbbells. Emma Goldman never changed and neither will I."

"I'm not interested in her future marriage. I won't have her bringing that rag into this house. She goes out of her way to thwart me. Her appearance is a disgrace. All that money wasted on a sheared beaver coat that she refuses to wear. She deliberately dresses like a bohemian, insults everyone we know with her radical ideas, and curses like a stevedore. Even Mattie complained to me that she's trying to teach her the "National Negro Anthem," whatever that is. I thought Negroes sang the "Star Spangled Banner" just the way whites do. And she drags home every stray dog she finds in the street."

Oh God, she hated him. How was it possible that a man who was so successful and so respected professionally could be such a total bastard at home? And Mattie's disloyalty in complaining to him really hurt. Her knees were trembling, but she forced herself to be brave like Jimmy. "How dare you call my friends stray dogs? How dare you burn up my property? I'm a person, not your slave. I'll read anything I please and think anything I like. I hate your reactionary politics and I hate the way you treat Mom. She's a person, not your whipping boy. You want everyone to be afraid of you. But why should we be? You're not J. Edgar Hoover. All you are is a capitalist lackey who became a judge because you know how to play the right political games. I hate everything you stand for."

Now that she had started, the floodgates were open and she couldn't stop. "You're a fascist tyrant. I have the only mother I ever heard of who doesn't know how to drive, doesn't have a checking account, has a tiny allowance doled out to her, and on top of all that, has to put up with your daily verbal abuse and rotten disposition. I just wish that all of your fancy friends could see what a son of a bitch you are to your family, while you put on that phony pose of compassion and wisdom for the world. I wish Mom would leave you. She has nothing to lose but her chains."

"Please stop," her mother bleated. "I don't mind. You're upsetting your father."

"I don't give a shit if I do," she sobbed, angry now also at her mother who would never fight her own battles. "Jimmy died in part because he was running away from him."

Now she'd done it. The composed, noble, calculatedly superior face of M. Alan Stern—noted Republican judge, life member of the Federation of Jewish Philanthropies, and chairman of the board of the Jewish Theological Seminary of America—blackened as his hand swooped out and smashed her full across the face, knocking her to the floor.

She pulled herself up and screamed again. "I hate you, I hate you. You bully! You fascist pig! Comes the revolution, all rotten capitalists like you will be exterminated, and when they put you in front of a firing squad, I'm going to stand there and cheer."

He stepped toward her again but she bolted, running to her room and locking the door. Then she threw herself across her bed, sobbing. She hated her family, she hated their boring friends, she hated their smug life. She had no one to talk to, nobody who shared her concerns.

Ever since Jimmy's death, she'd dreamed of escaping to an out of town college, but now because Claude was going off to war, her mother did not want her to be away, and her father was such a skinflint that he was undoubtedly delighted to save some money. So she was stuck at home for another four years and would have to commute to college on Long Island. Four more years of living with that fascist! There was nothing she could do about that, but the minute she graduated, she'd find a job, move out, and join the Party. She owed that to Jimmy.

"I won't forget you, Jimmy darling," she sobbed into her pillow. "I'll keep the faith. I promise you."

CHAPTER Three

Underneath Charlotte Lewin's clear, artless round blue eyes, porcelain skin, and mop of bright auburn hair, there was a deep and terrible grief, a heavy burden of sadness that she spent much of her energy hiding. Her mother was crazy. She had been crazy for as long as Charlotte could remember, but after Charlotte's brother died of polio, the madness had intensified.

Not only was she crazy in general, she was most specifically crazy in regard to Charlotte, begrudging her even the food she ate, refusing to buy her clothes, never permitting her to bring friends home with her. Her father, whom she adored, seemed to lack the will or energy to stand up to her mother. Each time she was hospitalized he struggled to get her home as soon as possible, instead of leaving her there so they could get a little peace. Some people might have called him saintly, but Charlotte thought he was weak, and anyway, what difference did it make which one he was. The net effect was exactly the same, and it made daily life as dangerous as inching through a mine field.

Charlotte's only joy in life was her painting. She didn't know if she had any talent. Maybe some, maybe none. But it didn't matter. The happiest moments of her life were when she was alone at work, creating something ordered and beautiful out of nothing.

They lived on the top three floors of a landmark brownstone in Brooklyn Heights. On the first floor was her father's dental office. The house symbolized her family, beautiful on the outside, chaotic within. People on walking tours sometimes stopped to admire the architecture of the house, but they had no idea of what lay behind its facade. The filth and chaotic housekeeping accurately reflected her mother's mental state. When Charlotte read newspaper reports about the Collyer brothers, who had saved everything for twenty years including their feces, she experienced a shock of recognition about the housekeeping of her mother.

Charlotte hid herself in her immaculate bedroom and tried to hide her soul in art. But she could not hide. One summer afternoon in 1941, when Charlotte was seventeen, her mother reached a new height of madness. With that special kind of canniness she often showed, she picked a day when Dr. Lewin had gone into the city for a meeting of his dental association. Charlotte sat in her room happily painting a still life of peaches, pears, and grapes, when her bedroom door burst open with a bang. She sat there trembling, paint dripping from the brush.

"Thief! Who said you could take that fruit?" her mother screamed.

Many times her father had warned her to say nothing, since anything she said could set her mother off; the only thing to do when her mother started to attack was to apologize. But just now she didn't feel like it. This was her room, her place, her refuge.

"You don't pay for the fruit," she snapped. "It's as much mine as yours."

"We'll just see about that!" Screaming like a banshee, filled with demonic energy, her mother dashed across the floor and grabbed the arrangement of fruit. "I'll show you whose fruit it is."

Screaming in fury, "There, there, there," she hurled the

fruit at Charlotte, hitting her precisely on her mouth, her face, her neck.

Charlotte could feel her lip split and blood begin to trickle down her chin. Before she could recover from that, her mother began to throw her easel, paints, and brushes out of the window and down to the sidewalk two stories below.

When she picked up one of the canvases, Charlotte began to scream, "Stop it. Stop it. Not my paintings," and she tried to wrest it from her mother's hands. She pulled and pulled with all of her might, but she was no match for her mother in a manic state. Then suddenly, with a cackle of glee, her mother unexpectedly let go and Charlotte tumbled head over heels and crashed against the corner of her bed, cracking her precious canvas as she fell.

She lay there weeping while her mother tossed the remaining canvases out of the window. When she was finished, she sneered, "That will show you whose fruit it is," and marched out, slamming the door behind her.

Still weeping, Charlotte struggled to stand up, and then she limped down the stairs to assess the damage. Her mother, sitting at the kitchen table, watched her pass with a baleful glance. Charlotte forced herself to hurry before her mother decided to throw something else at her.

Shaking with anger and depression, she surveyed the damage, too discouraged to salvage anything. Her thoughts were chaotic and murderous. I want to kill her, I want to kill her. I wish she'd die. She may be crazy, but not too crazy to time her viciousness. She deliberately planned this assault for a time when he would be away.

She began to clean up. As she worked, her depression deepened. Why was she so unlucky? Why was she different from everyone else? Other girls' mothers loved them. They made birthday parties for them, took them shopping, shared their joys and sorrows. But her mother always seemed angry that it was her brother who had died of polio instead of Charlotte. She had never made any secret of her preference for him while he was alive or after his death. Once she'd sighed to Charlotte, "Well, I guess only the good die young."

Charlotte had snapped back bitterly, "You're living proof of *that*."

She hated her mother, but her father was also to blame for perpetuating the situation. He reminded her of a character in a Sholom Aleichem story who had nothing all his life, and when he got to heaven and could have anything he wanted, asked only for a roll of white bread. Why did he ask for so little? What was it in some people that made them want to be martyrs?

Her father didn't have to live this way. Many times she'd begged him, "Please, Daddy. Get a divorce and take me with you." But divorce was a dirty word to him. He had a Victorian code of ethics that was destroying all of them.

"I have never turned my back on my responsibilities" was his standard, dumb answer. "That's the meaning of marriage. For better or for worse. Your mother is like my arthritic right hand. I wish it weren't arthritic, but it's still my hand." Oh, great. So he had his arthritic hand, and she had a home life that was hell.

Grief-stricken, she worked on, trying to numb herself in labor. When she had finished burying her precious work in the trash bins, she walked to the Esplanade to gaze across the river at Manhattan. That's where I want to live, she thought. Free and rich and protected in Manhattan.

If only she could escape, but there was no place to go and she was too young to join the war. It wouldn't seem so bad if she could go away to college in a year, but there was no way her father would have the money. He was supporting *his* parents in Florida and his wife's mother in an old folks' home. More of his ridiculous useless responsibility that was penalizing her!

Besides, there was a big mortgage on the house, and no matter how strapped they were he insisted on contributing to many charities. Even though he was a dentist, he wasn't rich. Professional men's incomes had suffered throughout the Depression because so many patients could not pay, and it was only since the beginning of the war that his practice had become more lucrative because the young dentists had been drafted. So she would have to live at home while attending college, but at least she would go to Adams College, which was a lot classier and more elegant than Brooklyn College. She would have to be satisfied with that. She had no other choice.

Her mother had gone to Adams, long ago, before she had turned crazy. She still remembered it with happiness. "You must join my sorority," her mother had told her. "Of course, they'll automatically pledge you because you're a legacy. We were all so pretty back then. And we had wonderful times. Tea dances at the Plaza, going in a group to the Easter Parade and walking down Fifth Avenue together. Oh, I had wonderful sorority sisters."

"Sisters!" Charlotte had revolved the word around in her mind. Sisters! She'd like that. She'd often longed for a sister to talk to. A sister would have been her ally against her mother. A sister would have been her friend. Maybe if she had sisters she would stop feeling like such an outsider. She ached to belong to something, to stop feeling so alone all the time. Many nights she would stroll around Brooklyn Heights, peeping into brightly lit windows and envying the happy families eating dinner together inside.

She stood there looking across the river, her pretty auburn hair blowing in the wind, her round blue eyes red from crying, feeling sorry for herself. Nothing ever seemed to work out right for her. All through high school she had been afraid to invite anyone home because of her mother's unpredictable behavior. The manic-depressive cycle was terrible. When she was high she was cruel and vicious like today, and when she came back down into the depressive phase she would be humble, tearful, docile, and pathetic, begging her family to forgive her, promising that things were going to be different, promising that it would never happen again.

And then gradually she would again begin to move toward her manic stage, and the madness would escalate. Only last month she had tried to run out into the street naked, and when Charlotte had attempted to restrain her, she'd blackened her eye. She should have let her go. She might have been hit by a car.

She sat on the Esplanade until dusk fell, shivering with hunger and fatigue but afraid to go home. Her father found her there. She ran to him with a glad little cry as he held out her jacket to her. Then he folded his arms around her, and she buried her face against his coat. "It's all right, sweetheart. It's all right. She's gone to the hospital again. I waited until the ambulance came."

"Do you know what she did today? The worst ever!"

"Some of it, and you can fill me in on the rest. Mrs. Busybody next door was waiting to complain about her screeching. But I didn't need her to tell me. I saw your canvases in the garbage can and knew that she was manic again. I found her sitting naked in the middle of the living room, tearing out her hair. I'm afraid they'll have to give her some more shock treatments. I hate what they do to her, but I don't know what else we can do. At least they bring her down."

"Oh, Daddy, it's all so awful."

"You don't have to tell me. Who knows better than I?"

He took off his thick glasses and wiped his eyes. "Let's go have some dinner, sweetheart."

She hooked her arm tightly in his as they walked to the local Chinese restaurant, feeling momentarily warmed by the touch. But once inside the restaurant, she felt sad again. Everybody else seemed to belong to a big, cheerful family. Why was everyone else so much more fortunate than she? Why had she been so deprived and cheated in life? If only she had someone to talk to about it. It was hard to discuss things with her father. She didn't want to add to his burdens, and he had never really been of much help. She'd like to see a psychiatrist, but even if they could afford it, she wouldn't dare. Suppose they told her that she would turn out to be as crazy as her mother. She'd kill herself if she ever thought that would happen.

They sat down and ordered the standard $1.35 dinner: egg roll, chicken chow mein, and fried rice. The taste and smells helped to revive her. She hadn't realized how hungry she was. After dinner, while they were sipping jasmine tea, her father took off his glasses, wiped his eyes, and looked at her with compassion. "I feel so bad about what happened today. I'll never leave you at home alone with her again. Sometimes I feel at my wit's end. I've failed her and I've failed you."

She refused to give him easy comfort. "You haven't failed her, but you have failed you and me. It's not your fault if she's crazy, but it is your fault if you continue to put up with it. She's destroying our lives."

"If only I could make you understand. Pearl wasn't crazy when I met her. She was sweet and loving and optimistic. She liked to sing. Why, she must have known the words to over a hundred popular songs. By heart! And she was a good housekeeper and cook. Every night when I would go upstairs from my office and find you kids and a good dinner waiting for me I would know how lucky I was. That's how I remember her. That's what she was like before your brother died. You can't just wipe all of that out with the word 'divorce.' I wish you could have known her then. And believe me, even though she acts crazy, deep down she loves you."

"It's so deep down that I can't find it. That's not love. It's hate. I don't need that kind of love. I'm glad she'll be away for a while. Where did they take her?"

"Where else? Kings County! I wanted to go with her, but it was more important to find you. She won't notice that I'm not there. They gave her a shot that will knock her out for the night, and I'll get over there first thing in the morning, before my patients come."

"I wish you'd leave her there permanently before she destroys both of us."

"Kings County? Permanently? I wouldn't wish it on a dog."

"A dog wouldn't throw out my paintings."

He looked at her with so much pain that she relented. "Nothing is your fault, Dad. You're the best man in the whole world. Let's have some fun for a change. Cheer ourselves up. Let's go to Radio City."

"I don't know. It seems wrong to go with your mother in the hospital."

"Please, Dad. What difference can it make to her? Think of it as medicine for us."

"Well, all right, if it will make *you* feel better."

"It will make us both feel better. And I want to suggest something else to you. Please hire a woman to take care of the house while Mom's away. It's so disgustingly dirty. In the afternoons, she could also help you in the office."

"That's a good idea, sweetheart. Your mother will come home to a clean house. And this weekend, why don't we go downtown and replace your art supplies?"

"No point in it, if she's coming home again."

She tried to talk reason to him on the subway into the city. "Dad. Do you believe in an afterlife?"

"No. I wish I did."

"Do you believe in reincarnation?"

"Of course not. Superstitious nonsense."

"That's the way I feel too, Dad. Then if you believe that this is the one and only life you'll ever have, why don't you try to make your life better? You're entitled to a little happiness. It hurts me that you spend all of your life working and worrying, and you still feel undeserving of any pleasure. Try to be good to yourself. Get a new suit, a new tie. You used to go to the theater. Buy some tickets. I'd love to go with you. I've always wanted to see a Broadway show. Most of the other kids I know have seen dozens of them."

He looked at her fondly. "My little girl is growing up."

Oh, for heaven's sake. He hadn't let himself hear a word she'd said. I'm going to have to save myself, she thought. I can't save him because he doesn't want to be saved.

However, as soon as they were inside the plush mirrored lobby of Radio City, her spirits rose. The marvelous art deco interior had been skillfully designed to achieve precisely that kind of relaxed feeling. There was something peaceful about this exotic temple in which people lowered their voices and felt like Sybarites for a few hours. Thank God for movies, she thought.

The movie that day was *Babes on Broadway* with Judy Garland and Mickey Rooney, another version of their familiar story about putting on a musical for the benefit of a settlement house. This time, in acknowledgment of the war, there was also a patriotic number about British refugee kids. How lucky they were, the kids in the movie: free, happy, not always concerned about a crazy mother. Even the refugee kids seemed happier than she. She sighed with the familiar yearning for peace and love.

As they walked home from the subway after the movie, her stomach began to contract with the familiar anxiety, and then suddenly she began to skip like a little kid. Yippee! Her mother wouldn't be there tonight. Maybe she would be away for a long time. She fell asleep happier than she'd been in a long time.

She'd always criticized her father for being undynamic, but the next day he surprised her. When she returned home from school, she found that he had hired Greta, a charming, young German-Jewish refugee with large sympathetic dark eyes, braids wrapped around her head, and a warm, loving heart. Charlotte adored her from the very first moment.

She arrived early each morning, and Charlotte would awaken to the smells of good food: fresh brewed coffee, eggs frying, and toasted bread. The three of them would eat breakfast together, laughing, talking, listening to the news and weather report on the radio, and then she would take off for school, her stomach full and satisfied, her clothes fresh and pressed and mended. During the day Greta would clean the house and office, shop, prepare and eat dinner with them, clean up, and finally hurry home to her bedridden mother with a portion of the dinner meal.

Charlotte could hardly wait to see her at the end of each day. Instead of huddling into herself at school like a turtle, she began to talk to other students, looking for interesting and exciting stories to share with Greta when she got home. Nobody had ever listened to her the way that Greta did now.

Greta was a marvelous human being. She could talk about anything: religion, sex, politics, love. For the first time Charlotte had a sympathetic older woman to confide in, an intelligent, rational, loving adult to help her come of age.

"How can you be religious, Greta?"

"Oh, I must be religious. It is my protest."

"But do you really believe in God? I mean someone up there with a long white beard?"

Greta's merry laugh rang out. "No, I do not believe in that kind of God. But that is not important to me. Religion to me is an act of defiance. They killed my father and brothers for this religion that we did not even observe in Germany. So now I observe."

"Were you a maid in Germany?"

"Of course not, liebchen. I was a student, a young girl like you. My father had a good business, and we had a fine house."

Charlotte gazed at her adoringly. "That's amazing. You never complain, I've never seen you cry, and you never take out your problems on us."

"It is bad manners to make others suffer just because I do. And of what use would it be? Even if you wept with me, it would not change the facts. So why should I burden you?" Greta even tried to ameliorate Charlotte's anger against her mother. "People who hate become shriveled inside. I agree that what she has done to you is unforgivable, but she is being severely punished. Who would wish to be crazy? What can be more terrible than to be out of control of oneself? Probably her life will never again be good, but you have all of yours still ahead of you. To forgive is to be happy."

"You might not feel so sorry for her if you met her. She's distinctly unlovable." Greta laughed and hugged her.

"But you, liebchen, are very, very lovable."

"I am? Really?"

"Of course."

For the first time in Charlotte's memory the house glowed with cleanliness and order. Greta washed drapes, repaired broken drawers, replaced light bulbs, and brushed down ancient cobwebs from corners of the high ceilings. And when they sat together at dinner each night, eating sauerbraten, red cabbage, dumplings, and apple cake, an unfamiliar joy would fill Charlotte's heart. This was what family life could be. Day by day she grew happier.

Greta went with her to replace the art supplies and made Charlotte her first dinner party. "I cannot believe that you are seventeen and have never had a party." She took her downtown to the A&S department store and helped her choose a party dress of navy taffeta and an everyday one of cotton madras.

Oh, it was so much fun to do the most ordinary things with Greta. Lunch at Chock Full o'Nuts of cream cheese on raisin bread and orangeade seemed like the best food she had ever tasted. She kept hoping that they would bump into one of the kids from school. She knew that no one would think that Greta was old enough to be her mother, but perhaps someone would think that she was her big sister.

On the night of the party, it was only Greta's presence that kept her from acting like a nervous wreck. But the three girls and four boys whom she had invited seemed genuinely glad to be there. The gleaming house was filled with the aroma of roast duck and apple strudel. They were all bright, alert young people, and they stayed far into the night asking Greta about her experiences. "Is it too painful to talk about the Nazis?" one of the boys asked hesitantly.

"Of course painful," she answered, "but necessary also, I think. The world must know."

"We're all enlisting," another boy said. "Right after graduation."

Without hesitation, she took his hand in hers. "I hope it does not have to be," she said, looking directly into his eyes with characteristic sincerity. "But if you must go, remember that you are fighting for freedom."

They talked late into the night, trying to understand Hitler's war against the Jews. "It is impossible to understand," she said. "A kind of mass psychosis. It has made me forever afraid. Even here, in this country, I am afraid. Some day, when my mother is gone, I will go and live in Israel. Maybe there I will not be afraid. Who knows? I may even find some relatives there who have survived."

At the end of the evening, Charlotte stood beside Greta, watching with quiet pride as Greta kissed each of the guests good-bye. "A great party. See you tomorrow, Charlotte," they called to her. She beamed with happiness.

"See you tomorrow," she answered their call.

"Come back anytime," Greta added.

One of the boys, Norman, hung back from the others, and when no one was looking, he grabbed her and placed a fast, nervous kiss on her lips. "See you tomorrow," he whispered, and then he fled.

She looked after him in wonder. It was the first time she had ever been kissed by a boy. Oh, joyous night! She had friends. She was no longer alone.

Greta closed the front door and looked at the clock. "Three o'clock. And work still to be done. I will stay in your brother's room tonight."

"I wish you lived here all the time, Greta."

"Oh, I do, too. How my mother would love this house."

Her father was putting the dishes in the sink. "You looked beautiful tonight, sweetheart. I like to see you happy. You go on up to bed. I'll help Greta to clean up."

"Are you sure?"

"Of course. We don't want you to work on the night of your party."

"I love you both." Happily, she kissed them each good night, then started up the stairs to her room. On the landing, she stopped to look back at them, and stood there transfixed. Greta was in her father's arms, and they were kissing passionately. Then they parted, and her father looked at Greta in joy. As she watched, it seemed to her that years slid off his back and she was looking at the boyish, enthusiastic man he must once have been. It made her want to cry. Then she turned, tiptoed into her room, and quietly closed the door, happy for them both. At last life was going to change.

She never told them that she had seen them together, but she went out of her way to let them know she would approve. First she would go to one, then the other. "I wish you were married to Greta," she'd tell her father. "I wish you were married to my father," she'd then tell Greta. It was the most wonderful three months of her life. No longer did she dread coming home from school. Each afternoon she would hurry to share the day's events with Greta, waiting for her with tea and homemade little *rugulech* filled with raisins and walnuts.

But one day in April, when she ran into the kitchen calling, "Greta, I was admitted to Adams," Greta was not there. She ran downstairs to her father's office. Greta must be there. But she wasn't. He was alone, sitting on his waiting room couch hunched over in the old position of despair, just staring into space. Fear clutched at her heart. "Where's Greta, Dad?"

"Gone." He spoke with difficulty, through a haze of pain. "She won't be coming back."

"Gone? But why? What happened?" She wanted to howl with grief, disappointment, loss, betrayal!

His face was ravaged with almost unendurable sorrow. "Your mother is coming home tonight. Greta left dinner for us."

So that was why Greta had run. "Oh, Daddy. How could you let this happen?"

"What could I do?"

"Run after her. Save us all. Oh, Daddy, I saw you kissing her on the night of my party. You love her. I love her. Don't let her go. Please, Daddy, save our lives."

"I can not throw your mother into the garbage."

"Why not? She threw all of my art in the garbage."

"Do you want me to act like her?"

"Oh, I don't know, Daddy. But *this* doesn't seem right." She burst into tears, and he held out his arms to her. "Oh, Daddy, Daddy," she cried as they held each other and wept together, "she was so generous, so noble. I loved her."

"And so did I, sweetheart. So did I."

Lumbering like a wounded animal, he stood up and walked to the door. "I'll go and get Pearl now." There was nothing more to say. With depression that matched his, she set the table and quickly put away her art supplies, remembering sadly the day when she'd gone to buy them with Greta. For the next two hours, she paced in agitation, unable to concentrate on her homework. At six o'clock, she heard the slam of a taxi door and quickly turned up the oven to warm the food Greta had left for them. When her mother came in, she was so suffused with hatred that she could hardly bear to look at her.

"I'm home," her mother called. "You two can't get rid of me even if you try." Charlotte hardly recognized her. The auburn hair, so like her own, was completely white, the blue eyes were glazed and dull, and she was puffy with new weight. Her father's eyes implored her to answer.

"Hi, Mom," she said dully. "Dinner's ready."

"Good! I'm hungry." Her mother plumped herself down and waited to be served. Charlotte's tears dripped all over Greta's good cooking. They finished dinner in twenty minutes, chewing away like robots; three strangers forced to be together, three strangers who did not like each other at all. Her mother stuffed herself greedily with three pieces of Greta's apple cake, belched loudly, then walked upstairs to her room.

"Want me to help with the dishes, sweetheart?"

"You know what I want," she said, making her voice cold.

He shrugged in despair. "I'm going downstairs."

"Who will keep your office clean now?"

"I don't know. And I'm tired of thinking about it."

She turned on the radio while she did the dishes. Usually Artie Shaw or Harry James could make her feel better. But tonight, nothing worked. She missed Greta more than she had ever missed anyone in her life. It was a physical pain.

After the dishes were dried and put away, she tried to concentrate on her homework for a few hours, but depression sat on her chest like a bad meal. She might as well get to sleep.

Before going to bed, she went downstairs to say good night. Her father was asleep on his waiting room couch. She leaned over to wake him, kissed his cheek, then froze in horror. Something was wrong. He was too cold. She shook him and shook him, then ran to get a mirror which she held against his lips. Nothing. Nothing at all. She sank down on a chair facing the couch struggling to control her mounting hysteria. Somehow she wasn't surprised. I felt it, she thought. I knew something awful would happen. Oh, Daddy! This is the end of your journey. And then, for the first time, she saw a note addressed to her on the floor beside the couch.

"Forgive me, sweetheart. I cannot live without Greta but I cannot abandon your mother. Dad." Her heart began to pound so thunderously that she feared she might faint. She put her head between her legs until the weakness passed.

The coward! He'd held happiness within his grasp and been too weak to seize it. He could have made life better for both of them, given her Greta to compensate for all the terrible years with her mother. Instead, he'd taken a coward's way out. Mingled with grief at his loss was anger at his defection. Weak all through his life, and now weak at the end. How dare he dump all of this on her shoulders?

Her wrath also enveloped Greta. Day after day they'd been loving confidantes, and yet she'd gone forever without even saying good-bye. She'd probably gone because she could not be dishonorable. Charlotte understood that. But even so, she had not done the right thing. Now she was all alone, her father was lying dead before her and her crazy mother was upstairs. She wanted to howl aloud in rage.

When she was finally able to pull herself together, she phoned the police, then reluctantly went to confront her mother, who was sitting on a rocking chair at her window looking out at nothing. Charlotte hovered before her with anxiety. How should she handle this? How could she avoid a hysterical tantrum?

Finally, she just told her the facts, trying to sound calm in order to keep her mother calm.

Her mother listened vaguely, unable to focus her eyes on Charlotte's. Then she finally understood. "Dead! Dead! What a bother. Why do these awful things always happen to me? I'm not supposed to be upset this way. How will I go to the funeral? I look terrible. I need a touch up. I'm not supposed to be upset this way. I don't know what to do. What should we do?"

"I'll call Daddy's lawyer, and then I'll call Riverside." That was where they had held her grandfather's funeral. "I'll call people tomorrow." She would have to notify relatives, their few friends, colleagues, and patients.

She sat in the kitchen shaking until the police came. They insisted on seeing her mother, but she had already taken her sleeping pills and could not be awakened. "You poor kid," one of them said. They were young, in their early twenties, and very, very kind. They sat with her until the body had been removed. "Go to sleep, kid," they said, before leaving. Fully dressed, she flung herself across her bed and sank into blessed unconsciousness.

The next morning, when she staggered downstairs, her mother had already gone out. "Back soon," said her note on the kitchen table. "I've gone to get my hair done for the funeral."

CHAPTER Four

Fate brought the three girls together. On a beaultiful fall day in 1942, the first day of school, Sarah got on the train to Long Island, looked about, and saw an empty seat next to an absolutely gorgeous girl, who was studying an Adams catalogue. She looked more like a model or an actress than a college student, and under ordinary circumstances, Sarah would have avoided someone who looked so bourgeois, but the girl looked up and smiled with such irresistible charm that Sarah was drawn to her. She sat down in the facing seat, and they began to exchange information.

They looked totally dissimilar. Wendy, tall, slim, exotic, was dressed in a black silk suit, patent leather shoes, matching purse, and little diamond stud earrings. Sarah was dressed in a handwoven approximation of a gunny sack that she'd bought in the Village, and large, free-form copper bracelet and matching earrings. And yet, they instantly felt comfortable with each other.

"You live at 88 Central Park West?" Wendy repeated in a marvelous, sophisticated voice that told Sarah she was not from New York. "That's super. We're practically neighbors. I have an apartment at the Century."

The use of the word "I" puzzled Sarah. "Your family lives there?"

"No. I live there. My home is in the Virgin Islands."

"Wow! Your folks let you have your own apartment? Lucky you. My folks are so overprotective you wouldn't believe it. They wouldn't let me go out of town to college. One of my brothers died in Spain and the other is in the Pacific, so I had to stay in New York. I wanted to go to Antioch."

Wendy took out a long cigarette holder, inserted a Pall Mall in it, and held out the pack to Sarah. "Want one?"

Sarah looked at the holder with admiration. How marvelously sophisticated! She took one of Wendy's cigarettes even though she'd only smoked a few times before. She wanted to learn to smoke. Everybody smoked. Servicemen, Humphrey Bogart in *Casablanca*, Paul Henreid, romantically lighting *two* cigarettes in *Now, Voyager*, and even President Roosevelt, always photographed with a long cigarette holder like Wendy's. War prisoners reputedly preferred cigarettes to food. It looked strong and modern and mature and sophisticated and gave you something to do with your hands at parties. She had to get used to it.

Wendy lit her cigarette with a gold Dunhill lighter, then looked at her soberly and said, "What a strange coincidence. You lost a brother and I lost a sister. She drowned. What was your brother doing in Spain? Bullfighting?"

Despite herself Sarah laughed. It was such a funny image. But immediately after her eyes filled with tears. Her brave, tiny brother. "Of course not. He died in the Lincoln Brigade."

"What's that?"

"You're kidding! The Spanish Civil War?"

"I think I vaguely heard about it. But I'm not sure."

Sarah tried not to let her disapproval show. Wendy was such a pleasant, friendly girl. So she simply said in a mild voice, "It didn't end until 1939. That's not exactly ancient history."

"Yesterday is ancient history to me," Wendy yawned.

"But aren't you interested in the world? Don't you read newspapers?"

"No, to both of those questions," Wendy laughed, tossing back her magnificent mane of black hair, her violet eyes flashing with amusement.

Wendy instantly knew from Sarah's face that she had shocked her, but she didn't care. Tired of always guarding herself and her secret, she had determined that in New York she would say, think, and be exactly what she wanted to be.

But despite her disapproval, Sarah was fascinated. She had never before met anyone like this. "Well what *does* interest you?"

"Jazz! Sex. Fashion. Travel. Theater. Nightclubs. Food. Wine."

Sarah's eyes widened. "That sounds so decadent. Kind of like Lady Brett Ashley."

"How wonderful that you know! She's one of my favorite literary characters. In fact, one of my models. I like to think of myself as an Epicurean, a Sybarite, totally committed to having fun. And New York's the place to have it. I've only been here a week and I'm mad about it already. I mean, my God. The men! Last night a friend smuggled me into the USO at Temple Emanu-El. Acres and acres of gorgeous officers. Do you go there?"

"I'd love to, but you have to be twenty-one."

"Who pays attention to such dumb rules? Want to go with me next time?"

"Sure. Why not? I guess so, if we won't get in trouble."

"But really! What can they do to us? And anything that's real fun must be a little dangerous. What do you do for fun?"

Sarah thought about that for a moment. "I don't think about having fun. I think about my responsibility to society."

"We'll certainly have to change that," Wendy grinned at her and Sarah grinned back. This beautiful girl was irresistible.

Wendy was telling Sarah about her hotel when they were interrupted by a cheery cry of, "Hi there." They looked up into a toothy Jinx Falkenberg kind of smile. "Adams freshmen?" the girl asked. They nodded. "Oh, super. I thought so. I'm Patti Parker, president of Tri Delt."

"A June Allyson look-alike," Sarah murmured.

"I know," Patti beamed. "Everybody tells me that."

"I'm Sarah Stern."

"I'm Wendy da Gama."

She checked off their names. "OK, Wendy. You can come and sit with us at lunchtime today." Wendy looked at her in surprise. She was not accustomed to receiving orders from strangers. But she decided to be polite for the moment.

"All right. Where do we go?"

"Not her! Just you."

Wendy arched her eyebrows and put on her most haughty, sophisticated expression. "Just me?"

The girl nodded.

"Would you mind explaining why?"

Patti looked at her in confusion, then said, "One of her own kind will come around to get her." Wendy looked at her in disbelief. She'd never encountered anti-Semitism on the island. How dare this little twerp act so smug. Besides, she already liked Sarah.

"Her own kind? You mean someone short?" Sarah's anger turned to amusement. Unlike Wendy, she knew all about this aspect of the sorority system, but she'd always just accepted its existence. Now, Wendy's surprise at learning about it made her see just how wrong it was.

"Of course not. Jewish, not short. There are two Jewish sororities on campus, and their representatives will be coming around to pick up their people. If you like, you could even come and sit with us now, Wendy."

"Why would I want to do that? I am sitting with someone."

"But we're Tri Delt. We have the top girls on campus."

"I doubt it."

"I assure you, it's absolutely true. Everybody knows it. So why would you question it?"

"Because they have someone as rude as you in charge. Now if you'll excuse us, Patti. We're having a private conversation."

Patti gasped in disbelief then stalked away. "Quelle horreur," Wendy laughed, wrinkling her pretty nose in distaste.

Sarah looked at her in admiration. "That was a really nice thing you did for me. After all, we've just met. I heard someone say recently that the definition of a friend is someone who'd hide you from the Nazis. That's the kind of thing you just did."

"I didn't do it for you. I'm half-Jewish myself, originally. But that's not the point. I can't bear smug, self-satisfied, totally insensitive little tyrants like that. I've spent a lifetime meeting people like that at our hotel. She's the type that complains constantly, makes all kinds of unreasonable demands, and then forgets to tip. My mother does not permit them back a second time."

Sarah was amused at Wendy's hotel-proprietorship perspective, but the encounter with Patti had left her uneasy. "You may have made an enemy. *We* may have made an enemy."

"That insignificant little twit? Who cares? That's another thing I learned at the hotel. Life is too short to be intimidated by bullies. I pegged Miss Ponytail as an officious little bitch the minute I saw her advancing with her clipboard. I wouldn't be caught dead in her sorority."

"But will you join a sorority?"

"I suppose. I'll give them their money just to be left alone. I don't intend to waste my life hanging around campus with a bunch of silly girls. Not with a city full of servicemen. What about you? Will you join one?"

"I suppose. You can't be a campus leader without doing it, and I want to lead the International Relations Club. So I guess I'll join. But after this, my heart isn't really in it. For the first time I realize that separating Jews from Gentiles is exactly what the Nazis are doing. It's wrong and stupid. And for me it's ironic. I don't even believe in religion. I believe in being a citizen of the world."

"I don't believe in religion either. Frankly, I don't know how anybody who is rational can. My mother converted to Catholicism, but she hasn't been near a church since my sister died. My father became fanatically religious then. He became obsessed with the idea that he was being punished because of the sin of pride. Can you imagine worshipping any god that would treat you that way? My poor father! He never recovered from my sister's death.

"But my mother's really marvelous. Strong! Like a rock. I couldn't wait to get to New York, but I felt bad about leaving her. She tried to reassure me. She said, 'Ultimately, people's salvation comes not from religion but from a strong sense of self-worth and a readily marketable talent. I have both, Wendy darling. So I'll be fine. You just go off to college and have a ball.'"

"She sounds wonderful. I envy you."

"She is wonderful. You'll see when you meet her. She puts all of her energy into running the hotel, and she keeps herself very, very busy. But she misses my father and sister terribly. What about your mother? Did she change after your brother died?"

"Oh, sure. She was always kind of humble and shy, but now I sometimes think she's living on a different planet much of the time. I wish she had something important to do with herself, like your mother. But she doesn't. She just waits for me to come home from school each day."

Just then the train stopped at Jamaica for the transfers from Brooklyn, and Charlotte entered their car, looking about her anxiously. She saw the two empty seats beside Sarah and Wendy, but hesitated. Would they want to sit next to her? One of the girls looked so magnificent in her couturier clothes that she felt intimidated, and the other girl looked kind of odd in a bohemian gunnysack. Charlotte felt plump, poor, and ordinary in her saddle shoes, bobby socks, pleated skirt, and Peter Pan collar. Wendy saw her hovering there indecisively and called out, "Hi. Are you going to Adams? Come on over here and sit with us."

She could hardly believe it. That gorgeous girl and the cute, small, dark-haired girl were beckoning to her. Her face lit up with pleasure, and she hurried to join them. "I'm Charlotte," she said shyly.

Wendy, using the social skills that she had honed at the hotel, drew her out as she had done with Sarah. When she told them that she too had lost a sibling, they looked at each other in amazement. "It's kind of spooky," Wendy said. "We may be the only three girls at the college to whom this has happened, and fate has brought us together."

"It's happened to many people in Europe," Charlotte said. "We had a housekeeper who lost her father and brothers in Germany."

"And the longer the war goes on," Sarah said soberly, thinking about Claude, "the more losses there will be."

"That's the line they keep handing out at the USO," Wendy laughed. "Kiss me baby because tomorrow I may be gone. Little do they know that they don't have to convince me."

"They don't?" Charlotte asked in astonishment.

"Certainly not," Wendy boasted. "Sex is my favorite occupation."

They looked at her in disbelief. Girls just did not talk about sex that way. "Attitudes toward sex must be a lot different where you come from," Sarah said.

"They call it the blessing of the islands," Wendy giggled. That was true, but it was the natives who called it that.

In a few minutes, another girl came walking toward them. Dressed in saddle shoes, socks, shetland sweater and plaid skirt, she was a brunette duplicate of Patti. "Oh, oh," Sarah said. "Here comes the Jewish contingent."

She carried an identical clipboard to the one Patti had carried. "Hi. I'm Susie. A E Phi."

"I'm a legacy," Charlotte said eagerly. "My mother belonged to your sorority."

Susie looked her over. "What's your name?"

"Charlotte Lewin."

Susie looked over her list. "Oh yes. We've heard about you."

The way she said it made Charlotte anxious. "What do you mean?" she asked.

"My aunt was a patient of your father's. She was at the funeral." Charlotte flushed, remembering the terrible scene at the cemetery when her mother attempted to jump into the grave.

Susie turned to Sarah. "And you are?"

"Sarah Stern."

"Aha," she checked Sarah's name. "Your father is Judge Stern, right?"

"Don't hold it against me," Sarah said.

Ignoring her levity, Susie looked at her lap. "Is that the *Daily Worker*?"

"It sure is," Sarah grinned. "Want to borrow it?"

"Certainly not." She looked at it as if it were a snake.

"Don't worry. It doesn't bite," Sarah said as Susie fled.

Wendy was amused. "We two have really made great first impressions."

Charlotte looked at them with concern but said nothing. She couldn't afford to be dubbed as either promiscuous or political. All she wanted here was a little happiness and acceptance to counteract the daily turmoil of life with her mother. But when the conductor called, "Adams. Adams

College," and they stepped off the train, Sarah linked her arm in hers, and there was something so kind and warm and friendly about her that Charlotte could not have drawn her hand away even if she had wanted to. Besides, it certainly seemed to be a plus to be at Wendy's side. Nobody walked past her without that quick glance of admiration. Even the conductor jumped down from the train, reached up, and helped her down. She batted those gorgeous lashes at him, smiled seductively, and they started off. It was enough to make anyone feel jealous.

"Oh, God, what weather," Wendy said, stretching her arms to the sky. "Indian summer. The first autumn of my life. We're off to a wonderful year."

She linked her free hand in Charlotte's other arm, and suddenly Charlotte felt free and confident and optimistic. She was not alone. Side by side, now a unit of three, they joined the long parade of girls strolling toward their future.

CHAPTER Five

Because Adams was a commuters' college, it had its own indigenous rush system. Since there were no sorority houses, the center of sorority life was the dining hall, where each sorority, depending on its size, had one or two long picnic tables assigned to it. For the first two months of school, September and October, incoming freshmen were permitted to eat lunch at whichever tables interested them, and during this period they were examined with all the microscopic intensity of someone about to be admitted to the British royal family.

Eventually, all freshmen broke down into three sorority categories. The automatically accepted, the automatically rejected, and those in between. Under ordinary circumstances, Wendy, Sarah, and Charlotte would have been automatically accepted.

Charlotte was a legacy, Wendy was beautiful, and Sarah

was smart. But Charlotte's family situation immediately moved her to an automatic reject, and Sarah and Wendy managed to offend as many people as possible during the weeks before final pledging.

Sarah's mistake was that she had expected to find girls as interested in politics as she was. But apart from winning the war, nobody really cared very much. And those few who cared, were violently anti-red. Her first lunchtime struggle came over the Spanish Civil War.

Knowing that her father was Judge Stern, one of the girls asked her, "How come your brother went to fight in that commie war?"

"Commie war? Don't you know anything? The Republican government was a legitimately elected government, and it was overthrown by that fascist Franco. Anybody with a brain went to Spain. Dorothy Parker, and Ernest Hemingway, and John Dos Passos, and André Malraux. It's just plain ignorant to call it a commie war. Fifteen hundred wonderful American men died there."

"Do you always get this excited about politics, Sarah?"

"What are you talking about?"

"Don't you think it's a little unladylike to get so intense about things?"

"Unladylike? I think it's unladylike to be dumb or unconscious."

Both Jewish sororities crossed her off their lists that day.

* * *

Wendy sprawled at a sorority table, smoking. "Since you're only half-Jewish," one of the sorority girls asked, "why have you decided to pledge a Jewish sorority?"

"I don't see that it makes a difference."

"Why do you say that?"

"I intend to spend as little time as possible on campus."

"Don't you think that you should make a contribution to sorority?"

"Oh, sure. How much? I'll write a check."

"Not that kind of contribution. A contribution of time."

The Sorority

"Certainly not. To tell you the truth, I'm more interested in groups of boys than in groups of girls."

All of the sororities crossed Wendy off their lists.

* * *

"Don't you have any questions to ask me?" Charlotte tried not to let her voice sound plaintive.

The sorority girls went through the motions. "In what way could you contribute to our sorority."

"I would do anything you liked."

"Do you have any special skills?"

"I used to paint, but I haven't done anything recently."

"That's it?"

She cast about wildly. "I'm a legacy. And I could help with party decorations." Then she said, suddenly angry and close to tears, "What kinds of contributions do you want anyway? How do *you* contribute to sorority?"

"We're the ones asking the questions," they answered. "Not you."

They didn't have to cross Charlotte off any lists. She had been crossed off before school even began that year.

On Pledge Day, a current of electricity ran through the college. In the dining hall, above each of the picnic tables, colorful brocade banners, embroidered with the Greek letters representing each sorority's name, had been proudly unfurled, and each table was decorated with floral centerpieces.

After three long months of endless teas, lunches, observing, questioning, debating, deliberating, and voting, the names of the new pledges had been posted that morning, and ever since, the college dining hall had been exploding with excitement.

Below these proud banners, shrieking, gleeful, euphoric, joyously weeping girls were jumping up and down in excitement, hugging and kissing as if they'd just won a sweepstakes. Glad cries rang throughout the hall: "I never thought I'd make it," "I'm so happy that you pledged me," and "Now you're one of us."

For those girls who had been pledged, it was the pinnacle of their lives. They had found success.

But for those girls who had not been pledged, their remaining years in college would be filled with reminders of their inadequacy. They were social failures, outsiders, and insignificant members of the power structure of the school. Nonaffiliates were untouchables, second-class citizens who were automatically excluded because of their insufficiencies from everything but going to classes, an activity regarded by the sorority girls as the least important aspect of the college experience.

There was much more to school than studying, and there was no way for nonaffiliates to pretend that they would not be missing a lot. Tri Delt had established a fund for exchange scholarships with Latin America. Delta Zet had been actively engaged in giving parties and dances for disabled war veterans. Pi Phi Alpha sent money, food, and clothing to the people of war-torn Italy and entertained servicemen at the Lido on Long Island. Sigma Kappa had taken over a seacoast town in Maine, and members drove up there to deliver aid to the local fishermen and their families.

But that was only the beginning. No nonaffiliated girl had ever been on Daisy Chain, been president of a campus club, acted as hostess to visiting celebrities, or served on important college committees. Wendy, unquestionably the most beautiful girl at the college, would not be Daisy Queen. Sarah and Charlotte would have to struggle for participation in the Art Club or International Relations Club.

In addition to that, Greek-letter organizations actually governed the college. Matters such as plagiarism, excessive lateness, failure to return library books, cheating, late fees, and so on were ruled on by sorority committees, and the disciplinary treatment of nonaffiliated girls was different and far less lenient and sympathetic than that meted out to sorority sisters.

Once a year the college president hosted all the sororities in his home on Greek-Letter Day without considering the feelings of nonaffiliates who never did get to see where he lived. And up until this time, nobody had ever dreamed of challenging the sorority system.

At a table at the far end of the dining hall, a group of girls slumped despondently, trying to become invisible. This table bore no proud flag, no happy faces. Here there was no laughter, no celebration, no congratulatory joy, no smiles, no excited chatter, no screams of newfound sisterhood. These were the girls who had been judged unfit by their peers. Their names had not appeared on the posted pledge lists. And there was no court of appeal.

The young pariahs sat there in silent shock, wrapped in transparent cocoons of misery, searching for balance and control in the face of this monumental public rejection, struggling not to cry or show how much they had been hurt.

Many of the girls at this table already looked like rejects. They were too tall, too short, too fat, too thin, too homely, too badly dressed, or too something. But Wendy, Sarah, and Charlotte, sitting together at one end of the table, did not look at all different from those girls who had been pledged.

"Well, they really socked it to us, didn't they?" Sarah said, trying to sound hard-boiled and sophisticated.

Wendy crossed her long, coltish legs, lit a cigarette, and said, "So much for being a smart aleck. I guess I shouldn't have told the Greek committee that I thought all religion was a fake."

"I was stupid, too," Sarah said. "I knew I shouldn't carry the *Worker*, but I didn't want to conceal my political views just to impress those conceited bitches."

Charlotte was the most distressed of the three. She dug her nails into the palms of her hands, trying not to cry. "It's an extra disgrace for me, because I was a legacy. They never turn down a legacy."

"They did this time," Wendy said. "Don't let them see you cry, Charlotte. Laugh at all this nonsense."

Sarah looked at Charlotte compassionately. I'm not devastated, she thought. She had always been a little uneasy about the concept of sorority, and in a way was glad that the decision had been taken out of her hands. She patted Charlotte's hand. "Wendy's right. Don't let them see you crying. Think about lynchings. Think about the war, about concentration camps. Think of the Nazis. Sororities are really bourgeois nonsense."

"I like bourgeois nonsense. In fact, I love it." Sarah and

Wendy burst into laughter, and in spite of herself, Charlotte joined them.

"Now listen girls," Wendy said. "This is not going to crimp our style. We're here in New York, wonderful, wonderful New York. This past month alone I've been to the Waldorf, the Stork Club, Toots Shor's, and 21. And I assure you that not one person in any of those marvelous, glamorous places ever heard of this dumb little sorority system."

"You're right," Sarah said. "Nobody at the Jefferson School ever did either."

"But we did," Charlotte said sadly. "That's the point. For the rest of our lives we're going to know that the leading girls on this campus didn't want to associate with us."

"Their loss," Wendy said in her throaty voice. "We have to tell ourselves that we really didn't want to associate with them very much either, so not getting in was a blessing in disguise. Frankly, I dreaded the very idea of their stupid hazing: wearing silly clothes, performing menial tasks, running wild goose chases. And all for what purpose? To wear an ugly Greek-letter pin? The important thing now is to act indifferent to the entire situation. If they think we care, then they really will have won."

Sarah agreed. "All that pious moralizing, smirking presumption, puritanical vindictiveness, and self-congratulatory philistinism! I hate such smugness. And what hypocrites! They pretend that they exist for social contributions, but their major purpose is really to get each other dates. And as far as I'm concerned, any system that leaves a small bunch of girls feeling like total failures at the age of eighteen is a rotten system."

Charlotte was inconsolable. Wendy and Sarah had compensations for this rejection, but all she had was her crazy mother. "We wouldn't think so if we'd been admitted."

"Oh, yes we would," Sarah insisted, "but we just would have hidden our feelings. We would have lived a lie for the next four years. I'm beginning to feel lucky that I don't have to."

Charlotte laughed, in spite of her depression. "Honestly, Sarah, you remind me of Pollyanna. What beautiful crutches!

You two are just saying all of these things to make us feel better. Like whistling in the dark!"

"Better than not whistling at all," Wendy quipped.

"Nevertheless," Sarah continued, warming to her topic, "it's unjust. Nonaffiliated girls pay exactly the same tuition as sorority girls, and yet they're treated like second-class citizens. I intend to draft a letter about this to the dean, and I expect both of you to sign it with me."

"Of course." Wendy blazed with the Spanish pride of her father. How dare they reject her!

"You're right," Charlotte said. " I'm sick and tired of life's unfairness. No matter what, we should stick together. That's what it really means to be friends. Like the *Three Musketeers*."

"That's a great idea," Wendy said. "I don't remember ever reading anything about three female musketeers who stick together, loyal and united against the world. But *we* can do it. In fact, we have to do it to survive here."

Sarah's face lit up. "Sometimes you sound so marvelously political, Wendy."

"God save me from that," Wendy joked, blowing out a smoke ring. "It's not political. It's commonsense."

Sarah was jubilant. "That's what we'll be. Our own sorority. All for one and one for all. We don't need Greek letters to make us strong. We'll be strong because we have each other. And we have to make a plan to get whatever we want out of this college, even without Greek letters. I want to be president of the International Relations Club. What do you want Charlotte?"

"I'd like to be president of the Art Club. What do you want, Wendy?"

"I just want to live it up in the city. I'll applaud and help the two of you."

Then, walking side by side, feeling strong in their own little group, they left the dining hall with heads held high.

They became inseparable, taking classes together whenever they could and meeting back at their table between classes if they were separated. And whenever they were away from school, they explored the city with Wendy.

But during that first year, it became increasingly clear

to Sarah that she could never be elected president of the IRC. She'd observed at other elections how the sorority girls voted for their own.

"So forget about it," Wendy said. "Why do you care?"

"Because the present IRC leadership is to the right of my father."

"So what?"

"Please Wendy. Don't make me more upset than I already am."

"I can get you elected," Wendy said.

"Stop bragging. Money doesn't do everything."

"That's what you think. I'm going to do something, but I'm not going to tell you what it is. Charlotte and I will do it together. We'll nominate you for the ballot, and then just watch my dust."

"You have to tell me."

"Nothing doing. You'll be pleasantly surprised."

On the day of the election, Sarah walked into the dining room to find Charlotte holding fifteen large, wonderfully attractive posters, each of them signed in large letters with the artist's name. She'd spent the past month making them. "What do you think?" she asked with a smile of delight.

Every one of them said the same thing: Victory Party for Sarah Stern at El Morocco as Guests of Wendy da Gama. Dates For All.

"They're gorgeous," Sarah said. "I don't know how to thank you for spending so much time on me. But Wendy, if I win, do you know what this will cost?"

"Who cares? My father's family practically owns the West Indies."

"Is it legal?"

"I don't see why not."

"You don't think it's bribery?"

"Of course it is. How do you think my father's family got so rich?"

"I'd rather win on my own merits."

"Don't be a dunce. You can't. The sorority girls don't win on their merits either. We're going to outsmart them at their own game. If the sorority girls vote for one of their own, it only helps her. If they vote for you, it helps them.

Nobody here has ever had a victory party like that. Don't worry. You'll win."

She did, of course. The defeated candidate and her sorority sisters grumbled that it was not fair, but nobody else wanted to contest it. El Morocco was too tempting a bait. Wendy was host to a hundred girls at the best party they'd ever attended. For years afterward, students talked about the victory party for Sarah Stern.

Thanks to her posters for Sarah, Charlotte became the next president of the Art Club without resorting to tricks, and after that, the sorority girls treated them with a certain grudging respect. But the nature of her victory made Sarah uneasy. "They resent us now," she said, "and they'll be biding their time."

"I don't think we have to worry," Wendy laughed. "I think we've permanently outsmarted them at their own game. There's nothing they can do to touch any of us."

CHAPTER Six

During the war, the largest USO catering to officers was located in the tremendous ballroom of Temple Emanu-El, on Fifth Avenue and Sixty-fifth Street, the grandest, richest temple of the old New York German Jews. As a child, Sarah had walked across the park to Sunday school, and both Jimmy and Claude had been bar-mitzvahed there. But Sarah had not set foot inside it for years because she associated it with her father who had been president and still was a leader of the congregation. Besides, she didn't believe in religion, "the opiate of the people."

To Charlotte, it was legendary, a place where only those Jews who had reached the pinnacle of social and economic success in New York City could belong. She had walked past it on her way to the Central Park Zoo and had gazed at it with longing but had never been inside. Now she was going there with her friends. She was excited but also frightened.

As they approached the building, on the first night that Wendy planned to smuggle them in, Charlotte vowed that some day she would rightfully belong there. Some day she would move to Manhattan and move in the best circles. Sarah's refusal to take advantage of all her advantages was incomprehensible to her. And even tonight, Sarah kept mumbling that she had made a mistake in coming when she could be home reading a good book or attending a class at the Jefferson School. They had finally talked her into it, but she was still registering her protest by refusing to dress up.

The girls found, as Wendy had predicted, that they had no difficulty in getting in. By now, everybody at the USO knew her and had fallen under her spell. Even though it was quite obvious that she was under twenty-one, she was so charming, beautiful, and captivating that she had easily obtained the requisite pass. And she smuggled her two friends in that night by dazzling the guard at the door with her usual charm.

Once inside, she led them to the coatroom. "There are only two rules here," she laughed. "Do not dance too closely and do not leave with anyone. I always ignore both of those rules and I expect the two of you to do the same. Here we go girls. Good hunting!"

They followed her inside to a whirlwind of sound: laughter, music, talking. She was instantly pulled onto the dance floor while Sarah and Charlotte huddled together watching her with admiration.

Her alabaster skin gleaming, her firm breasts thrusting themselves out of her dress, tossing her black hair, flashing her perfect smile, she danced the lindy with one man after another, always surrounded by a crowd, shoving, cutting in, vying for her attention, laughing, flattering, cajoling. Other couples stood aside to watch the grace with which she moved. No wonder she really didn't care about being in a sorority, Charlotte thought. The world was at her feet.

"I'd love to be sought after that way," Charlotte sighed. "Just once in my life."

"I wouldn't." Sarah looked at Wendy turning and smiling and flirting. "I'd hate to have people always looking at me. I don't know how she stands it. I don't want to be on stage. I don't give a rap about crowd pleasing. I can't even relate to that many people at one time. I want to be one of the masses."

"I see the masses every day on the subway and they reek from perspiration. You mystify me Sarah. I wish someone would ask us to dance. Do you mind standing here?"

"No. I like watching. Relax Charlotte. Someone will ask us to dance eventually. Wendy says there are about ten men here to every woman. I just hope I'm not stuck with a reactionary dope."

Charlotte laughed. "I don't care what their politics are. I just don't want to be a wallflower. Do you think I look all right?"

"You look great. But don't hunch over that way as if you have the cares of the world on your shoulders. Stand up straight and proud. Stick your chest out."

"My breasts are too big."

"And mine are nonexistent. But what the hell, Charlotte. Let's both stick them out."

Just then, as Sarah had predicted, two army lieutenants approached and held out their arms, and after that, caught up in the special sexual intensity of wartime, they whirled from one partner to another, doing the lindy, the rumba, the cha-cha-cha, having an absolutely marvelous time while the band played "What a Difference a Day Makes," "Tenderly," "Deep Purple," "Chattanooga Choo Choo," and "Don't Sit under the Apple Tree."

Behind the laughter, there was deep concern but it was part of having a stiff upper lip to conceal it. The war was going badly for the United States. Manila, Bataan, and Corregidor had fallen, and the Marines were fighting at Guadalcanal, but within this hall all was lightness and laughter and life. That was the unspoken rule. Nobody talked about the future.

The final dance was to "When the Lights Go on Again." Clinging tightly to each other, the young people sang along with the vocalist, and Sarah found herself close to tears. A lot of these men were going to die. Maybe even Claude!

The girls met the three men with whom they'd ended the evening outside the temple, and they walked across the park to Wendy's apartment, savoring the fresh Indian-summer night.

Charlotte's lieutenant put his arm around her. He had one of the most beautiful names she had ever heard. Nyall Moss! He was from the Midwest, had a master's degree in literature, and was slim, straight, and very blonde. "You're the first person I've ever met from outside of New York," she told him.

"And you're the first real New Yorker I've met," he said, looking at her with evident admiration. "If I told you that I'm a sucker for red hair and blue eyes and was falling in love with you would you believe me?"

"No," she laughed.

"If I told you that I was shipping out tomorrow would you go to bed with me tonight?"

Her blue eyes danced. "No. But I might write to you."

"Oh, big deal," he teased. "I thought New Yorkers were supposed to be sophisticated."

She giggled, and he turned to her and took her in his arms and kissed her. Her heart soared with pleasure. Warmth spread through her. "Wow," he said, when they finally broke apart. She felt gay and normal and pretty. Just like anyone else! Holding hands like two kids, they raced to catch up with the others.

Sarah was with a short, dark-haired captain from San Francisco. She liked him because he was sensible and read *The Nation*. He had a wife and three kids and was too mature to wear a mask of macho gaiety once they had left the USO. They walked together silently for a while until he finally burst out, "I have this deep conviction that I'm going to die. I dreamed that I saw my kids clustered around my coffin. Do you think that dreams are prophecies?"

"No. I don't believe in Jung and I don't believe in Freud. I think we just dream. It could be fear or indigestion. Sometimes I dream about the Nazis." She shivered.

"Maybe it is just fear or indigestion, but it worries me

anyway. I don't know how my wife could support the kids alone."

"You didn't have to go did you?"

"Not legally. Morally. I want to give it to that bastard Mussolini for screwing up the old country. When we march into Italy, I'll be liberating a lot of my relatives."

Wendy walked along with three officers, all trying to edge the others out in their own private little war. "Pretty snazzy," one said when they reached her apartment. "You live here all alone?"

"I'm never really alone, darling," she said, trying to sound like Tallulah Bankhead. "Just help yourself to drinks while I change into something a little less square." She changed to a strapless evening gown, and they piled into two cabs to Fifty-second street to hear Billie Holiday sing.

Drinking, holding hands, they felt a special kind of closeness at the haunting songs: "God Bless the Child Who Has His Own," "I Cover the Waterfront," and "Strange Fruit." Sarah's escort kept wiping his eyes. She held his hand to comfort him.

At three in the morning, Wendy's three escorts left with her, and Charlotte went home with Sarah. In the lobby Nyall bent and kissed Charlotte again, but differently from in the park. This time he pushed open her lips with his tongue, and for the first time in her life she was soul kissed. She could feel her heart pound and her body respond with passion. How wonderful it was to be touched, to be loved, to feel wanted. After her father's death, she'd thought she could never be happy again. But here she was, alive, normal, and with somebody who liked her. They stood there necking until they were overcome with fatigue, and then they sadly said good-bye.

"It's terrible," Charlotte said, "to think that we'll probably never see them again."

"I know. That poor little captain. He could have been exempt, but he felt he had to go. I worry about Claude."

When Wendy reached her building, she stood in the lobby flirting with the three officers. "Which one?" they begged, circling her like Indians around a wagon train.

She puffed away on her long cigarette holder and used

her Tallulah voice. "Sorry darlings, I hate to disappoint you, but I have a late date with a lieutenant colonel."

A collective groan went up from them, but they were outranked. Without further protest, one after another kissed her good-bye, trying to outdo themselves in passionate performance so she would remember. "I'll be back," each of them whispered.

"Darlings," she laughed, finally extricating herself, "you've smeared lipstick all over my face. I'll have to hurry now to put myself together again."

Beautiful, laughing, sophisticated, she waved good-bye, and the elevator man took her up to her floor. Then she sat looking out at Central Park until dawn, smoking and sipping brandy, depressed and despising herself for being a fraud and a coward. On every date, she really intended to go through with it, but each time she chickened out. Well, one of these days, sooner or later, she'd find the courage to live up to her bad reputation.

CHAPTER
Seven

The next three years were wonderful for the girls because they had each other. Each of them showed the others a different face of New York. Sarah took them marching in May Day parades and to hootenannies and lectures at the Jefferson School. "Only because I love you," Wendy sighed. "Quelle ennui. Nothing in the world can be more boring than Marxism."

Charlotte led them to the city's museums. Her favorite was MOMA, the Museum of Modern Art, where for the price of admission you could also see wonderful foreign films that rarely came to the regular movie theaters.

And Wendy, always providing them with escorts from the men who buzzed around her, took them to the Stork Club, the Blue Angel, the Rainbow Room, Eddie Condon's, and the other jazz places along Fifty-second Street, and the

Village Vanguard and Basin Street in Greenwich Village. She wanted to see every play, see every movie, and hear every folk and jazz artist in the city.

She was wild about Ella Fitzgerald and Billie Holiday and had a mad crush on Josh White. Because of him she had bought an expensive guitar and taught herself to sing "Three Meat Balls," spending hours approximating that little click in his voice. She sang it over and over again to her friends in a low, husky voice, trying to sound black. They didn't have the heart to tell her that she didn't.

Their academic records varied. Sarah was a straight-A student, even in those subjects like math that didn't interest her at all. After the end of her term as president of the IRC, she became president of the Debating Society and was admitted to Phi Beta Kappa in her junior year.

Charlotte's grades were far less consistent. In the subjects she liked, such as art, she would get A's, but when she didn't like something, she would find herself unable to concentrate, even when she knew she should.

Wendy just scraped by because she never did any homework. "If you can pass without doing homework," Sarah scolded, "just think how well you would do if you studied."

"I don't want to do better. I hate school. It's an interruption of my life. You two are the only things that make it semibearable."

During their junior year, they began to plan to spend the summer in Mexico City, studying Spanish at the University of Mexico. They would have preferred to go to France, but even though the war in Europe was over, Sarah's mother was terrified that some bombs might still remain in the Atlantic and that the converted troop ships now being used for tourists were not sufficiently seaworthy. She even objected to having Sarah fly. So to get permission, they agreed to go by train.

"It's just ridiculous," Wendy snorted. "Edita goes over regularly for her clothes."

"It's because Claude's still in the Pacific. He's still not safe."

"I can't imagine anything more boring than sitting on a train for three days," Wendy said.

"I don't care how we go," Charlotte said. "I've never been anywhere."

They worked hard at their Spanish, practicing with each other and studying everything about the Aztec culture. Sarah couldn't even talk about the conquistadores without getting indignant. "The nerve of them," she would scream, "to come to a foreign country and force their religion on the people who welcomed them."

Everything was just about set when Charlotte asked her mother for the money promised for her train ticket. Since her husband's death Pearl had become sufficiently stable to function in her daily life. She was still volatile and unpredictable, but no longer seemed completely out of touch with reality. Her manic-depressive swings had become less extreme although her behavior continued to be inconsistent, alternating between kindness and cruelty, and Charlotte could never be sure which would predominate on any given day.

Today it was cruelty. "I've changed my mind," she snapped.

Charlotte struggled against despair. "But I just bought a suitcase!"

"So give it back. You're not going to Mexico. You're not going anywhere. Why should you go? *I* never go anywhere."

"But you promised. And we've made all of our reservations."

"So unmake them. Your friends can go without you."

"But why? You said I could go. I asked you over and over again to make sure, or else I never would have begun to plan."

"If you weren't so self-involved you might guess. We're out of money."

"Out of money? But that's not possible. What about the life insurance?"

"I took it in a lump. It's gone."

"But Daddy left money for me to go to college."

"That's gone, too. I won't be able to pay your tuition next year. You'll have to drop out and get a job at the end of May. I'm renting out the office downstairs and the two top floors. You and I will have to move down here."

"Here? But there's only a kitchen, dining room, and living room. Where will we bathe?"

"Bathe at your rich friends' apartments. You spend most of your time there anyway. I don't want to hear another word about it. You're not going to Mexico, and that's that."

"I can't believe how cruel you are. I hate you."

"I should worry," her mother laughed.

She ran to her room and lay sobbing on her bed until the next morning. What was the use of struggling? This was the way things were always going to be. Every time she began to hope, her hopes were dashed! Greta, her father, sorority, and now this. Instead of a carefree, joyous summer with her friends, she would be living in terrible conditions with her mother, working at some crummy job, suffering through the subway rush hour, and she would no longer have even her own bedroom as a place of refuge. The whole prospect was unbearable.

The next day, struggling to hold back her tears, she told her friends what had happened. "No problem," Wendy said. "I'll pay your fare."

"I appreciate it, but I still couldn't go. I have to get a job right away. And I won't be back here in the fall."

"Not graduate? After all this time? That's awful."

"I know! I'm still in shock. The worst part of it will be living in such close quarters with my mother."

"I can help you with that, for the summer anyway," Wendy said. "Stay in my apartment. My maid will still come in to clean."

For the first time Charlotte felt some of her depression lifting. She was not going to Mexico, but she'd still have a summer of freedom. "I'll never forget this, Wendy. Not for the rest of my life."

"That's what our sorority is all about isn't it?" It was as difficult for Wendy to understand the cruelty of Charlotte's mother and the apathy of Sarah's as it was for them to imagine the generosity and kindness of hers.

"I'll try to get a little money for you, too," Sarah said. Her father kept her on almost as short a leash as her mother.

"I don't know what to say. You're both so generous, and

I have nothing to offer you in return. Some day, I promise I'll reciprocate. Just give me time, until I get a little money."

Sarah looked at her in surprise. "Of course you have something to offer. We're sorority sisters. Friendship is more important in life than money."

Not if you don't have any, Charlotte thought. Sarah always expressed contempt for money, and Wendy was indifferent to it, but they could afford their unrealistic attitudes. She knew better. Money was the beginning and end and meaning of life. Money was freedom. The kind of freedom that afforded the luxury of the two of them waltzing off to Mexico this summer while she stayed home. The kind of freedom that enabled them to pick their school clothes each August from *Mademoiselle* while she struggled to wear whatever she had for still another year. They just didn't understand, couldn't see life from her point of view. Overfed people couldn't feel the pain of hunger. But money was all that mattered, and some day she was going to have it.

The only way to get it was to marry a rich man, and somehow she'd do it. Some day she'd have so much money that she'd no longer be a victim or an outsider. Those were her two goals in life. To have money and to belong. To show those sorority girls. To have them woo and flatter and bow down before her. Some day she was going to have money, and then, perhaps she, too, could engage in the same unrealistic pretense as her friends.

CHAPTER
Eight

Wendy and Sarah were in high, crazy spirits from the moment they got on the train. "Freedom! Liberation!" Sarah exulted in the privacy of their compartment. "Isn't this fantastic. I love the design of this compartment. All these little parts fit together. What fun to do nothing but read for three days."

"You must be kidding. That's not what I intend to do."

"If you mean what I think you mean, all I can say is, not in our compartment."

"Killjoy. Admit that you intend to lose your virginity this summer. Olé?"

"Olé," Sarah laughed. "How can I remain a virgin with a nymphomaniac for my best friend!"

"You and Charlotte think any woman who's slept with one man twice or two men once, is a nymphomaniac." They laughed again.

It was wonderfully cozy and compatible, sitting there and watching the country roll by. For a while, they practiced Spanish, and when they got tired, Wendy played her guitar and they harmonized on "Los Quatros Generales," "On Top of Old Smoky," "Viva la Quince Brigada," "Eddystone Light," "No Hiding Place," and songs from *Oklahoma* and *Carousel*. As dusk fell they sat in companionable silence following a glorious sunset.

"In a way I'm glad my mother was so paranoid about flying. It's kind of exciting to go across America like the pioneers."

Wendy laughed. "You mean in an air-conditioned compartment?"

"You know what I mean. It's like returning to the womb. Everything we need is right here with us on the train."

"I *hope* everything we need is on this train. Just pray there are some cute men on board."

"Be serious for a minute. I still feel bad about all of this being so wonderful. I feel guilty about Charlotte. It was an absolutely rotten sadistic thing for her mother to do at the last minute."

"I feel bad, too. But we both did the best we could. It's almost impossible for me to understand her mother. My mother would starve to give me what I needed. Not that she's ever had to, of course. But she would. I love her so much. She's a rock, my fixed star in the universe. It's only because of her that I was able to survive the death of Paula and the death of my father and something else which some day I'll tell you about."

"Charlotte has to struggle to survive her mother," Sarah

said indignantly. "Rotten mothers shouldn't have children, but unfortunately for Charlotte, they do."

"That's why she developed that crush on Professor Shtall when she was studying *The Divine Comedy*. How anybody could worship that walrus with whiskers growing out of her chin."

"That's what she needs. The way I need my brother. What do you need, Wendy?"

"I don't know. My sister, I guess. And I've found that in you. And I need my mother. Thank God I still have her. She's my ballast."

"I wish I felt that way, but I don't respect mine. I can't respect weakness. And she has no philosophic base. If I asked her, 'Mom, what's important enough for you to die for?' You know what she'd say? She'd say, 'Bite your tongue.' Isn't that incredible. 'Bite your tongue.' Oh yes, another one of her favorite intelligent lines is, 'Shussh. The neighbors will hear.'"

Wendy laughed. It was droll, even though it was sad. "Maybe she was different once," Sarah continued sadly, "but now she's nothing but a hollow shell. My father has squeezed all the life out of her, but she let him do it. She never put up a fight for anything. Our generation will be different, Wendy. Men and women will be comrades. Friends!"

"You think so? I don't know. I've never had a male friend. Women are my friends. I don't even know how to talk to a man unless I'm flirting."

"I can't even do that comfortably. But everything is going to change for me this summer. I've decided to find a lover. Many Spanish Loyalists have fled to Mexico City. I might even meet someone who knew my brother."

"You'll have the chance to meet every important lefty in Mexico, if that matters to you. I have a letter of introduction to Juan O'Gorman. He lives in San Angel near Diego Rivera with his wife, Frieda Kahlo."

"Diego Rivera! Juan O'Gorman! Oh, my God. I can't believe it. Why didn't you mention this before?"

"I just received the letter from my mother yesterday. My folks met O'Gorman on a trip to Mexico and commissioned some work for our hotel. He's half-Irish, half-Mexican, and my mother says he's absolutely divine, a genius and a very lovely gentleman. He did the murals at the airport in Mexico City and in the City Hall at the Zocalo. I'll contact him as soon as we get in. San Angel is only about a half hour from Mexico City. I'll rent a car."

"San Angel? I know that name. That's where Trotsky lived."

"Who's he?"

"Wendy. You never cease to surprise me. He was one of the leaders of the Russian Revolution."

Wendy shrugged. "Sarah darling, that was hundreds of years ago, and it has absolutely nothing to do with me."

"You're hopeless," Sarah laughed, loving her. They sat in their compartment waiting for dinner and gradually more and more of their protective layers peeled off.

"No man has ever seemed to want me," Sarah confessed. "I guess I'm not the sexy type. Men don't like flat-chested girls. I've necked and kind of petted with a couple of guys, but it was never any big deal."

Despite their growing intimacy, there was one thing Wendy withheld. The true story about Paula's death. But she did tell Sarah about Uncle Mario, and somehow, in the telling, it became exotic and wildly funny. "I guess that's one way to lose your virginity without pain," Wendy laughed. "Get drunk on brandy. And it certainly developed my taste for brandy, but now I'm going to admit something else to you, Sarah, that I've never told anyone else. I haven't gone to bed with anyone since Mario."

"I don't think that's such a tragedy. I've never gone to bed with anyone at all. I always knew that there was less to you than met the eye. I knew you couldn't have time for all of those so-called exploits."

"Don't ever tell Charlotte, Sarah. Please. She loves disapproving of my bad reputation. And besides, I intend to make up for it this summer."

"Two sex fiends are being loosed on poor Mexico."

"Part of the Good Neighbor Policy."

"And what better way to really learn Spanish? But I don't want to just screw around. I want to find Mr. Right."

Wendy groaned. "How can anybody as rational as you believe there's only one man who was created for her? Especially since you don't believe in God. It's as illogical as Charlotte's temporary crush on Catholicism under Shtall. The world is full of interesting men, and I want to sleep with as many as possible, regardless of race, color, or creed. How's that for a political statement?"

They giggled together, but Sarah refused to be swayed. "You can do what you like, but I still believe in my astral twin."

"Darling, far be it from me to deprive you of your delusions. Life will do that. But what will you do after graduation if you still haven't found him?"

"I don't know exactly. I wanted to be a lawyer, but my father almost had a stroke when I mentioned it. He went into one of his usual self-righteous temper tantrums. 'Are you crazy? Women can't be lawyers. They're not smart enough. I would never have a woman in my firm. No self-respecting law firm would. Teach until you get married. That's a proper field for a woman.'"

"What an opinionated jerk. He should see the way my mother runs our hotel. Like a general."

When the porter knocked and said, "Last call for dinner," Wendy changed to an off-the-shoulder low-cut black lace dress, platform sole shoes, and dangling gold earrings. "You really look sexy," Sarah said. "Like Rita Hayworth."

She had changed to a cotton skirt, blouse, and flat-heeled shoes, called Shank's Mare, from I. Miller. "Is that the dressiest thing you brought?" Wendy asked. When Sarah nodded Wendy said, "Well, maybe I should change."

"Please don't," Sarah said, appreciating her concern. "We each have our own style, and I hate to be dressed up. I could go through the rest of my life in one pair of Levi's."

"Are you really sure you don't mind? I could change in five minutes to something more casual."

"Absolutely. You don't have to dress down just because of me."

"At least put on a little makeup. You can use anything of mine that you want."

Sarah laughed. "Wendy dear, you look beautiful enough

for both of us. Leave me alone. I don't have to get dressed up to eat, and I don't want to bother with makeup. I bet La Pasionaria doesn't care about clothes or makeup. Mrs. Roosevelt doesn't care either."

"You mean you actually want to look like Mrs. Roosevelt?"

Sarah punched her affectionately, then gave her a hug. "I'd be honored to look like her. Let's go. I'm absolutely starved. What fun! I never ate on a train before."

The dining car was elegant with snow-white tablecloths, centerpieces of fresh flowers, and amiable black waiters in immaculate, starched white uniforms. It was all wonderfully new and exciting to Sarah. Unlike Wendy, she had done little traveling. Her summers had been spent at a girls' camp in the Poconos. Her folks hadn't traveled much either, not even before the war, other than an occasional trip to Florida or Hot Springs. Her mother had once dreamed of romantic far-off places, but her father believed "Everything we need is right here in New York City." Her mother sighed and accepted.

The maitre d' came forward to escort them, and Wendy followed him, instantly attracting everybody's eyes as she glided proudly to her table. It continued to amaze Sarah that she could be so indifferent to the glances. Sarah scooted into her seat, but Wendy waited, poised regally while the waiter helped her into hers. "A double scotch on the rocks for me," she ordered. "What about you, Sarah?"

"You know I don't drink. I hate the taste of liquor."

"Do you like champagne?"

"I love it. I got drunk on it at my brother's bar mitzvah."

"A bottle of champagne, instead." Wendy ordered. "Forget about the scotch."

"Champagne's too expensive," Sarah protested.

"My treat. Don't worry about it. We have to drink to the summer." The waiter brought the champagne in a bucket, popped it open, and poured it. The two girls toasted each other.

"Delicious," Sarah said.

"There's hope for you, Ninotchka," Wendy giggled.

Sarah sat there enjoying her increasing mellowness, reveling in the sight of the passing towns, feeling young and free and pampered and happy.

"What are you going to order?" Sarah asked when the waiter brought the menus.

"Oysters, vichyssoise, and pork chops."

Sarah's mother kept a kosher house. "Oysters and pork chops are treyf." Wendy looked at her blankly. "Forbidden," she explained.

"Then you have to try them. Time to stop being provincial. If you're going to be liberated this summer, Sarah, you can't do it by halves. It's all or nothing."

"Are you sure I won't die?"

"If you do, we'll die together. Let's try everything we can. All right?"

"Absolutely. But remember I'm on an allowance. My father is such a tightwad."

"Don't worry. Life in Mexico is cheap, and we'll never have to pay for our own dinners."

"Who'll pay for them?"

"Men of course. That's one of their major functions in life as far as I'm concerned."

"Not as far as I'm concerned. I would only want a man who loves me to pay for me."

"For a leftie," Wendy teased her, "you certainly are romantic."

"Well of course. Why not? One has nothing to do with the other. I grew up reading about Mr. Rochester and Heathcliff. Did you ever see *Wuthering Heights*?"

"Yes, one time, thank goodness. I wish I could have seen it a dozen times. I adore Laurence Olivier."

"I saw *Pepe le Moko* ten times at the Apollo. Jean Gabin is the only movie star I've ever lusted for."

"I've never seen Gabin, but once I had a crush on Nelson Eddy. He came to the hotel."

"You're kidding? The great stone face?"

"I don't know about that, Sarah. Some of our Hollywood guests told us that he and Jeanette MacDonald had a thing going. His face may be stone, but I don't think the rest of him is."

The two of them collapsed in laughter at this. "You've

dated hundreds of men these past three years, Wendy. Have you ever been in love?"

"I thought I was, at times. But once they shipped out I never thought about them again. They all seemed interchangeable. For me, the best time with a man is when you first meet. God, that's exciting. You know, all that dreamy dancing at the USO." She hummed a few bars of "All, or Nothing at All." "What I like best is leaning against a man's chest and feeling my knees and stomach turn to water. Now my goal in Mexico is to pass GO and move directly from that feeling into bed. I think I'm finally ready. I won't be afraid anymore."

At the end of dinner, when the waiter brought their coffee, he said, "They's two gennemen down there who wants to know will you ladies join them in the club car after dinner?"

They followed his glance to a table at the end of the dining car, where two paunchy middle-aged men were puffing away on large cigars. When they saw the girls looking at them, they raised pudgy ringed hands and wiggled them at the girls. Sarah shuddered. "What nerve! They are super repulsive."

"They sure are," Wendy said. She deliberated for a moment then said, "But what the hell. Let's have a drink with them anyway. Just for kicks. We'll dump them if anyone more attractive appears."

"Absolutely no. They're old enough to be our grandfathers."

"Oh, come on," Wendy said. "It can't hurt just to have a drink. Where's your sense of adventure?"

"I don't want that kind of adventure. Suppose they're white slavers."

Ignoring Sarah's objections, Wendy tipped the waiter and said, "Tell them all right."

"Lady Brett Ashley wouldn't spend five minutes with such creeps," Sarah scolded.

"Lady Brett Ashley would never say no to adventure. Maybe they're marvelous, cultured art dealers."

"Fat chance. They're not marvelous, cultured anythings. I want to go back to our compartment and read."

"So go!"

"I don't want to leave you alone."

"Then don't!"

"All right. One drink and that's it."

"Oh, God," Wendy groaned. "I've brought my duenna to Mexico."

"You're going to have to do all the talking, Wendy. Thank goodness you learned how to do that at the hotel. I don't even know what I'd say to men like that. My first impulse would be to ask why they don't ask women their own age to join them."

"Why should they? They're probably married to women their own age. I don't think you have to worry about making scintillating conversation. They look like the kind of egomaniacs who just want pretty little girls to bat their eyelashes at them and listen. But if you find it absolutely unbearable, just start to talk the party line. They'll run out of sheer boredom."

"Oh, you." The two of them giggled nervously together.

After dessert, Sarah reluctantly trailed Wendy into the club car. The men, already seated there, stood up politely when they entered. They were both in their fifties and snappily dressed in expensive but tasteless, loud-colored suits, with awful, hand-painted ties. Both seemed unconcerned about their large, protruding bellies.

Up close, they were even more repulsive. Sam, the taller one, had dandruff all over his jacket and a gigantic wen on the side of his nose. He leered at them and said, "Have a seat, girlies. What're you drinking?"

"Scotch," said Wendy.

"Aha. A real drinker. And you girlie?"

"Coke."

"Coke? A party girl." Then he laughed so hard that his belly shook and his face turned red.

"Oh, God," Sarah muttered, "I'm having my first adventure with Sydney Greenstreet. Just what I've always wanted."

Wendy nudged her and tried to repress her giggles. Sam put an arm on the banquette behind her and began to devour her with his eyes. She batted her magnificent eyelashes, flirted, and giggled seductively, making Sarah increasingly uneasy. He kept licking his lips, and his fingers were like fat, white slugs. Imagine being touched by them! Horrible!

Bennie, the other, had five-o'clock shadow, was just as fat but slightly shorter, was totally bald and dank with perspiration. He lit up a cigar, and Sarah frantically waved the smoke away. "Please don't blow that smoke on me. I can't breathe."

"The best from Havana."

"I don't care where they're from. I can't breathe."

"So where are you girlies going? Texas or Mexico?"

"Mexico."

"First time?"

"Yes."

"Students?"

"Yes."

After eliciting only monosyllabic answers to a few more questions, Bennie gave up the attempt to draw her out and began to talk about himself, just as Wendy had predicted. Sarah sat there angry at Wendy and at herself. She felt defiled.

"We're in the import-export line," Bennie told her. "It's about time that damned war ended. It almost put us out of business."

"What a shame that you've been inconvenienced."

"It sure is." He was not as stupid as she had assumed. "Don't give me that superior glance, girlie. Nobody ever gave me nothing. Nobody sent me off to be a student in Mexico. I never had your advantages. I've been working for a living since I was eight years old. Now we can begin to get back the European markets and finish off the goddamned Japs. At least that we can do alone. It's a goddamned shame that we have to share Europe with the Russkies."

"Is that so?" Sarah snapped. "If not for the Russians, you might not be here now. In case you don't know, they lost twenty million people."

"So what? Still too goddamned many of them. We're going to have to fight them next."

Sarah stood up blazing with anger. "I'm leaving," she

snapped. "You," she scolded Bennie, "are nothing but a warmonger and an imbecile."

"Whoremonger," he said, "what the fuck are you talking about? Hey, gorgeous," he turned to Wendy, "what's the matter with your friend here? Is she a fruitcake? A nut case?"

"Wendy, are you coming?" Sarah asked.

"In a little while," Wendy said in that sexy, languid voice that drove men crazy. "I want to finish my drink."

"You quisling," Sarah snapped before she stomped out. Ooh, she should have done something. Poured a drink all over the disgusting little porker. Done something awful to show him. But after awhile, when her anger had somewhat abated, she began to feel depressed and stupid. She'd certainly handled that badly. Instead of teaching him something, she'd let him wiggle off the hook with the conclusion that she was "a nut case." She should have tried to teach him, to explain to him, instead of getting so upset by his stupidity. It was just that whenever she started to talk politics her anger at her father overpowered her.

She had accomplished nothing by blowing up that way. Some revolutionary she would make! She couldn't even engage in logical debate with some moron in a club car. Maybe if she'd been calm and controlled, he still wouldn't have changed, but at least she could have tried. She was absolutely furious with herself. And she was equally furious with Wendy for staying. It wasn't that she was unfair enough to expect Wendy to treat her enemies like her own. But leaving with her would have constituted a protest. Alone, she was a nut case.

Wendy came in an hour later. "Hi," she said. Her voice was slurred. "They made up our beds, I see. What a neat room."

Sarah turned her back to her and refused to speak but Wendy seemed unaware of Sarah's anger. "Wow! Have I got something to tell you." She carefully locked the door behind her and sat down on her bed facing Sarah's.

Sarah kept her back turned. It was so hard to resist those dancing eyes. "Guess what, Sarah. They made me a business proposition."

Sarah raised her eyebrows. "Oh, wonderful. As what?

A madam? They're probably just what I thought! White slavers!"

"Well, they're white," Wendy giggled, "but you can forget the second half. Just take a look at this!"

"Oh, all right." Sarah shrugged and turned around as Wendy turned her satin purse upside down and emptied the contents onto the blanket. Sarah's eyes widened. What absolutely magnificent jewelry! Her mother had some beautiful pieces, but she kept them in the vault. But here, casually flung down, were two magnificent rings with sunbursts of diamonds, a gold necklace with a sapphire-and-diamond pendant, and four diamond bangles.

"They look real," she said, hoping she was wrong.

"That's because they are. So how do you like them?"

"They're beautiful, I suppose, if you go in for that kind of thing. I wouldn't be caught dead in diamonds. Wearing jewelry is decadent and terribly bourgeois."

Wendy burst into laughter. "Sarah darling, you never cease to amuse me. How can you call stuff this expensive bourgeois? Every piece is just divine." She put the jewelry on, then revolved in front of Sarah, gleaming like a fairy princess. "See how they glitter and shine."

Sarah looked troubled. "I don't get it. Did you buy them?"

"Of course not. I'm the only girl in my family. I have enough stuff in the vault from my grandmother and aunts and mother to last for ten lifetimes. Sam and Bennie aren't involved in anything as wholesome as buying and selling. They want me to smuggle the pieces into Mexico for them."

"Smugglers? So I was right. I knew they were shady characters. I just felt it in my bones. Did you tell them you wouldn't?" But even as she asked the question she knew the answer.

"Of course not. I told them yes."

"But why, Wendy? Why would you have anything to do with such people? You might end up in jail. You just said you have plenty of jewelry at home. And you don't need the money."

"Money has nothing to do with it, silly. I only want to do it because it's so dangerous. It's like being in a movie. Like *The Lady Vanishes*. That takes place on a train, too.

And they'll let me keep one of the bracelets. I don't have a diamond bracelet like this one. But it's not really that. Mainly it's the idea of being a smuggler! It gives me goosebumps! It's absolutely thrilling! I've never felt more alive in my life. It's fun! That's what it is. Crazy, different fun! They asked about you...."

"Really? How thoughtful of them to include me. What did you say?"

Wendy laughed. "I told them probably not."

"Good! I'm glad you're not completely crazy. I won't do it and I don't want you to do it either. Please don't, Wendy. It must be dangerous or they'd take the stuff in themselves. Did they explain to you why they couldn't?"

"I didn't ask. I don't care. I imagine 'the stuff' is probably hot."

Sarah's voice was incredulous. "Hot? And you would carry it? How do those creeps expect you to get past customs?"

"By wearing them."

"That's also crazy! What twenty-year-old girl goes to school in Mexico wearing jewels like these?"

"Nobody will know I'm wearing them. They don't undress you at the border. I'll wear a long sleeved high-necked blouse. That will take care of the bracelets and necklace. And I'll put the rings in my skirt pocket. I'll be so casual about it that no one will suspect. And if anybody gives me a hard time, I'll just smile at him. That usually works."

"You're out of your mind! It only works in your world of privilege. Go out on a picket line some day and see how the cops or horses' hooves react to your beautiful smile. Please don't do it, Wendy. You'll be caught and thrown in a Mexican jail for the rest of your life. They have a terribly corrupt criminal justice system down there."

"Oh, don't be boring. They don't put girls like me in jail."

"Boring?" Sarah almost shrieked. "And you accuse me of being naive! Your problem is that you don't read newspapers. You don't understand the totalitarian mind. Girls like you are put in jail all the time. But they're raped first."

Wendy swept the jewelry back into her purse, leaned

back against her pillow, and lit a cigarette. "I may not understand the totalitarian mind, but I understand the minds of men and servants. And that's all that the police are down there. Men and servants. My mother told me all about Mexico's corruption. What makes you think you know so much, Sarah? You've never even been out of the country before."

"You don't have to go abroad to have a little common sense. The whole situation is illogical. It just can't be that simple, or they'd do it themselves. Why would they reward you with a diamond bracelet for a simple job that isn't dangerous?"

"Oh, you know men!"

"No, I don't. Not that kind, anyway. There's more to this than you understand."

"But what's the worst that could happen?" Wendy asked. "They'll simply confiscate the jewelry. I won't lose either way."

"They'll confiscate the jewelry and put you in one cell with your two fat friends. Imagine having to make conversation with them for an indeterminate sentence."

"Sarah darling, you have no sense of adventure. If the Russians had depended on people like you to man the barricades, the czar would still be in the Winter Palace. Let's stop talking about this. You don't have to be involved at all. But just in case I do get arrested, simply call my mother collect, and she'll call the consulate. No matter what you say, I think it's thrilling. Maybe some day I'll even write a book about it."

"If they give you paper and pencil in your cell!"

CHAPTER
Nine

Sarah was nervous from the moment they stepped off the train at Monterey into what felt like a scorching blast furnace. "It must be a hundred and ten, Wendy. Have you noticed the soldiers over there? Do you think they're here for any special reason? Like maybe a warm reception for our friends?"

"Of course not. Will you stop worrying, please. In Mexico soldiers always kind of stand around waiting to make revolutions."

"Somehow I don't think that's what they're here for."

As they lined up for customs, Sarah saw the eyes of the soldiers lustfully fixed on Wendy, licking and smacking their lips as they uttered the words, "un angel."

"I'm getting more nervous every minute, Wendy. Those soldiers think you're dessert. My Spanish teacher told us that the expression 'Que chingon,' which they use for, 'What a man,' literally means, 'What a rapist.'"

"Stop it. It's too late to do anything, so you might as well relax. This is absolutely the most exciting thing that's ever happened to me. Like riding on a roller coaster."

"It's also happening to me, and I hate roller coasters."

The line moved quickly as passengers at the front of the line quickly cleared customs and boarded the waiting old-fashioned, connecting train to Mexico City. Old-fashioned though it was, it looked like paradise to Sarah. She longed to get out of the heat, kick off her shoes, and order a tall cool glass of juice. Even the worst summer days in New York weren't this bad. Here there were no trees; suffocating dust covered everything; and the air was a solid mass.

She could see Sam and Bennie far in front of them on the customs line. The two officials automatically passed most of the travelers, but when Sam and Bennie stood in front of them, the officials jerked to attention in sudden recognition, and instantly the would-be smugglers were surrounded by soldiers with drawn guns. They stood shaking in the center of the circle, pathetically fat, and impotent like cornered rabbits.

Sarah clutched Wendy's hand and watched in horror as one of the soldiers, probably underpaid, underfed, and a little crazy from the virulent inescapable heat, raised his arm and smashed the butt of his gun down violently on Bennie's head, so hard that even at this distance Sarah could hear a sound like the crack of a dropped watermelon. Bennie crumpled to the ground, blood spurting out of his wound. "This can't be happening," Wendy gasped.

"I want to throw up," Sarah answered. "I knew those soldiers weren't just waiting around for a revolution. They were waiting for your new friends. Oh, my God. Look at that." They'd just pushed Sam down on his knees, and before their horrified eyes he lifted his hand and pointed directly at the girls.

"Why that ratfink," Wendy said angrily. "How dishonorable."

"If you wanted honor, you should have picked different friends. What are we going to do?"

"I'll appeal to their sense of chivalry. Oh, why didn't I learn Spanish better as a kid?"

The soldiers turned, looked at them, and began to gesticulate. "How do you say, 'I'm scared shitless,' in Spanish?" Sarah asked. This was it! The real, terrible world! Goons breaking the heads of Wobblies, Nazis beating Jews, mounted policemen bringing their horses' hooves down on the heads of strikers. Wendy just hadn't understood. Still wanting to throw up, she clutched Wendy's hand as the soldiers advanced toward them.

The other passengers, as if terrified of contagion, scrambled away, anxious to dissociate themselves from possible trouble. The girls were pariahs again. It was like the terrible loneliness of pledge day. Then the heat and her terror triggered a strange kind of click in Sarah's brain. Languor set in. She began to feel detached, almost as if she were watching a movie in slow motion. This was happening to someone else. But she was abruptly jolted back to reality as the soldiers surrounded them and barked, "Vamanos."

Bowed under the weight of their heavy suitcases, they slowly moved forward to a tin shed where they had taken Sam and Bennie. The heat jangled Sarah's nerves, and at every step she winced at the possibility of a gun also crashing down on their heads. Her neck ached with tension.

"Oh, my God," Wendy exclaimed as they entered the shed. "It's even hotter in here. At least 110 degrees. No wonder the soldiers are so crazy." She looked over to where Sam and Bennie sat handcuffed to a hard bench. Sam was dully watching the scene, but Bennie, slumped there, seemed unconscious and unaware of the flies feeding on his wound.

Managing to touch their breasts and buttocks several times, the soldiers pushed them to a table where an angry, mustachioed man, el cápitan, kept them standing for fifteen minutes while he glared at them. It was Sarah's first experience with the demoralization and intimidation caused by the absolute lack of power. He could play with them as long as he liked. He could keep them there while the train pulled away. He could do anything he liked. What was to prevent him? Who was to prevent him? Here, he was the law.

She kept visualizing fates of increasing horror. They could be fined, imprisoned, raped, tortured. They could be killed. Their parents might never know what had happened to them. Sweat was dripping down her neck, and the physical discomfort was maddening. She was going crazy with thirst. Suddenly el cápitan banged his fist down on the table, and both girls jumped in terror at the sound. Then, without a word, he held out his hand. Realizing that the men must have told him, Wendy instantly handed over the necklace, bracelets, and rings. "Nada mas?" he growled, and she shook her head.

He pointed a finger at Sarah, and Wendy said in freshman Spanish, "Ella no tiene nada. Ella solamente va a la universidad." He looked at Sarah suspiciously, barked out a few orders, and she watched, numbed beyond fear, as her luggage was savagely ripped apart, searched, then sloppily thrown together again. Finding nothing, one of the soldiers pushed her to a bench across from Sam and Bennie's, dumping her wrecked luggage at her feet. Wendy remained standing in front of el cápitan, swaying slightly, but retaining her poise. "Por favor, señor," she flashed her beautiful smile. "Una silla." He barked out an order, a backless stool was brought for her, and she sank down gracefully.

As soon as she was seated, el cápitan began to yell at her in English. Why that fake, Sarah thought, pretending to only speak Spanish. "You are estupida," he shouted, "and those men are also estupidos. They are stupid because they do not know we have been watching them. They have tried this very method before. They think that we will not remember. Why would you do such a thing for such men? A girl so beautiful and not poor. A student visiting us? Is this the way to treat a country that has permitted you to visit?"

Wendy's beautiful eyes filled with tears. "Lo siento mucho. Please forgive me." Tears spilled down her lovely face. "I did not understand. I was afraid of them. I know it was stupid. I'll never do it again. Forgive me please."

Wendy reached into her purse for one of her expensive lace handkerchiefs, wiped her lovely eyes, then put the handkerchief down on the table. After that, el cápitan barked out a few incomprehensible commands, and Wendy was helped up by a soldier who placed his hand under her upper arm, high up enough to touch her breast with the back of his hand. Still clutching her there, he led her to Sarah's bench.

"You left your handkerchief there," Sarah whispered.

"It won't be there long. There are good, green Yankee dollars under it."

"Oh my God, Wendy. Now you've done it. Bribery on top of smuggling. They'll lock us up and throw away the key."

"Let's just see what happens."

"How much did you give him?"

"I haven't the slightest idea. I just grabbed a pile of dollars. Maybe $500, maybe more, maybe less. But who cares? It's worth every penny if it gets us out of this mess."

"We didn't have to be in this mess in the first place." Sarah was depressed. All this time, she'd been kind of a phony. It was easy enough to scream fascist at her father, and of course he was. But she'd caved in completely in the presence of a real fascist. She was annoyed with Wendy and angry at herself, but there was nothing to do now but wait.

Suddenly everybody filed out of the shed except for one guard. It was siesta time. The train still waited in the station. Sarah sat there agonizing but Wendy lay down on the bench and immediately fell asleep.

Sarah looked across at Sam and Bennie. Bennie's eyes were closed, and he did not appear to be breathing. She had to do something. Perhaps he was dying. Reaching into her messed-up picnic basket, she took out two oranges that had been lovingly packed by her mother in another life, then stood up waiting to see if there were any reaction from the guard. He too seemed to be asleep. Then, her heart pounding in fear, she slowly inched over to the other bench.

"Bennie," Sarah whispered when she reached him. He opened painfilled yellow eyes and looked at her without recognition. Thank goodness! At least he was alive! Even though they'd brought this on themselves, she felt sorry for them. They seemed so old and defeated now. Maybe they were only doing this to support their families. She thrust the oranges into Sam's handcuffed hands, then scooted back to her seat, her heart in her mouth. It was the bravest thing that she had ever done. Now she felt better about herself. She'd done something. She wasn't only revolutionary rhetoric.

Back in her seat, she looked at Wendy. To her amazement, Wendy continued sleeping as peacefully as if she were in her own bed. That's poise, Sarah thought in amusement. She peeled her remaining orange, took a book out of her handbag and began to read *What Makes Sammy Run*, which the Party hated, but she secretly liked anyway. Hollywood's problems seemed so remote to her at that moment that it was like reading fantasy.

An hour later, el cápitan's return was announced with a burst of raucous laughter. "Wake up, Wendy. They're coming back for the Christians."

"Oh, God. I have to change my napkin. But I'll wait until we're on the train."

"How can you be so optimistic?"

"I've been tipping servants all my life. He won't be able to resist the size of the tip."

El cápitan barked out a few commands, and Sam and Bennie were dragged out to the sound of the soldiers' gratuitous cursing. Sarah shivered for them. As soon as they had gone, two policemen approached the girls. Well, this was it. The bribe hadn't worked. Her mind filled with a vision of the two of them, raped and starving on pallets of straw in roach-infested cells. She bent her head and waited. There was nothing to be done.

"Vamanos," one man shouted roughly, and she picked up her suitcases. Wendy snuffed out her cigarette and carefully replaced the holder in her purse. This gesture was the last straw. Sarah was suddenly filled with such anger against her friend that she couldn't look at her. It wasn't fair to be guilty by association. She hadn't wanted to be involved in any of this, and *she* hadn't done anything. She had always assumed that one day she might go to jail, but for political reasons, for demonstrating against injustice. That would be a noble reason!

But to go to jail for criminal reasons as if she were a member of the lumpenproletariat! That was unforgivable. Especially since she was innocent. And yet what could she have done? Could she have said, "Take Wendy, not me?" No, she could never do that, not even if she had been offered the choice. Not to a sister. Probably not to anyone.

Two soldiers pushed them back to el cápitan's table. He said nothing but looked lustfully at Wendy for a few minutes. Then, with a sigh of regret, he held out her empty handkerchief to her. A smile crossed her face. "Muchas gracias, señor."

Two soldiers carried their luggage to the train and helped them on, managing of course to touch their breasts again in the process.

They were on their way. Wendy sank back into her seat. She was jubilant. "Wow! What an unbelievably marvelous experience."

"Marvelous? You're out of your mind. It was not a marvelous experience. It was the most scary experience of my life. I've wet my pants, aged ten years, and along with every other innocent person on this train I've wasted almost half a day because of you." She shivered. "I wonder what will happen to Sam and Bennie."

"Who cares? Those creeps are criminals. El capitan told me that even if I'd succeeded in smuggling the things through, they wouldn't have given me anything, certainly not a diamond bracelet. I'm glad they're locked up. They won't try this again with unsuspecting girls."

"Unsuspecting! Honestly, Wendy, I think you have a screw loose in the morality department. You cooperated willingly. They didn't threaten you. And maybe they *would* have given you the bracelet. I wouldn't believe anything that corrupt el cápitan told you. But that's not the point. If they were criminals, then so were you. And even though you only did it for kicks that's just as bad. Whatever they were guilty of, you were guilty of also."

Wendy looked at her in perplexity. "I don't understand you. What do you want, Sarah? You want me to say I'm sorry. But I'm not. Sometimes I think that you have absolutely no sense of humor. It was exciting and interesting, and I may never have an experience like that again. So please don't be so square."

Sarah shrugged. Even with the best of friends it seemed that there were areas of perception that you just could not share. She turned to watch the scene from the train window, and her anger gradually dissipated in her pleasure at the unfamiliar sights; cactus, adobe huts, peons lounging against buildings with their large white hats down over their faces looking exactly like every travel poster she'd ever seen for Mexico. And finally, Mexico City itself, bustling, modern, and mysterious. It was exciting just to hear everybody speaking Spanish.

They had been warned that it might take them a few days to become accustomed to the extraordinary altitude, 7,240 feet in the sky, but they felt alert, alive, and exhilarated as they walked out of the station. The air was clear, fresh, and invigorating, and the temperature was perfect. A porter carried their bags to a cab, and after tipping him, Wendy bargained with the driver for a price, finally fixing on one that was half of what he originally asked.

"It embarrasses me to bargain," Sarah said. "Thanks for doing it."

"I don't mind. It's the way of life here. My mother gave me precise instructions about it."

In a few minutes they had reached a pretty, white, two-story stucco townhouse off the Paseo de la Reforma, two blocks from Chapultepec Park. Everything was seemingly back to normal, just the way it should be for two rich pretty American girls. But the memory of the shed and the image of Bennie covered with blood and flies still haunted Sarah, clinging to her like stale tobacco smoke.

At the boarding house, la duena greeted them, and the cab driver carried their luggage up to the room, a charming, cool, white-washed plaster interior with a high arched ceiling and a flower-covered balcony from which they could see the wide, verdant Paseo and the Castle of Carlotta and Maximilian, high up in Chapultepec Park. Sarah stood on the balcony for awhile, thrilled at finally being there.

"This is really strange for me," Wendy called to her. "It's the first time I've ever shared a room with someone. Do you care which bed and drawers I take?"

"No," Sarah called back. After years of summer camp, she was totally relaxed about room arrangements. When she went inside, Wendy was sitting on her bed looking at her unopened suitcases on the floor beside her.

"I can't do it," she said, throwing up her hands in exasperation. "I've never had to unpack and arrange things for myself before. They must have a maid who would do it for me."

"I doubt it. This place is for college girls."

"What will I do?"

Sarah laughed. "All right. I'll help you to unpack and put things away if you promise me no more dangerous adventures."

"And if I won't promise?"

"I guess I'll still help you."

"Oh, thank you, Sarah darling. And as soon as we're settled, I have a surprise for you."

Sarah began to work while Wendy fluttered about her. Finally she said, "Wendy, you're only an impediment. Go sit on your bed and get out of my way. It's a good thing I brought so little. If I hadn't, you'd have to keep half your stuff in your suitcases. I can't believe how much you brought."

"I know. I always travel with too much. But I need everything I bring. My mother's the same way."

When Sarah had finished, she sat down on her bed and asked, "OK. What's the surprise?"

"Close your eyes," Wendy said gleefully. "Now open them."

There, on the palm of her hand, reflecting the dying sun, was one of the diamond bracelets. "Ta-ta. Surprise! How's that for an accomplishment? I had it hidden in my bra all the time. I wasn't going to go through all of this for nothing."

Sarah gasped. "*You* weren't? What about me? How could you do such a thing? Bribing them with all that money to extricate us, and all the while risking even worse trouble. I just can't believe it. You're just a selfish, spoiled brat who thinks she can buy her way out of anything. You didn't think about my feelings or needs for even a second."

"Oh, darling," Wendy said, crestfallen before Sarah's anger. "You're absolutely right. Honestly, sometimes I can be so thoughtless and insensitive." With one swift gesture, she tossed the bracelet over to Sarah's bed. "Here. You can have it. My way of apologizing. I didn't want you to be involved. And I really do appreciate your unpacking for me."

"I wouldn't touch it." Sarah flung it back.

"Please take it, Sarah. I don't want you to be angry with me. I did try to extricate you. You heard me tell him that you weren't involved. Some day we're going to look back on this and think of it as a totally fabulous adventure." Sarah still didn't answer. "You're not going to stay angry all summer, are you? Why won't you take the bracelet? Somebody's fat Mexican mistress is going to get all the rest of the jewelry.

She didn't earn it. But we earned it. Sitting there sweating all afternoon!"

"I don't know how to make you understand, Wendy. I'm a nervous wreck from the whole experience. I will never look back on it as a fabulous adventure, and I will never wear diamonds."

"Oh, God," Wendy yawned. "We're back to the fur coat nonsense again. Who would you hurt by wearing diamonds? Not the South African diamond miners. They need the work."

"Let's just drop the whole thing. You'll never understand my point of view, and I certainly find yours totally amoral. So let's just forget it."

"Amoral? I don't even know what that means. Suppose you had gone to el capitan and announced, 'There are two smugglers on this train and my friend over there is helping them.' Is that what you'd consider moral? We three would have disappeared, you would have been alone for the rest of the summer, and Mexico would continue to be every bit as corrupt as before."

Sarah made one last attempt. "Some things are right, Wendy, and some things are wrong."

"And some things are just plain murky. Why was smuggling wrong in this case? Nobody would have been hurt. As far as I can see the only wrong thing was hitting Bennie. Those poor cream puffs! God knows what will happen to them now. But we're not responsible. They would have been caught sooner or later. Come on, Sarah. Where's your sense of humor? No harm was done. Some day you'll tell your grandchildren about it. And weren't all those repressed soldiers copping a feel absolutely pathetic?"

Now Sarah joined in Wendy's laughter. "I don't think they ever found *my* breasts."

She might as well drop it. There was no way she and Wendy could ever see this incident in the same way.

"Friends?" Wendy asked anxiously. She really didn't understand why Sarah continued to be so upset, although she did agree that being in the shed was awful. Especially in the middle of her period. But here they were, safe and sound, and the bribe she'd paid was insignificant in terms of the cost of the bracelet.

"Yes," Sarah finally laughed. "I may thoroughly disapprove of you, but I love you anyway. And you certainly are an original. Now please, no more adventures this summer. If you want to play the role of madcap heiress, please do it when you're not with me."

CHAPTER
Ten

Charlotte moved into Wendy's apartment the day after her friends left for Mexico. Even though money was tight, she had to order a cab. Her luggage and art materials were too cumbersome to manage on the subway. It was not until her mother saw the extent of her packing that she actually realized Charlotte was moving out and might not be returning.

"You can't go," she wept. "You can't leave me alone. Suppose I get sick again." When Charlotte didn't answer, she tried to woo her. "If you don't leave, I'll give you money for your tuition next year." So she could have stayed in school! Outrageous! This only hardened Charlotte's resolve. She continued to pack methodically as her mother became more and more abusive. First, she carried out the few paintings she'd done while Greta was with them. Then, with her mother pulling on her arm to stop her, she carried her suitcases and boxes out to the cab. After that, she said coldly, "Good-bye, Mother. I'm going now."

Her mother began to shriek, "You can't leave me alone. I'm sick. I can't be alone. You know that. You can't go. You ungrateful little bitch. After all I've done for you."

Charlotte looked at her with loathing. She was dressed in a filthy old bathrobe, her face was covered with pimples that she sat squeezing by the hour, and it was so long since her hair had been washed that it looked coated with tallow. "Good-bye," she repeated, desperate to escape.

"You'll be sorry," her mother screamed, running into the house, as the cab pulled up.

Charlotte stood beside the cab shaking with nervousness

while the cabbie loaded the trunk. Then he slammed it shut, looked up, and suddenly shouted, "Oh-oh, look out." But it was too late! Her mother was pouring a bucket of hot soapy water from the upstairs window directly onto Charlotte. "That will teach you," she screamed. "Good riddance to bad rubbish and don't think you can ever come back here again."

Charlotte burst into tears. One of the few good outfits she owned was now totally drenched. The cab driver took charge.

"Come on, kid. Get in before she does something else. Come on. Let's go."

"I'll wet your cab," she wept.

He opened the door and gently pushed her in. "You don't have to worry about this cab. I've cleaned up a lot worse things than soapy water. I've washed vomit and come off that seat lots of times. So get in and let's go. That woman gives me the willies."

He closed her door, got into his seat, and asked, "Where are we going?"

"Central Park West and Sixty-third Street."

He began to drive and asked, "What was all that about, kid? Try to leave without paying the rent?"

"No," she sobbed. "That was my mother. She didn't want me to leave her."

"A hell of a way to show affection. That's some mother you got there, kid. Listen, kid, I'll turn off the meter if you stop that wailing. It's making me noivous. Look, it's off. I'll charge you whatever you can afford."

"You don't have to. I have enough money for you."

"Nah, nah, that's all right. Here, take this rag. Not too clean, but you can wipe your shoes." Little by little, as she began to recover, she confided in him.

"You done the right thing, kid. Take it from me. You got your own life to lead. My kids've all left home. That's what's natural. Feeling better? OK, try to relax. Lean back, close your eyes, and I'll put on WNEW. Sinatra. He'll make you mellow."

By the time they got to Wendy's building, she had dried off a little from the warm spring breeze. But her hair felt sticky. She couldn't wait to get into the shower. The doorman had been alerted to her arrival, and the moment the cab pulled up, a team of porters rushed out for her luggage. She opened her purse, but the cabbie shook his head and motioned toward her luggage. "Lemme ask you something. Are those oil paintings?"

"Yes," she said, watching the men stack them in a dolly.

"Did you paint them?"

"Yes. But they're not very good."

"They look good to me. Listen kid. I can live without your few bucks, but I never owned a real, genuine oil painting done by a genuine artist. My wife hung up a calendar in the kitchen with sunflowers. I'd love to bring a real painting home to her. But listen, only if you want. I don't want to take advantage. . . ."

"Take advantage? After all your kindness to me? I'd love to give you one of my paintings."

"Only if you want. I mean, it's not like you owe me. . . ."

"I'd be honored to give you one. A lot of painters have used their paintings for barter but nobody's ever asked for one before." She reached behind her into the dolly and pulled out a canvas she'd done at cherry blossom time in the Brooklyn Botanic Gardens, with Greta sitting enraptured at her side. "This is my favorite. And here's my name at the bottom of a tree."

He held it reverently in his hands. "C. Lewin," he read. "It's gorgeous. Wait till the wife sees it. I'm going to keep it for the rest of my life, and then I'll give it to my kids. I'll be watching for your name when you get famous." He carefully placed the painting in his trunk, pointed a grease-stained finger at her, and said, "Don't go back to Brooklyn." Charlotte looked after him with gratitude. He'd saved this awful day for her.

She let herself into Wendy's apartment and felt her turbulent spirits calm as she stood there for a moment basking in the luxury. She'd visited many times before, but it was different now to have this whole wonderful place for her own. Quickly stripping off her damp clothes, she hurried into the shower, reveling in the thick rug beneath her toes, the fragrance of Wendy's expensive soap and shampoo, the quiet, expensive elegance. Oh, the peace! She remained in the shower for a long time as her past was washed away, and she was baptized into a new life.

Everything in the apartment was fresh and new. Sachets of potpourri in every closet and drawer, embroidered sheets, towels, tablecloths and napkins neatly stacked in the linen closet. Not a chipped dish in the breakfront, not a bent piece of silverware in the drawers, not a dented utensil in the kitchen. Wendy simply threw things out if they became damaged.

A polished set of copper pans and molds hung on the kitchen wall above a shelf of expensive cookbooks that Wendy had never opened. The immaculate refrigerator purred away, and there was not a speck of food or dust on top of the stove. Oh, my God, Charlotte thought, I'm in heaven. She shuddered, remembering the chaos and filth surrounding her mother, remembering the cleanliness and order that Greta had brought during her few months with them.

But even Greta's energetic polishing had not given her house the logic, arrangement, and design of this apartment. This had all been worked out, painstakingly and intelligently, by experts. That was what it meant to have money and a decorator. Everything was where it should be; the appropriate lamp for reading, the convenient table for setting down a drink, the aesthetic logic of the arrangements of paintings on the walls. Everything planned and coordinated. No clutter, waste, or disorder.

On the terrace overlooking Central Park there were freshly planted window boxes filled with hardy roses. Their perfume caressed her as she stretched out on a comfortable chaise longue, feasting her eyes on the park, letting her hair dry in the pleasant breeze. Money was everything. Money could pay for a life like this. Nothing else mattered.

Oh, it wasn't fair that for so much of her life she'd lived with screams and dust, a dirty bathroom, a smelly, noisy refrigerator, and a filthy, food-encrusted stove from which gas escaped. Nobody, looking at her, could imagine the disgusting pigsty from which she emerged each day. Nobody knew how hard it had been to look immaculate at school.

That was why it still hurt to have been rejected by a

sorority. She'd always tried so hard. Other people seemed to have compensations for the bad things that happened to them. Take Wendy! Even though she had lost her sister and her father, she had a wonderful mother who adored her and gave her everything she wanted. She had always been loved and rich. That was why she could afford to be so generous. It was hard to be generous when you had to shiver over every penny but Wendy wasn't concerned about any possible damage to the apartment. If Charlotte were to spoil something, Wendy would just throw it out and replace it.

She was consumed with a sense of the unfairness of things. Why should Wendy have all this and she have nothing? She had to admit that she was jealous of Wendy even though nobody had ever been more generous to her. She knew it was illogical, but that was how she felt. Nothing would ever make up for all of her deprivations. Her girlhood had been stolen from her and even if she did get rich, all of her terrible experiences would be forever embedded in her memory. But damn it, she was going to try to make something of her life. There was no way she'd let herself turn out like her mother.

The first thing was to find a job. And so, early the next morning, carrying a portfolio of her drawings, she began to make the rounds of advertising agencies. By the end of the week she was hired by the art department of the Marshall Berman Advertising Agency on Madison Avenue. The salary was low and she was at the bottom of the ladder, an apprentice really, but she was euphoric. She had a job and was living in Manhattan in a beautiful apartment. Her luck was changing.

It was a cool, early June day, and the city was still fresh with spring. Enchantment lay around every corner. It was the city where she had always wanted to live. Now she was here, and some day she would really belong—have charge accounts everywhere, be invited to the best parties, be welcomed by name by the maitre d' of every expensive restaurant. Her soul soared upward with hope.

Each morning she left early and strolled leisurely to work—across Central Park South, through the elegant lobby of the Plaza Hotel just to look at the people, down Fifth

Avenue past the windows of Bergdorf Goodman and the Tailored Woman, across Fifth to Saks, east at Saks to Madison Avenue, and then into her lobby—feeling unfamiliar communion with the world.

She wrote to Sarah and Wendy. "Thanks to your generosity I'm feeling better about myself and my life. I still haven't caught sight of your maid, Wendy. It's like the story of the 'Shoemaker and the Elves.' My bed is changed, the laundry ironed (even my bras and underpants), drawers are straightened, and holes mended. She comes after I leave and is gone by the time I get home. Each day in your beautiful apartment is especially precious. I like my job, too.

"The girls with whom I work at the agency are a totally different breed from the sorority girls. None of them have gone past high school, so they're respectful and a little flattering about my three years of college. Most of them are just marking time until their men return from the Pacific. They all know a lot more about advertising art than I do, and they're generous and go out of their way to help me."

Patsy, a cheerful Italian girl who worked beside her, was especially friendly. She chattered away constantly, filling Charlotte in on company gossip. "You'll like Mr. Berman. Everybody does. He's a good boss. I know lots of people say no boss can be good, but he is. He's been away a month, trying to get over the death of his wife. Did you read about it in the papers? No? Well I don't know about the *New York Times*, but it was a front-page story in the *Daily News*. Just one of those crazy freak accidents that happen in New York all the time. She was standing on the corner across from the Plaza, holding her little boy, Teddy, by the hand, and a car went out of control, up onto the sidewalk, and killed her instantly. The kid wasn't hurt at all, but can you imagine him seeing all this happen? I mean, just standing there screaming, 'Mommy, Mommy.' I tell you, it gives me the creeps."

In a flash, Charlotte remembered bending over her father, planting a kiss on the cold, rigid cheek. Many times in dreams she'd found herself kissing a skeleton that had wrapped its bony hands around her neck while its legs encased her body, imprisoning her, squeezing tighter and tighter and tighter. She was choking, choking to death. She couldn't breathe. "Hey." Patsy was shaking her by the shoulder. "Are you OK? You turned so pale."

"Yes, I'm all right. What happened to the little boy?"

"I don't know exactly. I think the grandmother is taking care of him. Isn't that typical of life? A loving husband, a beautiful kid, and all the money in the world, and zap. Dead at thirty. Mr. Berman's about five years older."

"All the money in the world?"

"Sure. This is a very successful agency. He's a real winner."

Listening to Patsy talking about him, she felt a certain sense of anticipation, and when he sent for her on the first day of his return, she could instantly see why his employees admired him. He looked like a corporate president should: slim, erect, intelligent, self-contained. A thin face with fine sharp features, good-humored brown eyes, and a well-shaped mouth. Nice teeth. A small mustache. Not handsome in a conventional way, but well put together, groomed with care. He was dressed in an impeccably tailored navy suit, a creamy hand-stitched white shirt, and an expensive-looking silk paisley tie. His gold cuff links matched his Patek Philippe gold watch, his black leather shoes gleamed, his nails were manicured, and his light brown hair was perfectly cut.

She liked the look of his clean neck. Her father had always looked like a slob. Well, poor thing, he'd had nobody to take care of him. It was far easier to look nice if you had an invisible maid like the one Wendy had, doing all of the dirty work for you.

When he spoke, his voice was polite, cultivated, Ivy League. "Welcome to the company, Miss Lewin. Sorry I couldn't personally greet you before today. Everyone here is quite pleased with your work. I hope that you'll be happy here." Any emotional distress could only be deduced from the fact that he chain-smoked, lighting each fresh cigarette from the burning tip of the one he was discarding. He's like me in a way, she thought. No matter what we're going through, we still try to look neat and well-dressed. It's a kind of protection from the world.

"Thank you," she said shyly, struggling to hide the remnants of a Brooklyn accent in her voice. He evoked in her a sudden sense of bittersweet nostalgia. She was Jay Gatsby looking across the bay to Daisy's mansion. Clyde Griffiths wanting Sondra in *An American Tragedy*. He represented everything she had always wanted: strength, position, success, money, class. He epitomized the kind of man she wanted but despaired of ever getting. Sarah could get such a man. Wendy could. But how could she get such a man? What did she have to offer? No father, a crazy mother, no money, fat legs, no college degree. Although she'd never expressed this thought to her friends, she'd never blamed the sorority girls as unequivocally as Wendy and Sarah had. Why shouldn't they have rejected her? She might have rejected herself if she were in their position. Why should they have liked her? She didn't like herself.

She lingered, trying to think of something appropriate to say, wanting desperately for him to approve of her. "Thank you, Mr. Berman. I'm grateful for the opportunity. And may I express my condolences. I'm very sorry about your wife. And your little boy...." Now she could see clearly that beneath his professional mask he was in terrible pain, but he was the type of gentleman who would never inflict his suffering on other people. Then, with a rush of compassion, remembering the familiar ache for her father, she said the right words instinctively.

"I know how he must feel. I lost my father, and life has never been the same for me since. It makes you feel branded, different. Guilty. Somehow to blame." She shivered involuntarily.

He looked at her in surprise. She'd reached him. "Yes," he sighed. "Poor Teddy. I don't think a three-year-old has the vocabulary to express such horror, but I know he feels it. Right now he's a little numb, sucks his thumb, and doesn't say much. But I worry that a time bomb may go off in the future." He shook his head in sorrow. "God knows I'll do my best to try to prevent it. What helped you to get through?"

"Of course I was much older, but my two college friends saved me. They still are. I'm living in one's apartment."

What a lovely girl, he thought, noting her diffident manner, beautiful skin, lustrous auburn hair, and exquisite neatness. He liked employees to look like this.

When she left his office to return to her desk she was filled with unaccustomed peace and happiness. He knew who she was.

CHAPTER
Eleven

During the next few days, she saw him infrequently and only from a distance, but one night when she had been working late because she had no money to do anything else, they unexpectedly bumped into each other at the elevator. "What a pleasant surprise," he said courteously. "Have you had dinner yet?"

She shook her head, too shy to answer.

"Well then, do come and have a bite with me. I really don't like to eat alone."

She walked shyly at his side along Madison Avenue, wondering nervously what to talk about during dinner. Here was the kind of opportunity to know him that she would not have dared to dream of, and she was terrified. Please, God, she prayed to herself, don't let me bungle it. Her mind darted about feverishly, and the shields of her dress were wet with perspiration. She bit her lip to keep it from trembling. They walked north to Fifty-fifth Street, then west half a block to Le Pavillon. "Le Pavillon," she gasped. "I can't go in there! I'm not dressed right."

He looked at her seriously with honest concern about her feelings. After a moment of careful scrutiny he smiled encouragingly. "You look fine. Very pretty. Not a thing to worry about."

She looked at him worshipfully and let herself relax. Could anything be more wonderful than the aura of a powerful man? He would take care of her, not let her be embarrassed. She had not felt so protected since the long walks of childhood along the Esplanade with her father.

As soon as they entered the restaurant, her senses were awhirl with the sight and smell and sound and feel of comfort and privilege. She felt wistful, as she had on entering Wendy's apartment. She was only a visitor here, but Mr. Berman waited with the unmistakable stance of belonging, as the maitre d' rushed up and greeted him by name. Ignoring the fact that they had no reservation, he immediately led them to a banquette. Marshall's eyes lit up with pleasure as Charlotte reverently touched the snow-white tablecloth, and then, with childlike spontaneity, bent forward to smell the fresh roses. He found the combination of woman and child totally captivating.

"What would you like to eat?" he asked after they received the menus.

"Please order for me. Any little thing would be all right." She wouldn't want him to think she was imposing on him. He smiled at her use of the words, "any little thing," then ordered champagne, Beluga caviar, Perigord foie gras, quenelles and oeufs à la neige. It was the best food she had ever tasted.

"I never thought I'd eat here," she said shyly. "I have two friends who have. One of them, Wendy, eats here all the time. The other one, Sarah, could afford to eat here all the time but she won't. She wants to be one of the proletariat."

He laughed aloud at that, and she was glad that for a moment she could help to banish the terrible sadness in his eyes.

"Her father is Judge Stern. Have you heard of him?"

"Yes, indeed. The Torquemada of the right. No wonder she wants to be one of the proletariat. It must drive him wild."

"It does drive him wild. But she doesn't do it just to anger him. She has an exceptional social conscience."

"Are you that way too?"

"No. I've been too busy trying to survive to worry about the rest of the world." She noted that he was smiling. "Are you laughing at me?"

"Of course not. I was smiling because I was so amused by your honesty."

As they ate, she said little, preferring to listen to him, fastening intently on his every word, trying to learn the language of his class. His conversation was an urbane mixture of current events and the social and cultural happenings of the city. He was the archetypal upper-class New Yorker, a culture consumer, leading the kind of life for which she'd always yearned, the kind of life that Wendy and Sarah took for granted.

"Do you like opera?" he asked.

"I don't know. I've never been to one."

"Perhaps you'll go with me some time. My parents were opera lovers. They had the same box I now have. Of course, once you get a good box for Thursday nights, you never give it up."

"Oh, of course," she echoed lamely.

"Some day Teddy will have the box. My wife loved opera as much as I. She also loved all the ritual surrounding the box! The cheerful little maids rushing to greet us, unlocking our box, hanging our coats in the little anteroom, then wishing us a good evening. During intermissions, friends would come to visit us." He sighed. "We had only ten years together. Such a freak accident. It haunts my dreams."

Charlotte tried to comfort him. "You were lucky to have a good marriage even for ten years. I don't think my parents ever felt that way about each other. Maybe at the beginning, but not in my memory.

"And things really got bad after my brother died. It was awful to see him in that iron lung. I wouldn't even go into the room. I'd rather die than be imprisoned in one of them. Can you tell me the sense of keeping a body alive like that? It's like being in a coffin."

"I've often thought so myself."

"After he died, my mother started to get kind of crazy. If you don't mind my saying so, Mr. Berman, that's one of the things I admire the most about you. Your wife died and it didn't make you crazy."

"That's what you think." He smiled then changed the subject.

He also loved the ballet. He told her about it, mentioning romantic, unfamiliar names: Alicia Markova, André Eglevsky, Nora Kaye, Hugh Laing, *Giselle*, *Petrouchka*, *Swan Lake*. "Ballet can make you cry, you know. I've cried for Petrouchka, a puppet. Imagine that! A puppet! And the Stravinsky music is marvelous."

"I feel so ignorant," she said, surprised by her own candor.

"It's not as if you'd had the opportunity. But you needn't feel sad. You have your whole life ahead of you. I'd like to see your face the first time you weep at *Giselle* or *Swan Lake*." He stopped abruptly, as if he'd said something improper, then recouped with, "Well, everybody weeps the first time. Especially at Markova. It's incredible. Such grace. Such lightness. As if she has defeated gravity."

His favorite art form was solo piano, and his favorite pianist was Artur Rubenstein. "I don't know how anyone can prefer Horowitz," he said with some heat. She'd never heard of either one.

"I'd like to ask you something about music," she said, moved past self-consciousness by delight in having someone to discuss these things with. "I took a symphony course in college, and I loved Tchaikovsky's symphonies. Especially the sixth. And his piano concerto. But my teacher said he's too melodic."

He laughed. "I'm familiar with that pose. It's in right now. I have the greatest respect for his music. There's nothing wrong with melody, and Tchaikovsky has some of the most beautiful. I like a wide variety of music. I have eclectic taste." Yes, she thought, that described him. So very smart, but also flexible.

He walked her home along Central Park South. "I'm living in my friend's apartment," she said. "I think I told you that. I have to find another place in September."

"Really? Let me work on it. I have a friend who teaches at Columbia and is going to France on sabbatical for a year. He's looking for a tenant who'd take good care of his things."

"Oh, I would. I'm very careful and very neat."

"I knew that, the moment I met you." She didn't say

anything more about it. Somehow she knew that once he made a promise, it would be fulfilled.

"Well, here we are," he said when they reached her building. "I'm afraid I've kept you up far too late. Thank you for helping me to spend such a pleasant evening. Perhaps I'll be able to get to sleep now."

"How can you thank me? It's I who am grateful to you. I'll never forget tonight." Then, overcome with emotion, she hurried to the privacy of the elevator, where tears of happiness rolled down her cheeks.

She lay awake for hours, remembering every single moment of the evening's enchantment. I'm in love, she thought. I'm in love with him. He's everything I've ever wanted; he's stable, strong (not weak like my father), cultivated, successful. He could bandage all the sorrows of my past life and protect me from any future ones. Please, God, she prayed, let him love me. Let him marry me. I'll never ask for anything again.

But when she went in to work the next day, he was no more accessible to her than before. In the afternoon, she glimpsed him from a distance, and he smiled and casually waved to her before disappearing into an office. Nothing more. The hollow, familiar feeling of disappointment and deprivation swept over her. What a fool she was to ever set herself up for joy. Better never, never to dream.

She went through the next few days wrapped in her familiar despair. But then, on Thursday morning, he stopped by her desk and asked her to have dinner with him that night. It would have to be early because the following day he would be going out to the beach with his son. It was impossible for her to act casual about this, so she said what immediately came into her mind. "Oh, thank you. Thank you for making me feel important."

He was surprised by the vehemence of her words and dazzled by the worship in her eyes. Unaccustomed to such naked admiration, he was a little embarrassed. But he was also flattered. He was, after all, bereaved, lonely, and bruised himself. She had helped him to almost forget his tragedy during their dinner together, and he liked teaching her.

After that, they had dinner together several times a week.

Gradually, she became comfortable with him, with the best restaurants in the city, and with appropriate behavior patterns for his way of life.

Trying to understand what was happening, she wrote to her friends: "Can he possibly be romantically interested in me? I honestly can't figure it out. What can I offer such a man? I know he thinks I'm neat and smart and pretty. Once he said that I'm as fresh as a country morning. I think he likes my youth. But right now he's one of New York's most eligible bachelors. He belongs to Temple Emanu-El and the Harmonie Club, and he must know dozens of women who are rich and chic and sophisticated. Sometimes I think that if he likes me, perhaps there's something wrong with him. But thus far, I've been unable to find a single drawback to his character or personality.

"Wendy, my dear, to anticipate your usual question, I'm still a virgin. He's never so much as kissed my cheek. I can't tell if it's because he's still in mourning, because he's a perfect gentleman, or because I don't attract him that way. Maybe he spends time with me because it's safe. I mean, I don't have the right to expect anything of him. I'm grateful for anything.

"Remember when we read *The Devil and Daniel Webster*, we used to talk about what was worth selling our souls for? Well, I'd sell my soul to marry him and reach safe harbor. I'd even give up my art for marriage to such a man who would always protect me, delight me, think about my needs, surprise me with gifts on every birthday, every anniversary, and every other holiday, too. He's that kind of man.

"I keep learning from him. I like listening to everything except his interminable stories about Teddy. When he starts to recount every inane little saying as if he's the most brilliant child in New York, I have to control my restlessness. Actually, that's the only thing wrong with him. He has his little boy on the brain. He feels guilty about him, as if it's his fault that he's deprived of a mother. It's totally illogical, but there it is.

"I would prefer that he didn't have a child but I guess if he had to have a child I would have preferred a girl. I've always thought they were easier to handle than boys. But it really shouldn't matter much either way. He has three servants who have been with him forever, really like aristocratic family retainers, and if I were ever lucky enough to marry him, of course a nanny would take care of Teddy, so that would not be a problem for a new wife.

"Which I would die to be.

"I'm anxious to hear about all of your exploits. Love."

CHAPTER
Twelve

Wendy read Charlotte's letter aloud to Sarah. "She's going to snare him. I feel it in my bones."

"Oh, I hope so. She needs that so much. The way she said 'To reach safe harbor.' Just think. She'll probably be the first one of us to get married."

"And maybe the first one to get divorced."

"Oh, Wendy. Why do you pretend to be so cynical? You know you're really not that way at all. I think you're a latent idealist."

"You mean *you're* not that way at all. I like to have as few illusions about people and life as possible. We'll see. Underneath Charlotte's sweet exterior, there's an awful lot of anger. I wouldn't want to be that little Teddy."

"Why do you say that? I'm sure that all of her mother's cruelty would lead Charlotte to be especially loving to a child who's been through such a terrible experience."

"Well I'm not. She needs so much attention and coddling herself. It's like Snow White. And besides, Charlotte has never had the model of a good mother."

"Models can be changed. Look at the Russian Revolution."

Wendy laughed. "As far as I can see nothing's changed there, either Sarah. You just have a new group of terrible people in power."

"This is not a joking matter to me," Sarah said firmly. "If I didn't believe that cycles could be broken I just couldn't go on. I don't want to be my mother or my father, and I have to believe that if I can do it, Charlotte can too."

"Maybe," Wendy shrugged. "I suppose it's necessary to hope."

They had fallen in love with Mexico City, walking everywhere, west from the Zocalo along Avenida Cinco de Mayo and Avenida Francisco Madero, along Avenida Juarez, and the magnificent Paseo de la Reforma from the Plaza de la Republica to Chapultepec Park, where they climbed to the castle of Carlotta and Maximilian.

Every day brought glorious new experiences. The only thing that bothered Sarah was the virulent, inescapable poverty all around them. Outside their boarding house lay a fly-covered Indian woman nursing a diseased-looking baby, lying right on the concrete with nothing beneath her. Beggars were everywhere, diseased, deformed, tubercular, with missing limbs. Starving children pressed hungry faces against restaurant windows, making her ashamed of eating. In dreams she saw their distorted faces, bloated bellies, toothless mouths, withered breasts.

"I can't stand it," she told Wendy.

"I know! It's really awful. But I don't think there's anything we can do about it. There are just too many poor people, and this isn't even our country. So why insist on torturing yourself? You didn't make the world. And you can't change it. No matter what the Marxists say, the poor will always be with us. It's not our problem."

"Yes it is," Sarah said soberly. "I think we can make a difference. I think that's what we were born for. I'll never forget that at his bar mitzvah my dear brother said, 'Playing safe is an unethical and contemptible policy. No cause can succeed if people play safe and wait for the success of the cause. We must sacrifice ourselves like Abraham did and actually make the attempt to realize the cause.' He said that's what it means to be a good Jew."

"Could he be a Marxist and a good Jew?"

"Marx *was* a Jew."

One day they went to Amecameca where people were living in clay hovels on floors of cooled grimy volcanic cinders. That night, escorted by Indian guides, they rode burros up Popocatepetl to watch the fiery, destructive beauty of the volcanic explosions from the neighboring peak of Ixtacchihuatl. Shivering in the unexpected, piercing cold, thinking of the paradox of the beauty of the shower of fire and the devastation it caused in the valley below, Sarah felt an aching sense of cosmic loneliness. Nature was indifferent, and most people didn't care.

She had to do something. She had no extra blankets, but when they returned, she gave the woman on the street in front of the building a large bath towel and some jars of baby food. Then she filled her pockets with pesos and chocolates and gave them to every child beggar she passed that summer. In the long run it could not make a difference. But it made her feel a little better.

* * *

A few weeks after their arrival, they were invited to a party at Juan O'Gorman's house, and it was there that Sarah met the love of her life. O'Gorman's house was an ultramodern, light-blue structure, high in the air on wooden stilts, surrounded by a variety of tall cacti that resembled the shape of cypress.

That night, the marvelously festive glass house was filled with laughter, dancing, the romantic sound of Spanish voices, the tinkle of glasses, and the wonderful, joyous music of the mariachi. As the girls entered, people turned to look at Wendy, a vision of old Spain in an off-the-shoulder black lace dress, her hair piled high on her head with combs, a few soft tendrils tumbling down around her face. Diamond studs gleamed in her ears, and the diamond bracelet glittered on her arm. Their host, a warm and charming man, came hurrying toward them. "Ah, the beautiful Wendy," he smiled, kissing her hand. "You are the image of your mother."

After she was introduced, Sarah stood listening to Wendy, so poised and secure in her position, wealth, family, and beauty, comfortably chatting away about Edita and the hotel. As she stood there talking, the usual ring of men began to form around her. Bored, Sarah slipped away to admire the extraordinary art that filled the magical house: paintings, sculptures, drawings, pre-Columbian jewelry and terracotta figurines from Teotihuacan and Tlatelolco. She saw Diego Rivera, a mountain of a man surrounded by a coterie of acolytes. Imagine! Diego Rivera, just sitting around, like an ordinary mortal. It was thrilling.

This was exactly the kind of milieu she had always longed for, the milieu of progressive, creative leftists who cared not only about their art, but also about art as political expression. Mexico had Rivera, Siquieros, Tamayo, but she knew of only one artist in the United States, Ben Shahn, who also viewed his art as inseparable from his politics. She liked the idea of art as political expression. I'll never know what people see in abstract art, she thought.

She wandered happily about, looking at the artwork, listening with pleasure to the heated political conversations, so absorbed that suddenly she went head over heels across the outstretched legs of a young man.

"Oh, God, I'm sorry," he said. "I shouldn't have been sprawled out that way." As he helped her up, she fell forward against him, and instantly, her body tingled with total awareness of his masculinity. He smelled good, familiar, like someone she had always known, and his hands were strong, sinewy, and warm. For a moment they stood absolutely still and held each other, looking into each other's eyes, and she felt in just that split second, in the intensity of his glance, that she was approaching a destination toward which she had been traveling all her life. Then rocked by the intensity of her feelings, she pulled away.

"No. It was my fault," she said. "I just wasn't watching."

"Please sit down here. Let me get you a drink. Don't go away. What would you like?"

"Anything other than tequila, pulque, or cerveza."

"Aha. The Orange Croosh type." The Orange Crush commercials, "Cerveza no. Orange Croosh sí," were inescapable that summer, omnipresent on the radio, blaring throughout the city.

He returned, balancing two enormous Margueritas. "You can't toast our first meeting with orange croosh. It's just not romantic enough."

"You're right," she laughed, looking directly into his eyes. "It isn't." Her face flushed with unfamiliar daring.

He held up his brimming glass, rimmed with salt. "To Mexico. To you. To? What's your name?"

"Sarah," she giggled, flirtatiously clinking her glass against his.

"To Sarah," he said. "Eternity was in her lips and eyes."

"Ooh. *Antony and Cleopatra*. And you are?"

"Hal Gordon. The guy with the too long legs."

"To you, too, Hal." They clinked glasses and drank together for the first time. Then she told him, "Nobody has ever quoted Antony and Cleopatra to me before."

"You can't imagine all the tricks I have to seduce little curly headed girls. Why, I can say all of *Prufrock* by heart."

She laughed. "Add the *Manifesto* to that, and you can probably have me."

"Is that a promise?"

"N-no. I'm just kidding around. Don't make me nervous."

"Why not? I'm nervous. You think girls have cornered the market on nervousness?"

"I don't know about other girls, but I'm certainly nervous. See my friend over there?" She motioned toward Wendy. "She's never nervous about men."

He looked at Wendy reflectively. "No. I bet she isn't. She certainly is beautiful, but I wouldn't be part of that adoring circle. I'm not a worshipper by nature."

"No? What are you?"

"I'm a lover." Oooh! Her stomach turned over and she gulped down the rest of her drink. "Back in a jiffy with refills," he said. "Now don't go way."

Her knees were trembling. "I'll be right here waiting."

When he returned, he handed her the drink, sat down on the floor at her feet, lit a cigarette, and looked at her. Without coyness, she looked back. Why did she find him so attractive? An ordinary guy, brown eyes, craggy features, light brown straight hair, pitted skin, dressed simply in slacks and a shetland v-neck sweater with a shirt beneath it. She liked the fact that he was so simply dressed. It made her feel comfortable about her own simple plaid cotton dress, which was really more suitable for a picnic in the country than for an elegant evening party.

And there was a quality about him that she warmed to. A certain evident niceness, an intelligence, an absence of malice. She also liked the fact that he was not too tall. Five feet eight or nine at most. She'd always felt dwarfed, uncomfortable, overwhelmed by big men, as if they might squash her flat in bed. But he was not too big, not too broad, and not too handsome. She felt comfortable with his looks. He was her vision of a working-class hero: Tom Joad, Joe Hill, the Wobblies.

"How old are you?" he asked. "You look about sixteen."

"I'm twenty. And you?"

"Thirty going on fifty. I've been around. And I was wounded in Normandy. But don't get depressed. I'm fine now. Nothing important was injured."

She gulped down her drink, and he immediately reached for the empty glass. "I should warn you," she said. "I'm not a good drinker."

"That's not a warning, kid. That's an invitation."

Oh, my, she thought, as her stomach contracted again. I never have known how to make sexy repartee. To change the subject, she asked, "Tell me what you've seen in Mexico."

"I've seen a lot. I've been all over. Oaxaca, Guadalajara, Acapulco. And I've seen Trotsky's tomb. Poor old guy. Exiled to Mexico, totally powerless, just another poor old hounded Jew, and all he wanted to do was live out the rest of his life in San Angel. And Stalin, with all the power of the Soviet state, couldn't let him go. It bothered me when it happened, and it still does. Why such fanatical pursuit? It reminds me too much of the way the Nazis wanted to exterminate every last Jew, as if they were cockroaches. I broke with a lot of my old friends over poor old Trotsky."

The mariachi had begun to play again, and people were dancing. "Would you like to dance?"

"I'd love to."

"You'll have to be patient. I'm still a little stiff from my wounds. I never was a great dancer anyway. It's really just an excuse to get you in my arms."

"I know. I feel exactly the same."

They danced wordlessly for a few minutes, melting into each other in pleasure. "La ultima noche que pase contigo, quiero olvidarlo pero no he podido," the marachi sang. She trembled against him, light as a bird, and she could hear the wild beating of her heart. Then the music changed, everyone sat down, and two men began to dance a funny, pretend bullfight in the center of the room. "That's Cantinflas," Hal said. "The Charlie Chaplin of Mexico."

"I've never heard of him."

"That's not surprising. There's a basic contempt in the U.S. for everything south of the border."

They sat there watching the mock bullfight, his arm around her shoulders. She leaned back against it. No strangeness. No fear. No distance between them. She was hungry to know everything about him. "How did you happen to come to this party?"

"It's a long story."

"I have all night."

"Did you just say what I thought you said, or am I hearing the tequila?"

"I said it."

"Please don't take it back. Now where shall I start?"

"At the beginning."

"All right. If you get bored, it's your own fault. My father owns a candy store in Brooklyn. When I was seventeen, I dropped out of New Utrecht High School, ran away from home, lied about my age, and joined the Lincoln Brigade."

"Oh, my God, my God, I felt it." Tears filled her eyes. "Tell me, did you ever meet a boy named Jimmy Stern?"

"I sure did. He died in Madrid. A good kid."

"He was my brother."

He put his arms around her. "I'm sorry. Now that I know, I can see a definite resemblance. Small, quick, those same apple cheeks and eager eyes. Ah, don't cry, love. He didn't die for nothing. That war was a good fight. I never doubted it. That's a fixed star in my universe. And he passed the torch to you, didn't he? All right. Go ahead and cry. That's something worth crying for. To cry is to remember. So go ahead and cry." She leaned against him and even through her distress was conscious of the warmth of his arms and the heat of his hands, holding her and comforting her and healing her.

"Did you see him die?" she asked when she could speak again.

"No. I was injured myself. Shot in the leg. They found out my age and sent me home. Then came Pearl Harbor and I was drafted, wounded again on D-Day in the Normandy invasion, spent some time in the hospital, and got out three months ago. I came here to look up some friends from Spain, and I've been here ever since, trying to figure out the rest of my life."

"The rest of your life?" she echoed. "What do you mean?"

"I don't know. I seem to have lost my way. I've seen so many terrible things, and it's hard to come to terms with the evil of mankind. The question is how the hell do you live a life of dignity and purpose in such a world? I could go to college on the G.I. Bill, but I feel too old. Besides, I've looked at a few catalogues and found that they don't teach the kinds of things that interest me. In literature classes, they don't teach Ilya Ehrenburg, Bertolt Brecht, or Steinbeck. In history, they never mention Sacco and Vanzetti or Tom Mooney. They don't teach anything about the American Indians or the Mexicans in the barrios. They don't teach about lynchings or the Poll Tax or the racism of our country. They don't teach what I want to know. They don't teach the truth.

"So my mind goes back and forth, forth and back, trying to figure out what I can do despite a bum leg and a bad back, and just about the only thing that would suit my character would be to run a bookstore. Once I learned the ropes, I think I could get a G.I. loan to open one of my own. So there you have it. I'm thirty years old and I'm nowhere. Maybe your tripping over me was fated. You were sent to me to help me figure out the rest of my life."

She caught her breath, dizzied by the sensations that shot through her. "I may have some very good ideas about that," she said thinking, I can't believe I'm saying these things.

He grinned back at her, a sexy, crooked grin that tore at

her heart. "But I hardly know you," he joked. "Better tell me a little bit about you first."

"There isn't very much to tell. I just finished my junior year of college. I'm majoring in a combination of literature and history, and I love going to school. I'm a straight-A student. Jimmy's death was the worst thing that ever happened to me. Let's see. What else? I was rejected by the sororities at my college, probably because I was too left wing. I thought I'd meet lots of left-wing kids at college, but I haven't met a one. My friend Wendy and I are at the university for the summer, studying Spanish. Oh, God, this is all so dumb and unimportant that I'm embarrassed to tell it to you. I know I haven't made much of a difference to the world yet, but I want to some day. I really care about people."

"That's the torch I was referring to. Tell me some more."

"Let's see. What else? I live on Central Park West, my mother is a housewife, my brother Claude who's in the Pacific is a lawyer, and my father is a judge. Judge Stern."

"Judge Stern? You're kidding! That reactionary bastard?"

"I'm afraid so. That's the one."

He pulled his arm away from her shoulders as if he'd been burned. "Wow. When I make a mistake..." He shook his head. "Judge Stern! I think maybe you tripped over the wrong gent, kid." He stood up.

She felt as if he'd thrown a glass of ice water in her face. It made her angry. "I don't believe this," she scolded. "The sins of the father? That's not fair. I can't stand my father and neither could Jimmy. Would you have held my father against Jimmy, too?"

She stood opposite him, quivering in anger, her hands clenched into fists, and he ached to take her in his arms again. "All right. All right. I apologize. I reacted without thinking and I was wrong. But you still tripped over the wrong guy. I can just picture you bringing me home to daddy; penniless, injured, uneducated, no trade, and with a father who owns a candy store. Let's say good-bye right now. I'm just not looking for any more heartache."

Distress made her bold. She could not lose him, now that she had finally found him. Her voice trembled. "Please don't run away. Can't you tell that I would never make your heart ache? My father isn't here in Mexico, and even if he were it wouldn't matter. As far as I can see, there's no one in the world right now but you and me." She reached her arms up to him imploringly.

"No one," he echoed. And then, finally, finished with foolish denial, they kissed for the first time, a gentle kiss of such ineffable, unbearable sweetness that her throat choked with tears. He sat back on his heels and gazed for a moment at the miracle of her, his eyes also moist with tears of wonder, and then he fiercely pulled her against him and kissed her again, and then again, kissed her tender lips and her fragrant neck and her tip-tilted nose, kissed her over and over again, with the intense, blazing passion she had known only in her dreams. "Don't leave me," she whispered.

Brushing his cheek against her curls, he whispered in Castilian, the language of love, "Ah mi amor. Te quiero. Te he buscado toda mi vida. No temas. Nunca estare lejos de ti."

"I love you," she echoed. "I've been waiting all my life for you, too."

"You'll never be rich with me," he whispered.

"Oh, there are different kinds of rich." Her voice was tremulous with joy.

"Time to go?" he asked, standing up and pulling her up with him.

She swayed against him in simultaneous surrender and possession. "Yes. Time to go."

CHAPTER Thirteen

Before leaving, Sarah took Hal's hand and shyly introduced him to Wendy. He smiled. She smiled. They said, "Hi," and that was all. The meeting was brief, courteous, and indifferent, but Sarah was too euphoric to notice.

What does she see in him, Wendy wondered, looking after them as they left. A nice guy, probably, but strictly ordinary. I wouldn't spend five minutes with someone like that. This was the first time she had ever seen Sarah react this way to a man, and she certainly wanted her to be happy, but as she watched them walk out into the perfumed night, clinging joyously to each other, she was rocked by a feeling of bereavement that simultaneously surprised and upset her. What's wrong with me? she wondered. All this time I've been urging Sarah to find a lover, and now that she finally has, I'm upset about it. That just doesn't make sense. But her logical mind could not quell her turbulent emotions.

Behind her beautiful, fixed smile, her mind raced about, trying to understand why she was filled with such despair. Certainly it was not because Sarah had left without her. If she'd met someone she liked, she would have left the same way. That was implicit in their relationship. All girls operated under that unwritten law. It was all right to leave, if you met a man. No one ever questioned that. And she'd done it many times, to both Sarah and Charlotte.

Was it possible that she was a little jealous? But how could she be jealous of Sarah? She loved her. And besides, there was nothing to be jealous of. Although Sarah was a straight-A student, she couldn't care less about that, and she had to admit objectively that Sarah was on the plain side. As for Hal, he had bad skin, was poorly dressed, and wasn't even tall.

So why should she be feeling so jealous and abandoned? It was just that not one of the men surrounding her was looking at her in the way Hal had looked at Sarah, with a kind of reverence and respect. She looked into the eyes of her admirers, glittering with undisguised lust, and suddenly she felt sickened. They were a band of wolves, wild animals waiting to devour her, their jaws spread wide in hungry smiles that showed their teeth and lascivious tongues. Only the restraints of civilization kept her safe from them.

She thought of how Sarah had gazed at Hal as if he were Prince Charming. How could she so easily have felt all that trust? How could she be so quickly in love? Wendy had never been in love. Not even the least little bit. All of her adventures had really been attempts to feel what it was like to be in love. But she'd never found the key. Standing there, she became increasingly agitated.

She had to be alone for a few minutes. "Excuse me," she said to her adoring circle as she dashed out to find a quiet place where she could think and breathe. She fled into the first dark, empty bedroom, sat on a corner of the bed, and, to her surprise, burst into tears.

"Why, what's the matter, honey?" a man's voice asked.

"I beg your pardon. I thought I was alone." She switched on the nightstand lamp. Sitting in a large easy chair, looking steadily at her, was the most magnificent-looking black man she had ever seen. Tall, strong, broad, powerful. With blue eyes. She suddenly thought of Paula's words so long ago. "Like an African sculpture." But she wanted to be alone. "You shouldn't have been watching me that way."

"Everybody watches you and don't you just love it. I've been watching you all evening, teasing on all those poor suckers."

She was too depressed to talk. "Please go away," she begged. When he didn't move, she forced herself up.

"Ah, I'm sorry, honey. Don't get mad. Stay and talk to me for a minute. I've never seen anyone as beautiful as you up this close, and I might never get the chance again. Come on, honey. Sit down again and I'll be nice. I'm Maurice McBain and I'm studying dentistry here. And you're Wendy and you're at the university for the summer."

"How do you know?"

"I told you. I've been watching you all evening. That is, along with everybody else."

She put a cigarette in her long holder and looked at him. "You don't look like a dentist."

Instantly, he tensed up. "What do I look like? A porter?"

"Of course not, silly. I was thinking you look like an African king, except for those blue eyes, of course."

"Blood of some damned slave owner." He leaned forward to light her cigarette, and also lit one of his own. His eyes caressed her face. "And you," he said, "look like forbidden fruit."

"I don't want to talk about things like that. Tell me about you."

He was from Philadelphia. "I've never been there," she said. "Perhaps I should plan a trip when I get back to New York. The Liberty Bell. Independence Square. It must be a beautiful city."

"Beautiful? Well, I tell you honey, it depends on where you sit, and I didn't exactly sit on Rittenhouse Square. No, for me it wasn't exactly great back there, but it was better than where I went afterwards."

"Where was that?"

"Georgia. In the good old South. Let me tell you, honey, that place made Philadelphia seem almost good." His face clouded up, became dark, gloomy, and impenetrable, and his strange cobalt eyes flashed like steel knives.

"What happened in Georgia?"

"What didn't happen? First I was Jim Crowed out of my mind, then I ended up in the stockade. Girls like you don't know nothing about that kind of thing."

"So tell me."

For the first time that evening her interest was aroused. There was a sexy, dynamic, and exciting quality about him, and she liked listening because he was talking about something significant instead of just flirting.

"Back home," a cloud darkened his face, "I couldn't even be sitting here talking to someone like you. I bet you never sat talking to someone like me before either."

She looked at him and thought of Paula. He was right, of course. They had never had a black guest at the hotel.

All of the servants were black, but that was just the way things were. Edita had no prejudices, but the subject of having black guests had just never come up. All of their guests were referred by friends, and no black person had ever tried to make a reservation. It was strange that she had never before thought about it at all.

She changed the subject. "How did you happen to come here to school? Because of prejudice? For more freedom?"

"It was the only school that would have me, but there's not much freedom in Mexico. This is a sick country, stinking with crime, and most of it is done by cops who get away with it. The government is a joke. It's an agency for economic plunder and corruption.

"I have to admit that it's better for me here than at home, but you have to be just as wary here. They don't especially mistreat blacks. They mistreat anybody who isn't rich. The only color they really love here is Yankee-dollar green. Everybody here is on the take. They call it la mordida."

"Oh, I know all about that." She smiled, touching her bracelet. "Will you go home when you're finished with school?"

"I suppose. My mother misses me and I don't think I can make a living here. It's a real dilemma."

"Well, don't be discouraged. My friend Sarah knows everything about current events, and she assures me that after the war all prejudice will come to an end because people will associate prejudice with Hitler."

He threw back his head and laughed, a husky bittersweet sound that made her think of the song, "Laughing to Keep from Crying."

"You two innocents sound straight out of never-never land. I once almost believed that garbage myself. So did lots of other blacks. That's why we enlisted in the white man's army even before we had to. The irony of it is that they segregated us by race to fight against Hitler's racism, and then to prove that they were really in favor of democracy, they put the Japs out west in concentration camps."

"Concentration camps? You must be joking. The United States would never do anything like that. How come I've never heard about it?"

"There are lots of things that people like you never hear of. You don't have to know them to survive. The Japanese are still in the camps. The government picked them up and shipped them out to the desert like parcels of garbage. They lost everything they'd worked for all their lives—houses, businesses, greenhouses, fishing boats. It doesn't surprise me. It's the same as what Uncle Sam did to the American Indians."

His bitterness hurt her. "Things will get better after the war."

"The hell they will! Life's going to be different and better and richer for all the white boys coming back, but it won't do a thing for us. You ever hear of that Senator Bilbo?" She shook her head. "That mean, old, fat white man told the Senate he wanted all niggers deported to Liberia and said every red-blooded white man should use any means possible to keep the niggers away from the polls. In the Senate of the United States! And they let him."

"That's really awful," she said. "I can hardly believe it."

He laughed again. "You really are an innocent. Beautiful and nice, but you sure as hell don't know what's going on in the world. Well, I guess girls like you don't have to. Tell me, honey, have you ever heard any black poetry?"

"I don't think so."

"Langston Hughes? Countee Cullen? Paul Laurence Dunbar?" She shook her head. "Of course you haven't. They don't teach him in school. They only teach poetry about trees, graveyards and fences, not about real people. Black poetry tells the truth. Here's a good one to start on. It's by Langston Hughes and it's called 'Ku Klux.'"

>They took me out
>To some lonesome place.
>They said, "Do you believe
>In the great white race?"

>I said, "Mister,
>To tell you the truth,
>I'd believe in anything
>If you'd just turn me loose."

> The white man said, "Boy,
> Can it be
> You're a standin' there
> A-sassin' me?"
>
> They hit me in the head
> And knocked me down.
> And then they kicked me
> On the ground.
>
> A klansman said, "Nigger,
> Look me in the face—
> And tell me you believe in
> The great white race."

She wrapped her arms around herself and shivered. He sat there looking off into space. Oh, please, she wanted to say, please don't torture yourself. Don't tear at the scab. But she understood that it was impossible for him not to, and her heart ached for him.

"You don't know black poetry, and I'll bet you don't know what's going on with blacks back home.

"Do you know, up until the year before last all blacks employed by the Philadelphia Transit Company could only hold the position of laborer? Well, that didn't look so good since that was supposedly the kind of thing we were fighting against in Germany. So the Justice Department ordered them to employ eight black trolley-car conductors. Know what happened? There was a citywide strike. Roosevelt had to send troops in just so those eight guys could drive. Some democracy! Needing troops to protect a lousy job!

"And right this very minute, all over the U.S. and Europe, there are riots between blacks and whites who are fighting together against the Japanese. I tell you, it's not our war. Why should we fight the Japs? Why should we fight anyone! Killing ourselves for nothing. After the war the white man will get all of the good jobs just like before."

She looked at him sadly, feeling his pain as acutely as if it were her own.

"I wish that I could make it better."

"I wish that you could, too."

But I can't, she thought. There's nothing to be done about prejudice. That's just the way people are. It's like what I told Sarah at Amecameca. You can't change poverty either. Some people are poor and some people are rich, and all you can do is to be as nice and kind and generous with your money as possible. It's just the way life is.

He continued to talk. "Let me tell you some more about Georgia. One day, some white sergeant, getting his shoes shined by a little colored kid, rubbed his knuckles across the kid's head, 'for luck.'"

"For luck? How strange! Why?"

"Beats the shit out of me. It certainly didn't make the *kid* lucky. The son of a bitch was wearing a real heavy ring, and he rubbed so hard, digging it in, that the kid began to cry just as yours truly happened to be walking past. After months of my first exposure to the deep South, I was looking for trouble. I just went crazy. I woke up in the stockade, and there I stayed for one year, in solitary confinement, with no trial, until I was dishonorably discharged."

"No trial? Are they allowed to do that?"

Again his deep laugh rumbled up. "Oh, honey," he said. "You sure are refreshing. Don't you know that they can do anything they want to colored people? That's what it means to be colored."

"I think that's absolutely outrageous."

"Welcome to the club. But hey, listen, I don't want to talk about my fucked-up life. I'm depressed enough already. Why don't we get out of here and go some place."

Oh, dear, she thought. Here it comes. The usual pitch. And she wished he wouldn't spoil this, that his story wouldn't turn out to be just a prelude to a pass, merely a variation of the fevered pleas at the USO. "Love me tonight, baby. Tomorrow I may be dead." Not that she didn't find him attractive. Of course she did. But it seemed important to her that he also see her as a person, not just an exceptionally beautiful girl to be conquered. "What kind of place?" she asked suspiciously.

"A jazz place. Friend of mine is playing at a little nightclub in the Plaza Insurgentes. Do you like jazz?"

"Like it? I love it," she said happily. "I've been to all the places on Fifty-second Street in New York. I love Dixieland and I'm crazy about Josh White and Leadbelly. I adore Billie Holiday and I wish I'd heard Bessie Smith. Have you heard her?"

"Of course I have. I've heard everybody on the chitlin circuit."

"What's that?"

"Music you poor deprived white folks never get a chance to hear."

"I never even knew there was such a thing. Please teach me all about it."

"Oh, honey. What I wouldn't like to teach you." She felt her heart turn over. He stood up and stretched, a magnificent six feet five, and she wanted to reach out and touch him.

"How did you get here?" he asked. "I came by bus."

"I have a car."

"Solid. Let's go."

"I'll just say good night," she said, "and I'll meet you outside."

"Why outside? Afraid to be seen leaving with me?"

"Of course not. Don't be silly. It's just that I meant you might like to say good night to some people yourself."

"If I did, I wouldn't have been sitting in that dark room alone." Without another word he strode out. Was it possible that he wouldn't wait for her? Well, she shrugged, if he didn't it would be the first time a man hadn't.

Fixing on her public smile, she said good night to her host and tried to pull away from the group of men who immediately surrounded her again, calling, "Wendy, Wendy," while expressing excessive grief at her departure and begging for the possibility of her favors. It was ridiculous and irritating. Their hot hands grabbed at her, and the kisses of their slavering lips left a sticky residue on her hands.

It took fifteen minutes before she could extricate herself, and she was almost frantic as she ran outside. Suppose he hadn't waited. But there he was, outlined by the full moon, smoking, and gloomily pacing back and forth. He was beautiful, like an athlete, a discus thrower. Really, prejudice was absolutely crazy. And suddenly a thought occurred to her for the first time. It was prejudice, nothing but prejudice, that had killed Paula. She ran up to him out of breath. "Sorry I'm late. It was like an obstacle course. I was afraid you might not wait."

"And I was afraid you might not come." He ground his cigarette under his heel, looked down at her face and then, in gentle wonder traced her beautiful features with his finger. She put her hands on his shoulders, and looked at him with her violet eyes. Her perfect lips parted, she sighed, then waited. He also sighed, but didn't touch her. Why he's trembling, she thought, feeling his broad shoulders under her hands. This big, strong man is trembling.

And then she stretched to reach him, tilted her face up, and gently brushed her lips across his.

"First time I've ever been kissed by a white girl." His voice was husky.

"Try again," she laughed, trying to play down the rush of feeling that suddenly blazed through her. "I don't bite."

"Oh, baby. You can bite me any time." Now he bent down and kissed her back with such intensity that she felt her knees buckle.

"Now that was a kiss," she teased him. "I think I felt the earth move."

Oh, they were young and happy and alive.

"You're going to pay for that levity, girl."

"Make me pay," she murmured. "I can hardly wait."

CHAPTER
Fourteen

She held out the car keys. "Would you like to drive?"

"I would but I can't afford it! Driving in this country's a rich man's sport. One guy I know had his car towed from a legal space by the police and had to pay the police la mordida to get it back. Another got stopped for making a legitimate left turn and also had to pay. One hit a cow with his car and spent the next three months in jail because he couldn't pay la mordida. They never heard of bail down here. This must be the richest country in the world because with fifty-million thieves they still haven't been able to steal it all."

She laughed in amusement. He had a way of recounting really awful things and making them sound funny. "Besides," his voice softened, "if you drive I can look at you, and that's got to be one of the most beautiful sights of my life."

"You mustn't stare at me while I drive. You'll make me nervous."

"You're making me so nervous I'm apt to explode," he said, pulling her against him again. "Come on baby. Let's go. You drive and I'll sing you the blues."

"Super! My favorite kind of music." They set out, and he sang "Part-Time Love" to her in a deep, true baritone.

> "My baby came home this morning.
> I asked her where she'd been.
> Don't ask me no questions, Daddy,
> I got to leave you soon again.
> That's why I've got to find me
> find me a part-time love."

"Is that what you'd like?" she teased him gently. "A part-time love."

"Not with you, baby. A lifetime with you."

"Sing it again so I can learn it." This time she sang along with him. Isn't this strange, she thought. Hundreds and hundreds of dates, at all of the best places in New York, and this is one of the best times I've ever had. "Now sing me another."

"No more songs just now. I want to know something about you. I . . ." He paused, searching for words. "Here I am, with a beautiful, rich white girl who is like from another planet. Tell me something that'll help me know you. Tell me about when you were a little girl."

She hesitated as a tide of homesickness washed over her

unexpectedly, then she described the beauty of the island and of the hotel. "I'm afraid I sound like a travel brochure," she apologized, finally.

"Is that where you live now?"

"No. I don't go home very much at all. It has bad memories for me."

"What kind of memories?"

"Sadness. Death. I don't like to be sad, and yet so much of the time I am."

"You didn't look so sad back there, grinning at that bunch of jerks."

"My sister and I were trained to appear cheerful, smiling, enthusiastic. Like stewardesses. You have to wear a mask if you run a hotel. And besides, my mother considers it good breeding."

"I wouldn't know anything about that," he teased. "I'm just a po' black boy."

"Nonsense. Anybody can be well bred."

He threw back his head, and laughter rumbled up from his stomach. "Easy to be well bred if you're running a hotel. Not so easy if you're scrubbing the floors."

"That's ridiculous. Every single one of our servants is charming and polite. Why they're our friends. I love my nurse Carmen like a second mother."

At this, he began to laugh so hard that tears ran from his eyes, and he pounded his feet on the floor of the car. "You can laugh," she said indignantly. "I don't care. It doesn't mean that you're right."

"I'm sorry, honey." He was contrite. "I'm not really laughing at you. I'm enjoying you. You're so totally out of my experience that it seems funny to me. Hey, pull over to the side here. Let's have a smoke and talk some more."

"Very well." She pulled out her long holder, and he lit her cigarette. "What would you like to talk about?"

He sat looking at her. "The shape of your lips. Most of all, that's what makes you so beautiful. Even without lipstick they're perfect."

"Thank you." She was still annoyed at his mockery.

"Ah, don't be mad, honey. It's just my way. But put yourself in my shoes. Try to see how funny it seems for a girl who has everything to play at being melancholy. It's a romantic act, a pose. At the same time I'm laughing, I want to eat you up."

"I don't want you to laugh at me, and I don't want you to eat me up." She thought of the way that Sarah and Hal had looked at each other that night. As people, not as objects.

"You said I have everything. What does that mean to you?"

"Don't put me on. You know what it means! Young and rich and gorgeous and white. You don't have to put up with nothing from nobody. You can tell the world to go fuck itself. That's having everything."

"That's not at all what it means to have everything." She searched for the right words to express the nostalgia that haunted her. "To me, having everything is having innocence. Once I lived in a Garden of Eden, and I had a mother and a father and a sister I loved and an uncle I trusted. I did have everything then. My sister's coming-out party was the most beautiful night of my life, a fairy tale. That was the last such night. That very night we were struck by lightning and Eden disappeared. I could never again find my way back to paradise. So please don't say that I have everything. I have my own sorrows."

"Why, honey! Everybody comes to the end of innocence sooner or later. It happens to colored kids the day after they're born. Count yourself lucky if you lived in paradise for fourteen years. And when you look at the rest of us, you're still doing OK. In the newsreels you see people walking back and forth all across Europe? Wave after wave of refugees all looking for the same thing as you, trying to forget about death and return to paradise. But at least your paradise is still there. Those folks have nothing to return to."

She could not make him understand. "It's not as simple as you're trying to make it. Let's drop it!"

He put his arms around her and pulled her close to him, burying his nose in her fragrant hair. "Why don't you tell me about it now, while we're alone on this purple Mexican night."

"I've never told anyone." Suddenly she was hungry to tell.

"I'm not anyone. That is, not anyone who can ever matter to you. Chances are our paths will never cross again after tonight. So you can tell me. Pretend you're speaking to the wind. Why not get it off your chest?"

She leaned her face against his shoulder, not wanting to look into his eyes, and then she told him every detail of that tragic night, every detail from the beginning to the terrible end. "I can still see it," she wept. "Still see her body hurtling down." He held her in his arms and gently patted her shoulder with his large comforting hands. She felt as if she were back nestled in Carmen's arms.

His voice was filled with sorrow. "To die because of one poor little colored baby! Is that why you're here with me right now? Because your sister had a colored lover?"

"I don't know. I don't think so. But it wouldn't matter anyway, would it."

"Yes it would! Of course it would! I want us to be here for good reasons, not for sick ones. I'm me. Not your sister's lover. Try to forget the past. There was nothing you could do. So let's try to have some fun. No more sad stories. Let's drink and dance and laugh and listen to great jazz piano. But we have to make tracks before the club closes. Do you feel well enough to drive?"

"Watch my dust." Released, suddenly euphoric, she drove at seventy, all the way to Mexico City where they found that the club was still open. It was a dark, basement-level grotto with garish red lights, a haze of smoke, and some of the best piano playing she had ever heard.

During a break, when a small combo took over, Maurice introduced her to his friend, the pianist, who stared at her as all men did. "What's he got that I don't have," the pianist joked.

"Me," Wendy joked back. "I think he's got me."

Maurice stood up and held out his arms. "Dance?" She nodded. "Do I have you?" Again, unable to speak, she nodded.

They began to move to the music, and she leaned against him, frail and trembling within the circle of his arms, her insides on fire with electric shocks of desire zigzagging across her body. How glorious it was to want someone so much. She felt no ambivalence. No more would she huddle in fear at the remembered reverberation of Edita's shots. With him, she knew instinctively, everything would be just fine.

At closing time, they left, stumbling against each other, stopping to kiss with wild abandon in the street. He was hard, pressing against her body, and she felt mad with desire.

And then something strange and totally unpredictable happened. An old street peddler, rushing home at the end of a long day, saw them standing there and hurried over with her box of wares. "Mira Señor," she said, flipping up the top. Inside, they could see by moonlight, were rows of Aunt Jemima dolls, all laid out in rows next to each other.

His large, powerful fist rose toward the sky in fury. "Get out of here," he shouted, "before I break every one of those damned dolls."

The poor old woman, terrified, scurried away frantically, and Wendy looked at him in shock. "What was that all about?"

"If you have to ask me, you wouldn't understand. Get in the car. Let's go."

"Yes sir," she responded angrily to his anger. "Where shall I take you, sir?"

"Just drive to your own house. I'll walk home from there. At least in Mexico I don't have to worry about being stopped by the cops for being black."

"Whatever you say!" She struggled to regain her habitual air of insouciance, but this was too much. Just as she had started to feel something, she'd been stopped cold. It left her confused and angry.

They did not exchange another word. When she reached her street she parked in the usual place, turned off the ignition and stepped out. The beggar woman, asleep with her baby in her arms, lay on the cold concrete in front of the house with nothing beneath her and nothing covering her. A pile of rags for a pillow!

Maurice looked at the woman with an expression of mingled disgust and horror. "Want to know what it's *really* like to be expelled from paradise. Take a look at her! That's the real, unvarnished human condition. It's not a game!"

"Thank you for the education. Good night." She turned her back to him and walked into her building.

It was late and she was tired. The booze and marijuana were wearing off, and she could feel depression rising. Why had he made such a fuss about an Aunt Jemima doll? Oh, she knew well enough that educated Negroes regarded it as a stereotype although lots of women on the island looked just like that. But it wasn't a negative stereotype. It was a comforting kind of doll. Like Carmen! And what did that poor ignorant peddler know? She only sold the things that tourists bought. But he had acted personally insulted, and that kind of wild flailing out accomplished nothing. It only made people more prejudiced. She could understand his feelings, of course she could, but not his lack of control.

She felt even more depressed when she found that Sarah was not yet home. Depressed *and* lonely! She had grown up surrounded by crowds of people. Always there were voices: the gay brittle gossipping voices of their guests and the singing, bantering voices of the servants. She had never lived alone before coming to New York, and now, after living with Sarah for a few weeks, she realized that she'd often been lonely in her New York apartment. Being with Sarah reminded her of all those happy years with Paula. She needed Sarah to talk to now, to help her understand the whole strange interchange with Maurice. Could she have handled him differently? Was there a way she could have diffused his sudden burst of anger? Or would anything have been futile? The trouble was that she'd really liked him, really been turned on by his moody intensity.

Unable to sleep, she walked out onto the balcony. And then she saw him. There he was in the street below, leaning against the catalpa tree, outlined by the moon, shrouded in darkness except for the red glow of his cigarette.

"Maurice?" Not quite believing, she called to him in a stage whisper, afraid la duena would hear her. "Is that you?"

"It's me!"

"What are you doing down there?"

"Brooding. I wanted to talk to you. Can I come up?"

"Of course not. No men are allowed here. I'd be tossed out."

"Then come down."

She hesitated, still angry, but her heart yearned for his warmth, and she was so very lonely.

"Please. Even for five minutes."

"Will you be nice to me?"

"Oh, baby," he groaned. "Do you have to ask? What do you think I'm doing here?"

"All right." Her hands trembled as she dressed, but she felt alive again as sudden wild joy swept through her. She was free and she was happy and she was going downstairs to make love to this man. She left a note for Sarah who also might not be back before morning. They'd both have to be very careful not to get caught by la duena. But she didn't worry about that now.

Carrying her shoes, she tiptoed down the stairs, quietly closed the heavy door behind her, and stood on the top step, her white cotton dress blowing above her long legs, the lantern above the entrance door creating a halolike aura about her. He raised his arms to heaven, like a conqueror, like the king he should have been, then lowered them and held them out to her. With a glad little cry, she ran to him, and he folded her against him. She reached up and pulled his face to hers, and his lips covered hers in so intense a kiss that for a moment she thought she might swoon. Then he picked her up in his strong arms and carried her to the car.

"I know a place," he said, slipping into the driver's seat, all fears of la mordida temporarily driven from his mind.

They drove for a lifetime of fifteen minutes to a low, sprawling cluster of one-room buildings, a Mexican version of a motel. He disappeared for a moment, then returned with a key. Mad to touch each other, they hurried to the room, unbuttoning their clothes as they ran.

The moment they were in the room, they flung their clothing to the floor and joyously dove into the enormous bed. The muscles of his strong, sinewy hands were like steel, and his chest was hard and smooth against her breasts.

"Oh, feel how wet I am," she said, taking his hand and

putting it between her legs. "I want you inside me now. No leading up, no holding back. Maybe later, but not now. Now I don't want anything except the feel of you inside me." She spread her legs and felt him move inside her, gently sliding deep, deep into her, and she let out a sigh of total joy. "Oh, God, I'm happy."

Her body arched through space toward his in an atavistic fever, whirling in delirium, in an indescribable ecstasy of mating, in a glorious fulfillment and completing she had been waiting for all these years. And then she began to come and come, each orgasm deepening in intensity until she had completely lost herself and there was nothing in the world except his cock deep inside her. Nothing but the shuddering, cataclysmic vibrations of their two bodies exploding with the volcanic force of long-repressed, subterranean energy, filling her with red-hot molten lava, searing her belly and spilling down over her thighs, until shuddering and shivering, the volcano sank into smouldering dormancy.

And then they lay still, still clasping each other tightly, as if afraid that something might come between them.

She reached out her tongue and licked the sweat off his neck. He laughed, pushed her back, and reached for one of her nipples with his lips. Each time he gently bit her she could feel her loins contract. "Oh, come inside me again," she moaned, and with a glad cry he mounted her and thrust himself deep, deep inside her, and again they moved in total harmony, until finally, with cries of triumph they exploded against each other again. And then they were still.

"Oh, my God," she exulted. "How wonderful! What a waste! All these wasted years...."

He threw back his majestic head and laughed, the low deep rumble that so delighted her. "Now don't worry honey. You have the rest of your life to catch up. It won't be hard. I kind of think you have a natural talent for this."

She joined in his laughter, then grew serious. "I've been afraid to love, afraid that if I loved something, I would lose it. That could happen to us." He raised himself on one elbow and gravely looked down at her. In his broad throat a vein pulsed tightly.

"Maybe so! But at least let's give them a run for their money."

She pulled his dark, hard, sculpted body against her. "We'll give them a run," she whispered, touching him.

"See what you do to me!" His voice trembled.

"Come show me again," she whispered. "And then again and again."

When they awakened, the sun was up and they hurried to dress. Just before leaving, his hand on the doorknob, he stopped uncertainly for a moment and looked at her with questioning eyes.

"When?" he asked hesitantly, afraid that what had been between them in the darkness could not stand up in the light of day.

Her heart went out to him. She wanted him to feel trust in her so she tried to strike a light note, to pretend she was not aware of his fears.

"Tonight!"

"Tonight?"

"Of course tonight. Every night. Morning, noon, and nighttime, too. But can anything ever live up to last night?"

Now he laughed, proud and secure again in his masculinity. "Why, honey, we're just getting started. It gets better and better all the time. I regard it as my solemn duty to help you make up for all that wasted time."

"How noble of you to sacrifice yourself that way."

He laughed and pulled her against him, then bent to kiss her one more time. "Tonight," she repeated, trembling again with passion, wondering how she could wait until then.

CHAPTER
Fifteen

Sarah and Hal took a bus to Fortin for three days, just to be alone somewhere in beautiful surroundings with a good double bed. They registered as Mr. and Mrs. Gordon, feeling slightly shy and embarrassed at the beaming congratulations of the other guests who assumed they were a honeymoon couple. They had chosen the perfect place. They swam in the gardenia-covered pool, explored the hacienda with its extraordinary variety of unfamiliar tropical flowers, danced, made love, and grew sunburned and healthy. Gardenias were everywhere—in the pool, on the dining-room table, on their pillows at night, and in Sarah's hair. "I suppose this fragrance could become cloying after awhile," she said. "But right now I love it. Gardenias and you. For the rest of my life the scent of gardenias will remind me of you." He held her in his arms and breathed the smell of her hair and her skin and the gardenias, still not daring to believe in his good fortune.

From the first night they had been totally comfortable with each other. He didn't think her breasts were too small, didn't even notice until she mentioned it, and so for the first time in her life she, too, stopped caring.

"I never want to sleep alone again," she said, snuggling against his body. She rubbed her feet along his legs. To think that every touch could be so lovely—feet, legs, arms, bellies, backs. It wasn't only sex. Every part of him was part of her. Naked skin against naked skin. No other sensation like it in the entire world.

"I'll try to oblige." He smiled at her as, light as sunshine, she straddled his body, bent forward and covered his face with kisses.

"I can't believe how much I love you." Her voice was filled with awe. "More and more every day."

"I can't believe it either. It's almost enough to make this old atheist believe in God. Almost enough, but not quite."

"What do you believe in?"

"You! Me! Us! This moment! The struggle. I've learned not to have big, long-range dreams."

"I'll dream for us, Hal darling, for both of us forever."

They fell asleep wrapped in each other's arms until suddenly, at three in the morning, they were shocked awake by strange cracking noises, and their bed began to shake.

"Is this your effect on me?" she asked, clutching him.

"Not to denigrate my effect," he joked, to reassure her, "but I think we're in the middle of an earthquake. It's only a mild tremor. I've felt them before."

"Hold me tight." Her voice quavered. "I don't care if we die as long as we're together."

"We're not going to die. I didn't come through two wars in order to die suffocated by gardenias." She clung to him in terror for an eternity of five minutes, while everything else in the room groaned and shook and cracked around them. Then suddenly the shaking stopped, the noise subsided, and the earthquake was over.

Gently he freed himself from her arms. "All clear now." He kissed the tip of her little nose, then reached to the night table for his cigarettes.

"Is that all? Oh, it's too bad that I was so scared. Our one chance to make love during an earthquake."

He put out the cigarette and pulled her to him. "It's not too late. We can make an earthquake of our own." She felt as if her heart would break with love of him.

On Sunday night they had to return to Mexico City. She felt unaccountably weepy and depressed. "I don't want to go. I feel as if this was our honeymoon. Promise me that there will be other times."

"Of course there will be. You and I are just beginning our journey. Don't be afraid, my love." But he was, too.

When they stepped off the bus in Mexico City they saw the terrible headlines. The atomic bomb had been dropped on Hiroshima. "I am become death," Robert Oppenheimer was quoted as saying. World War II was over. The atomic age had begun.

They did not find another chance to get away that summer. And besides, neither one of them had the money. One day near the end of August, they could no longer avoid discussing the future.

"Only one more week," she mourned. "Summer's over and I'm afraid. I wish we could stay here, and never go back. I'm so afraid that when we go home I'll lose you."

He spoke with bravado but was as worried as she. "You'll never lose me. But what will your folks think?"

"I've told you that my father's impossible. But if you just stay away from politics maybe we'll get through."

"Liar. You know there's no way they'll think I'm good enough for you."

"I don't really care if they do or not. I won't let them interfere. Nothing's going to separate us. We love each other and we're going to get married. They'll have to accept you when they see that I won't be stopped."

He wrapped his arms around her. "All that resolve in such a tiny girl. And if they don't?"

"We'll get married anyway."

"On what? I don't even have a job."

"As soon as I get back to school, I'll register for education courses and student teach in the spring. Then I'll be able to get a job as a teacher the moment I graduate. That will give us an income until you're settled."

"You'd be sorry afterwards," he warned.

"So I'd complain. I'd complain and complain until you move your body into mine like this, yes, exactly like this, and stop my lips with kisses. Yes, yes, just like that. Oh, God, Hal. I love you, I love you. That's all that matters. We have to be together."

* * *

"Do you and Hal have a good sex life?" Wendy asked her one day.

"I don't want to talk about it."

"But, Sarah, you and I have never had secrets from each other. I've told you about Maurice and me."

"It's not that it's a secret. It's just that it belongs to both of us, so it doesn't feel right to discuss it with anyone. But please don't be hurt, Wendy. If I did discuss it with anyone, of course it would be you. Maybe I'll feel differently about it after we're married."

"You can't marry him," Wendy said. "Why do you keep on pretending that you can? You know your folks will never permit it."

"I don't care what my father thinks."

"But what about your mother? You love her."

"I do love her, but I love Hal even more. I have to be with him. There's just no choice as far as I'm concerned. Only one more week. I wish we could just stay here forever."

"Maurice wants to come back to New York with me."

"What do you mean come back with you? Doesn't he have to finish school?"

"I suppose. But he says he can't let me go. He wants to come to New York and live with me. He's just as adamant about me as you are about Hal."

"That's impossible, Wendy. Your building will never permit it. They'll send him to the back door. The other tenants will complain. They'd complain even if you were living with a white man to whom you weren't married. But a black man? And what will he do with himself every day while you're at school? Push a rack in the garment district?"

"He's an adult. He wants to be with me. If things get sticky, he can always leave and come back here to school."

"I still don't think you should take him. There's just no point to it."

Wendy became coldly annoyed. "Sarah, you don't know everything. I could ask the same question of you. What's the point of you and Hal?"

"It's completely different, and you know that it is. I intend to marry him. Can you say that about Maurice? You haven't even said that you're in love with him. Are you?"

"It's quite possible! I've never loved anybody more than I love him. He isn't the easiest person to get along with. He's moody and changeable, but I'm usually happy when we're together, and we have a great sexual relationship. Obviously I care for him a lot, or I wouldn't take him home with me."

Sarah's face showed her disapproval. Wendy was disconcerted and annoyed. "Oh, for heaven's sake, Sarah. I don't understand you. He makes his own decisions. He's an adult!"

"He's an adult who's so bedazzled by you that he's stopped thinking. I'll bet neither one of you has checked this out with the school. Are you sure that he'd be able to return whenever he likes? He should at the very least have a letter stating that he can. He's so close to the end. Why not leave him here, and he can join you when he's finished?"

"I've just told you. He wants to be with me so he'll come to New York whether I let him live with me or not. And I'd love to have him there with me. It will be so much fun to show him New York. We'll have wonderful times together."

"All right. I suppose I should butt out. It's just that I love you and I care about him too. I'm worried."

"There's nothing to worry about. Everything will work out just fine. You'll see. There's absolutely nothing to worry about."

CHAPTER
Sixteen

Just before Labor Day, Marshall asked Charlotte to marry him. Although they now spent almost every evening together, the proposal took her by surprise. After all, he'd never kissed her on the lips, never said, "I love you," never shown the slightest passion or desire for her. Occasionally he held her hand at the theater. That was all.

The evening he proposed started out as no different from any other evening they'd spent together. They had dinner, returned to sit on the terrace, and she listened as usual to his talk about business, Teddy, and the end of the war.

"Terrible thing, that atomic bomb," he said. "Some journalists say it saved a quarter of a million American lives, but others say the Japanese were just about to cave in anyway, that it was unnecessary. I don't know. I've heard all of the logical arguments for it, but still it feels wrong to me."

"They should have dropped it on the Germans instead."

"But I don't think it's been operational until now. Well, in any event, thank God it's over."

"Did you ever doubt that we'd win?"

"No. Not for a minute. We had to win. Amazing that it took so much time. It's still hard to believe that three damned countries almost brought the world to its knees. I wish my wife could have known that we've won. Every relative in Europe has been murdered. But our side won."

He lit a fresh cigarette from the embers of his old one, and gazed out over Sheep Meadow, remote from her for a few moments. It depressed her that he was thinking about his wife. How was she supposed to respond to his wish that his wife could have known? If she said, "I do too," it would be a lie. If his wife were alive, he wouldn't be sitting there with her. His wife's death had enabled Charlotte to live.

But if she said the truth, "I'm glad she's dead so that you're here with me," he would be shocked at her unkindness. He was always so very kind. In fact, so kind that she could never really be herself with him.

He didn't know her. He had a surface image based on her role as a timid, grateful employee who was all freshness and sweetness and docility, but the truth of the matter was that she wasn't either sweet or docile, although he did manage always to bring out the best in her. It was a terrible strain always to play the role he seemed to expect, but she would have done anything to make him happy.

He didn't really know her and perhaps she didn't really know him, because she hadn't realized that he still thought about his wife. The evidence that he still did, even when he was with her, blanketed her with the chronic depression that always lurked beneath her surface, waiting to rise up and torment her.

For once she didn't bother to act perky and cheerful. "Only two more weeks here," she said morosely. "I'm glad my friends will be coming home, but I hate to leave this apartment. Of course," she added hastily, "I feel very lucky to have your friend's apartment to move to."

Then, he took her hands in his, and said, in so offhand a manner that at first she thought he was joking, "You don't have to move there. You could marry me."

"That would be kind of a drastic solution to the apartment shortage," she quipped, trying to feel her way.

He laughed with her, then said, "I'm quite serious about this. I'm asking you to marry me. I've thought about the age difference a great deal, but I'm never aware of the age difference when we're together, and I don't feel as if you do either. Am I right?"

"Of course. I never even think about it. You've taught me so much. You're so kind, so wise. You've been my teacher, my mentor. You've saved me."

"I didn't think I would want to marry again," he continued, "and certainly not so soon. But being with you this summer, with all of your freshness and enthusiasm, has been like a rebirth for me. I need someone to love. I've never been inclined to run around and chase. I like coming home at night to one woman who's in my corner. I have many acquaintances, business associates, and colleagues, but I really don't have any close friends. My wife was my closest friend. That's the way I like to live, with a loving friend, and I think I can find it again with you. So what do you think? Will you marry me?"

Oh, my God, she thought, I can't believe it. I can't believe that I could be so lucky. She felt as if her heart would burst with joy. She was safe. Nobody would be able to hurt her any more. Filled with gratitude, she took his hand and pressed it to her lips. Her eyes filled with tears of happiness and her voice trembled. "Of course I'll marry you. I'd be honored to."

His kind brown eyes twinkled into hers. "I hoped you'd feel that way." Reaching into his pocket he took out a little box and held it out to her. She flipped open the cover and gasped. An emerald-shaped diamond, at least five carats, bigger than any she'd seen on the fingers of the sorority girls. She threw her arms around his neck and pressed her lips to his, unaware in her joy that she felt absolutely nothing for him sexually, nothing at all like what she'd felt for the officer at the USO. But even if she had possessed such awareness, it would not have mattered. Nothing mattered any longer except the fact that she had just become a winner. The diamond winked and glittered on her finger and proclaimed to the world that her prayers had been answered.

They sat together for hours, planning the future. "I can't wait for you to meet Teddy," he told her, "but I think he must be eased into this new situation gradually. We can't do anything to shatter his stability. It's fragile enough as is. I don't think it would be wise to separate him from my mother-in-law until he gets to know you. She's been with him night and day since my wife's death, and they're deeply attached to each other. She saved him, not I. She's quite an extraordinary woman."

"I wouldn't want to separate them either."

"I knew you'd feel that way and it really won't be a problem. She'll only stay until Teddy has adjusted to you, and the apartment is so vast that you'll have all the space you need. She isn't old, you know. Only fifty-five. She was widowed two years ago, but she's always lived in New York and has quite an active social life. I know she's anxious to return to her own apartment, so the minute you give the word, she'll be off."

"Does she know you want to remarry?"

"Not yet, but that won't be a problem. She'll never stop grieving for her daughter, but she's a good, kind, generous woman. She would want us to have a normal, happy home life again."

The very thought of living again with *any* kind of mother frightened Charlotte, but nothing could dim her joy. Everything would work out. Nothing in her life would ever go wrong again.

"When will you tell her?" she asked.

"I thought I'd tell her this weekend, and then perhaps you'd like to come to the beach with me over Labor Day. I have new neighbors that I'd like to invite to dinner. Arla and Lenny Wine. He's not too pleasant, kind of rough and coarse, but he's just given us his account, and it's a rather large one."

"What kind of business is he in?"

"Real estate! Construction! He owns dozens of old buildings, and now he's building several new luxury apartment houses, and he wants to attract the best people to them. He's pretty awful, but business is business. Arla, on the other hand, is rather sweet and sad. She's southern and not sophisticated, and she feels out of the social swim. She needs a woman friend, and it will be pleasant for you to have a friend next door."

"That's wonderful. I would like a friend out there." She was sure that she would also be intimidated for a while in the Hamptons, so it was good to know that she would have a friend who wouldn't threaten her.

"I don't feel a big wedding would be appropriate," Marshall said. "Would you feel deprived if we had a small one?"

"Oh, no. That's exactly what I'd like, too. I have no relatives and only my two friends to invite. And both of them have boyfriends. Four guests! That's all! But I would like a wedding dress if that's all right with you."

"By all means. What would you think of a small ceremony in the rabbi's study at Temple Emanu-El and then a buffet dinner at the apartment or my club? Would that be all right?"

"Perfect! That would be fine. Anything you say."

They decided that there was little point in her moving now to Marshall's friend's apartment. "Would you mind living at my apartment until the wedding?" he asked. "It's so large that you'll have complete privacy. Your own room and bath and sitting room."

"That would be fine, of course," she said gratefully. She felt that he was trying to reassure her, to make her understand that everything would be proper, by the book. He would not attempt to make love to her until after they were married.

"Only one thing worries me," she said. "My mother was a terrible example to me. I don't know anything about children. Do you think I can be a good mother?"

"Of course you can. You're sweet and kind and intelligent. You and Teddy will adore each other."

After he had gone, she sat on the terrace, staring at her ring. It all seemed impossible. A deus ex machina, a machine from the gods. She would have a husband, she would be rich, she would be protected. She, who had always been unlucky, had suddenly found gold.

Three months ago she had come to Manhattan, as soaking wet as a newborn babe, penniless, without family support or college degree, pretty enough but not extraordinary like Wendy, and miraculously she had triumphed. The only problem she could foresee was Teddy. She was not nearly as certain as Marshall that she was competent to be a mother at twenty, but she vowed that she would give it her all. That was the very least she could do for this wonderful man who had saved her.

CHAPTER
Seventeen

Wendy and Sarah and their lovers left Mexico City just after Labor Day. Hal and Maurice, planning to spend the days in the girls' compartment, which had two facing couches when it was made up, bought the cheapest coach seats and joined the girls as soon as their tickets had been punched. Wendy had ordered a picnic basket from Sanborn's, filled with wine, beer, cheese, red bananas, and assorted chicken, turkey, ham, and roast beef sandwiches.

Maurice held Wendy's hand in his and gently sang to her, "I've got the world on a string."

Despite their joy at being together, all four of them were filled with apprehension about the future. But they pretended to be gay and optimistic; drinking, eating, kissing, laughing, and having such a festive time that they were unaware the train had slowed until it suddenly jerked to a stop. Hal raised the shade and looked out. "Marshall, Texas." His voice sounded grim.

"So?" Sarah asked. Why was he looking perturbed?

"It's a bad place. This is where those lousy Texas deputies turned back the Oakies, beating them, shooting them, burning their tents." He flashed a warning glance at Maurice. "We may be in for a spot of trouble."

"Honestly, Hal, sometimes you can be paranoid." Wendy tried to joke away his fears. "No one would dare to bother us. And besides, our door is locked." But Maurice's eyes met Hal's with equal concern. Then all four of them started nervously at the sound of loud banging on the door. "Open up in there. Sheriff!"

Wendy grabbed her wallet and opened the door. "Here goes. They can't be any worse than those Mexican cops. Let's see if the same technique will work."

"Be very careful about offering them money," Sarah whispered. "I don't think you can buy American cops off."

"We'll just have to see." Calmly, Wendy opened the door and stood in front of the sheriff and his deputies, proud and tall in her imperious beauty. Smiling radiantly, her voice sultry, she asked, "What can I do for you, sir?"

He moved forward inexorably until he was inside the doorway. Then he looked at Maurice. "We heard there was a black boy in here cohabiting with white girls. Stand up, boy."

Maurice shot up, banging his head on the ceiling. Then he stood there waiting, his forehead covered with perspiration, his face impassive.

Sarah clutched Hal's hand in agitation. His eyes blazed into hers warning her to be quiet.

"Cohabiting?" Wendy's laugh rang through the compartment. "Why you must be joking."

"Then what's he doing in here?"

"Well, isn't it obvious? He's serving us lunch. He's my servant." She flashed her most enchanting, dazzling smile. "I'm Wendy da Gama and my family owns the Virgin Isles da Gama. It's a very famous hotel. Just a minute. I'll show you a picture of it." She reached into her purse and pulled out a picture postcard.

"Do you like fishing? Well, we have the most marvelous fishing on the island. Blue marlin."

"When does he go back to his seat?"

"As soon as he cleans up." She flashed that devastating smile again. "You have my word of honor."

"All right," the policeman said. "See that he does."

Wendy closed the door, and the four of them sat there looking at each other, not daring to speak until the train took off again.

"The nerve of that little twerp," Wendy said putting her arms around Maurice. He pulled away and shook his head with an ancient grief. It was Hal who comforted him. He sat beside him and patted his hand. "You did just right," he said. "This wasn't the place to fight. Not for either of us."

Maurice sat there grieving while Hal held his hand, reminding Sarah of two war buddies who have just been forced to witness destruction that was not of their making.

"Come on, kids," Hal said lifting a bottle, "let's get smashed and say the hell with them all." Just then, a sudden knock at the door made them all freeze again.

This time Sarah, her temper taking over, angrily yanked the door open, a tiny whirlwind of fury. "What is it now?"

"Hold on, hold on," came a soft black voice. "You don't have to bite my head off." She gasped in relief. It was the porter assigned to their compartment.

Looking a little worried he said softly, "You folks can't come to the dining car together. Why don't I just bring your meals here? No point in getting folks riled up."

They looked at each other in dismay, but he was right. "That's very kind of you." She banged the door shut again, angry not at him but at the situation.

Wendy was equally angry. "Nobody minds if we sit with awful crooks like the two we met on the way to Mexico, but a fine man like you, Maurice..." She brushed a kiss across his cheek, but he stared out of the window, refusing to meet her eyes. "Are you angry at me because I said you were a servant?"

"Of course I'm not angry at you. I'm angry because you *had* to say that, not because you did. I'm not angry. I'm sick to my stomach. Three years away from the good old U.S. of A. and I'd forgotten. How could I forget? How could I let myself forget? How did I ever kid myself that things would be different now? It makes me sick to have to cringe before a redneck son of a bitch like that. To have to be defended by a woman!"

Hal tried to comfort him. "Don't even think about it that way. What matters is not who defended you but that we got through. They could easily have taken you off the train. Let's try to put this behind us. Things will be better in New York."

Maurice shook is head sadly. "Things will never be different anywhere. This fucked-up world just won't let us alone."

"Please don't let that awful sheriff get to you." Wendy put her arms around him.

He sighed, looked at her and smiled his world-weary smile. "That awful sheriff or his brothers or his cousins have been getting to me from the day I was born."

"I'm beginning to feel very guilty," Wendy said. "I should have urged you to stay in Mexico."

"Would you have stayed with me?" he asked.

"No. I promised my mother to finish school."

"I promised my mama too. But I couldn't have stayed without you." She held him close to her, guilty because he had done what she would not. The enormity of his sacrifice had not been clear before. Sarah had asked her if she loved him. Now she knew in one flash of illumination that she did.

"I'll make it up to you," she whispered. "I promise that I will." He turned away from them and, curling himself up on the narrow seat, willed himself to fall asleep while the three of them whispered around him like the anxious relatives of a convalescent.

Wendy covered him with a blanket. "Summer is over." She shivered with a sudden chill.

"I feel about a hundred years older than when we left New York," Sarah answered.

"I do too. It's kind of eerie isn't it? Smuggling jewelry in and smuggling Maurice out. I'm going to make this up to him. I'll buy him new clothes and a good watch. And I'll take him to see *The Glass Menagerie* and to the Philharmonic and the opera and to hear all of the good jazz on Fifty-second Street. For the first time in his life he won't have to worry about money. We'll have so much fun that he'll forget all about anything bad that ever happened to him."

Hal looked at Maurice to make sure that he was still asleep. Then he whispered, "He might want to do something more with his life than accompany you, kid. And besides, how long can you support him?"

"I have no idea. I just write checks and they're covered."

"Do you even know how much rent you pay?"

"No. My mother's lawyer handles that. But I know that I don't have to worry about money. Thank goodness I have enough to make this up to him."

"Do you think she can?" Sarah asked Hal.

"Not with money," he answered.

Sarah leaned her head against his, filled with forebodings about the futures of them all.

CHAPTER Eighteen

Sarah and Wendy rushed to Marshall's apartment the day after their return. Charlotte was so impatient to see them that she was pacing right outside the elevator. They fell into each other's arms, hugged and kissed, and jumped up and down in excitement. "Oh, God, I have so much to tell you," each of them screamed.

"What a beautiful apartment," Sarah said, happy for Charlotte.

"I owe you both so much," she answered. "If I'd had to return to Brooklyn each night I wouldn't have been so accessible, and Marshall and I might never have come to know each other."

Before lunch she showed them her new wardrobe. "All Christian Dior. See! The new look. The bosom, shoulders, and hips round and the waist tiny. Best of all, with skirts twelve inches from the floor, they cover my legs. This style was made for me. And wait until you taste lunch. Marshall's cook is superb."

At lunch while they drank champagne and ate salade Nicoise with thick chunks of tuna and fresh string beans, tiny homemade rolls and strawberry mousse, they talked about the wedding. "I'm not having my mother." Charlotte's voice was defensive, as if she knew they'd disapprove. "I told him I was an orphan. I couldn't tell him the truth. He's so kind that he would have insisted on inviting her, and I won't let her spoil my wedding."

"She's bound to find out," Wendy warned. "She'll trace you through the wedding announcement in the *Times*."

"The 'obits' is the only section she reads. But please let's not talk about my mother. I'm nervous enough. Even the mention of her sends cold chills up and down my spine. Let's talk about sex. I can't believe that you're both sleeping with guys."

"Well, aren't you?" Wendy asked. "You're living here."

"No! Marshall hasn't so much as touched me. Or soul-kissed me! He's a very moral man, so he's waiting until after the marriage. He respects me."

"Oh, God, save me from that kind of respect," Wendy teased her. "I don't call that moral, I call that repressed."

"You know that your sexual attitudes have always been peculiar, Wendy."

"I find yours even more peculiar, darling."

"Tell me about you and Hal, Sarah. I'm used to Wendy's promiscuity but I can't believe you're finally doing it."

"I don't really like to talk about sex," Sarah said. "All I can tell you is that it's wonderful, and I love him, and we're going to get married just as soon as we can."

"Aren't you afraid that perhaps he won't marry you now that he's slept with you?"

Her friends rocked with laughter. "Honestly, Charlotte, you're overdoing this strange new need to be super bourgeois," Sarah teased.

Charlotte looked at both of them, feeling a faint tinge of dismay. How had they managed, in just two minutes, to make her uneasy because she *wasn't* engaging in premarital sex? They were the ones who were out of line, not she.

Sarah broke into her thoughts. "I still can't get used to the idea that you won't be back at school with us."

"But I am coming back. We had to get special permission, though, because I'll be married. Isn't that ridiculous?"

"It's in keeping with the rest of that convent," Wendy said.

"I just can't wait for those sorority girls to see my ring and all of my new clothes and find out whom I've married. I not only have a mink coat, I've ordered a casual mink in the Eisenhower jacket style. And Marshall's chauffeur will take us there each day. That will show them."

"If they bother to notice," Wendy yawned. "I hope that showing them is not the only reason you're going back to school. They're not worth it."

"That's a big part of it," she admitted, "but I want my degree, too. And I want to get back to painting. Time is going to be a real problem, though. Marshall wants me to be involved in all kinds of charities, and of course, there's this place to run, although his butler really does most of the supervision. There's a lot to learn about running this kind of establishment. Both of you have had experience with managing servants, but I haven't. And I want to do everything just right for him. I'm so grateful to him. Do you feel that way about Hal, Sarah?"

"Grateful to Hal? Of course not. I'm grateful that I've found him, but I don't feel grateful *to* him. I just love him. He's coming for dinner next week to meet my folks. Daniel in the lion's den. It'll be a total disaster."

"Your father's reaction to Hal should be great theater," Charlotte said, amused. "I wish we could be there to help you."

"I wish you could too. I'll need some support. But it would be too complicated. Claude's home and he's bringing his new fiancée for dinner. I haven't met her yet, but naturally she's the right sort. Incidentally, Claude thinks it was great to drop the bomb on the Japanese. It got him home."

"Your father's son," Charlotte said.

"I know. Would you believe that in my whole life, Claude and I have never had a conversation? But talking to Hal's like being back with Jimmy. He listens with a kind of wisdom that comes out of pain and suffering. He respects people."

"Well, I look forward to meeting both of your guys at the wedding," Charlotte said. "Please don't go out of your way to tell people that you're living together, Wendy. Nobody would understand."

Wendy's eyes flashed fire at her, and Sarah quickly changed the subject. "You're so lucky to have a little boy. I adore children. Where is he? I'm dying to meet him."

"Probably in his grandmother's room. He clings to her. I know what he's been through so I try not to feel bad about it, but he doesn't care for me at all. It makes me very sad."

"I'm sure he just needs time," Sarah tried to comfort her.

"Poor little thing." Wendy shuddered. "Nothing is worse than seeing someone you love die right in front of your eyes."

The girls were still there when Marshall arrived, and they both liked him at once. He was self-composed and erect, splendidly dressed in a gray flannel suit and immaculate white shirt, which was still fresh at the end of the day; he was well-built, without an inch of fat on him, not young or vibrant like Hal or Maurice, but kind, sensitive, and rational. It's interesting, Sarah thought. It's as if each of us has looked for a man to replace what we've lost. Charlotte, the security of her father, Wendy her childhood, and I my brother.

As president of a big company, Marshall was accustomed to dealing with people, and he immediately put them at ease. Wendy, admiring his urbane sophistication, thought, there's something to be said for older men; they have their problems under control.

From the moment he came in, Charlotte seemed like a person they hardly knew. She ran around trying to make him comfortable, asking him about the day's events, trying to anticipate his needs. When he spoke, she dropped everything to listen to him with admiring intensity. I hardly recognize her, Wendy thought. Is it real or just a big act? But Sarah found the transformation completely believable. Charlotte was happy at last.

To Sarah's delight, despite his bourgeois appearance and the fact that he was a businessman, Marshall was not reactionary.

In answer to her questions about politics, he looked

amused. "I've been a New Deal Democrat all my life. If you don't want me to have preconceptions about the Left, you must extend the same courtesy to businessmen. I believe in absolute freedom of speech and belief, and that's a lot more liberal than the Communists I've encountered. In fact," he grinned, "I'm so liberal that I think even Communists should be free to speak and meet and study their boring pamphlets and tracts. Since I've never known a Communist with any power, I've never been able to understand why all the big boys in Washington get so excited about them."

"Oh, it's just a red herring," Sarah said passionately, "to distract the people from making real improvements and changes in their lives."

"You're probably correct," he said mildly. She was totally delighted with this interchange. It was the first time she'd ever been able to have a political discussion that did not end in hysteria and animosity. What a great guy!

"And now that we've finished with politics, let's talk about something important. What do you think of my son?"

"We haven't met him yet," Wendy said.

"He's with his grandmother," Charlotte explained.

"I'll get him. You two will love him. He's making exceptional strides." He hurried out, and Charlotte looked after him with an anxious expression.

"Relax," Sarah whispered. "We'll help you. Little does the poor kid know he's getting three new mothers." Charlotte hugged her. Suddenly the problem of Teddy did not seem so overwhelming.

Marshall returned in a moment carrying Teddy, a shy little three-year-old with round brown eyes and curly brown hair. "Hi, Teddy," Charlotte said, but he turned his face away and clung to his father.

Sarah held out her arms and he went to her. "Call me Aunt Sarah." She handed him a parcel, which he quickly unwrapped while sitting in her lap. "A momkey doll," he crowed in pleasure.

Then Wendy held out her arms, and he also went to her. Charlotte sat there struggling not to cry. What would Marshall think?

"My turn to kiss!" Wendy handed him a big stuffed teddy

bear. "A teddy bear for Teddy," she said, kissing his little chin.

"Ooh. You're pretty," he said. "I wish you were my mother instead of her."

Charlotte tightened her lips, and her blue eyes filled with tears. He didn't like her. Most people didn't like her. All her life she'd been unpopular. What was it? Why was it? Almost as if she exuded some kind of unpopularity essence. It wasn't just in college, after her father's suicide, that she got this reaction. She'd even been unpopular in elementary school. She still remembered how awful it was when they lined up in twos—she was always the one without a partner. Her mother hadn't loved her, and now it was Teddy.

He would never let *her* touch him, but now Wendy was tickling his neck, and he was shrieking with laughter. "I wish I had a little dumpling exactly like you. The next time I come I'll have an even bigger present for you."

Wasn't this typical of the way Wendy so easily got everything just because she was beautiful. A three-year-old kid took one look at that beautiful face and wanted her instead of Charlotte.

She looked at Marshall with a frightened expression, but he seemed unaware of Teddy's attitude toward her. No matter what, she had to keep trying. What would she do if she lost Marshall's love?

CHAPTER
Nineteen

Sarah took the subway down to the Lower East Side to see where Hal lived. She had never been that far downtown before. The farthest south she had ever been was to Greenwich Village. Of course, her father's office was on Wall Street, but that was completely different. And she'd gone there by cab or car, never taken the subway.

Nobody she knew ever visited the Lower East Side. Most

of their crowd wanted to get as far as possible from their humble immigrant beginnings.

When she stepped out of the subway, she felt as if she were in another country. The streets were filled with pushcarts, bustling people, children racing around, and the sounds of Yiddish. A kind of energy and excitement filled the air.

I like it here, she thought. It's alive. This is where everybody started. My mother's parents and my father's too, although he would like to forget it. They came directly from Ellis Island to right here.

Hal was watching her in front of his tenement, nervously smoking and pacing about. She ran and threw her arms around him. "I like it here. Honest I do."

"Not so fast. Just reserve judgment for a little while."

He unlocked his door and sheepishly showed her inside. She hurried to put him at ease. "I like this too. I really do. I've never seen so many books and records. I'll love being here with you. You'll see."

He dropped a kiss on her upturned face. "Know what I love the most about you?"

"My politics," she teased him.

"Guess again."

"My intellect?"

"Guess again."

"I give up. It certainly can't be my flat chest."

"I even love your flat chest. Why do women assume that all men are obsessed with large breasts? No, what I love the very most about you is that you're so damned sweet. One of the world's innocents. A romantic radical. My romantic radical."

"I'm not so sweet. You've never seen me on a picket line. I'm a spitfire."

"I know what you are. And I know that it would be wrong to take advantage of your innocence. My darling impractical love, we should pack it in. Try to be realistic. A girl like you can't live in a place like this."

She hugged him fiercely. "I can live anywhere with you. Nothing is going to separate us. We'll manage somehow."

"I don't know. I honestly don't know if I can take the responsibility for this."

"It's not your responsibility to take!" She drew herself up to the full length of her tiny body. "I'm an adult, and I take the responsibility for whatever I do. And one thing I've learned from politics is that anything worth having is worth fighting for."

"What if your father says we can't marry or see each other?"

"We might have to sneak around for a while, degrading as that would be, the way Jimmy and I always did about the Jefferson School and political rallies. But I hope that once he sees that I won't be swayed, he'll let me live at home and finish up the school year, then give us a proper wedding. Maybe everything will be all right."

He sighed, dreading the evening. "I don't think it will. You know there's no way that he'll approve of me. It's going to be a terrible evening and all to no purpose."

"We have to try. We'll go step by step. If he doesn't accept you, then we'll worry about what to do next."

"I'll do my best to ingratiate myself, to make you proud. I even bought a suit."

"Oh, darling." Her heart turned over. "You make me proud every single day." They looked at each other and she felt her breath quicken with passion and her stomach melt.

"Do you think we have time?" he asked.

She reached for his belt. "I can't possibly get through dinner without it."

* * *

On the surface at least, the dinner at Sarah's home that night looked like a happy, pleasant family affair. Her mother, father, and Claude greeted Hal with the courtesy they would extend to any guest. Sherry and caviar were served in the library, Claude played a few Chopin études for them, and they discussed the exceptionally humid September. At eight, dinner was announced.

Claude's fiancée, Ann, was the only daughter of the Goldman Department Store family and a perfect social match for him. Both families already knew each other from their country club and were delighted with the engagement. She chattered away completely at ease.

However, it was quite different with Hal. He sat there ill at ease, his head cocked slightly to the side, feeling that they were speaking a foreign language, unable to hook on to their frame of reference, hopelessly out of his depth. Sarah's heart ached at his discomfort. She saw Claude and her father look disdainfully at his cheap suit, then at each other, and wordlessly dismiss him as 'not our kind.' In under five minutes he had been judged, condemned, and dismissed.

She felt his despair as her father questioned him about matters deemed essential in a suitor for his daughter's hand, quickly learning that Hal had not gone to college, had no money, had no significant career ambitions, suffered from war injuries, and came from poor and uneducated parents. His questions answered, Judge Stern proceeded to ignore him for the rest of the meal.

Smarting from their disdain, Hal sat there forcing himself to eat. Sarah tried to catch his eye, but he would not look at her. Her mother sat there in her usual silence while the judge talked to Claude and Ann about wedding plans.

It was one of Mattie's classic dinners; brisket, wild rice, fresh string beans, salad, apple crumb cake, and coffee, but Sarah was too distressed to eat anything. It was evident to her that Hal had not really understood just how luxurious her home would be, and, given his political sentiments, she was also embarrassed to have him see their black maid. After coffee, while they sipped Cherry Heering and Drambuie in the living room, her father suddenly made an announcement. "I have a surprise for Sarah." She looked at him distrustfully. What kind of surprise?

"Some time ago," he sipped his liqueur, "Sarah indicated that she would like to go to law school. At the time, I rejected the idea. I didn't think then that women had the requisite intelligence for law, and I still don't think they have the intellect for higher levels. Women are emotional, rather than analytical.

"But things are changing. Now that the war is over, this society will explode with growth, and many new lawyers will be needed. Women can do the routine work that will free men for more important tasks. As a matter of fact, a young woman did some research for me the other day that was quite satisfactory for a woman. I was pleasantly surprised. I thought, if she could do it, so could Sarah. So there it is. Fill out your applications, Sarah, and you can go to law school next year."

He's bribing me, she thought with longing, and how I'd love to do it, but his offer's come too late. He could offer me the sun, the moon, and the stars now and still not separate me from Hal. She kept her face impassive. "Thank you. I appreciate the offer. I'll think about it."

Then her father stood up and looked at his watch. "If you will excuse me, I have work to do."

Hal also stood up. "I'd like to speak to you for a few minutes alone, Judge Stern."

"I don't think we have anything to say to each other." He turned his back to Hal and walked out without another word.

Hal stood there feeling humiliated, rebuffed, and impotent, looking like a crestfallen child. "Come on, Hal," Sarah said, taking his arm. "Let's go for a walk."

"Please come back soon, Sarah," her mother said. "I want to talk to you. Good-bye, young man."

Sarah looked at her in surprise. It was rare for her mother to make any demands, even one as simple as this.

"Oh, Sarah," Ann said. "I'm disappointed. I was hoping you and I could talk about my shower. Do you think Tavern on the Green would be a good place for it?"

Hal was already walking out of the door. Without responding, terrified that he might just take off, Sarah ran after him and caught up with him as he was getting into the elevator. She grabbed his arm and held it tightly, not releasing it until after they'd crossed Central Park West and sat down on a bench outside the park. Then she moved close to him and put her head on his rigid shoulder. "I'm no saint," he said angrily, "and I don't like to be humiliated."

"Oh, I could kill them. They're so damned smug."

"They're not smug. They're right. Sarah, my love. Give it up. I knew the truth even before I saw myself through their eyes. I have absolutely nothing to offer you. Go to law school or marry some rich boy and live happily ever after."

"Absolutely no. I love you and that's all that matters. I love you and I won't be denied. I like all the good things of life. Of course I do. Who doesn't? But that's not what I want the most. I've always wanted to find someone like Jimmy, someone who lived according to a moral imperative, someone with logic and empathy who cared about people as ends, not means. And you're the only person I've found like that.

"On the train, Hal darling, terrible as that experience was, part of me was happy because we were going through it together. I knew that you felt the same impotence as I because we couldn't protect a friend. As bad as I felt, it was better because you were there.

"I want what you are. A man of conscience. A man who will always give money to those less fortunate than he is no matter how little he has, a man who cares about all the right things. I like to talk to you and dance with you and laugh with you and cry with you. I like to sleep all night with you, the two of us twined together like pretzels. I like to wake up with you, feeling your body there beside mine. Just the two of us there together making a universe. No matter what they say or do, I'll never let you go."

"Let me think about it alone," he said. "I can't think when I'm with you." He bent over and gently kissed her. "Better go home, love. Your mother will worry. I'll call you tomorrow."

Sick at heart, she watched him walk away.

Her mother was hovering in the foyer, wringing her hands. As soon as Sarah entered she clutched at her and whispered, "Let's go to your room, I don't want your father to hear." Sarah followed, saddened as always at the defeated slope of her mother's stooped shoulders. Oh, Mother! What availeth it to sell your soul for a rich husband?

Once inside, her mother quickly shut and locked the door and sat down on the edge of the chair, tearing at her cuticles. I feel so bad, Sarah grieved, because you've never been happy. And I owe you so much. Your unhappiness has given me the courage to fight for my own. Her mother bent forward and in a hoarse whisper asked, "Sarah, darling. In Mexico this summer. You and that young man?" She stopped in confusion and Sarah waited.

She cleared her throat several times then began again. "Sarah darling, are you still a virgin?"

"Why, Mother." She flushed with embarrassment. "How can you even ask me such a personal question?"

"Between mother and daughter there should be nothing personal. So tell me. I have a right to know."

Sarah looked at her and debated. Should she protect her by lying? No. She couldn't do that. It just didn't seem honorable. But she wanted to be gentle. "The answer, Mom, is no. But you don't have to worry. I love Hal and he loves me. We're going to get married."

Her mother's lips trembled and her eyes filled with tears. "Oh, Sarah." Her voice broke. "How could you have done this to me?"

"To you, Mom? What are you talking about? What have I done to you?"

"You know perfectly well. Your father will blame it all on me. For being too easy with you! For trusting you! How could you do such a thing? To throw yourself away on such a man, on a nothing! I don't understand it. I just don't! A girl with everything. What will we do now? No decent man will marry you. But maybe it isn't too late. You must tell me. Are you in a family way? Is that the problem?"

"No. I'm not pregnant."

"Then it's not too late. Thank God. You must never see him again. We'll just have to lie to the man you marry."

"Don't be silly. What would you do? Show him the sheets? But anyway, you don't have to worry about my virginity." Her mother winced. "There won't be a different husband. I love Hal and I'm going to marry him. If I can't have him, I don't want anybody. Don't you understand? I love him."

"Oh, love! Love! You think I never was in love? You think I never wanted someone? But there are people you want and people you marry, and they're not the same. Let me tell you a story. When I was a girl, we used to go to Cuddebackville for the summer. And I was a very well brought-up girl. I listened to my parents. If my father said, 'Jump,' we all jumped. And no questions asked.

"One day, I went to a stream to look for watercress. I can still remember the dress I was wearing. A white dress, with blue stripes and a sailor collar. It had gold buttons and it was down to my ankles. I always loved the sailor look.

"While I was looking for watercress a man came along in a canoe. Of course I never talked to strange men, but he had a nice quality. Blue eyes! An open face! He was a watercolor artist. I saw he had some of his work in the boat, so I wasn't afraid. He spoke to me as if he knew me. 'Get in and I'll take you for a ride,' and just like that I got in. I had never done such a thing before in my life. I got in. It was warm, and I trailed my hand in the cool, clear water. We ate the watercress, the sun shone on the lake, and the sky was so blue. We talked and talked about everything, and I knew at that moment, Sarah, that I was happy.

"But I did what your grandpa told me to do and I married your father. Everyone knew even back then that someday he would be a judge! And then one day I saw that artist's name in the paper. He jumped off a roof because he could not feed his family."

"Oh, Mom, how can you not understand? Maybe you would have been happy with that man even for a few years. This way you've never been happy."

"Of course I've been happy. I've been happy in my children. That's where most women find their true happiness. But then Jimmy died, and now you want to throw yourself away, too. If you marry this man, then my life will be nothing. My whole life will have been a waste if you do this to me."

"Mom. Listen to me. It's a whole different world. People marry for love. That's the only thing that matters. Dad will have to accept that eventually."

"No. He will never let you marry this Hal. He said that if you do, we'll sit shivah for you. You will get no money and he won't even let me see you. Oh, Sarah! Please don't do this to me. I always dreamed about when you would get married. That's the best time for a mother and daughter. A shower at the club, an engagement luncheon here for all of the relatives, and a beautiful wedding at the Pierre. I always imagined us picking out patterns together and planning a trousseau. Then a baby shower! And every Friday night all of us having dinner together; husbands, wives, grandchildren. Each year, bigger seders. Grandchildren looking for the affikomen. Grandchildren kissing me, touching me with their little hands and saying, 'Grandma, Grandma.'

"But now Jimmy is gone. I will never have his children to love. And Ann is all right, but a daughter-in-law is not a daughter. So all there is for me is you. And now you want to take that away from me."

"Oh, Mom, you know that's not what I want. I do want us all to be together. If only Dad would talk to Hal alone, get to know him. He would see what a fine man he is."

"Once your father's made up his mind that's it. He will never change it."

Sarah buried her head in her mother's lap, and the two women wept together.

CHAPTER Twenty

Her hand resting lightly on Maurice's arm, Wendy strode into the Copacabana trying not to show her dismay at the angry glances. It was nothing new to be looked at. From the moment she arrived in New York to go to college, she'd found that there was no way to avoid the attention her beauty aroused. So she'd learned to ignore it, to ignore the murmured whispers of strangers in the street, the catcalls of construction workers, and the insulting invitations shouted from cars. Women looked at her, too, envying her flawless skin, her carriage, the tilt of her perfect nose, and the hint of sadness that gave depth and mystery to her violet eyes. But nothing she'd ever encountered before equaled the hostility aroused by the simple act of peacefully walking down a street with Maurice.

"I can't believe it," she'd told Sarah. "Right here in New

York City, not the deep South, but in liberal New York, strangers have called me nigger lover. It's all right when we go to the Blue Angel or the Village Gate, but the other night, after all these years, the Stork Club wouldn't give me a table. Do you know how much money I've spent there?"

Maurice had become increasingly uncomfortable about their evenings out. "I know you mean well, but I don't like going where they look at us like freaks. I'm so uncomfortable that I can't even concentrate on the shows. I know you want to brazen it out, but it makes me damned uncomfortable. They hate me for myself, and they hate me even more because I'm with you."

Wendy looked at him in perplexity. They couldn't just sit home night after night. She'd die of boredom. "Do you want to go back to Mexico?"

"Of course I do. But not without you. Come back with me, Wendy. Nobody will bother us there."

"Just let me graduate," she begged. "I promised my mother."

But it was uncomfortable, and the situation came to a head that night at the Copa. She'd called to make a reservation, and as they entered she slipped a ten-dollar bill to the maitre d', and everything seemed all right. They had a good table, fast service, and after they'd ordered, they got up to dance. Both of them loved dancing, and they moved well together, almost like professionals. "Are you having a good time?" she asked.

"Just fine, thus far."

Then violence burst upon them so quickly that neither of them saw it coming. A hulking thug suddenly barred their way and said, "You bumped into me, nigger."

"He did not," Wendy snapped. "Get out of our way."

"Whore." He grabbed her beautiful Hattie Carnegie taffeta dress at the neckline and violently ripped it to the waist. My God, Wendy thought, I'm naked. She pulled the ripped top back up, trying to cover her breasts as Maurice unleashed a savage roar.

Letting loose the frustration of a lifetime, he punched the man so hard that Wendy could hear the crack of a jaw breaking. Then, watching in horror, unable to move freely because of her dress, she saw three bouncers jump on Maurice, drag him to the ground with screams of "Get that black ape," and with flashbulbs going off, proceed to beat and kick him while Wendy screamed hysterically, "Stop it! Stop it! Help him! Somebody help him!" But nobody did anything, and when the police finally arrived he was lying on the floor unconscious and bloodied. Shaking with shock, she knelt beside him weeping, "Maurice, Maurice. Speak to me. Wake up, Maurice. Talk to me. Oh, my God, is he alive?"

"Of course he's alive," one of the cops said. "You can't kill them. Skulls made of rock."

Two of them grabbed the unconscious Maurice under the arms and proceeded to drag him out, with Wendy following and screaming, "Get him a doctor. He needs an ambulance."

Ignoring her, they tossed his body in to the back of a paddy wagon, which immediately drove off, leaving her standing in the street, trying to hold her dress up. I have to hang on, she thought, I have to hang on for his sake.

Signaling a cab, she hurried to her apartment and dialed Charlotte. "Quick! I have to talk to Marshall." She continued to weep as she told him the story, and as soon as he understood the situation, he said, "Charlotte will be right over to stay with you. I'll call the police and find out where they took him."

She paced back and forth, weeping hysterically, until the doorman announced Charlotte. The girls fell into each other's arms. "Take a hot bath," Charlotte said. "That always calms me down." She drew a tub and helped Wendy into it.

Wendy was inconsolable. "The injustice of it! Why can't people leave us alone?"

"Oh, please, Wendy. You brought it on yourself. Not even someone as beautiful as you can buck society. Everybody tried to warn you, but you wouldn't listen. I'm surprised you didn't take him to a dance at the DAR. There are rules..."

"The rules are wrong," Wendy said and began to cry again.

"Of course they are, but that doesn't matter." Charlotte helped her out of the tub and into her terry-cloth bathrobe, then seated her in the living room with a stiff drink. After that, all they could do was wait.

At six that morning Marshall finally appeared with Maurice in tow. His head was bandaged, his arm was in a cast, and his face was covered with bruises. He stumbled like a punch-drunk boxer and seemed barely conscious. "Oh, darling," Wendy wept. "I'm so sorry, so very, very sorry. Are you all right?"

"Yeah! Great! Can't you tell?"

"Let's get him to bed," Marshall said. He passed out again when they started to undress him, so they only covered him and tiptoed into the living room to talk. Charlotte made coffee for them while Wendy, still distraught, paced back and forth in fury.

"I want to sue somebody," she said. "In fact, I want to kill somebody. Did you see what he looked like? What they did to that beautiful man?"

"He's lucky it's no worse," Marshall said. "Only his arm is broken, and they didn't book him."

Charlotte looked at him with quiet pride. "How did you achieve that?"

An impish grin appeared on his face. "Oh, I have all the right connections. I called Sarah's father."

Charlotte looked at him in surprise. "He did it? How did you accomplish that? Promise to run him for governor? He'd be horrified if he knew about their relationship."

"He didn't do it for Wendy and Maurice. He did it for me. I told him Maurice was usually my driver, not Wendy's, and that I needed him at once."

Wendy paced furiously again. "That's what I had to do on the train from Mexico. Oh, it's absolutely outrageous that the only way we can protect him is by pretending he's a servant."

"We have to accept what we cannot change."

"Oh, bullshit! Sarah always said we have to fight to change things, and now I know she's right."

"I'm also concerned about this, Wendy." Marshall held out a copy of the *Daily News*. On the cover, under the headline of "Chauffeur in Copa Brawl," was a picture of Wendy trying to hold up the dress over her bare breasts.

"You look gorgeous," Charlotte said.

Wendy looked at it in disgust. "I give up. He'll have to go back to Mexico where he's safe."

After they left, she threw away the paper so Maurice wouldn't see it, then fell asleep on the living-room couch. He was still asleep when she tiptoed in to look at him at nine. The sight of his battered face sent waves of anger spiraling through her again. She hated to leave him, but he would probably sleep all day, and she'd already missed too many classes. Tired and depressed, she kissed him gently and left a note saying that she'd be back by three.

She walked out of her lobby and found her friends outside her building in the car, waiting to drive to school. "Well, I guess my father finally did one good thing inadvertently," Sarah quipped. She put her arms around Wendy as soon as she was in the car. "Poor darling," she said. "What a terrible experience for you both. Why didn't you call me?"

"I was afraid to disturb your father. I still can't believe it." Wendy's face expressed remembered horror. "They kept kicking him and kicking him. They wanted to hurt him, they really did. Remember how that Mexican brought his gun butt down on Bennie's head and everybody looked the other way? That's the way this was. Not one person cared about a man who was being beaten just because he was black. Not one person saw him as a human being. No one tried to intervene. It was even worse than when the Mexicans hit Bennie because they only hit him once, but those bastards kept kicking and kicking Maurice.

"You know what I thought of? I thought of the sorority girls at school. They also wanted to hurt us because we didn't conform. That's what I thought of. In all my eighteen years on the island, I never saw such wanton cruelty and indifference as last night."

"Sometimes," Sarah comforted her, "you feel ashamed of the human race."

"That's what Mark Twain said," Charlotte added. "He said something like, 'I'm not prejudiced against any race, color, or creed. All I have to know is that a person's a human being. Can't get much worse than that.'"

Wendy uttered a bitter laugh, then leaned her head against Charlotte's shoulder and dozed all the way to school. When they reached their table, she found a note waiting for her. She was to report immediately to the Penalty Board, the sorority committee responsible for fostering obedience to the Students' Association's rules and regulations. "What do you think it is?" Sarah asked.

"Probably my rotten grades again. Oh, God, my head is splitting. I should never have come today. That's exactly what I need this morning. Another confrontation!"

Charlotte ran to get aspirins and water, and Wendy inserted a cigarette into her holder, trying to stop the trembling of her hands. Charlotte tried to bolster her. "We've never shown weakness to those girls yet. Don't let them get you now. Remember who you are."

"We'll be waiting right outside," Sarah added.

Suddenly Wendy felt a vast apathy sweep over her, the same feeling that had dominated her existence for months after Paula's death. She was so tired that she could hardly stand up. The hell with everything! The hell with her grades! She wasn't surprised that they were down. She hated studying, and since Maurice had been living with her she'd been doing even less than before. She didn't care about school. She never had! All she wanted was to finish this last year, get her diploma for Edita, and say good-bye forever to so-called higher education. This was not the first time she'd met with this committee. They would probably put her on probation again, and what good would that do? She didn't care enough to raise her average, and her fatigue and anger this morning did not dispose her to negotiate diplomatically with them.

She tossed her beautiful head, squared her shoulders proudly, and entered the Star Chamber. Instantly, all conversation stopped, as her judges stared at her with expressions of mingled curiosity and horror. She looked back at them with equal distaste. Sorority girls! Squeaky clean in their bobby socks and saddle shoes, and not a friendly face in the bunch. Mealy-mouthed, prissy little conformists.

Beside the girls sat their advisor, Professor Barley, a mediocre teacher who got her stroking as advisor to the Greek Council.

"Sit there." She pointed a long, bony finger toward a stool where Wendy was to face her accusers.

I'm back in Mexico with el cápitan, Wendy thought wryly. Gracefully sinking down onto the stool, she took out her long cigarette holder, lit a cigarette, insouciantly blew out a puff of smoke, and asked with total indifference, "Well, what is it?"

"We would prefer that you not smoke during this investigation," Professor Barley said.

"I would prefer that I do. Now will you please tell me what this is all about?"

"Really," snapped Patti, who had never forgiven Wendy for that initial put-down on the train. "Are you going to pretend that you really don't know?"

"I don't share all of your marvelous talents, Patti. I'm not a mind reader."

"I must insist that you refrain from insolence, Wendy," said Professor Barley, "and give this hearing the respect that it deserves." Wendy smiled and blew a smoke ring.

Professor Barley's pasty face grew white. "No matter what the circumstances, there is no excuse for poor manners."

Wendy blew another smoke ring. "Is sending for me this way and keeping me in suspense supposed to be good manners?"

"Typical," Patti snapped angrily. "You've always thought you were too good for this institution."

"Not this institution. Just little toadies like you."

"That does it. You are entitled to absolutely no consideration." Patti pulled out a copy of the *Daily News* and held it up with disgust. So that was the reason for this hearing!

"Would you care to explain this?" Professor Barley asked.

"It looks self-explanatory to me."

Professor Barley shuddered as if she'd peered into an abyss. "It seems that you appeared at the Copacabana with your chauffeur and created a disturbance. Is that correct?"

"He's not my chauffeur. He's my lover. We live together."

A collective gasp went up from the group. Professor Barley's shocked voice indicated disbelief. "Let me try to understand. You are living with a man to whom you are not married, and this man is black? This violent person in the picture is, in fact, the man you are living with?"

"That's absolutely right."

"Yccch," said one of the girls. "How disgusting. Being kissed by thick black lips."

"A black man in clean white sheets!"

"She probably has syphilis or gonorrhea by now," one of the girls murmured. "They all have it."

"Can this be true?" Professor Barley's voice quivered. "Can it be true that a girl who looks like an angel is living a life of such total depravity?"

"It can indeed! It's absolutely true," Wendy said.

Professor Barley again pointed her bony finger at Wendy, like the Old Testament God warning the inhabitants of Sodom and Gomorrah of retribution. "I have no words to express my horror. How could you have done something so tasteless? You might have brought dishonor to our campus. Thank heavens *we* were not mentioned in this scurrilous article. But that is no thanks to you. You are hereby expelled as of this very moment. Leave this campus at once!"

Wendy drew herself up proudly. "Oh, I'm glad to go. I never learned anything worth knowing here anyway."

"Out," Professor Barley pointed, the way one would to a dog. "Out right now. Do you hear me? Out I say! I never want to see your face again."

"I don't relish seeing yours either." She stood there tall and proud and beautiful. "What a shame. My mother was going to endow a chair here in memory of my sister for a quarter of a million dollars. I'm certain that this little group here can come up with the money now from some other source. Ta-ta."

She marched out of the room, and Sarah and Charlotte threw their arms around her. When she told them what had happened, Sarah said angrily, "We'll take you home right now. Those lousy hypocrites."

"I'll phone for the car," Charlotte told her. "We'll boycott classes for today, and tomorrow we hire a lawyer. Marshall will take care of it."

"No, it's all right. Both of you should stay for your classes. I can catch the next train back to New York. I don't want to wait for your car to get here. I'm anxious to see how Maurice is feeling anyway. He'll be delighted that I can go back to Mexico with him now."

"Are you sure you'll be all right?" her friends asked.

She continued her show of strength for them. "I'll be fine. All I need is a good night's sleep."

All of her bravado evaporated on the train, and she felt foolish and depressed. It wasn't that she cared about those witches or getting the degree. But Edita would, and she hated to disappoint her.

CHAPTER
Twenty-One

She could hardly wait to tell Maurice. Everything would work out now the way he had wanted. They would be together in Mexico. "Maurice," she called as she unlocked the door. "Guess what? I have exciting news for you."

But he wasn't there. She looked through the apartment, then found a note on the entrance table, weighted down with his apartment key. "Going back to Mexico," he'd written, and nothing more. "Going back to Mexico." That was all! Just like that?

She sank to her knees and wept. It was as if he had died. It was like losing Paula all over again. "Oh, Maurice," she wept, "I loved you. Didn't you know that?" When she was able to calm herself, she poured herself a large brandy and sat on her terrace mourning him, his loss now slashing at her with a sharp, insistent pain. She kept remembering them together: that first night in Mexico, making love, listening to good jazz, dancing, walking across the park hand in hand and laughing with sheer joy at being alive.

She remembered everything, even silly little things like when she'd introduced him to a tongue sandwich and he'd tried to teach her to ice skate. Charlotte had Marshall, and Sarah had Hal, but she was all alone again. Thank God she still had her dear mother.

She wanted Edita's arms around her, wanted to weep on her shoulder and have Edita put her to bed. She wanted to tell her the bad news in person, not on the phone. She went inside and dialed the hotel. "Mama, Mama darling, I'm lonesome. I miss you."

"I miss you too, darling. Why don't you come home for Christmas?"

"No I can't. I don't want to. Besides, my friends are here. Could you come to New York?"

"You know I can't darling. It's our busiest season, and I hate the cold." A wave of nostalgia swept through Wendy as she remembered how Mario had told her about Edita's search for a place where she would always be warm.

"Why won't you come home, darling? Is it still because of Mario?"

"That, and Paula and Papa."

"They happened to me too, darling."

"You're much stronger than I am, Mama."

"No! I'm really not. But I have no choice. I don't like the way your voice sounds. Is something wrong?"

"No, Mama. Everything's all right. But I miss you."

"Think about coming home, darling. Even a weekend visit! But if you can't, I'll be there April first for your birthday. Make a reservation at the Plaza, and we'll take your friends to lunch. And we might just whisk over to Paris for the spring collections if you can get away from school."

Wendy smiled ironically to herself. "I'm sure I could arrange that, Mama. I love you. Even if I don't come home, just knowing you're there gives me the strength to go on."

"I feel the same, darling. See you in April."

After she hung up, Wendy reached for the phone. "I'm back in circulation," she told each of the delighted men who answered. Within an hour she had filled every night for the months ahead. But it was without joy. I am the hollow woman, she told herself sadly, and she reached for the brandy to ease her pain.

The following week, Charlotte also decided to drop out of school. It was not customary for girls to remain in school after they were married. Besides, the sorority girls had seen her in all of her finery, and it had not made the slightest difference. In fact, things were even worse than before because now she and Sarah had to cope with snide remarks about Wendy, so they were constantly embattled.

Although she never expressed it, she resented having to defend Wendy on this issue. Why should they have to defend Wendy's spoiled behavior? She had been wrong to deliberately provoke the college. She expected to get away with things that nobody else could, just because she was rich and beautiful. And it wasn't fair.

She never paid for the things she did. Only one week after Maurice had gone she was dating three men a day. The problem was that Wendy had always had it too easy. She had never been forced to propitiate anyone as Charlotte had been forced to do throughout the years with her mother.

And the truth of the matter was that she was still propitiating, out of love, not out of fear, but propitiating nevertheless. It was Marshall whose needs came first now. She was living his life, not her own. She had not picked up a paint brush since her marriage. The pattern of their life together did not leave time for it.

Her only connection with art at present was the fact that they collected. Never having had the money for it before, she had to admit that she loved it. Everyone said she had a fine eye. But it was not the same as producing.

I really can be an ungrateful bitch, she chided herself. Just the way my mother always said. How can I resent Marshall for even one moment after all he's done for me? I was nothing without him, and I'd still be nothing if I were poor and single. That's more important than my painting.

No, she had no right to complain. Marriage had endowed her with the key to the New York life she'd always envied and dreamed of. Department store charges, successful friends, furs, jewels, a chauffeur, membership in Young Presidents, dinners at 21, travel, the box at the opera.

Anyone who wasn't satisfied with all of that really was no good, really deserved to be punished. I'm a troubled person, she told herself. My mother messed me up for the rest of my life.

There were things wrong with her marriage that money couldn't fix. The first problem was Teddy. She had done her best, but he still did not like her, and day by day she found herself hardening against him. He epitomized all that had always been wrong with her life, all of her undeserved victimization and unpopularity. Sometimes she almost hated him. But how could you hate a bereaved, defenseless little boy? It was wrong and she knew it.

And her second problem was sex. Her distaste for sex almost equalled her distaste for Teddy. What did everybody else see in it? Wendy regarded it as great fun and Sarah seemed to find it some kind of holy, religious sacrament. But to her it was dirty, smelly, and disgusting. A penis was a slippery snake secreting noxious, stinking slime. She was unable to fall asleep on sheets still wet with foul excretions! The only way she managed to cope with that was to put a towel under her until morning, to protect her body from touching the disgusting mess. Of course, she had their sheets changed daily.

Why was she missing what other people found? It wasn't fair! Typical of her luck! But she wanted to make Marshall happy, so whenever they made love she breathed heavily and thumped her body around like a beached fish. Unfortunately, Marshall liked to keep the lights on, so she had to guard her face at all times. She tried to compose her features into an imitation of Rita Hayworth's parted-lip sensuality, and that seemed to satisfy him. She tried to get him very excited so that it would be over soon, and then, as soon as he was finished, she would hurry to douche and take a perfumed bath, scrubbing to wash every bit of the awful odor away. But even so, she often had the sickening sensation that the smell of sex clung to her, and even the slightest whiff of it, real or imagined, was enough to turn her stomach.

Because there was nobody to whom she could talk, she often found herself brooding about her sexual problem. She never doubted that she loved Marshall completely. He was ten times neater and better looking than Hal. But Sarah acted as if her union with that ordinary man were free of physical nastiness. How could it be? Didn't every man excrete disgusting semen?

What was it her friends had found in sex? Each time she and Marshall made love, she grew more alienated, with the kind of loneliness that reminded her of standing on a deserted subway platform at three in the morning, with a chill wind blowing torn newspapers about.

Sarah refused to discuss sexual details with her friends, but Wendy did, nonchalantly saying such things as, "The only real kind of orgasms are the vaginal kind. Clitoral orgasms are all right; but I can do that for myself. I need a man for vaginal orgasms." Of course, Wendy was a little crazy. Who else would ever talk about masturbation so freely? Anyway, masturbation was every bit as unsatisfactory as intercourse. She didn't like to touch herself down there. It gave her a lonely, dirty feeling.

She knew that no marriage was perfect, and given a choice between having good sex with paupers like Hal or Maurice, or poor sex with a rich businessman like Marshall, she would always choose the latter. Besides, it was not only the sexual aspect of humanity that disgusted her. Most of the physical side of life turned her stomach. That was why she had been so attracted to the spirituality of Catholicism when she'd studied Dante in her sophomore year with Professor Shtall.

She hated mess and bad smells and disorder. She hated the naked, unadorned human body unless it was in a painting. She hated people who smelled from perspiration, had greasy skin, crusted eyes, and dirty hands. She hated the smell of menstrual blood and rotten teeth. She hated the stink of humanity.

It was things she loved—furniture, rugs, jewelry, art—things that were all clean, beautiful, controlled, and permanent. Her friends knew that she was a neatness fanatic but never realized to what extent because she was circumspect, knowing they would find her behavior neurotic.

She was actually rather relieved about being out of college. Maybe she would have a baby, preferably a girl, who would love her and be her friend for the rest of her life.

* * *

Sarah felt terrible about facing the last semester without her friends. "Now it will just be me alone every day, having to walk past those awful girls, listening to them make catty remarks about the two of you."

"You can probably get out by Christmas," Charlotte said. "If you have a hundred and twenty-five credits you don't have to stay for graduation. That's what they told me when I decided to come back. They really didn't want me going to classes. They still believe that all of their little charges are virgins. They seemed to be afraid that I would discuss marital sex openly. I wish I'd known about the hundred and twenty-five credits before. If I'd taken more credits, I would have been able to get my degree."

Sarah was jubilant at finding a way to leave. "I have at least that many credits. I always took five courses instead of four because there was so much I wanted to learn. I'm thrilled. I didn't want to stay without you two anyway.

"So none of us will have a formal graduation! It's strange in a way, but symbolic. We never felt that we belonged there. We always felt like outsiders. I can't wait to get out. I feel as if we're graduating *to* something, not graduating from something. I don't think anything much happened to me in college. The only thing that really matters is that we found each other."

PART TWO

Careers

CHAPTER
Twenty-Two

Sarah made arrangements to leave college at the end of the fall semester and then told her mother about it. As usual, Mrs. Stern became unhinged at the thought of any deviation from established plans.

"Sarah, you are giving me a heart attack. Each year I understand you less. Why do you want to leave college early? You don't have to be monkey see monkey do. You don't have to leave college just because your friends are doing it. It's different for them. Charlotte already has a wonderful, rich husband, and you should only be so lucky. If you had such a husband I wouldn't say a word. And Wendy's crazy. She's nothing but a bum. Please, for me, have a normal graduation."

"Wendy's a wonderful friend, and she's not at all crazy."

"Oh no? You could have fooled me. I couldn't believe that picture in the *Daily News*. Who walks around with no underwear and takes a chauffeur to the Copacabana? Only a crazy girl, a bum, a tramp would take Marshall's chauffeur to the Copacabana with no underwear on, and on a school night too."

Sarah restrained her amusement. "Chauffeur?" Her mother would have a heart attack if she knew that Wendy had been living with a black man. Her mother droned on.

"I didn't like her from the first minute, and her mother must be just as crazy to give her all that freedom and money. Who ever heard of an eighteen-year-old girl coming to New York alone with a mink coat and her own apartment? She was crazy when she came to New York, and in three-and-a-half years she's become even worse.

"She never cared about school or grades, but it's different for you. You're smart. At the top of your class. I would have been so proud. And what's the rush? What can you do for the next six months but bum around with her? You can't enter law school in the middle of the year. Your father will be furious when he finds that you're leaving before graduation."

"But I'll have my degree."

"It's not the same. The graduation isn't just for you. You have no right to be so selfish! Who paid for college? We did. You owe us something. You're graduating for your family. So give us the chance to be proud. Not even Claude was a straight-A student like you. What difference does it make if your two so-called friends aren't there now? It's a school full of girls, and girlfriends don't last anyway. They come and go. After I was married, I couldn't even remember the names of my old girlfriends. A husband and children are what matters, not girlfriends."

Sarah looked at her mother and sighed. How did such a stupid woman produce a straight-A radical? Really, it was a miracle. All these years Sarah had blamed her father for making her mother stupid, but somewhere along the line her mother had cooperated. And yet she loved and pitied her. Nothing was worse than living that way, surviving by self-deception and denial of reality. Perhaps the only thing she'd really learned from her was how not to live. Oh, well! She hated to hurt her, but there was no way to avoid it. Her mother would simply have to survive.

"Mom, I have to tell you something. Just be glad that I can get my degree and get out. The fact of the matter is that I'm pregnant."

Her mother looked at her as if she had an advanced case of leprosy. "Pregnant," she whispered, "your father will kill me. How can you be pregnant? In September you told me you weren't."

"In September I wasn't. But that was three months ago."

"You mean all these past three months you were living under our roof and carrying on with that good-for-nothing?"

"I'm getting sick and tired of this, Mom. You have to show a little more respect for people. Wendy is not a tramp, and Hal is a wonderful man, and both of them are a lot smarter than you are."

Then, for the second time in her life, her meek, mild mother smashed her across the face. The first time had been a ritual slap when she'd had her first menstrual period, but this slap was one of anger. "I will never forgive you for this disgrace," she wept, trembling like a leaf. "Never. You've ruined my life."

What life, Sarah wondered. You ruined it yourself by selling out, little by little, year after year.

"Come with me to the judge's study. We have to tell him right away." Her mother always referred to him as the judge when she was especially upset.

When her father heard the news, he didn't explode. He turned to ice. "Pack your bags," he said coldly. "I want you out of here tonight. Out of my sight. Go and live in Russia with your Communist lover."

"Tonight?" her mother interposed, trembling violently. "How can she go tonight? Where will she go?"

"Sit down," he barked. "Not another word, you stupid woman. All of this is your fault."

"Don't call her stupid," Sarah shrilled. "You're the stupid one, not Mom. A normal person would be delighted at the prospect of a grandchild. It's not as if I'm going to have an illegitimate baby. I love Hal and he loves me and we'll get married right away. Why can't you look at it that way? He's a wonderful man. Good and kind and gentle and intelligent and exactly the kind of man I would want for the father of my daughter."

"Please, Sarah darling, don't scream. The neighbors will hear you," her mother begged.

"I don't care who hears me. I hope all of New York finds out what a lousy, unforgiving fascist he is."

Ignoring both of them he continued coldly, "I see sluts like you before my bench every day. From now on you are dead to us. You are not to call your mother or bother her for money. You are never to enter this apartment again. I no longer have a daughter. Now pack your things and go."

Sarah looked at her mother. Fight back, Mom, she thought. Fight back this once and save your soul! I need you, Mom. I'm scared to death. Hal was waiting for her in the lobby totally innocent of the situation. How would he react when he not only found out that she was pregnant but that he also had to take her home with him?

And then, miraculously, her mother did fight back, but it was too late. Ashen-faced, shaking, she spoke up. "I won't let you do this. I won't let you throw my daughter out."

He sat there calmly pressing the fingertips of each hand against those of the other in a mockery of the gesture of prayer, looking at the two of them with a sadistic little smile. "Oh, really? Then why don't you go with her. Yes, that's exactly what you should do. How unfortunate that you will have absolutely no way of supporting yourself. Perhaps you can live in cozy squalor with your daughter and her commie boyfriend in their tenement, although I can't for the life of me see why they would want you."

"Bastard," Sarah spat at him as Mrs. Stern burst into tears, then sank down again shaking. Sarah knelt on the carpet at her feet, threw her arms around her and kissed her. "Thank you for trying, Mom. I'll never forget it. Please don't cry. Everything's going to be all right. Don't cry, sweetheart. Be happy. You're finally going to become a grandma. You'll like that, won't you? You always said you wanted grandchildren. So don't cry. I love you. Everything will be all right."

She picked up the house phone, asked the doorman to tell the gentleman waiting for Miss Stern that she would be a little delayed. Then she quickly packed the same two suitcases she had taken to Mexico and phoned for a porter. Her father had locked himself in his study, but her mother hovered about her weeping.

"I'm going now, Mom. I'll call you tomorrow." The two women clung to each other.

"What have I done with my life?" the older woman whispered. "Forty years of marriage and I have no money of my own to help my daughter. Forty years of marriage and I have no voice. Go, Sarah, darling. Run. Make a good life. This Hal can't be worse than your father."

"I'll phone you tomorrow," Sarah repeated. Then without a backward glance she followed the porter to the lobby where Hal was pacing around looking anxious. She burst out of the elevator and into the shelter of his arms.

"What's going on?" he asked, looking at the suitcases.

She was trembling too violently to talk, so he put his

arms around her and waited. She fluttered in his arms like a panicked bird but gradually calmed down as she felt the rough tweed of his jacket under her face and smelled the dear familiar fragrance of soap, starch, and tobacco. His warmth flooded into her cold, frightened body, and she thought how lucky she was not to be alone like her mother.

Seeing that she was calmer, he again asked, "What happened? Why the suitcases? Another political argument?"

She shook her head, pulled his face down to hers, and gently kissed him on the lips. "Oh Hal," she said, "I'm going to have a baby." Then the wonder of it swept over her and her words became an exultant paean of joy. "I'm going to have a baby. I'm going to have *your* baby. Oh, Hal. Take me home now and make love to me. I'm going to have your baby."

With an answering cry of triumph he lifted her into his arms and carried her to a waiting cab.

CHAPTER
Twenty-Three

Three months after Charlotte's wedding, her mother-in-law had a fatal heart attack. Charlotte was devastated. "I never realized that you were so fond of her," Sarah said.

"But I was. She was so good to me. Much better than my own mother. I don't think a day passed that she didn't weep about her daughter, but she never took it out on me or Teddy. She really wanted all of us to be happy. Now I'm upset about Teddy. All of the responsibility is going to be dropped on my shoulders, and he doesn't like me at all. He's practically a basket case after losing both his mother and his grandmother, and all he wants to do is hang on to Marshall. He won't let me come near him."

"You'll have to be patient," Sarah said. "The poor child is traumatized. Whatever he does, you can't take it personally."

"How can I not take it personally? He's the youngest

person who's ever disliked me. He evokes all of my old feelings of inferiority."

Sarah tried to cheer her up. "Now you can get really close. You'll have wonderful times with him. Wendy and I will help. We can take him to elephant rides at the Bronx Zoo and to see the Rockettes at Radio City. It's wonderful to see the world again through a child's eyes."

"Every time I think of what that child's been through I could weep," Wendy said. "He needs love so desperately."

"I hope you're not implying I don't love him."

"Do you?"

"No!"

"Well damn it, you should," Wendy said irritably.

"Oh, easy enough for you to talk," Charlotte snapped back at her. "You never do anything you don't want to do. You have nobody but yourself to ever think about."

That's the problem, Wendy thought to herself. That's exactly the problem. Nobody else to think about and too much time to brood. Her longing for Maurice was a daily source of pain, and other men couldn't help to dim his memory.

She couldn't even remember all of the men she'd slept with since he'd gone. Not one of them had interested her enough for a second date. Most of the time she only slept with them for company or as a sedative, although she often preferred brandy.

"Please don't you two start to fight." Sarah quickly tried to head them off. "It's not that you're not a good mother, Charlotte. It's just that we feel so sorry for Teddy. I think it's a miracle that he's functioning at all. He's such a tender child. I love the way he wraps his arms around my neck. I wish that he was mine."

"So do I. You can have him."

The butler came in carrying a large, heavy silver tray. "Well," Charlotte said consulting her new diamond watch. "It's time for tea. I hope you like cucumber sandwiches."

Wendy was amused at her affectation. "Cucumber sandwiches! Where did you get that idea?"

"I read about them in *The Importance of Being Earnest*."

"It certainly is nice to be back in Merrie Olde England

with the aristocracy," Wendy teased. "If you don't mind I'll have a drink."

"Has your mother seen Hal's apartment yet?" Charlotte asked.

"Not yet. Poor thing! I want to spare her. She'd have a heart attack."

"Any normal person would," Charlotte said.

"Especially those of us who were to the manor born," Wendy teased.

"You can scoff at me all you like, Wendy, but you would never in a million years live in Hal's apartment."

"What does that have to do with anything?"

"It has to do with everything. If you won't try to stop Sarah, I will. It is absolutely crazy for her to insist on downward mobility. Normal people want to get rich, not poor."

Sarah laughed. "What would a 'normal' person do?"

"Go to Cuba and have an abortion. I can't think of anything more insane than having a baby when you have no money and no job. It's one thing, Sarah, to have radical political tendencies and sympathize with the working class, but it's quite another kind of thing to opt for martyrdom. Why must you insist on suffering? It's just pointless, like refusing to wear your fur coat at college even when you were freezing. How did that help the working class? I hope you took it, by the way. You'll probably have to sleep wearing it, but even so, I don't know how you'll be able to survive without heat. And how can you deal with a baby in a cold water flat?"

"We'll manage."

Charlotte made one final attempt. "Go to Cuba. We can both chip in for it. Let's all go and make it a gambling vacation. Get rid of the baby and make some money."

"Don't be stupid," Sarah snapped. Instantly, tears filled Charlotte's eyes and Sarah was contrite. It was easy to forget, even after all this time, how abnormally sensitive she could be.

"I was only trying to help. It's for your own good."

"I know. I know. But you really have no understanding at all of my feelings. I don't want to have an abortion. I'm ecstatic about having Hal's baby. Then I'll have a part of him that belongs to me for the rest of my life. Nobody will ever be able to take it away from me. I want this baby. I wouldn't have an abortion even if we weren't getting married."

"But you have no money," Charlotte repeated. "I'm just trying to help you, Sarah, to give you the benefit of my experience. You have no conception of what it means to be poor. It's not the slightest bit romantic no matter how much in love you are. There's nothing worse than having no money."

"Nonsense. There are millions of worse things. Being locked in a boxcar. Being tortured. Having medical experiments performed on you. Having an atomic bomb dropped on you. All of these things happened to people who were just as good and deserving as we are. And all of them are a lot worse than being poor."

"Please don't be political now, Sarah. Nobody's dropping an A-bomb on you at the moment. I'm trying to discuss important things with you."

"We'll manage. The baby's due in August and I'm taking the New York City Board of Education exam for September placement. Hal will work evenings in the bookstore and watch the baby until I get home from school."

"But how can you have a baby in an unheated apartment?"

"We'll buy a heater."

"Since Charlotte's making the wedding," Wendy said, "I'll buy the layette. And we'll both contribute until you get on your feet."

They looked up to see Teddy at the door peeping in at them. He held up chocolate covered hands. "I made chocolate pudding," he said.

"Hi, Teddy." Charlotte held out her arms. Ignoring her, he went to Wendy and stood before her adoringly. Charlotte's eyes filled with tears. Wendy bent and gave him a kiss, and Sarah said, "I want a kiss, too. And I want you to come to my wedding, Teddy."

"Can I, Charlotte?"

"I told you to call me Mommy."

"You're not my mommy." His hand darted toward the tea sandwiches. "Can I have one of those?"

"Not until you wash your hands."

Ignoring her again, he reached out and grabbed a handful. Instantly, Charlotte reached out and slapped him, knowing that she was doing it not for the sandwiches but because he wouldn't accept her.

"I hate you," he said. "You're not my mommy." And grabbing another handful he swiftly ran out, leaving Charlotte in tears.

"I don't know why it is," she sobbed, "but nothing ever seems to work out right for me. Honestly, it's like in *Rebecca*. Marshall's first wife haunts me."

"Aren't you overdoing this a bit?" Wendy asked.

"I certainly am not, though I don't expect you to be sympathetic. All of Marshall's friends and associates liked his first wife better than they like me. I can feel it wherever we go and whatever we do. Even the servants liked her better."

Sarah, tender-hearted as usual, immediately tried to comfort her. "Please don't cry. I know it's a hard adjustment for you, but after all, he's only three years old. Think of how bewildered he must be. I'm sure he really does love you."

Charlotte wept on.

"Will you please stop," Wendy said. "You can't take a three-year-old's rejection seriously."

"I'm not just crying about that. The fact is, I'm also pregnant."

Sarah clapped her hands. "But that's wonderful. You won't have any of my problems."

"But I don't want a baby. I don't want to be a mother. My figure looks great for the first time in my life and I've had all those wonderful new clothes made. Pregnancy is disgusting. Swollen breasts, sagging bellies, awful thick ankles, varicose veins, and morning sickness. I don't want to be a breeding animal. I'm too young to have a baby."

"On the islands they start to have them when they're ten."

"Very funny," Charlotte wept.

"Be happy," Sarah urged. "We'll have our first children together, and they'll be friends for the rest of their lives, just like us. The next generation of the sorority. Just think, Charlotte dear. Once you have children, you're never as lonely again. You'll have your own family. You'll love that. You know you will."

Charlotte sighed. "I always did think I wanted children until I had Teddy dumped on me. Do you remember the 1939 World's Fair in Flushing? I went one day with two other girls from school. I never could invite anybody home with me because my mother frightened them away, and I didn't have friends, so I was thrilled when they asked me. My father gave me five dollars to spend there.

"At first it was wonderful, a large, grand party. The loudspeakers kept blaring Glenn Miller's 'Moonlight Serenade' over and over again, and I was happy and excited."

"That's still one of my favorite songs," Sarah said. "I want to dance to it at my wedding."

"Let me finish. I had to go to the bathroom, and when I came out the girls had disappeared. Just like that! I ran around and around wildly, calling their names until I was hoarse. Maybe I should have been furious, but instead, I was ashamed. I figured that in some crazy way I deserved to be left. I was too ashamed to go home early so I wandered all day listening to 'Moonlight Serenade' and feeling that nobody in the whole world was as alone as I. Later I found out that they'd met two boys and simply gone off because I was an extra girl. So maybe you're right about the baby. At least I'll never be alone again."

Sarah hugged her. "That's a terrible story," she said.

I'm tired of being alone, too, Wendy thought, and of sleeping around. It was time to find a husband, but she tired of men so quickly. Everyone but Maurice.

She was glad that Edita was coming to New York. "I can't wait for you to meet my mother," she told her friends. "You'll both adore her. She's good and kind and smart, and she understands everything. And if you want her to, Sarah, I'm sure she'll be glad to give you away at the wedding."

"Really? I'd love that," Sarah said. "I don't think my poor mother will dare to come."

Idly, Charlotte wondered how her mother was getting along. She hadn't communicated with her once since leaving home. She probably should check on her. Suppose her mother had died? She was her only heir, and real estate in Brooklyn Heights was quite valuable. But Marshall had plenty of money, and she'd rather inherit nothing than to have her mother know where she was. Life certainly was ironic. She'd escaped from the problems of a crazy mother to find the problems of a disturbed kid.

"I just decided what I'm going to ask my mother to do for my birthday," Wendy told them. "I'm going to ask her to go with me to Mexico and help find Maurice."

CHAPTER
Twenty-Four

That spring, for her daughter's twenty-second birthday, Edita made her first of what was to become an annual pilgrimage to New York to celebrate with Wendy and her friends, before whisking her off to Paris for a shopping spree. The girls had been dazzled by Edita from the moment they saw her at Sarah's wedding. They had never known a mother quite like this chic and vibrant woman. She was the first successful career woman they'd ever met, but that was not as astonishing to them as was her relationship with Wendy. Wendy loved and respected her. Sarah pitied her mother, and Charlotte hated hers, and neither one of them had ever thought of a mother as a friend or role model. Edita was both for Wendy.

When Edita entered the Palm Court of the Plaza Hotel for the birthday luncheon, people turned to look at her in the same way they always looked at Wendy. Magnificently regal, her dark hair piled high in a chignon, her long neck and body straight as a girl's, she carried herself like a queen. Her exquisitely tailored, black silk suit had been made to order for her by Yves St. Laurent, and she wore diamond and sapphire earrings and a matching brooch.

She hugged and kissed each of the girls warmly. "What a lovely time to be here!" Her husky voice with its faint Russian accent wrapped them in a spell of exotic sophistication. "Spring in New York at my favorite luncheon place. Sometimes at home I dream of this julienned chef salad. I've tried to have our chefs duplicate the dressing, but we just can't seem to find the secret."

They all toasted each other with Dom Pérignon. Sarah had put on too much weight for her tiny frame, and she rolled a bit when she walked. But she was merry and optimistic.

Charlotte looked nothing like the girl she'd been a year before. Her red hair was worn in a fashionable poodle cut that accentuated her high cheekbones, her maternity suit was a Chanel that had been adjusted for her, the perfect pearls in her ears matched the double strand around her neck, and all traces of her Brooklyn accent had disappeared. But despite the external changes, she watched Edita and Wendy with a hungry heart.

Edita quite openly adored Wendy and didn't hesitate to show it. She kissed her from time to time, listened to anything she said with respect and held her hand on top of the table. She had not one word of criticism for Wendy about the college fiasco. Instead, she was angry at the college.

"What she does out of school," she said, her beautiful dark eyes flashing with disdain, "is none of their business. I thought Adams was a college, not a convent."

My mother was never on my side, Charlotte thought sadly. Unaware that her mother was unbalanced, the high school dean had sent for her once to complain that Charlotte never smiled. She was about to be installed into Arista, the high school honor society, and the dean was anxious for each new member to smile enthusiastically when she went up to accept the Arista pin.

"She always looks so unhappy and doleful," the dean had complained. "Would you please practice smiling with her at home?"

"Certainly," her mother had said through bared teeth. "I don't know why she doesn't smile. Nobody could have a better home life." As soon as they were out of sight of the school, her mother had turned to her and punched her in the face. "How dare you embarrass me," she'd screamed. "Smile, damn it. Smile." Ever since, there had been something strained about Charlotte's smile. It wasn't warm, open, and sexy like Wendy's or friendly like Sarah's. Her smile was always only a step away from pain.

But Edita was in Wendy's corner. She probably would have punched the dean, not her daughter. She was tough and strong but also feminine, an unusual combination, and she had the dignity, poise, and presence of a great actress. Kind of like Katharine Cornell. This was the kind of mother you could learn something from, the kind of mother you could be proud of, the kind of mother you could love. Charlotte's heart burned with the old sorrow and envy.

"And how is your art coming along?" Edita asked in her low throaty voice that was much like Wendy's except for the faint traces of a Russian accent. She smiled into Charlotte's eyes and Charlotte smiled back, wanting her approval.

"It isn't. I haven't touched a brush since I got married. But I haven't left art. Marshall's on the board of the Metropolitan Museum, and he's always been a serious collector. I'm becoming one too."

"Wendy tells me that you have infallible taste," Edita said, and Charlotte's day was made.

Then she turned to Sarah. "And how does Hal like working in that bookstore in Greenwich Village?"

"He loves it. Not much money, but he's learning the ropes. He says the hardest part of it is restraining himself from just hiding in a corner and reading."

They sat there for three hours, drinking, talking, and laughing. Then they accompanied Edita upstairs to her suite, where she ordered more champagne for herself and Wendy and coffee for the other two. "I didn't smoke or touch a drop of alcohol when I was pregnant," she said. "That's the way to produce beautiful babies."

"Have you ever thought of remarrying?" Charlotte dared to ask. "You're so beautiful and alive, and you must meet many eligible men at your hotel."

"I seem to be a one-man woman. The way my daughter

seems to be with this Maurice. So I've decided to cancel Paris and go to Mexico City with her to find him."

"Oh, Mama," Wendy said, throwing her arms around her mother. "That's the best birthday present you could have given me."

The next day they flew to Mexico City, were met by a chauffeured limo, and taken immediately to the Maria Isabella Hotel. This time Mexico City was a totally different experience for Wendy. They were driven everywhere, ate only in the best restaurants, and managed to be insulated from Mexicans except for when they went to the university, where they spent an entire day going from office to office, until they were finally certain that Maurice had never returned to school and that the school had neither a home address nor a forwarding one for him.

Wendy wept in her mother's arms for hours that night. "Oh, my poor darling," Edita tried to comfort her. "I hate to see you so unhappy. Do you want to hire detectives?"

"I don't think so, Mama. We've done enough. He shouldn't have just gone off the way he did. No matter how upset he was he should have thought a little bit about how I'd feel. Now he'll just have to find his way back to me."

"What will you do now, my darling? No school, no love."

"Don't worry, Mama. I have my friends and a wonderful social life in New York. I'll get involved in charity work, take a few courses, maybe do some traveling."

"But I do worry. You seem so rootless to me. Your friends will be busy now having babies, and they won't have as much time for you. Why not come home, darling, and work with me at the hotel?"

How wonderful it would be always to have the comfort of her mother and Carmen, but those feelings were immediately replaced by the memory of the body hurtling down from the cliff. And even if she could transcend that memory, she knew instinctively that if she returned it would be like moving back to childhood. She would be coddled, catered to, and cosseted, but she would never grow. "I can't, Mama. The island's too small."

"New York's an island, darling."

"No, it's a whole world."

Edita kissed her tenderly. "I'll always be there for you whenever you need me."

CHAPTER Twenty-Five

In the summer of 1946, Charlotte had a girl whom she named Kitty, Sarah had a boy named Jimmy after her brother, and Wendy, a favorite subject of every society column in New York, came to epitomize what was known as café society. Four years later in the spring of 1950 Edita made her annual pilgrimage to New York for the ritual celebration of Wendy's birthday, her twenty-sixth. It was the same joyous reunion as ever. Seemingly, nothing had changed.

"How are the children?" Edita asked Charlotte and Sarah. "You must bring me up to date. How fortunate you both are. I wish my darling daughter would also get married and give me a grandchild. Wendy darling, I don't think a notebook of your press coverage is quite the same thing." They laughed together.

"You're absolutely right, Mama, darling. Be patient a little longer. I just haven't found the right man yet."

Edita looked at her soberly. "I'm trying to be patient, but time is running out. Now Charlotte, tell me about your family."

Charlotte sighed. "Teddy is seven and uncontrollable. I'm afraid that he'll be kicked out of Collegiate. Kitty is nearly four, and you can't imagine how brilliant she is. We were having dinner at Laurent, and the waiter suggested chicken breasts with sherry. Kitty looked up and said, 'I don't like chicken and cherries.'"

Edita laughed politely, but Wendy said, "I don't think that's especially witty. Teddy has always been much smarter."

"That's your opinion. I think Teddy's psychotic."

"Oh, please," Sarah begged. "It's awful to label children. I'm sure that's not what his therapist says."

"He hasn't made the final diagnosis, yet," Charlotte said

coldly, wishing they'd mind their own business, wanting not to look bad in front of Edita, who now turned tactfully to Sarah and asked, "And how is Jimmy?"

"Oh, he's wonderful. Everything is going along just fine with us. We've moved to low-rent housing in a building called Knickerbocker Village, and I'm teaching English in a junior high school on West Forty-eighth Street. It's a wonderful job, and we have one of the largest Teachers' Union chapters in the city."

"Sarah organized them," Wendy said proudly.

"And I have great neighbors, too," Sarah continued. "The Rosenbergs. They have two little boys, and they're wonderfully cooperative and have the right politics. We're really lucky."

"Oh, God," Charlotte sighed. "It's like Pollyanna talking about the beautiful crutches."

"And what about your mother? Do you see her?"

"More than I expected. She finally had the gumption to tell my father that she was visiting her grandchild. She babysits a lot and Jimmy adores her. Whenever she can, she slips me a few dollars, but my father's still doling it out to her."

"What a terrible way to live," Edita said. "Hard for me to understand why anyone would be so docile. I was lucky in Francisco. He loved to give to me and the girls. Oh, well! Let's not talk about that or I'll get sad. Tell me what's happening with Hal and the bookstore. Wendy told you that I would be willing to stake you, didn't she?"

"Of course she did, and we'll never forget your generosity. But we've dropped those plans for the present. Hal's wounds still bother him from time to time, and it would require more stamina than he has for him to be an owner. It's really better all around for him to go on working nights at the bookstore. That way he can cover Jimmy until I get home from school, and they have a great relationship because they're together so much. I think it's just as important for a father to spend time with a child as for the mother."

"It certainly is." Charlotte's voice was resentful. "I get fed up with the total responsibility for our homes and the children. Would you believe that Marshall doesn't even know where the dishes or toilet paper are kept?"

Edita tactfully reproved her. "But it was exactly the same with me. Francisco could run a famous hotel but he couldn't find a cuff link." For a moment her luminous dark eyes misted over. "But you know, my dear, none of that really matters. I would give anything to have him back again. Being alone does give one a different set of priorities. I know it's hard when you can't be yourself, but be patient. Some day you'll return to your art."

This time the luncheon did not last for three hours, and Edita did not invite the girls back to her suite. After only an hour she complained of fatigue and asked to be excused. "I would like to see Hal and Jimmy," she told Sarah. "May I visit tomorrow?"

"Of course! That will be wonderful. They'll be delighted."

Charlotte felt rebuffed almost to tears. Why hadn't Edita asked to visit her? She loved Edita so much, but Edita preferred Sarah. She was depressed for the rest of the day.

Edita always hired a chauffeur and limo when she was in New York. The next afternoon they drove to Knickerbocker Village where Hal was waiting downstairs for her. "Welcome," he said, kissing her warmly. He adored her as much as the girls did, not only for her generous offer to finance the bookstore, but also for serving as surrogate mother to Sarah at their wedding.

The chauffeur handed Hal a large box for Jimmy from F.A.O. Schwarz, and then she followed him to their apartment. "I've been listening to Senator Kefauver and his Special Committee to Investigate Organized Crime," he told her, switching off the television. "It's a historic event. The first time any such investigation has been televised. I never thought television could be such a benefit to man."

She sank down into a chair. Hal thought she looked tired and pale. "Sarah will be home from school soon and her mother is out with Jimmy. He'll be thrilled to get a present. What's in this enormous box?"

"His first fire engine. He can ride around destroying your furniture."

"On this furniture it won't even show. Would you like some tea?"

"That would be fine." He looked at her again. Her voice had none of the enthusiasm and vibrancy of the past.

They sat there companionably sipping tea and talking. Edita automatically practiced her hostess skills, honed over many years at the hotel, of making people comfortable in her presence by drawing them out and discussing their interests. She did this now in her usual fashion, but it seemed to Hal that she was less vital and vivacious than usual. She asked him about the bookstore. "Is it doing well?"

"It's hard to know exactly. It changes from day to day. Some publishers are making gloomy predictions that TV is going to blow them right out business, but I'm not so sure. Paperback books are sweeping the market, and no real intellectuals pay much attention to television. We only have this one here because your generous daughter gave it to us. But how could television ever compare with the *New York Times*."

"Oh, the *New York Times*!" Edita's charming laugh rang through the apartment. "Wendy tells me that it's an obsession here, that people line up to get Sunday's on Saturday night. She once met a man who said he preferred reading it to making love."

"If he said that to Wendy he was crazy. She's the most beautiful girl in New York. And not only that. She's good and kind and not the least bit conceited."

"But she's alone and it worries me. And despite all of her so-called worldly experience, there are aspects of her that are quite unworldly. At times she seems so innocent and childish to me. For example, she hasn't the slightest idea of how to deal with money. It's my fault, of course, for always handling everything for her, and it's too late to remedy now, but I wish I'd had the foresight to make her more responsible and independent."

"It's never too late for you to teach her," he said.

"Yes, it is," she answered. Puzzled by a strange note in her voice, he changed the topic to politics. They spoke about the Korean War. "I don't understand it," she said. "Do you?"

"I think so. It's all part of this country's dementia on the subject of Communism. We have a paranoid country here. Building bomb shelters! Bomb drills in schools! Hiding under desks! Dumb slogans like Better Dead than Red! It's all to keep from focusing on what's wrong in our own backyard."

"People don't even know what it means to be Red. They respond like children if you ask them. Red equals bad and bad equals Red, and they get incoherent if you ask them to explain what they're talking about. I look at my little boy and wonder if he's going to have a world to live in. We've seen the effects of the A-bomb, and even so, Truman's told the Atomic Energy Commission to go ahead with the hydrogen bomb. The super bomb. Why, why, why? It's all sheer insanity. Einstein knew the score. He thought that politicians should never have been allowed to get their sticky fingers on atomic energy. He warned Truman that we risk general annihilation next time. What an irony! The end result of our extraordinary technological accomplishments is the ability to destroy the world."

"We all have to die sometime," Edita said vacantly.

He looked at her in surprise. That's a strangely stupid response, he thought, suddenly disturbed.

Just then Sarah came tumbling in, distraught about what had happened that day. Her junior high school was in the Holy Cross Diocese, and her pupils were an interesting mixture of the children of longshoremen and itinerant unemployed actors who were holed up with their families in the rundown brownstones of the Times Square area. She held out the front page of the *New York Post* and pointed to the picture.

"This is one of my students who accidentally shot one of the theater kids yesterday. They were playing with his father's gun and didn't know that it was loaded. Oh, it's a rotten shame that those longshoremen have to keep guns for protection. That shapeup is so corrupt. What they really need is a Harry Bridges in New York. Now there's one kid dead, and the kid who shot him may have been destroyed for life. I'll have to go and visit him tonight and see what I can do to keep him out of reform school. He shouldn't be blamed."

"It's terrible to keep guns around where children can get at them." Edita's voice sounded like a soundtrack running down.

Instantly, Sarah was alert. She sat down beside Edita and looked into her eyes. "Something's wrong! This isn't just a social visit!"

Edita sighed deeply. "I'm afraid you're right. There's no point in beating around the bush, Sarah, dear. I have cancer of the liver. At most I have a few months to live. Maybe less."

"Oh, no." Sarah threw her arms around her and they cried together. "Oh, poor you and poor Wendy. I'm afraid she'll fall apart."

"I'm worried too. That's why I'm here. When I go, she'll have no family other than you four, and she'll need you all desperately."

"What can I do to help?"

"I'd like both of you girls to be at her apartment when I tell her tomorrow and then to accompany us to the hospital. I don't want her to be alone. Can you do that?"

"Of course! I'll take the day off." Sarah held Edita in her arms and tried not to cry.

Just then Mrs. Stern came in with Jimmy, and Sarah introduced them. Her mother, unaware of Edita's fate, was totally intimidated by her style and beauty. Oh, life was sad and strange, Sarah thought. No one should ever be envious or intimidated by facades.

But even so, even under sentence of death, it was better to have led Edita's life than her mother's. At least Edita had known love, respect, accomplishment, pride, and satisfaction. At least she had owned her soul.

"Time for me to go," Edita said. "I'm getting tired." Sarah kissed her good-bye and Hal escorted her to the limo. As soon as they were out of sight, Mrs. Stern turned to Sarah, nervously swiveling her head around as if fearful that the apartment might be bugged. She spoke in a frightened whisper.

"I heard the women in the street talking. They've arrested your neighbors."

"What neighbors?"

"You know! That quiet couple! The Rosenbergs!"

"Impossible! Who arrested them and for what?"

"The women don't know exactly. They think it was the F.B.I. and that they're Russian spies. You should never have been so friendly with them. Now you and Hal had better watch your step. When they come back from jail don't have anything more to do with them."

"Mom, it's ridiculous. It can't be true. Forget about it and don't worry."

But she was worried herself. At a time like this, it was just crazy enough to be possible. As soon as Hal returned she told him, and his anxious face reflected her own odd premonition. After her mother had gone, they knocked and knocked on the door of the next apartment, but nobody answered. It was silent as a grave. They held onto each other and shivered.

CHAPTER
Twenty-Six

Numb with horror, her eyes red and her face ravaged by days of weeping, Wendy sat in the paneled, opulent Park Avenue office of Dr. Robert Kingman III, reputedly the best oncologist in the city.

She felt as if she too were dying. Edita's illness had reawakened all of her old guilt, agony, and frustration because she'd been unable to save Paula. This time, she was determined to stop at nothing. She began to cry again. Oh, Edita! My dear, dear mother! Always so strong! Always there for me! My rock! My fixed star! How can I go on without you?

Struggling for control, she lit cigarette after cigarette in her long holder, until finally the receptionist showed her in.

She was surprised to see so young a man planted behind the massive mahogany desk. Perhaps she should have looked for someone older. But Marshall, who had obtained his name, had informed her that both his father and grandfather had been noted society doctors and that he had an unimpeachable reputation. She sat down and looked at him closely.

His expression was reflective and mature. Everything about him inspired confidence, from this quietly opulent office to his sober demeanor. He was quite evidently a man one could depend on. For a moment, a tiny flame of hope flickered up in her heart.

Trying to keep her hands from shaking, she lit another cigarette and tried to speak coherently. "Save her. Whatever it costs. Please save her."

How old was he? In his thirties it seemed, but he carried himself like General MacArthur, ramrod-straight back, opaque gray eyes, short brown hair, a firm mouth, and a firm speaking voice. Jack Armstrong, the all-American boy, so totally in control of his face and body that she wondered if he'd gone to military school. Here quite evidently was a man who knew who he was and what he could do, a man you could trust to take charge. For the first time in days she was able to breathe. He braced his shoulders. Telling patients the truth was always the hardest part. "I visited your mother this morning. I cannot save her. Nobody could. Cancer of the liver is terminal."

She could feel her heart cracking. "No," she screamed as she began to faint, pitching forward out of the chair just as his arms caught her, held her, then lifted and carried her to the couch. She kept her eyes closed until the attack of faintness passed, and when she opened them, his gray eyes were gazing down at her.

Gasping for air, she struggled to sit up. "I can't breathe. I'm suffocating. Brandy please." He rang his nurse to bring her some, then watched intently as her lovely lips curled round the tip of the glass and a little color flooded back into her smooth, perfect cheeks. She began to sob, and he took her hand and waited.

When he thought she could listen, he began to talk again. "I'll be with her as much as possible, and I promise that she'll feel very little pain. I'll prescribe as much medication as she needs."

"No pain?" she whimpered.

"No pain. I promise." She took his hand and rested her cheek against it.

And then the long, terrible vigil began. He was true to his word, and most of the time Edita was sedated and slept. Charlotte sat there with Wendy during the day, and Sarah usually relieved her each afternoon as soon as she had finished with school. But Wendy hardly noticed their presence. She saw them through a fog, a haze, a long, long telescope. She felt so strange. Like a condemned prisoner in a cell watching free people outside walking around, laughing, talking, doing all the things that normal people do who are not under sentence of death. And her poor mother was alone and isolated in another cell, and neither one of them could help the other. Sarah understood how she felt.

"I felt that way when I read that while the Nazis were sitting on top of the walls of the Warsaw ghetto taking pot shots at Jews inside, Polish people in their Sunday best walked right past the ghetto walls to go to church. But that's the way the world is. We just don't think about such things until they hit us."

"Yes, that's exactly it. Cancer never existed for me before. It was one of those things that happened to other people. Statistics had nothing to do with me. But this entire hospital is filled with cancer patients, and now nothing exists for me *but* cancer. The worst part is her daily deterioration. I want her to die before it gets worse. I wish I could just give her a shot and end it painlessly right now."

"I do, too, but we'd never get away with it here. Too many nurses and attendants always snooping around. Besides, I'm not sure that either one of us *could* really do it."

"I could. Of course I could. I'd do anything to spare her from further suffering."

For Sarah, it was also a time of terror outside of the hospital. The Rosenbergs were in jail, their children had been taken somewhere, and she was refused permission to visit the jail. She felt angry and depressed and impotent each time she walked past their apartment. In addition, many of her Teachers' Union friends were being fired by the Board of Education for refusing to sign the loyalty oath. Oh, what a ridiculous device that was! Any genuine spy who was a threat to national security would sign the oath without a moment's hesitation.

But the school system was losing some of its most-dedicated teachers because of it. She and some of her colleagues had refused to sign the oath on the grounds of conscience and freedom. After escaping from her father's tyranny she was not going to let other petty dictators pry into her personal political beliefs for their own sick purposes.

But lying awake night after night, she worried about her decision, wondering how they would manage if she lost her job as so many of her friends had done. And it was certainly possible! She was on the mailing list for every radical newspaper and magazine and had signed every petition printed since the one for the Joint Anti-Fascist Refugee Committee. Unimportant as she was, there must be an encyclopedic-length dossier on her at the FBI. She assumed that there was also a vast dossier on Hal. All of the men who had fought in the Lincoln Brigade were suspect, but he would not lose his job. The bookstore owner was also a radical and a friend. The problem was that his job paid so little that they couldn't really manage without her salary.

Well, perhaps if Adlai Stevenson were elected in 1952 the country would return to Roosevelt's high ideals. The problem was how to survive until then.

For Wendy, the outside world did not exist. Each day Edita grew smaller and smaller, changing before their anguished eyes to a whimpering bundle of pain that often did not seem quite human. Sometimes she spoke quite lucidly, telling Wendy, "Be careful with your money. Do not marry a fortune hunter. Do not give it to your husband. It must remain yours."

But at other times she would start to ramble incoherently. "You and Paula must remember to greet every guest tonight. We must never take our guests for granted. Where is Paula, darling?"

"She'll be here in a little while, Mama."

"Such good girls. I love you both."

"We love you, Mama."

Charlotte fretted about Wendy. She told Sarah that she was drinking a fifth of brandy a day.

"You're exaggerating."

"If I am, it's not by much."

"Well, Dr. Kingman said Edita only has a few days now. Then we'll dry her out. I'll take her home with me and put Jimmy in our room."

"Don't be ridiculous. That awful apartment would make her feel worse. Roaches in the kitchen! One bathroom for all of you, and where would she sleep? On that broken couch in the living room? Forget it! We'll take her out to the Hamptons and fix her up. That's a proper kind of environment: sea, sand, and interesting people."

Sarah restrained herself from answering. Didn't Charlotte ever listen to herself? Sometimes she was such a solipsistic bitch. She seemed to have no idea that she might hurt Sarah's feelings by speaking about her apartment that way. Not that she wasn't right! The apartment was dilapidated and cramped, but it was a big improvement over Hal's original apartment, and they tried to make the best of it. But this was not the time to quarrel. What a strange mixture Charlotte was of insensitivity and generosity, humor and anger. You had to love and accept her for the good things—her generosity in making the wedding, her willingness to bring Wendy back to health—and forget how truly irritating she could be at times.

On the last day of Edita's life, a Saturday, Sarah agreed to cover in the morning and Charlotte in the afternoon. Dr. Kingman would be there in the evening. Sarah tiptoed in and saw Wendy sitting on Edita's bed, tenderly holding the sleeping, shrunken body in her arms, like Mary holding Christ in Leonardo's *La Pieta*, rocking her, and gently crooning, "Hush, little baby, don't say a word. Mama's gonna buy you a mockingbird." While she sang, tears flowed down her face continuously like rain. As Sarah was about to say, "I don't think you're allowed on her bed," she was suddenly struck by how absurd that would be. What the hell difference would it make she thought savagely. Without saying anything, she walked over to the bed, bent over, and kissed Wendy's cheek. "I like the way you sing. I always have."

"Mama always did, too, didn't you, Mama? Carmen used to sing that song to Paula and me to put us to sleep."

Edita sighed in her sleep and Wendy gently put her down and slipped off the bed. Then she raised her ravaged eyes to Sarah's. "Just before you came in she was talking to my father and Paula. She said, 'Wait for me, my darlings. I'm coming to you. Wait for me.' Isn't it wonderful to think that she's really seeing them, that they're beckoning to her and she won't be somewhere all alone? Oh, Sarah, I can't bear the pain. I want to die, too. I don't want to live in a world without her. Nobody will ever again love me the way she did."

"I love you. Charlotte loves you. Your future husband and children will love you. Edita had a wonderful life, better than most women. You know that! Think of the blessings. A good marriage, a loving family, plenty of money, beautiful clothes, jewels, a fine career. All her life she was proud and beautiful and respected, not frightened or repressed like my mother or crazy and cruel like Charlotte's. She was a proud, successful woman and a great model for all of us. You know that she wouldn't want you to fall apart."

Wendy began to weep again. "I want to fall apart. I want to be unconscious. I wish I was still a little girl. Our nurse Carmen would brush our hair for fifteen minutes at a time. I can still hear the swish-swish of that brushing, see the hummingbirds outside and smell the flowers. Every year Edita replaced the brushes in London because Carmen would wear them out. I miss having my hair brushed. I miss Carmen's scolding. I miss everyone so much. I never thought I'd end up with no family."

Sarah held her. "You have us. Our sorority. I know it's not the same. But we do love you."

Just then, Charlotte came in, magnificent in green-flowered chiffon, with large diamond studs in her ears, her red hair carefully cut and shaped to her face, trailing a cloud of Joy perfume and carrying a beautiful, woven picnic basket of chicken in aspic, raspberries, and a good bordeaux wine.

"I thought maybe you'd want to eat. I loved her too. Better than my own mother."

Sarah looked at Wendy. "When was the last time you ate?"

"I don't remember. But I can't."

None of them could. Death was in the room. They sat there holding hands, keeping watch while the sun set over the East River. And some time during the early evening, without making a sound, Edita passed away.

CHAPTER
Twenty-Seven

Wendy spent the month of July recuperating at Charlotte's house in East Hampton. "I miss Sarah," Charlotte said. "And I hate to think of the three of them going to that awful Coney Island every day by subway for their vacation. We have plenty of room. I'm going to invite them out for August."

When she asked Marshall, he was delighted. "Plenty of room for all," he said, "but I'd like to ask you to do a favor for me in return. Ask Arla Wine to lunch."

"Do I have to? I've tried to get friendly, but she can't even carry on a conversation."

"Then let her come over here and just be with you and Wendy. Make her feel welcome. I don't want to offend her husband."

Charlotte tried to phone her but her phone was out of order. "Would you like to walk over there with me, Wendy? It's so pleasant to walk on the beach."

"No," Wendy answered in the dispirited voice she'd used since Edita's death. "I'm tired and depressed and when I'm depressed, beaches only make me more depressed. I think about my sister."

"All right. I'd like to take a walk. I'll walk over there and invite her for tomorrow."

"And for the Labor Day dinner, too," Marshall called after her.

She walked along the beach trying to be her better self. Marshall asked so little of her that she shouldn't resent this request. And, after all, what was good for Marshall's business was good for her. But she had made friendly overtures the previous year, and Arla had shown quite clearly that she was not interested. When Teddy went to her house to play, she sent him right home, even though Charlotte had often given her boys lunch.

Three times her husband Lenny had come to their parties without her, and she'd failed to appear for two luncheons. In addition to that, the woman was dumb and sloppy and dirty looking. She looked like Appalachia, like po' white trash. She was an emaciated blonde, her hair was lank, greasy and dirty; her skin was mottled; and there were often ugly black and blue marks on her body. When Charlotte asked about them, Arla said weakly, in that dumb southern accent, "Ah jest bruise easy."

She was kind of weird. Even on the beach, she wore thick, pancake makeup. When Charlotte had said, "Everybody on the beach is brown except you," Arla had answered, "Ah jest sunburn easy."

She always carried with her a big shopping bag of movie magazines and paperback romances, and she had once told Charlotte, unapologetically, that they were the only things she ever read and that she had never thrown one away. She had thousands of them stacked up in her basement. Imagine saving such trash!

Anyone Charlotte had ever known, if they did read movie magazines and romances, would have been ashamed to admit it. But Arla obviously did not know any better. She frankly admitted that she had not even finished high school.

Money certainly wasn't her problem. They lived on lower Fifth Avenue in the city, and their beach cottage was even larger than Marshall's. And yet, she had no servants, and her house was badly furnished, dark, gloomy, and dirty.

If you could get past her idiosyncracies, she was really rather sweet. There was nothing malevolent about her, and it was evident that she admired Charlotte. But as far as

Charlotte was concerned, she was just kind of dumb and flaky, and they had absolutely nothing at all in common.

The boys were playing outside. Stewart was nine; Mark was seven; and Peter, five. They were as dirty and mangy as their mother. Stewart was really a menace, far worse than Teddy. He'd been hit by a car near Washington Square Park when he was six, and he'd been a little strange and sadistic ever since. Other children feared him, and he still couldn't read.

"Is your mother inside?" she called brightly. The boys ignored her.

She walked up the porch stairs, made her way through a maze of broken toys and bicycles on the porch, and rang the doorbell. She waited a few minutes, and then, when Arla didn't answer, she walked through the house to the kitchen, stepping right into a dish of chocolate pudding on the floor.

"Damn it," she swore. "My new sandals."

Arla was sitting at the kitchen table, her head buried in her arms. The phone was off the hook.

"Hello," Charlotte said softly. Arla lifted her head but kept it turned from Charlotte.

"I tried to call you to invite you to lunch, but your phone is off the hook."

"I know." Arla turned and looked at her. Charlotte stared back in shock. Both of Arla's eyes were black and blue and blood oozed from her cut lips. For a moment, Charlotte was back in her girlhood, looking into the terrible, battered face of her mother after shock treatment. "What happened to you?" Her voice was unsteady. She felt faint, nauseated, tainted by just being here.

"I fell down the stairs. Lost my balance."

"Shouldn't we call a doctor?"

"No. Please don't. I'll be all right. I thank you kindly for inviting me, but I can't come to lunch. I just have to wait to feel a speck better."

Charlotte stood there indecisively. "I'll call you when you feel better," she said. "We're having a big Labor Day party, and we'd like you to come."

"I'll have to ask Lenny. I'll let you know. Thanks for

coming over. It's right neighborly. Please don't worry. I'll be all right."

Charlotte shot out of the house and fled back to her own clean, beautiful one. She didn't know what was wrong with Arla. Perhaps she drank. But whatever it was, she wanted nothing to do with it. She wanted no reminders of the ugliness of her past.

CHAPTER
Twenty-Eight

Marshall sat beside Wendy on the long veranda of his house in East Hampton. Below them, Hal, Sarah, Jimmy, Charlotte, Kitty, and Teddy romped on the beach. "You've done nothing but sit around and drink for a month," he scolded gently. "Won't you come down for a swim? It will do you good."

"Not today. Perhaps tomorrow."

"Not perhaps! Definitely! You've had a month of grieving and that's all allowed. Tomorrow you will be baptized back into life in the waters of the Atlantic Ocean."

"I'll try, Marshall. I'll try. But I feel so empty, so tired. I have no energy. I couldn't even make a conversation with Robert the other day. I feel lost, in limbo. I don't know what to do with the rest of my life. The hotel has been sold and I have no family. What do you think? Any words of wisdom?"

"You can do anything you want to do. You're rich, beautiful, charming. You can marry, work for charity, travel, rent a house in the South of France, undergo psychoanalysis, learn to fly a plane, rent a villa at St. Moritz, make the cover of *Confidential*. The world lies open before you like a sea of dreams. Is there anything you really *want* to do?"

"I don't know. I'm confused. I do know that I don't want to go to Europe. Every place reminds me of Edita. I have this terrible knot of loneliness in my stomach all the time. That's why I've been drinking so much."

"I understand how you feel. After my wife died, I would sometimes stand alone in my study and howl with grief, like a wolf. Just howl and howl until my throat was sore. It's the worst feeling I've ever had."

That was why he'd married again so quickly, she thought.

"Have you been lonely since you got married?"

"Not for five minutes."

"That's what I should do. I need a solid, stable base. I need structure. Married people don't have to make decisions about what to do each day. Their lives provide the pattern. I'm tired of thinking. Too much freedom seems empty."

"Nevertheless, I would love to have your freedom," he said.

"Really? Why?"

"To become a pianist. Concertize. I played as a boy, and I've just begun to take lessons again. Of all the things I've done in my life, nothing equals the joy of music. But I never get enough time to practice."

"Charlotte always said that music was important to you, but I didn't realize that you wanted to *make* music. I just thought you liked to listen, go to concerts and the opera."

"It's far more to me than that. The most profound experiences of my life have been connected to music. Once, my wife and I were visiting Zion National Park in Utah, and just as we were leaving, after days of getting nothing but hillbilly music and pop, I turned on the radio and the glorious chorus of Beethoven's Ninth came streaming out. It was one of the great moments of my life. I pulled over to the side of the road, and we just sat there in the sunlight, holding hands in ecstasy." He sat there for a moment, traveling back in time.

"Better not discuss my interest in concertizing with Charlotte yet," he added. "She'd be terribly upset if she thought I wanted to retire to make music. She gets such a kick out of being a president's wife. Well, in any event, it's a long way off."

"I love music, too," she said. "But jazz more than classical. I used to love lots of things; theater, museums, funky little nightclubs, the Paris collections, but only music still gives me pleasure. I listen to Charlie Parker's 'After Midnight' over and over again. But everything seems hollow and pointless when all that's waiting for us at the end is death. I feel as if I'll never be happy again."

"Of course you will. After my wife died, my doctor said I was suffering from anhedonia."

"Anhedonia?"

"It means the inability to feel pleasure."

"Really! How interesting. I didn't know there was a word for that. But that's exactly what it is. No joy. And sometimes I have trouble breathing. It's like a fish's mouth opening and closing in desperate agony before it dies. Gasping for air."

"That will pass too. I promise you that." His kind brown eyes looked directly into hers, warming and protecting her.

"You're the first man in my life, Marshall, that I've ever been able to talk to like a girlfriend."

He laughed. "I take that as a compliment."

"What do you think about Dr. Kingman? It was you who recommended him."

"Why do you ask?"

"I think he's interested in me."

"I had a feeling. Are you interested in him?"

"I don't know how I feel. I admire his competence and his caring. Busy as he is, he was with me at the hospital every day. He's a good doctor, and he's strong and stable, and I think he'd make a good father. He's never been married and he's very rich, so I wouldn't have to worry about *my* money. That was something my mother was always worried about, right up until the end. She thought I was impractical. He is somewhat humorless but perhaps I could loosen him up."

"That's a singularly unromantic summation. Shouldn't you feel more excitement, more enthusiasm? Shouldn't you at least feel as if you're in love?"

"I'm too numb to feel anything much. My major goal now is simply to find safe harbor."

"Why not invite him back out for the Labor Day weekend? Spend a little time with him. See how he interacts with your friends."

They were interrupted by Charlotte's screams of "You

come back here," as Teddy streaked up onto the porch and cowered behind his father.

Charlotte, breathless, her eyes flashing fire, came running up behind him and tried to get at him. "Don't let her hit me, Daddy, don't let her hit me," Teddy screamed. "I didn't do anything. I didn't do anything."

"Of course she won't hit you," he said. "You know I don't believe in hitting children."

"I don't hit him," Charlotte protested.

"She hits me," Teddy shouted. "She's mean to me all the time when you're not home. You just don't know, Daddy."

Charlotte could have wept at the unfairness of things. "Why you lying little bastard. The problem with you is that you don't get hit enough."

"Calm yourself, my dear. Please don't speak to him that way. Let's try rationally to find out what the problem is. Exactly what happened?"

"He threw sand in Kitty's eyes. Deliberately! He's a menace! He tries to hurt her in any way he can because he's so consumed with jealousy."

"Liar, liar," Teddy shouted. "I love Kitty. I wouldn't hurt her. We were just playing around."

Terribly disturbed, Wendy watched the scene but refrained from interfering and complicating it further. It was all a vicious cycle. Teddy had never accepted Charlotte, and her anger about it constantly simmered below the surface so that when it erupted, normal spats turned into earthquakes. And Marshall never really dealt with it. He seemed to think that calm words would make conflict go away. How was it possible for someone who was so successful a businessman, who could so easily extricate Maurice from the clutches of the law, prove to be so ineffectual within his own family?

He was using reason now to put out the fire. "I'm certain, Charlotte, that you've misinterpreted his motivations. All boys are high-spirited. He's not a jealous child, so please don't put ideas into his head."

Charlotte stood there shaking with rage. "You always take his word against mine and make it impossible for me to discipline him. You're so besotted with your damned music that you can't even see how disturbed your precious son is. I've tried and tried but he'll never love me. It's so damned unfair. I just can't bear it."

She ran into the house weeping, and Marshall turned to Teddy. "Try to be nicer to Mommy," he said. "When I come out next Friday I'll bring you a new toy from F.A.O. Schwarz. Anything you like. What would you like?"

"I don't want a toy. I want my real mommy. And I want this one to die instead!"

Wendy put her arms around the boy. "That is not nice, Teddy. Charlotte loves you. We all love you. And you should love her."

"I love you, Aunt Wendy, but I hate her."

"You know you don't mean that," Marshall gently reprimanded him. "Now go back and play. I'll watch you from here."

"I do so mean it," Teddy shouted, running off. "I mean it, mean it, mean it."

"I'm sorry you have this conflict," she said as Teddy ran back to the water.

"It looks a lot worse than it is. It will press itself out. People say things in anger that they don't really mean. Their relationship gets better all the time. And now, if you'll excuse me, I'll go and comfort Charlotte. I wish you'd take a swim."

Later Wendy tried to discuss it with Sarah. If only Charlotte weren't so thin-skinned. It was true that Teddy wasn't easy, but after all, he was only a child. "I don't like to be critical," she said. "It seems so ungrateful. She saved my life by having me here, and she's a generous, loyal friend, but I keep thinking there must be another way of handling him."

"I feel the same way as you about criticizing," Sarah said. "She's saved our summer, too. It's so wonderful to see Hal and Jimmy playing on the sand. But I do think she could try harder. She forgets that he's a child and treats him like an adversary. I've spoken to her about it several times, and she really wants to do better. Each time she vows not to let him get to her, but he always does."

Wendy lay awake that night thinking about Marshall and

Teddy. What really went on in Marshall's head under the bland exterior? Didn't he see that Teddy was becoming more and more difficult and disturbed? What good were his money and success if he could not help his son? Did he ever let himself think, even for a moment, that he should have married a more mature woman, perhaps someone with a child of her own who would not have resented his child? Did he ever permit himself to think that he had made a mistake? It was impossible to tell. He still seemed to be deeply in love with Charlotte, but even if he were not, he would view it as a breach of good manners to permit anyone to know.

And what should she do about Dr. Kingman? She wasn't sure she wanted him. She wanted Maurice. She would always want Maurice. But she might never see him again.

Would she be making a terrible mistake if she married out of loneliness? But perhaps that was why most people married. Of course he wasn't the only man she could marry. She could return to the city at the end of the summer, get back into circulation, and try to find someone who excited her more. But the truth of the matter was that she was tired of that life, tired of being up late every night, sleeping until noon, and then spending the remainder of the day getting ready for the evening.

Her mind went back to the years of her childhood, those enchanted years in Eden. She saw them all going to chapel on Sunday—Francisco, so strong and straight and proud, his age betrayed only by his white pointed beard and a streak in his dark hair, and Edita, a vision of loveliness holding his arm. Edita had looked up at him with passionate love until the day he died. That's what I want, she told herself.

For the first time she thought of her mother, not as the beautiful secure woman she later became, but as the frightened girl who had the courage to look for the sun. She must have been lonely too, Wendy thought, and I never realized it before. How brave she was. She came to a strange land where she couldn't even speak the language, and she made a wonderful life. If she could do it, so can I. Just before she fell asleep she made up her mind to accept Robert

Kingman, and afterward she dreamed that Edita was glad she would no longer be alone.

CHAPTER
Twenty-Nine

On the last Thursday in August, Wendy and Sarah sat on the beach sunning and watching the children. Charlotte was in the house working on the preparations for the Labor Day weekend. She had scheduled only a small dinner party for Saturday night because the annual barbecue for all of Marshall's employees would be held on Sunday. On Tuesday everyone would return to the city, and only the servants would remain behind for a few days to close up the house until the following summer.

"I love it here," Sarah said. "I'll hate to leave. Sand, sky, sea. No money worries. The world becomes so simple. I'm very grateful to Charlotte. Even with servants, it's a lot of trouble and expense to have guests all summer long. I once read that a sign of love is willingness to share one's space. She's certainly shown that kind of love to us."

Charlotte had not permitted her to chip in for the food or even to pick up a check when they went out to lunch, a summer stock performance, or the movies. Hal had spent his two-week vacation here and had come out on weekends with Marshall. He looked healthy and sunburned and better than ever. Without her friend's generosity they would have spent the summer suffering through the city's baked concrete and rotten air.

"Are you pleased that Robert's coming out?"

"I suppose. This weekend's a test, although he doesn't know it. He really is so boring, Sarah. Lots of times I don't even know what to say to him. It's so hard to make conversation. Well, if we finally go to bed this weekend the problem will be solved."

"How will that solve the problem?"

"I've never found anybody really boring in bed."

"Do you love him?"

"I hope so. I want to get married."

"He's so different from us, Wendy. So social register. I hope he won't take you away from us."

"That could never happen. I could never marry anyone who'd force me to make that kind of choice. So don't worry."

She looked up and saw Teddy looking at them. When she smiled, he came closer. Then, without a word, he slowly sidled closer and closer until he was leaning against her. The poor kid. All of his body language said, "Love me. Love me please."

She put her arm around him. "Get a book, darling, and I'll read to you." He ran to get a book and then ran back, scrambled up on the foot of her chaise and stayed that way in rapt attention while she read.

* * *

"I want this Labor Day dinner to be perfect," Charlotte told her friends. An individual arrangement of yellow roses was placed at each setting, and the yellow tablecloth and napkins and black and gold Crown Derby china completed the color scheme of black and yellow. She painstakingly calligraphied each place card and matching menu, which listed lobster bisque, boeuf en croûte, spinach salad, fresh string beans, and coup marrons. Surveying the table she thought wryly, I get more sensual pleasure from the accomplishment of this perfection than from making love.

By eight o'clock, the children had been taken upstairs, the French windows were opened and a soft breeze gently blew across the dining room. The electric lights had been turned off, and all of the illumination was provided by candles in hurricane lamps.

After champagne and beluga caviar on the terrace, her guests entered the dining room to the elegant strains of baroque music. This was Marshall's surprise for them. Four musicians in velvet knickers and white wigs provided background music.

"I feel as if I'm in a royal court," Sarah said to Hal. She

looked at the table with admiration. This one dinner party cost more than she spent on food in a month. Maybe much more. How good it was of Charlotte to extend herself this way.

Looking chic and beautiful, Charlotte sat at one end of the table wearing a black strapless cotton gown and polished David Webb coral jewelry. Marshall, resplendent in his white dinner jacket, sat facing her. Sarah and Hal and Arla sat on one side and Wendy, Robert, and Lenny on the other.

Charlotte had explained to her friends that Lenny was a boor and a client and that Arla was pathetic. "She's a basket case. And Stewart! He set fire to a wounded gull the other day."

Robert Kingman, dressed in white flannels and a navy blazer, sat beside Wendy, looking in rapt adoration at her face. She had never looked more beautiful. Clouds of yellow chiffon billowed about her, and she wore Edita's magnificent emeralds.

She was pleased by his generosity. He had brought Charlotte wheels of brie and gourmandaise and a case of Mouton-Rothschild. Everything about him was correct: his speech, his movements, his carriage, his manners, his breeding. He was unfailingly pleasant and courteous. But he was difficult to converse with and hard to know.

Hal had tried to engage him in conversation and given up. "A dull fellow," he said to Sarah, "with nothing to say apart from the topic of medicine. He'll bore Wendy to death."

"Maybe not," Sarah answered. "She might just loosen him up."

"Do you really think so?"

"No," she laughed. "But if Wendy marries him, we're just going to have to learn to like him, reactionary though he is."

She looked with curiosity at Charlotte's neighbor, Arla, who looked just as Charlotte had described, with lank blonde hair, and frightened, watery blue eyes. Her lipstick had been applied unevenly and mascara was smeared around her eyes. She sat there hunched into herself, nibbling on her cuticles, a pitiful sight.

Lenny and Robert instantly and instinctively hated each

other. Lenny was a big man, over six feet tall and weighing two hundred pounds. His long hands dangled at his side like a gorilla's, and despite his expensive clothes he seemed low-class and coarse next to Robert. Caliban and Ariel, Sarah thought. There was an air of menace to him, a feeling of danger, the unmistakable warning that he was a man not to be crossed. He brought an aura of tension with him. Everyone in the room felt it.

He hated not only Robert. He hated and wanted Wendy. The naked lust with which he looked at her was almost palpable and coexistent with it was anger, a terrible anger, because despite his enormous wealth he could never own a woman like her. Then he looked across the table at Arla with such contempt that Sarah winced. Arla hunched further into her pathetically thin concave body.

Sarah did not see in Arla the mental illness that Charlotte suspected. If there was one thing she had learned from her parents it was how to recognize a bullied and defeated woman. That was what Arla was. Frightened, like Sarah's mother.

Lenny turned his gaze back to Wendy, undressing her with his eyes. Robert, too cool to show anger, especially to what he considered scum, protectively put his arm around her, and she leaned back into the shelter, wanting desperately to feel some kind of electricity from his touch, but glad of it anyway.

Lenny, angered at this show of possession, took an expensive cigar out of his pocket and lit up just as the lobster bisque was served. Charlotte looked at Marshall, but he would not reprimand a guest. However, Robert had no such compunction. "Kindly put that out," he ordered in his superior, prep-school voice. "It interferes with smell and taste."

"Listen, chum," Lenny blustered. "You've been looking for trouble the minute I walked in. I know your type. Let me tell you something. Nobody ever gave me nothing. I'm a self-made man."

"Well, obviously," came Robert's bored voice, "you did a very poor job."

Lenny drew back his enormous fist and clenched it. For a tense moment, no one spoke. Then Charlotte in a voice like steel took over. The hell with whether he was a client or not. This was her party. "Please put out the cigar, Lenny. If my cook smells it, she'll go on strike, and you won't get the rest of this marvelous dinner."

"Ah, the hell with it," he said, furiously grinding the cigar into his plate. "You're all against me. I can tell when I've lost."

"Nobody's against you," Marshall said warmly. "We're all friends here. Now, let's drink and eat and have a wonderful time."

Sarah looked at him in puzzlement. No balls! He should have told the man off before Charlotte did. It was exactly the same kind of weak behavior he manifested in regard to Teddy, and she despised it. Damn it, she thought, I'm a fighter. And right now I feel like kicking that Lenny in the balls and helping Arla.

"Where do you come from, Arla?" she asked. "I love your southern accent."

"Jackson," she whispered. "Do you really? Lenny doesn't like it."

"Nobody likes it, mush-mouth," Lenny said. "Southern accents sound dumb. Did you ever hear a big movie star with a southern accent?"

"It didn't hurt Faulkner," Sarah said tartly. "He just won the Nobel Prize with *his* southern accent."

"Faulkner?" Arla echoed.

"He writes about the South," Sarah explained. "You might like his work."

"A Nobel Prize writer!" Lenny hooted. "You've got to be kidding. All she reads are romances and movie magazines."

"Then maybe it's time for a change. I have a collection of his short stories in my room. If you come with me after dinner, Arla, I'll lend it to you."

After dinner, when the group adjourned to the terrace for espresso and cognac, Sarah took Arla's hand. "Let's go for the book," she said. Once inside her room, she locked the door and motioned Arla to sit on a chair.

"I don't really have the book," she said.

"You don't? Then why did you bring me here? What will I tell Lenny?"

"Oh, who cares. Just tell him I couldn't find it. I brought you here because I wanted to talk to you alone."

"Alone? Why? Did I do something awful tonight?"

"Of course not. I wanted to talk to you because you seem so frightened. I don't like to see anyone bullied. You remind me of my mother, and she's been terrified of my father for forty years. I've been looking at you all evening, trying to figure out why you wear such thick makeup. It's to cover bruises, isn't it?"

Shamefaced, Arla looked at the floor and nodded.

"I thought so. Why do you stand for it?"

"Girls like you just can't understand. I saw the way your husband looks at you. Like something sacred. Robert looks at Wendy that way, too, and Marshall's just the sweetest thing. But you see, my folks were poor as dirt, and I didn't even go to high school. Lenny's ashamed of me. That's why he gets mean."

"That's the most ridiculous thing I've ever heard. Do you think every woman who didn't go to high school gets beaten? And Lenny doesn't strike me as the world's greatest intellectual. I'm sure nobody forced him to marry you. He strikes me as a man who does exactly what he wants to do. And nobody forces you to stay with him."

"My kids do. I couldn't take care of them—no money, no job, no education, and no place to take them. So that's the way it is. But I thank you kindly for your concern."

"That's not the way it has to be. You can fight back. You have nothing to lose but your chains. I'll call you in the city. I live in Knickerbocker Village, so you're only about fifteen minutes away."

"I don't know. He doesn't like me to have girl friends..." Arla looked so miserable that Sarah wanted to shake her.

"I'll call you after he leaves for work. I'm not going to give up this easily."

"It's a long time," Arla said, "since anyone's been so nice to me."

"All three of us are going to be nice to you. Wendy, Charlotte, and I. You need us and we're going to help you.

We've always helped each other get through everything. You'll see. Tell me about you. How long have you been married?"

"Ten years. I came to New York to get modeling work, but there was lots of girls prettier than me. So I started to waitress, and that's how I met Lenny. I was seventeen. He'd been married three other times. It was all right at the beginning. He bought me clothes and introduced me to some of his friends. But after Stewart's accident he changed. He said it was because I wasn't watching careful enough."

Stewart had darted out into traffic to get his ball and been hit by a car. "I wanted to die right then and there, Sarah. The sight of that poor helpless child suffering so bad, screaming, 'I hurt, Mommy. I hurt, Mommy. Make it stop hurting.' I get sick every time I think about it.

"After he got home from the hospital he was a different boy. He forgot how to read and write, and he started to wet the bed, and Lenny started to hit him, and the more he hit him, the meaner Stewart got. I wasn't strong enough to make Lenny stop.

"He said Stewart wasn't dumb because of the accident, that it was all my fault because I was an ignorant hillbilly with inferior genes."

Sarah laughed and Arla looked at her with a hurt expression. "I'm not laughing at you. I'm laughing at him. There's no such thing as inferior genes. That's exactly the kind of thing people in power always tell those they repress in order to justify the repression. It makes them feel easier about the awful things they do."

"I don't know much about politics."

"It's not politics. It's common sense."

"Well, anyway, we'd better get back," she said nervously. "I don't want to make him angry."

"Someday," Sarah said, "you won't be afraid. I promise you that."

Hand in hand the two women walked back to the others.

* * *

Lenny controlled his pent up anger until they were walking back along the beach to their house. Then, still smarting from Robert's rebuffs, he began to work himself up. "I should never take you anywhere," he stormed. "You didn't say one intelligent thing all evening. I was ashamed of you."

She began to tremble. "I'm sorry, Lenny. I really tried my best. I didn't want you to be ashamed of me."

"Did you hear the way that son-of-a-bitch Kingman spoke to me? Supercilious son of a bitch. I think I'll have him roughed up."

"You can't do that. Please don't do it, Lenny. Wendy said she was going to invite us to the wedding."

"Listen, you cunt. I'll do whatever I want. Nobody's going to make a fool of me. I'll get that bastard."

"He doesn't mean anything to you, Lenny. Forget what he said. And please don't hurt him." She was trembling so hard that she could hardly speak. "If anything happens to him I'll tell. I'll go to the police. I will. I will."

"You bitch." He turned and smashed her so hard across the face that she fell to the sand and lay there for a few seconds trying to get her breath. Before she could rise he had pinned her to the ground on her stomach with his knee in the small of her back, ripped off her panties with one hand and spread her buttocks with the other.

She began to cry and beg. "No, Lenny. Please, no. The doctor said you shouldn't. It hurts me too much, and we don't even have vaseline here."

"Shut up." He opened his fly and jabbed his engorged penis into her so hard that she could hear her body ripping. She let out a scream of pain, and he pushed her face down into the sand to stifle the sound. *I can't breathe*, she thought as the sand filled her mouth and nostrils. *I can't breathe. I'm dying.*

The horror of being unable to breathe became so overwhelming that it transcended the ripping pain. And then finally, with a mighty thrust that almost rent her in two, he came and collapsed on her body, and with some atavistic instinct for survival she found the energy to turn her face to the side to breathe, gasping for air just before she blacked out.

All the next day, she struggled not to kill herself. She

couldn't bear to leave the boys alone with him. He'd destroy the younger two as surely as he'd destroyed her and Stewart.

CHAPTER Thirty

Robert and Wendy sat on the terrace talking, long after everyone else had gone to bed. "This summer has been good for you," he said in a professional tone. "I was somewhat concerned about you after your mother died."

"I guess everyone was. I really loved my mother."

"That was evident. Everyone at the hospital admired your devotion." And then, without further preliminaries, he asked, "Would you consider marrying me?"

"I don't know, Robert. Why do you want to marry me?"

"I love beauty. The quest for the ideal. I was interested in you from the first moment we met. Didn't you feel it?"

"I suppose I did." She thought sadly for a moment about the instant chemistry with Maurice, then forced it from her mind. "We don't know each other very well."

"In my case, there's not much to know. I've led an ordinary kind of life. St. Paul's, Harvard, Harvard Med School. I'm thirty-five years old, belong to Piping Rock, the New York Athletic Club, and the Knickerbocker. I love sports, travel, my work. I have no bad habits. I have a very large family that I'll inflict on you little by little. Well what do you think?"

"But what about love? Do you love me?"

"That goes without saying. I fell in love watching you with your mother. Even at your most distraught, you were beautiful. A Goya! The other night, thinking about you, a line from Walt Whitman suddenly popped into my head. Imagine that! I haven't read Whitman since college."

"What was the line?"

"'I am he that aches with love.' That describes the way I feel. I ache with love for you. It's the first time in my life. It's what I've been looking for."

His words made her breath quicken. "It's hard to resist a man who quotes Whitman, but you don't really know me either."

"Of course I do. I saw you day after day after day. Grace under pressure."

"But I have many faults."

"Really? Such as?"

"I'm accustomed to having my own way. I like to smoke and drink and screw around. I'm a rotten student and I'm not great at sports, although back home I learned to ride on little Arabian ponies, and I can play a fair game of tennis. I'm lazy and like to sleep late in the morning. I'm very, very extravagant and have an absolute passion for jazz. I listen to it day and night. I have absolutely no career desires."

"None of those things sound very bad to me, although I would expect you to be faithful. Would you be?"

"Yes. I want stability. I want children. That's what I want most of all. Lots of children."

He took her hand in his. "I do too. So why don't you say yes?"

"I'm not sure I love you. I'm still numb. I don't know how I feel about anything."

"Let me make the decision. Say yes! Risk it! I'm willing to take a chance on your loving me."

He stood up, pulled her to him and kissed her. She kissed him back, and she could feel the kisses getting increasingly passionate, but it was as if they were happening to someone else. This entire thing was happening to someone else. She was in a dream, and the only strong emotion she felt was one of fatigue, of a need to rest, of a desire to get this over and settled once and for all and be done with it.

"All right," she said. "I accept. I'll be happy to marry you."

"I knew that sooner or later you'd see it my way," he said.

They told the others at breakfast. Sarah exulted, throwing her arms around her. "I'm so glad you won't be alone any longer."

"Me, too." Wendy whispered back.

"That's wonderful," Charlotte said. "Let's have champagne to celebrate."

The maid brought the champagne and everyone toasted the engaged couple, then poured the rest of the champagne into a pitcher of orange juice. "You're all getting like me," Wendy laughed. It felt very good to be engaged at last.

They laughed and talked and planned, and the air was filled with electric excitement. Nobody could have known how depressed Charlotte felt. Robert was a much better catch than Marshall. He came from a prominent social-register family and did not bring with him the baggage of a crazy child or the memories of a beloved wife. Life was so unfair! No matter what she achieved she could never catch up to Wendy. The race had been skewed from the start.

She felt, at that moment, just as unhappy and deprived as before her marriage. She and Marshall had a lousy sex life, and he was boring. And now he was obsessed with music. But that always was the way things turned out for her. Once she got the things she had longed for so desperately, they turned out not to be the things she had wanted at all.

Ashamed of her thoughts, she quickly asked, "Would you like to be married at our apartment, Robert? Sarah was married there."

"Thank you, no. We will be married at St. Bart's, and the reception will be at the Knickerbocker or the Carlyle, depending on availability. That's the way we do things in my family."

"May I know the date?" Wendy teased him.

"I'll check and let you know."

Sarah's eyes met Hal's. No sense of humor! He's not right for her, she thought. She's dated many pompous bores like this one, and none of them ever got to first base because she always said they were no fun. But she's tired and lonely and vulnerable. She'll probably be bored to death in six months, and then what?

"I had better warn you," Marshall told Robert, "that you're not marrying one girl. These three come in a package."

"Really?" Robert casually dismissed his remark, and Sarah

looked at him in dismay, hoping he wouldn't alienate Wendy from them. It would be a struggle if he tried, but it was evident to her that in common with Wendy, Robert had long been accustomed to having his own way.

CHAPTER
Thirty-One

Somehow, when the phone rang, by some strange intuition, Wendy knew who it would be. She started to tremble as soon as she heard his voice. He didn't even bother identifying himself. All he said was, "So you're getting married."

"Maurice? Maurice. I can't believe it's really you. Where have you been all this time, and how do you know I'm getting married?"

"Just by accident. Someone left the wedding announcements section of the *New York Times* on a subway seat."

"The *New York Times*? Do you mean to say that you're here, in New York?" Then without waiting for him to answer, she rushed on, "How long have you been here?"

"I just got out of jail. I need help, Wendy."

"Jail! How awful! You know I'll help you. Where are you?"

"In your lobby."

"Come right up." She began to tremble. Six years. Six years since he'd left her that way, and never a word. All these years he hadn't given a damn about how she felt, and here he was turning up this way. The least she could do was to listen to his story. Then she'd give him a good kick.

But despite her anger a bolt of joy shot through her. That was the way it was. Some people stuck to you, got under your skin, and others didn't. She had promised Robert that she wouldn't screw around and she wouldn't. All she wanted to do was see him, talk to him, tell him that no one had ever meant as much to her as he had, tell him that she had gone back to hunt for him to no avail, tell him he made her think of home, tell him she had never stopped feeling responsible, had never stopped loving him. Her hands shook with fever and her knees turned to jelly at the memory of his magic. Everything came flooding back. The memory of his dark skin, of his magnificent strength, of the beads of sweat on his smooth brow, of the way he would croon to her when they made love. The idea of him swept her back to Carmen, her childhood, the comfort of the islands. When the bell rang, hardly able to breathe, she pulled open the door, then stood there in shock.

Maurice? This couldn't be Maurice. The man who stood before her was ragged, humble, shambling, bent over, defeated. His baggy old chinos had holes at the knees, and the leather was rubbed off his shoes showing sad patches of white. His cheeks were hollow, and he could not have weighed more than a hundred and twenty-five pounds. He had shrunken, withered, diminished, just as her mother had done.

"Maurice?" She tried to hide her shock and disbelief.

"No one else." An ironic smile crossed his face, and he held out his hands. palms upward, in a gesture that was simultaneously sheepish and despairing. She tied the belt of her robe into a double knot as the involuntary tears that were always so close to the surface since Edita's death began to slide down her face. He reached out and gently touched her cheek. "Why are you crying?"

She would not play games. "You've changed so much."

He shrugged. "Well, that's the way it is." He looked around the apartment with appreciation. "Hard to believe I once lived here."

"Would you like some breakfast?"

"I'd like to take a shower first if that's OK with you. I'm not all that hungry."

He was in the shower for a long time, and when he finally emerged, wearing Robert's terry-cloth robe from the Paris Ritz, he looked a little better—not the man she had known, but the grin was the same. "You and that cigarette holder. That was my first sight of you. The most beautiful girl I'd ever seen up close. Still the most beautiful."

Tears started to flow again. "As if that matters." She shook her head sadly. "What would you like to eat?"

"Coffee. With a slug of your wonderful brandy."

"I don't have any. I'm on the wagon. I started to drink too much while my mother was dying." She poured some coffee for him and passed him the bowl of fresh fruit and a plate of assorted cheeses, but he ignored the food and lit a cigarette.

"So your mama died! I'm sorry. I know how much you loved her. Mine died too! While I was in jail." Could that account for his present condition? She doubted it. He hadn't been very fond of his mother.

"What's wrong with you, Maurice? Why aren't you eating? You used to love to eat. And you're so thin. Are you sick?"

Again that heartbreaking ironic smile crossed his face. "I'm not healthy. That's for sure."

"How did you get into this condition? Why did you leave me that way? Where did you go?"

He'd gone home to Philadelphia where he'd proceeded to have blackouts from the beating at the Copa. "Add that one to the Georgia beating," he grinned bleakly, "and it was just one too many beatings for even this hard nigger skull to absorb."

She winced but let him continue uninterrupted. She hadn't found him in Mexico because he hadn't gone back to school. His vision had become impaired, and he began to suffer from maddening headaches. Besides, he couldn't seem to concentrate. So he'd become unemployable. No VA pension, no medical coverage, no social security, nothing.

"It's so hard for a black man to get a toehold on the ladder," he said bitterly, "that it's real easy to slip off and fall back to the bottom. And once you do, it's almost impossible to get back up again. You know, I saw that *Death of a Salesman* once, and I didn't give a damn. That sniveling idiot held a job most of his life, and he had a wife and kids and a house and a car. That's being rich to most black folks. So he was unemployed after sixty. Big deal! He was so dumb and so incompetent that if he'd been black, he never would have had a job in the first place. Most black people go straight from grade school to unemployment for the rest of their lives.

"Yep. That Willy Loman sure was stupid. But I'm pretty stupid, too. One day I found a wallet in the street. Practically new. Cartier. Beautiful leather. No cash, but credit cards. I was so broke that I got stupid. I tried to use the cards. They looked up my army record and gave me the maximum. Four years."

"Why didn't you call me, Maurice? Maybe I could have helped. Maybe Marshall could have."

"I don't know." The gap seemed to widen.

"Broke my mother's heart that I didn't make something of myself," he added.

Then she told him about what had happened on the day he disappeared. "Thrown out of school because of me? I'm sorry."

"The worst of it was that you weren't here to comfort me. If only you'd called me. Everything might have been different."

"I had to go. I was tired of being your toy. But while I was in jail I read about you from time to time in Earl Wilson, and once I saw your picture in *Look* and cut it out and hung it above my bed."

Her lovely violet eyes filled with tears, and she reached out and took his hand. "I could have helped you financially. You know that. I'll help you now. I'll send you a check every week. And I'll pay for you to get the best medical care available. I'm certain it's not too late to restore your health."

"Your future husband going to treat me?"

She flushed. "He's not that kind of doctor and he doesn't know about you. But after you're restored to health I'll help you to get a job."

He looked at her with a cynical grin. "What kind of job would you get me? Head of a hospital? President of an advertising agency? College teacher? The only job I could get is pushing a rack in the garment district. There's nothing for me here. I just want some money to go back to Mexico."

"I can't believe it's that bleak."

"You don't want to believe that. It makes you uncomfortable. But be honest, Wendy. You always used to be. If you were to refer me to your fancy friends, what jobs would they offer me? When was the last time you saw a black man who wasn't in a menial position? I'm not sure I would even have made it as a dentist. How would I have ever put together the money for equipment?

"Here, I want to show you a book. One of the guys in jail gave it to me before I left."

She turned the book over in her hands: *Invisible Man* by Ralph Ellison. "Let me read you something," he said. Then in a ghostly reminder of the rich, vibrant voice with which he'd recited poetry to her so many years ago, he began to read the prologue. "I am an invisible man. No, I am not a spook like those who haunted Edgar Allan Poe; nor am I one of your Hollywood-movie ectoplasms. I am a man of substance, of flesh and bone, fiber and liquids — and I might even be said to possess a mind. I am invisible, understand, simply because people refuse to see me...."

She listened and cried.

He put the book down suddenly and gripped the sides of his head in pain.

"You must see a doctor," she pleaded. "Please don't leave New York. I don't want to just give you money and never see you again. Let me try to help you. I'll speak to Robert and get you admitted to the best hospital. He's a wonderful doctor and he has all kinds of connections."

"You'd tell him about us?"

"Of course not. He wouldn't understand. I'll just tell him you're somebody from home. And after you're feeling better, I'll help you get a job. I promise you. But you must help me to help you. Will you do that?"

He was too exhausted to argue. "I can't talk. Would it be all right if I took a nap before I go? But I wouldn't want him to walk in and find me."

"Yes. It's all right. I'm not supposed to see him until tonight." She reached for her purse and took out her Vuitton wallet. "All I have is a hundred dollars. You go to sleep, and I'll slip out to the bank and get some more. When I get back, I'll call Robert. He gets to his office at ten. Go to sleep now. I'll be back in fifteen minutes." She handed him the money.

He took it and put it on his pile of clothes. Then they

walked into the bedroom together. "No one would ever believe that a bum like me once lived here with you. I always loved this apartment. The first nice place I ever lived in. Will you and your husband live here after you're married?"

"No. I'm giving it up. We've bought a town house on Seventy-first Street just off Fifth. But I'll still have my own phone listing under Wendy Kingman. So you won't have any trouble finding me."

"I'll always have trouble finding you. Even when I held you in my arms, I had trouble finding you. You were always a dream."

His voice faded out as he sank down, burrowed into her cream-colored satin sheets, and was instantly asleep. She lit a cigarette and sat there looking at him for a few minutes. Whatever passion she had felt for him in the past was not here now. Her heart burned with pain, with sorrow, with sympathy, with a tragic heartbreaking sense of something of rare value that had been lost.

Well, she couldn't do anything about the past, but she could help his future. She quickly threw on some clothes and hurried to the bank. Then she hurried home again, opened the door, and tiptoed into the bedroom. It was empty. Damn it! He'd done the same thing again. Just popped off without a word. She could hardly contain her anger.

On the breakfast table he'd left a note. "I have to do things my own way. For what it's worth I love you. Guess I always will. Half of me hopes your marriage will be lousy, but the other, better, half of me says that you deserve the best. So all the best to you, beautiful Wendy. Thanks for the money."

Open, beside the note, was *The Invisible Man*. He'd underlined some words. "O well they picked poor Robin clean, O well they picked poor Robin clean. Well they tied poor Robin to a stump. Lawd, they picked all the feathers round from Robin's rump. Well they picked poor Robin clean."

And farther down he'd marked one more line. "Please hope him to death, and keep him running."

She couldn't bear to think about it, so she closed the book and put it away.

She tried to call Sarah and Charlotte, but neither one of them was home. When she realized that she couldn't phone Robert and have him understand, she felt even more depressed. She put on Billie Holiday's record "God Bless the Child," remembered how she and Maurice had listened to it. She sat on her terrace, looking out at Sheep Meadow, thinking about the unfairness of life.

Robert had spent his entire life insulated in a cocoon of wealth and family and privilege. He was at the top and Maurice was at the bottom. His fate had been determined from the moment he was born, as surely as Maurice's. And he took it for granted. Everyone he knew or treated was rich and successful, and the poor and downtrodden simply did not matter in his scheme of things.

Maurice had once told her that being born black was a political statement. She now saw that it was also a political statement to be born Robert Kingman III, and that in order to get married she would have to overlook the fact that she did not especially like or admire the political statement he represented.

She would never have the wonderful solidarity in her marriage that Sarah found with Hal. Political activism would not dominate her marriage. Materialism would.

Needing music, she put on Mildred Bailey singing, "Old Rocking Chair's Got Me," phoned the liquor store, and asked for some brandy to be sent up.

CHAPTER
Thirty-Two

When Robert arrived to pick her up for the evening, she was naked under a revealing, black-lace peignoir. She reached up and kissed him passionately. "Let's go to bed," she said.

"Have you been drinking?"

"I sure have. All day!"

His gray eyes narrowed. "You promised me to stop," he said sternly. "Why did you break your promise?"

"I was sad, lonely, blue. I thought about my family, all the people I used to love who are gone."

"It's foolish to be morbid, Wendy. Everybody dies."

"Let's go to bed."

"Certainly not. There's not enough time. I had a very hard day, I rushed home to shower and dress, and you know how I hate to be late. You should be dressed. Please get dressed."

"Don't you love me?"

"Of course I love you. But there are priorities. My parents are anxious to meet you, and it will take us well over an hour to get out there, and more if there's traffic."

"If you love me, why don't you want to make love to me?" She got into bed and pulled the covers over her head.

"Please don't be childish, Wendy. I'm dying to make love to you. If you get up and dress I'll stay with you tonight."

"Who could resist such a passionate declaration," she said, beginning to dress.

She dressed in a Balenciaga with no back, covered herself with diamonds, and was ready in fifteen minutes.

"You'll have to change. You look like a hooker in that dress."

"Oh, for heaven's sake. What would you like me to wear?"

"Wear that yellow dress you wore at Charlotte's dinner. It makes you look like an expensive buttercup."

He helped her on with her chinchilla stole, then looked at the two of them in the hall mirror. "Perfect," he said. "We make a handsome couple."

She tried to talk to him in the car, but he would not discuss anything significant in front of his chauffeur. "Ask him to put on a jazz station," she said.

Robert ignored her and settled back to listen to chamber music on WQXR. So she sulked all the way to Locust Valley. That does it, she told herself. I'm ending the engagement.

But she felt better as soon as they reached Robert's parents' home. It was large, charming, magnificent: a Tara in

Nassau County. And she instantly loved Robert's mother, Margaret, who threw her arms around her and, with tears in her eyes, said, "You cannot imagine how happy this makes us. He's been married to his work. I was afraid he'd remain a bachelor."

Robert's father, the retired doctor, was drunk. "My God, you're a beauty," he said, plunking a wet kiss on her cheek.

"I also have a beautiful mind," she joked.

"Who cares about that?" Like father, like son, she thought wryly.

The only other guests that night were Margaret's two sisters and their husbands. After dinner, the women withdrew to Margaret's suite to plan the wedding. Robert had secured the church for June 15. They were so enthusiastic, so kind to her, that as their planning progressed the idea of breaking the engagement receded to the back of her mind. The wheels were in motion and there was no way she could stop them.

They had already planned a shower for her at the Colony Club, an engagement party at the Knickerbocker, and arranged to give her one aunt's villa in Cap d'Antibes for the honeymoon. And, to Wendy's delight, one of the aunts had been a guest at her hotel and remembered her mother and father very well.

"I never had a daughter," Margaret said. "Thank you for letting me fuss over you."

Wendy's eyes filled with tears. "Go right ahead and fuss," she said. "You cannot imagine how much I miss my mother."

"I know. Robert told us all about it."

Both she and Robert were more mellow on the way back to the city. "My family adored you," he said. "I was proud of you."

"I loved them too."

When they reached her apartment, he dismissed the chauffeur and came upstairs with her. "Now," he said, "I believe we have some unfinished business."

"Unstarted business," she said, dropping her clothes on the floor. He turned off the lights, carefully placed one sock in each shoe, emptied his pants pockets, hung his pants carefully to retain the crease, neatly placed the contents of his pockets, his watch, and tie on the dresser, and finally folded his underwear and slipped into bed beside her.

"You're lucky I haven't fallen asleep yet," she said with barely controlled annoyance.

"It is rather late."

"Oh, Robert. Don't be such a stick."

She reached for him and they made love. He did everything just right. Five minutes of foreplay, five minutes of fucking, and five minutes of cooling down with his arms around her.

Feeling depressed and unsatisfied, she bent to take his penis in her mouth. The second time would be better. But he gently disengaged her.

"I really don't like to unless we've both taken showers immediately before. Besides, my dear, I really must go to sleep. I have an early squash game. That was really wonderful. I love you."

After he had fallen asleep, she lay beside him worrying. Sex was never really great with him but tonight had been the worst. Well, maybe he'd improve with time. You couldn't expect every sexual encounter to be marvelous. He was competent and had a marvelous body, and she liked having his body there beside her in bed. She hated to sleep alone.

It was foolish to base a relationship on sex, wasn't it? She and Maurice had made celestial music, but she couldn't have married him. It was time to stop acting like an immature butterfly. She had to center her life. Sarah and Charlotte were increasingly busy with their own families and concerns, and fond as she was of Arla, the girl still had a long way to go. Every time they met for lunch she trembled with fear that Lenny would find out. She had begun to read voraciously, but she still was not smart.

The die was cast. She would marry the most eligible bachelor in New York, become part of his family and his circle, have a dozen children, and do her best to live happily ever after. And she loved his mother. That was very important to her.

Their June wedding was the social event of the season. Old sorority girls from Adams, reading about it in the society columns, noting that nobody seemed to care about that old episode at the Copa, and needing funds to expand, commented with regret, "We should never have let that one get away."

CHAPTER
Thirty-Three

One school day in May 1954, Sarah was unexpectedly summoned by messenger to the principal's office. She panicked. Something was wrong. It must be Hal! Hal or Jimmy! Something terrible had happened to them. She ran down the hall struggling to control her incipient hysteria.

But it was Wendy on the phone. "Get up to Charlotte's right away. Teddy's out on a ledge, threatening to jump. Take a cab and I'll reimburse you."

Thank God! *Her* little family was all right. Then immediately she was ashamed of her relief.

"I have to leave right now," she told her principal. "Emergency."

His face turned red with rage. "You can't do that. It's not fair to ask someone to cover your class at the last minute this way. You'll have to wait until dismissal."

"Sorry." She grabbed her jacket and began to run, unable to take a cab or bus because she had exactly five cents in her purse. She ran and ran, across Fiftieth Street to Park and then up to Sixty-ninth. Even before she reached the street, she heard the shouts, the sirens, the tumult.

Firemen stood poised below with outstretched air bags, and an excited, sensation-hungry, open-mouthed crowd filled the street, impeding progress, ignoring futile attempts of several policemen to keep people moving. "Ghouls," she snapped at the crowd, forcing her way through.

She looked up in horror at the sight of the skinny child plastered against the building.

She shouted, "I'm the boy's aunt." She broke through the police cordon, dashed into the elevator, then into the apartment where Charlotte sat weeping on the sofa under her magnificent, life-size portrait that Marshall had recently commissioned. Wendy sat beside her holding her hand, and Marshall stood at the window pleading with Teddy. Sarah ran to the window and stood beside him. "What happened?" she asked.

"I have no idea. I was in my study when I heard him and Charlotte yelling at each other. Then he went out there."

"The child's crazy," Charlotte sobbed. "He's only doing this to upset me. Now maybe everyone will begin to understand what I go through."

Without thinking, Sarah quickly took off her shoes. Her feet were almost as small as Teddy's. She stepped out onto the ledge and gingerly began to inch toward him while holding on to the window frame with one hand. When she'd moved to the limits of her reach she called, "Teddy," struggling to keep her voice calm and reassuring. "It's me, Aunt Sarah. I want to talk to you. Please listen. Do you hear me? You don't have to say anything yet. Just nod if you're listening."

He didn't answer, and a jagged knife of fear shot through her. She had always felt guilty about not doing more for him, especially since she was a teacher who really cared about kids. "Teddy," she begged, "please say something or nod to me. I'm scared to death out here. But I don't want to go back inside and leave you here alone. Are you scared too?" Suddenly she realized how foolhardy she'd been. Her first duty was to Hal and Jimmy, not to Teddy. But she'd moved instinctively and here she was.

Sick to her stomach, covered in perspiration, forcing herself to remain calm, she waited for a response. Then, finally, the child nodded. It was almost imperceptible, but it was a nod. They were communicating. What should she say next?

Then, dimly, she heard shouts floating up from the street far below. She listened for a moment, afraid to look down. What were they saying? They seemed to be warning her about something. She tried to listen before speaking again to him. It might be important. Suddenly, horror-struck, she made out the word. It was the same word, over and over again. "Jump," they were calling. "Come on, jump." She shuddered with anger, and the anger increased her strength.

"Teddy," she called, "just nod up and down if I say the right thing and shake your head if it's wrong. But do it very gently so we don't fall. Do you understand?" He nodded. Thank God he was at least that rational.

She felt a sudden rush of nausea go through her. "Teddy, dear, I know that you came out here because you were upset. Is that right?" He nodded.

"If you help me to figure out why you're upset I promise that I'll help you to fix it. Whatever it is, I can help you. You know that I'm a teacher and I help children every day. Do you understand that?" Again he nodded.

He clung there shivering, and she continued to speak calmly and rationally, forcing herself not to look down. "Now turn your body slowly, so you can see me and we can talk. Very, very slowly. Tell me why you're so upset, Teddy."

He shifted his body so abruptly that her heart plummeted. The slightest gesture could send him over. Now she could see the poor, woebegone, tear-streaked face, and such sadness swept through her that it took all of her strength not to weep.

Then he finally spoke. "She hates me. And I hate her. She's sending me away to school, and she said I could never come home again because I cut off all of Kitty's hair. Never! Not even at vacations! But it wasn't my fault. Kitty asked me to do it."

"I'm sure she didn't mean it. Most people say things they don't mean when they get angry. I do! And I bet you do too! Don't worry about Kitty's hair. It will grow back. She'll be fine, and boarding school can be a lot of fun. Lots of new friends."

"Suppose I hate it there? What if there are vampires? Suppose demons suck my blood and pick my bones?"

"Listen to me, Teddy. I guarantee you no demons. And if you don't like it, you can come home. You can call your father collect any time you like, and he'll come and get you right away. And if he's not home, you can call Wendy or me, and I promise that we'll come. I promise you, and I never break a promise."

"Maybe she wouldn't let you. She controls the world. And maybe it's too far away. At the end of the world where the north wind blows. It's where the ice queen lives."

"No, it isn't. It's in Connecticut. You know that's only an hour and a half away. It's very close. Closer than East Hampton. Please believe me. I'll come and get you whenever you like. And you can come and stay with us whenever you like and play with Jimmy. He's your friend. You know that! He loves you. I love you."

Still Teddy hung there. "Please come in," she begged. "We all love you. We don't want you to get hurt."

Marshall, taut with tension, stood at the window shaking, afraid to say anything that might interfere with the delicate connection Sarah was trying to weave.

"Look Teddy. I'm holding on to the window frame with one hand and reaching out the other to you. I want you to move slowly along the ledge until you're touching my fingers."

"I'm too scared to move."

It was time for firmness. In her best teacher voice she said, "You got out there, so you can get back in. Come on, Teddy. It's time to move. I'm waiting. Don't look down. Move toward me. Come on. You can do it." With agonizing slowness he began to inch toward her. She held her breath, then exhaled it in a gasp when they finally touched.

"Oh, it feels good to touch you," she said. "Now I'm going to open my hand, and I want you to move a little closer and put your wrist in it." As soon as she felt the boy's wrist, she closed her hand tightly around it. "I've got you, darling. Now we're going in together. Just move slowly. I won't let you fall."

In a few moments, she was inside the window, and Marshall stepped forward and lifted the boy down into his arms. "Teddy, Teddy." his voice broke. "Thank God you're safe. Don't you ever do anything like that again. You really frightened me. Oh, Teddy, don't you know how much I love you?"

They stood that way together for a few moments, weeping and trembling. Far below, the crowd cheered, and some of the people in the room applauded.

Sarah's knees were shaking with tremors of after-shock, and Wendy raced to her with a snifter of brandy as she sank down onto the sofa unable to control the sudden shudders that were now racking her body. Wendy hugged her and proudly patted her back. "Tiny but tough. You were marvelous. I could never have done that in a million years."

Oh, Sarah darling, she thought, you've saved somebody. If only I could have done as much with Paula! I never would have thought of going out onto the ledge. I never would have thought of going out onto the ledge to save Teddy.

Charlotte looked at Teddy in Marshall's arms and fled to her bathroom where she vomited over and over again in nervous foreboding. Everybody would blame her for this: Marshall, the servants, their friends. Suppose it made the newspapers. After all of her careful building, everything was in danger of going down the drain.

She rinsed out her mouth and threw herself on the bed trying to control her feeling of dread. Teddy might have committed suicide. Suicide! Like her father! The very word made her shake. She felt the same mingled anger and horror that she'd experienced at his death.

She lay there weeping, consumed with guilt. She should have been the one to save him, not Sarah. But it was because of her that he wanted to jump. It wasn't her fault. He'd been a problem child, an albatross since the day of their marriage. He hated her. He hated her the way she'd hated her mother. But it wasn't fair. She'd tried. Really she had. She spent every bit as much money on him as she did on Kitty.

Why couldn't he be like Kitty? Kitty was an enchanting child who had not given her one moment's concern since the day she was born. But Teddy had to ruin everything. It was the same old pattern of her life. No matter how much she tried, things had a way of turning out badly.

Apart from Teddy, everything had been going along so very well. She and Marshall were making a difference to the world. Not in the same way as Sarah and Hal, but in their own way. Marshall had always been a big contributor to charities, and now she worked tirelessly for his organizations, receiving as much benefit from them as they did from her. It was wonderful always to be needed. She made speeches, ran charity functions, arranged luncheons, and did everything so well that she was always praised. "If you want a perfect luncheon, ask Charlotte Berman."

Her hungry soul basked in the barrage of appreciation. They were big contributors and frequent visitors to the new state of Israel, and they were on the board of the American Jewish Committee, B'Nai B'rith, and *Commentary* magazine.

But Marshall's generosity went far beyond Jewish affairs. He was a major contributor to the New York Philharmonic and the Metropolitan Opera as well as a good friend and campaign contributor to the mayor and governor. Sometimes she worried that perhaps he was contributing too much, but money never seemed to be a problem.

Her proudest accomplishment had come the previous year. As a reward for continuous contributions, she'd been appointed to the Board of Trustees of Adams College. Finally, finally, she'd beaten those sorority bitches.

She would never forget the glory of sitting on the platform at graduation that past June, dressed in a Chanel suit, and looking down to see some of the old sorority girls in the audience, who looked drab and ordinary. She was the only member of her class to become a trustee. Charlotte Lewin, the despised! She! Not the sorority girls!

She loved the circles they moved in now. She had met Sarah's father and brother socially on several occasions, and it still seemed unbelievable to her that Sarah had so easily tossed away what she had struggled for. Nobody doubted that Hal was a nice guy, but he was strictly ordinary, a dreamer, a bookstore clerk. And poor Sarah worked so hard trying to teach poetry to those longshoremen's children whose vocabulary seemed to be limited to one word—fuck. She'd been wearing the same winter coat for ten years, and she actually seemed happy. It was a mystery!

Charlotte assumed that close as they all were, she was also a mystery to them. When she'd exulted about being on the Board of Trustees, Wendy had asked in amazement, "Do you still care about those sorority girls? Why?"

Stung, Charlotte had flung back, "It's not just that. I want to be of service to society."

Wendy had exaggerated a yawn. "How very public-spirited. I hate meetings. As far as I'm concerned, most charity work is designed to keep aimless ladies busy. I'd rather contribute money than fight with caterers. I watched my parents go through years of that kind of thing: worrying about pilferage, placating guests, checking details. No thanks."

Sometimes Wendy made her furious, and since her marriage to Robert she'd become impossibly arrogant. Sarah disagreed about that, but she insisted on always seeing the best in people. Trying to control her anger, she'd answered Wendy, "Your cynicism is just an excuse for your own laziness."

But she could never get to Wendy. "Maybe so," Wendy had smiled coolly, "but so what? *I* don't have to prove anything. I like being lazy."

"What do you mean *prove*," Charlotte had shrilled. "What do *I* have to prove? My husband is just as successful as Robert even though we're not in the social register. I'm trying to benefit society, but you always try to tear down everything I do."

"Come on, Charlotte. This is me! I know you! Do what you like but at least be honest about it. You love the power." Being married to Marshall had given her the confidence to ignore such gibes from Wendy. And then, out of nowhere, this awful debacle today.

While she lay there weeping, Marshall came hurrying into the room. He crossed quickly to the bed and sat down beside her. "There, there." He gently patted her heaving back. "It's all over. He's all right. We didn't lose him, thank God. His therapist is with him now so please calm down, dear. Kitty's just come in from school, and we don't want her to know what happened. We've all had a terrible fright, but it's over."

She turned and threw her arms around him. "I love you

so much, I would never want anything to come between us. I was afraid you'd blame me."

"I don't blame you; I blame fate. You didn't cause the accident. I thought we were doing all we could, but perhaps there was something more. Perhaps we should have sent him to a special school years ago, but I thought he needed family. Or perhaps we shouldn't have had another child so soon. He needed all of our attention. But there's no point in recriminations about the past.

"Somehow, I always assumed that he'd eventually grow out of things. Terrible things happen to lots of children and they survive. Children have survived the concentration camps. There was no way we could have known. Nobody's to blame!"

Then his habitual optimism asserted itself. "I'm sure the worst is over. His therapist assures me that he's going to the best school available for disturbed kids. I'm certain they'll straighten him out there."

Charlotte held him tightly to her, feeling grateful that she was married to such a kind, nonjudgmental man.

CHAPTER Thirty-Four

On June 19, 1953, Sarah and Hal and six-year-old Jimmy stood among five thousand Rosenberg sympathizers near Union Square, holding aloft a placard that read We Are Innocent. All over the world people were demonstrating against the death sentence. From France, descendants of Alfred Dreyfus cabled to ask that the Rosenbergs be kept alive for "the inevitable review of their trial."

Sarah had not been able to eat for days. They could not be spies. They were neighbors she had seen every day. Good people whom she had admired for their intellectualism and social conscience. Spies got paid, theoretically, and as far as she could determine they had even less money than she and Hal. And they wouldn't have endangered the lives of their children.

She was haunted by the memory of their meek, mild demeanor, of their tenderness toward their children, and of their kindness to her. This was not something abstract she was reading about in the papers. These were people she knew—friends! Totally innocent and framed by bullies without conscience like that lousy, corrupt Judge Kaufman, who had been unnecessarily vindictive. He was like the Judenrat, sending other Jews to their deaths in the foolish belief that this would make him less Jewish. Probably he would suffer no more guilt over what he had done than the Nazis had at the Nuremberg trials.

She had nightmares that it was she who was in the death house, she and Hal who had been unfairly accused and unjustly convicted. In the middle of the night, she would awaken in terror to find Hal trying to calm her. It was only by chance that her father had not presided at the trial, but he would have been equally cruel because that was what the government wanted.

"I have trouble sleeping," she said wryly, "but I'll bet nothing disturbs Judge Kaufman's sleep. Thank God my father wasn't the judge. I could never have lived down the shame of that."

It was a bad time. The previous year Teller had produced the H-bomb, and now people were building bomb shelters and stocking them with Bibles and cases of scotch. Her friends, the leaders of the teachers' union, had been fired; Robert Oppenheimer had been broken; and people in films, radio, and television were blacklisted and unemployed. Everyone was frightened. Several of their friends had thrown out the left-wing books from the New Masses Book Club, fearful of unexpected visits from the FBI. Others had moved to England or Mexico.

More terrible things seemed to be ahead. The *National Guardian* had written that concentration camps were being prepared for all progressives, and if the rumor were true, they would certainly get to her and Hal. They had thick dossiers on the men who'd fought in Spain, and she routinely signed every progressive petition. The government had shown no pity for the Rosenberg children. What would happen to Jimmy?

She was feeling terribly discouraged. The bad guys always seemed to win. Poor Alger Hiss was in Lewisburg Federal Prison and that bastard Whittaker Chambers was a social lion. The demagogue, McCarthy, had made a series of speeches throughout the country in which he questioned the loyalty of Adlai Stevenson, daring to claim that Stevenson was part and parcel of a conspiratorial group that included Hiss and Owen Lattimore. Twice during that speech he had referred to Stevenson as "Alger—I mean Adlai."

So Stevenson had been defeated, and Nixon, who had built his career on dirty tricks and the downfall of Alger Hiss, had become vice president. She thought back to the joy and optimism of V-E Day when the Soviet and American soldiers finally met. Now all of that was gone, and only fear, hatred, and suspicion remained. It was like those lines from William Butler Yeats's poem "The Second Coming": "The best lack all conviction, while the worst / Are full of passionate intensity."

Sarah was tormented by the injustice of it all. The Rosenbergs stood for peace, justice, humanity, everything she believed in. But what good was integrity if it led to the electric chair and orphaned children? She thought of the summers in East Hampton, of bicycle rides along peaceful, shaded lanes, of the sheer physical joy of sun and sand and good food. Sometimes she almost wished that she could turn away, or convince herself as her friends had that the Rosenbergs were guilty and deserved their terrible fate. But of course, she couldn't turn away. There was no way that either she or Hal could deny their connection to the rest of humanity.

She was suddenly jerked back from her thoughts by the crackling of a loudspeaker and the sound of a woman's sobs.

"Listen everybody," she wept. "Listen. It's past eight o'clock. Past eight. The Rosenbergs have been executed. It's all over, all over, all over."

A wave of nausea swept over her, and she thought she could smell the burning flesh of the electric chair. More

Jews were burning. Not even the gas ovens had satisfied the wicked.

Strangers in the crowd threw their arms around each other, desperately seeking some kind of warmth and affirmation to help them go on. They held on to each other and wept. And then, slowly, with shoulders bent, numb with horror at the incomprehensible cruelty of the state, moving stiffly with cracked hearts, people began to separate again and, like convalescents, move back to the reality of their individual lives.

Sarah wept as they walked. "Wendy's always said we can't save anyone. She's right! She's right! What's the use?"

Holding Jimmy on his shoulder with one hand, he put his other arm around her. "You saved Teddy."

"Maybe I did and maybe I didn't. Maybe I just saved him for the moment. Maybe it's all writ like in *Appointment in Samarra*. Remember, the man rides to Samarra to avoid death but he meets death there."

"I'll never believe that. Nothing's writ. We can always make a difference, and we made a hell of a try. But the other side had all the money, all the influence, all the big guns. It's like Spain, love. Our side lost, but at least we tried. That makes it easier for me to live with myself. We gave them a run, and history will record the truth of this some day."

She shivered and cried again as they walked past the Rosenberg's apartment. All night they clung to each other, finding renewal as always in their love. Dawn was breaking when she finally began to drift off to sleep. He looked down at her, gently stroked her hair, and whispered tenderly, "Rest my little warrior. There will always be other battles to fight, but this one is over."

CHAPTER
Thirty-Five

Wendy became pregnant on her wedding night. She was absolutely unprepared for how sick she would be. Both Sarah and Charlotte had sailed through their pregnancies with a minimum of illness. But her pregnancy was absolutely terrible. Whenever she got up, she would begin to hemorrhage, and she was so dizzy and nauseated most of the time that she did not mind staying in bed. She miscarried in her third month.

The next time she miscarried, she was in her fourth month. During each of her pregnancies, it was Arla who came to sit with her as soon as her children had gone to school. Sarah worked all day and took courses toward her M.A. degree at night, and Charlotte was completely occupied with her charity work, but Arla loved being there. She worshipped Wendy.

When she first started to appear, Wendy hoped her visits would be short. But after awhile, she was rather glad to see her when she tiptoed in each day. She had never known anyone quite so self-effacing or so worshipful. It was strange. Sometimes she'd look up and see Arla looking at her with an expression that was close to adoration. Back in college, she'd sometimes seen freshman sorority girls develop crushes on the older ones, but it had never happened to her.

Arla didn't speak much. She just sat there reading, observing, learning, struggling to understand. She was not at all dumb, as Charlotte had thought. She was oppressed and repressed, and Wendy was her college education.

Lenny had not hit her in a long time, she told Wendy. Maybe that part of her life was over.

"Have you told him how much time you spend with me?"

"I had to. He's never let me spend whole days away from home before. He hates Robert, but I told him that I never see him. I think he lets me come because he admires you so much. Maybe he hopes I'll get to be more like you."

Each day, when she left, she would humbly thank Wendy for letting her sit there. "When I'm with you," she said, "I feel as though I'm something." That brought tears to Wendy's eyes. There were so many oppressed people in the world. Women like Arla! Men like Maurice! She would not allow herself to be unhappy about her bad pregnancies. There were worse problems.

The third time she became pregnant she carried through and was in labor for over thirty-six hours before they finally performed a cesarean. By then, the walls of her womb had become so weakened that the doctors had to do a hysterectomy.

When she regained consciousness, Robert, sitting beside her bed, told her what had happened. They held each other and wept. "At least we have our child," he said. "A son! Robert da Gama Kingman IV. I thank you for that."

"Oh, Robert, I wanted a football team."

"At least we have one. And he's perfect."

She had to comfort herself with that.

Until little Bobby's birth, Wendy and Robert had been one of New York's golden fun couples, jet setters who led a rich, upper-class socialite life that was duly reported in all of the leading society columns. Wendy was usually referred to as that great beauty, Wendy da Gama Kingman, and everybody knew that she had been the model for the nude statue now on display at the MOMA. Their homes had been photographed for the *New York Times Sunday Magazine* and *House Beautiful*.

It almost drove Charlotte mad with jealousy and even made Sarah a little wistful at times. There were so many things she would never be able to see, so many places she and Hal would never see together. But she rarely permitted herself to dwell on this. New York City was the world in microcosm, and if they couldn't see the pyramids, they could go to the Egyptian collection at the Metropolitan Museum of Art; and if they couldn't see Rome, they could eat in Little Italy. It was their city, and it was wonderful because they were together.

After Bobby's birth, the Kingmans became reluctant to spend their summers in Europe. They worried constantly about the baby, hovering over him, fearful of germs and childhood diseases, concerned about proximity to the best doctors. And so they bought a house on Gin Lane in Southampton to be near her friends.

One Friday afternoon in the summer of 1956 the three friends sat on the veranda of Charlotte's house. Marshall and Robert were playing tennis, and Hal was on the beach playing with Jimmy. The au pair girls watched the other children, their portable radios blaring songs by Elvis Presley.

Wendy put down *Peyton Place* to listen to the music. As always, it raised her spirits. "I absolutely adore Elvis." She hummed along for a few minutes. "The most exciting entertainer I've heard in years. And so sexy."

Charlotte wrinkled her nose. "I think he's vulgar. But you always did like low-class music, Wendy. I love the music from *My Fair Lady*."

"Of course, dum-dum. I like that too. And jazz isn't low class."

Two-year-old Robert Kingman IV sat apart from the others with his English nanny. "Wendy, you fuss over that child so much he has to turn out neurotic," Charlotte said.

"Well, if anyone knows how to turn out a neurotic kid, Charlotte, it's you."

Sarah smiled at the familiar bickering as she rocked the carriage and cooed to Maggie, her new baby. She hadn't planned on another child but she and Hal were overjoyed with their little accident. How foolish they'd been to hold back all these years because of finances. Somehow they'd manage. And Jimmy was thrilled to have a little sister.

Wendy looked sadly at her son. "Poor little Bobby," she said. "He'll always be alone. The way I was."

Charlotte had little patience with Wendy's moments of gloominess. "I don't think your problems are so bad. After all, you do have all the money in the world. You can always adopt a Korean child if you're crazy enough to want one. As far as I'm concerned, one child should be just about enough for anyone. As for the hysterectomy, I wouldn't mind if *my* periods stopped. In fact, I'd be ecstatic. I go through hell each month. You're still beautiful, and you and Robert know the most interesting people in the world, so I don't think it's all that tragic."

"Thank you for that concerned, compassionate, considerate statement, Charlotte."

"I'm the one with real problems. I have to talk to you two about Marshall."

Aha, Wendy thought. He's finally wised up. I'll bet he has a girlfriend. I wouldn't blame him. Charlotte is such a royal pain in the neck sometimes. But she also felt a sudden, unaccountable disappointment. She had always found him so exceptionally honorable. "Another woman?" she asked.

"Of course not. Honestly, Wendy, everything with you begins and ends with sex. It's not a woman, but it might as well be. It's his damned music. I think he needs therapy as much as Teddy."

He was taking three lessons a week, had bought a second Steinway concert grand piano so that he could practice concertos with another pianist, was talking about reserving Carnegie Hall, and was spending increasingly more time with his ridiculous scales and less and less time with his business.

"We hardly go out together anymore," Charlotte said angrily. "I have to sit home night after night listening to that infernal practicing. It's just not fair. I gave up my art when we got married."

Wendy hooted with laughter. "Come off it, Charlotte, you're talking to us. You can't blame him for that. Remember that first luncheon at the Plaza? My mother told you to keep up your art."

"But she didn't tell me how to find the time. Anyway, right now, Marshall is engaging in enough art for us both."

"Everybody but me wants to be a serious artist," Wendy said. "Take Marilyn Monroe. She wants to play Grushenka in *The Brothers Karamazov*."

"Ridiculous. She's just pathetic," Charlotte said. "They say she's the hottest sex symbol of the decade. Do you think she's sexy?"

"It should happen to me," Sarah laughed, looking at her breasts that were still small despite her two children.

"I admire her," Wendy said. "You have to give her credit for working herself up."

"On her back," Charlotte snapped. Her two friends looked at her in surprise.

"My God," Sarah said. "You're beginning to sound like a member of the vice squad. I don't like to hear women pull down other women. Nobody ever says that about men who make good."

Then Charlotte asked them something she'd been wanting to ask for a long time. "Do you two still have good sex lives?"

Sarah answered first. The mystical unity between her and Hal continued to grow and deepen, but she had no easy words to describe it. "It's not something separate from the rest of our life. We love each other."

"May we know why you're asking?" Wendy asked.

"First answer."

"Very well. On the occasions that Robert and I make love, it's unfailingly competent. Not earth shaking. But competent."

"What about sex in the morning?"

"What about it?"

"I hate sex in the mornings. I don't feel clean. I like to get up, bathe, brush my teeth. Do you do it?"

"You may not believe this," Wendy teased her, poker-faced, "but on occasions we've actually made love before brushing our teeth."

Charlotte shuddered in distaste. "You both smoke, so maybe it's not so unpleasant. But since I've stopped smoking, I simply can't bear the smell of tobacco on Marshall's breath. You two should also stop smoking. It's really a disgusting habit. Marshall burns holes in things all the time."

"Tell us the truth, Charlotte. What's this all about? Are you frigid?"

"Just the kind of question I'd expect from you. Anyone who isn't a nymphomaniac is frigid."

"You are so impossibly thin-skinned. I wasn't trying to put you down. But if you would be honest, maybe we could help."

"All right. The truth is that I don't like sex. I've never liked sex. But that doesn't make me frigid, does it?"

"It certainly doesn't make you sexual," Wendy said.

"I don't think you should worry about it," Sarah tried to comfort her.

"But I do. So many things seem to elude me. It's like an orgasm. Just as I think I'm getting there, it slips away."

Wendy looked over to where Bobby sat with his nanny and thought of all the children she'd planned to have. "You're not the only one. Things seem to elude us all."

CHAPTER
Thirty-Six

Arla's children had begun to quarrel on the beach. "Where's Arla?" Sarah asked. Nobody had seen her that day. Apparently the children had come over alone at breakfast time and stayed for lunch.

"I'll go and get her," Sarah said. "Maggie's asleep, and I'd like a little walk. Please keep an eye on her but don't wake her up to hold her, Wendy."

"I'll make sure she doesn't do that or blow cigarette smoke all over her," Charlotte promised.

Sarah walked along the beach to Arla's house, knocked, and when no one answered, opened the unlocked screen door and walked in. "Arla," she called. "Arla? Are you here?"

"Are you alone?" Arla called.

"Yes."

"Then you can come up."

She was lying on her bed staring up at the ceiling. Sarah looked at her in horror. "Not again! I thought he'd stopped. This can't go on. You have to leave him."

"He hasn't hit me in three years."

"So what? Is that supposed to be some kind of wonderful record? Normal people *never* beat up women. He's a sadistic beast and he belongs in jail. Even my father, who used to beat my brother Jimmy so badly, wouldn't do this to a woman. I'll call the police."

"No, Sarah. Please, please don't do that. It will only make things worse. Maybe he'll be all right now for a while."

"That's the most ridiculous thing I've ever heard."

"He'll kill me if the police come."

"It looks to me as if he almost killed you already. It's absolutely outrageous. You can't let him get away with this. There must be something we can do."

"No, there isn't. There isn't anything anybody can do. And you three talk brave and tell me to leave, but nobody's figured out yet where I should go. I'm not here because I like to suffer. I'm here because there's no place to go and no way to support my kids."

"What set him off this time?"

"I started to talk to him again about getting my high school degree and going to college."

"That bastard. He's just afraid that if you have a way of making a living you'll leave him. I still think we should call the police."

"No."

* * *

Sarah walked back along the beach clenching and unclenching her fists. There had to be something they could do to help. The three of them planning together would be able to think of something. I'd like to take out a contract on that bastard, she thought. Hal and Jimmy were just coming out of the water, and at the sight of them she felt the familiar explosion of joy. How lucky she was! Hal smiled and waved to her, and she began to run toward them, anxious to shut out the horror of Arla's existence.

And as she ran she saw it happen right before her eyes. With his hand still raised in greeting, the smile on Hal's face suddenly turned to a look of surprise and he crumpled to the beach.

"Hal," she screamed, "Hal, Hal, Hal." She kept running for an eternity until she reached him. Her friends, watching from the terrace, also began to run while Marshall frantically phoned for an ambulance. Gasping and sobbing she dropped to her knees and lifted his head in her arms.

"What's wrong with Daddy?" Jimmy asked in a frightened voice.

"I don't know, I don't know," she said, rocking him in her arms.

"Hal," she begged as she rocked. "Hal, darling. Wake up. Wake up, Hal. Talk to me darling. What is it? What's wrong. Say something. Talk to me."

She stayed that way begging him to talk to her until the ambulance attendants pried him from her hands and forced her to understand that he had died of a heart attack.

Her friends took her into the house and put her to bed while Marshall got dressed and drove into the city to arrange for the funeral. "I'll call the doctor to give you a shot," Charlotte said.

"No."

"Do you want a drink?" Wendy asked.

"No. I just want Jimmy."

He ran to her, and she held him tightly in her arms. I want to die, she told herself. I want to die but how can I die with two children? How can I leave them alone? She and Jimmy sobbed in each other's arms until they fell asleep.

The next day they all returned to the city, and Sarah and her children went to Wendy's house. Charlotte was offended. "Why not come home with me?"

"I was married there. I couldn't bear it."

Marshall came over that night to talk to her about the funeral. "I want the cheapest pine box," she told him.

"That's not necessary, Sarah. I'll assume all the expenses."

"He would have wanted the cheapest box. He always said that wasting so much money to put a box in the ground was obscene. And I don't want a rabbi. He was not a religious man."

"Whatever you say." Marshall's voice broke.

Charlotte called her on the morning of the funeral. "I don't think Jimmy should go to the funeral. It's too upsetting for a child."

"I want him there," she said. "We have to be together."

"I don't think he should be."

"Well, that's where we're different."

"What about your family?" Wendy asked, during breakfast.

"Only my mother, if she wants to come. I couldn't look at my father or Claude. They probably wouldn't come anyway."

She felt so faint and nauseated when they entered the chapel that she could not walk alone. She leaned heavily on Marshall's arm and she held Jimmy tightly with her other hand. Her mother, Wendy, Charlotte, and Arla walked behind her.

She was surprised to see how many people had come. Hundreds! She hadn't realized that Hal knew this many people. I must tell him how many people came, she thought irrationally, before she remembered and bent her face to weep.

Marshall left her side and moved to the front of the room to begin the service. "We come together today," he said, "to celebrate the life of Hal Gordon. He was..." He stopped for a moment, too overcome with grief to continue. Then he went on. "He was a righteous man. A truly righteous man. And all of us are poorer for his loss. He would not have wanted a religious service. We ask instead that his friends come up to speak about him, to bear witness to his life."

Then, one by one they came. Friends, neighbors, acquaintances, customers from the bookstore, buddies from the Lincoln Brigade and World War II—all of them spoke the same words; generous, committed, loyal, compassionate, politically aware. He had died owning nothing but the love of everyone who had come his way. He had made a difference!

Marshall spoke again after the last speaker had finished. "He was an old-fashioned kind of man," he said. "A man who was contented as long as he had three things: his wife and children near him, a cause to fight for, and a good book to read. Yes, an old-fashioned man who cared about politics and ideas and friends more than about power and possessions. We will not see his equal soon again."

Sobs echoed through the room, and Sarah held Jimmy close to her. My poor little boy, she thought. To lose such a father. In her mind, she kept talking to Hal. Oh, darling, she grieved, who will ever love and understand me the way you did? How will I face the rest of my life without you?

Then Wendy rose, and in her clear, sweet voice she sang the songs Sarah had requested. "Viva la Quince Brigada" and "Los Cuatros Generales." She ended with "Joe Hill," and at the words, "I never died said he," weeping again filled the chapel.

Oh, darling, Sarah mourned, it was a good fight. And then she repeated the words he had said to her when she had worn herself out weeping on the night of the Rosenbergs' execution. "Rest, warrior. The war is over."

After the funeral, she insisted on taking the children and returning to her home. Her friends filled the refrigerator. And her mother stayed with her.

CHAPTER
Thirty-Seven

The week after Hal's funeral, as unexpectedly as he'd called her before, Maurice called Wendy. "Can I see you?" he asked.

Her first impulse was to say, "No." What was the point of seeing him? He would light for a moment, then fly off, and she would be left feeling disgruntled and discontent. But to her surprise she heard herself saying, "I suppose. For an hour or so. Come for lunch."

She was angry but curious. Where had he been and why had he called her after all this time? Would he look as bad as he had the last time? His voice had sounded strong on the phone, and the way she first remembered it. It would be interesting to hear his story.

When her butler led him out to the garden in back of her

house where she sat reading, she looked at him in surprise. He was back to his old weight, was well-dressed, and was healthy looking. And he had a new air of confidence about him.

She motioned him to a chair and her butler served lunch. Then she mournfully told him about Hal. "He was a good man," Maurice said. "As free of prejudice as any white man can get."

"May I ask why you called me?"

There was a new hardness about her that surprised him. "You sound hostile," he said.

"I hate the way you always disappear," she scolded, "like your invisible man. It's so damned unreliable and so inconsiderate. Why do you do it?"

"I don't know and that's the truth. I start to think about explaining things, and then it seems easier to split."

"That's cowardly."

He grinned in his new security. "Maybe so. I am a coward about some things. About a lot of things."

"Is that supposed to excuse your behavior?"

He did not answer but only looked about him while he sipped a drink. "This place is something! It's hard to believe that people live this way right in the middle of New York City. Pools. Paths. It's a jungle out there but inside these walls is paradise. People like you never see the jungle."

"People like me? Don't oversimplify. I have my own problems."

"Not like my people."

"Don't try to evade your own bad behavior by talking about 'your people.' Let's talk to each other like two human beings. Where did you go when you left me?"

"I checked into a VA hospital. I figured they owed me. I got hurt the first time in their army, so their army should patch me up. I was so spaced-out that they never even asked for my papers. Just led me to a bed."

"I was there for a year," he continued, "had three operations, and married my nurse. We just had a baby."

Feeling let down, she lit another cigarette and poured herself some brandy. So what if he were married? Why should that bother her? After all, she was married too. Surely she had not expected him to stay single for the rest of his life.

"When I got out of the hospital I still had to figure what to do with the rest of my life. Couldn't live off my wife."

"What *did* you do? You look fine. New suit, fresh shirt. Just as handsome as when I first met you."

"A few more scars. Do you still not read the papers?"

She laughed. "I've always read the papers. It's just that I don't read the news. I read about books, fashion, music and theater. The news depresses me."

"Have you ever heard of Martin Luther King?"

"I did hear something. I think Sarah and Hal once mentioned him, but I don't really remember what they said. Who is he?"

"He's a great man. A preacher in Montgomery, Alabama, and I'm working with him. I'm here this week to speak at a few churches about his work and do some fund raising. But I'm based in Montgomery."

"A preacher? Have you become religious?" She was joking but he was serious.

"Something led me to him. After I got out of the hospital I had an urge one night to stand outside in my backyard, naked in the rain. I stood there and raised my arms to heaven because I needed some kind of guidance about my life, and then I had this revelation that I should go and work with him, that he would be my salvation and my destiny. And he has. I never turned back."

She resisted an impulse to quip, "Are you sure they cured you in that hospital?" Well, what difference did it make what he believed? Obviously he had straightened up and was involved in significant work. "Tell me more about him," she said.

"It all started in Montgomery last year. They arrested a Negro seamstress who refused to give up her seat on the bus to a white man."

"I vaguely think I heard something about it."

He laughed and took her hand. "Oh, Wendy! Vaguely!"

"Are you laughing at me?"

"Only a little. Mostly I'm just remembering you. Anyway, that was the last straw for Montgomery's Negro community. They'd been putting up with this kind of crap for years, but they never could seem to get together. This time was different. All of the black leaders met to organize a one-day bus boycott to desegregate public transportation, and King emerged as the leader. That one-day boycott is still going on now, one year later. But it's war down there. He teaches nonviolence, but the whites just see it as weakness. Last January they bombed his house."

"Why did they bomb his home if he teaches nonviolence?"

"*We're* nonviolent. They're not. We're scared stiff all the time."

She shivered. "Must you be involved in this? I'm frightened for you."

"You have a choice in life. But I don't."

"I can't believe that. Everybody has a choice."

"Oh, Wendy, you have no idea what's going on in the real world. You don't have to know. You can buy your way out of everything except sickness and death, and even those two are easier for the white and the rich." He made a sweeping arc with his hand that encompassed the beautiful setting. "You live here on another planet, so safe and insulated. . . . So fucking safe."

"Stop patronizing me. I'm not safe."

He uttered a bitter laugh, and she felt tremendous anger well up in her. "How dare you laugh at me. You know goddamned well what my history has been. You were the first person I ever told about my sister. And last time you came I told you about Edita. But you like to have your myths. You think I'm safe? Well listen to this you egocentric bastard. I've had a hysterectomy. A hysterectomy, do you hear. At the age of thirty-one. I'll never have another child. But you think it doesn't count if it happens to a white person."

She wasn't just railing at him. She was railing at death and sadness and aging and loss. He stood up and pulled her against him, patting her back and trying to soothe her, and gradually, despite her anger, she was back in the past, melting into his arms, wanting desperately to find shelter there, and never wanting to let him go.

"Of course I think it counts. Anything that happens to you counts. You must know that. You must know how much I loved you. I left school for you. And I'll always love you. Nothing will ever change that." He tilted her lips to his and kissed her.

At the touch of his lips she exploded, tottering before the hurricane of her emotions. Her insides melted with the passion he had always evoked, and her soul soared in exultance at the reawakening of the old intensity. His powerful hands burned through her dress, and the familiar feel and scent of his skin—as she covered his face and neck with kisses—made her shiver with emotion. Oh, my God. I'm alive again, alive again. Happiness and well-being made her giddy. She threw back her head and laughed for joy.

Time flowed backward, and he was waiting for her in a halo of light beneath her balcony in Mexico. "Come," she said feverishly, unbuttoning her silk blouse as they walked. She led him to the elevator and pressed the button for her bedroom floor.

He didn't ask, but she explained, "My son and his nurse are on a different floor."

As they ascended she stripped off her clothes, and when the elevator stopped she was totally naked except for the large diamond studs in her ears and the sapphire-and-diamond ring on her finger.

His eyes caressed her willowy body. "That operation doesn't mean a thing. You're still the most beautiful woman in the world."

"Oh come, my love," she said, leading him to her bed.

He lay beside her, holding her in his strong arms, and the years fell away. She was back in Mexico, young and beautiful and strong and sure. She closed her eyes in dizzying ecstasy, her breath caught in her chest, and an ineffable feeling of sweetness filled her heart as she wrapped her long, champion's legs around him, and they began the old familiar ritual that was always new.

"Nothing's gone," she said in wonder. "Nothing's lost."

"Nothing's gone," he echoed in his deep, strong voice.

They moved together in equal joy, passion, abandon, and harmony of body and mind and spirit. They couldn't get enough of each other. Movement flowed into movement, orgasm into orgasm, until at last they lay together in her satin sheets, spent, exhausted, but still touching.

"I told you that operation wasn't anything," he said. "Maybe it made things even better. No worry about a little black baby."

A little black baby? She shivered and held tight to him. Poor Paula. Dead so many years because of fear of a little black baby. "I would have liked to have your baby," she said, meaning it.

"I would have liked it, too. I would have loved it. I love you," he said. "I've loved you from the first moment I saw you, and I'll love you for the rest of my life."

"And I you. Forever and ever."

They stayed together, talking, laughing, making love, until dusk was falling over the city. Then they dressed, and she took him to see Bobby. He picked the little boy up in his arms and swung him high in the air. "The most beautiful child I've ever seen. As beautiful as you."

They had brandy in her study before he left. "Tell me," she said, "did you come to ask me for money?"

"Yes. We need it. But that wasn't the only reason. You know that."

"I know. It's all right. I want to help and this is the way I can do it. I've been looking for something meaningful to do. I'll help you regularly."

She went to her desk and wrote out a check. "I don't like people to be pushed around. That's what started our sorority, you know. We didn't want to be pushed around."

He looked at it and let out a low whistle. "Five thousand dollars! Wow, I must have been good." She punched him lightly, and he doubled up and said, "oof."

"It's not for you, you conceited idiot," she teased back. "It's for the cause. In memory of my sister. I told you, I don't like people to be pushed around."

He put his arms around her. "*You* can push me around whenever you like."

"You'll have to stay in touch for me to push you. Will you?"

"I sure will try."

She had to be satisfied with that. But whether he did or not, she felt happy. She was alive again, for the first time in years.

CHAPTER
Thirty-Eight

Sarah could not adjust to Hal's death. Even though she had always been brave and feisty in political demonstrations, daring the hooves of policemen's horses and the catcalls, hoots, and incipient violence, she had no courage now to face life without him. She could not get out of bed, had taken sick leave from her job, could not take care of the children, and simply turned her face to the wall wanting to die. Day after day she lay there weeping and remembering every moment of their lives together; the way they had found each other in Mexico, the first time they had made love, the way she'd clung to him during the earthquake in Fortin, and the triumphant way he'd carried her to the cab when she'd told him she was pregnant. Oh, Hal! He'd envied no man, had worn the same winter coat for all the years of their marriage, and asked nothing for himself but the love and companionship of his wife and children.

She could not adjust to sleeping alone without the warmth of Hal's body. "I'm cold all the time," she told Charlotte, and two days later an electric blanket came from Bloomingdale's that helped her begin to sleep again. Her mother and friends took care of the children, but they could not get her out of bed.

She could not raise her body. "I am too weighed down by grief," she said.

Her friends let her lie there for a week and then decided that it was necessary to take action. She dozed off one day and when she opened her eyes she saw her father sitting beside her bed. And sitting beside him looking at her anxiously was Jimmy. "Look who's here, Mommy. It's Grandpa. Look what he brought me." He held out his wrist and proudly showed her a Mickey Mouse watch. That did it. Her temper began to wake her up again.

"Jimmy, darling, would you go outside for a minute please. I want to talk to Grandpa alone."

As soon as Jimmy was gone she laced into him. "How dare you come here to gloat."

"Don't be stupid, Sarah. I've come to see my grandchildren."

"They're not yours and you can't see them and I want you to get out of my apartment this minute."

"I want you and the children to come home, Sarah. You can't make it alone."

"Home. This is my home." He looked about him at the broken window and cracked ceiling and shuddered.

"You know what I mean, Sarah, so don't act stupid. Whatever else you were, you were never stupid."

"If you think I'd expose my children to a reactionary fascist like you, you're even crazier than I always thought. You hated Hal. You're glad he's dead. Chalk up another victory for your side."

She stood up on unsteady legs and proudly drew herself up to her full five feet two inches. "Out," she said pointing to the door.

He remained seated there as unflappable as in his own courtroom. "You have to listen to me, Sarah. There is no way that you can go to work with a ten-year-old boy and a new baby and no money to hire a maid for them. You're in no condition to go to work all day and then come home to this tenement and take care of your children. How can you force them to live in this terrible environment when the whole apartment on Central Park West stands empty. Come home with us for just a little while. As soon as you're strong enough to leave I promise that I'll help you find a better apartment in a proper location, and I'll help you with the rent."

"I have to think about it. Please go out and send my friends in," she said. "I want to talk to them."

When he heard the door open, Jimmy came running back in. "Want to go for a walk, Grandpa?" Jimmy clung to his hand needing a male figure and the sight filled her with confusion. A wave of weakness swept over her, and she lay down again as Wendy and Charlotte came in, leaving Maggie in the living room with Sarah's mother.

"Nice that you're back in the land of the living." Wendy sat down on the bed and gave her a hug. "He certainly got your temper going again, didn't he? I wonder if this should be reported in a medical journal."

"He remembered meeting me at several functions," Charlotte reported. "You are so lucky to have a famous father, Sarah. Nobody in my entire family was ever famous."

Wendy asked, "Tell us what he wants, Sarah."

"He wants me and the children to go and live with them."

"Thank God you're saved," Charlotte said. "You'd be crazy not to take him up on his offer. Your choosing to be wretched and poor when you were a girl was your affair. But now it affects your children. There's no life for you or them here. You don't have a single piece of furniture in this entire apartment that isn't chipped or broken. And nobody lives this far downtown. You have to accept. You can help the proletariat just as well on Central Park West."

Wendy laughed. "After fifteen years, Charlotte, you and I finally agree on something. Go home with them, Sarah darling, and take another semester's sick leave. Don't worry. If he keeps you prisoner we'll help you to escape."

And so it was decided.

CHAPTER
Thirty-Nine

For the first time in her life, Wendy found herself as interested and emotionally involved in current events as Sarah. She watched the news each night in terror, always afraid for Maurice and Dr. King. When they were arrested in a sit-in to desegregate the Rich's department store snack bar in Atlanta, Wendy organized a phone campaign to urge President Kennedy to have them released from Reidsville Penitentiary.

Once in 1961, she thought she saw Maurice among the Freedom Riders who were being beaten mercilessly with lead pipes, baseball bats, and bicycle chains while the police stood by doing nothing, and she immediately telegraphed money to provide bail for the Freedom Riders who were languishing in jail in Jackson, Mississippi. She was almost obsessed with the struggle.

Sometimes she could not bear to watch. It was too painful! She wondered how Coretta King could live this way day after day, never knowing what would happen to her husband, never knowing if he had been beaten, killed, or jailed.

"Can you believe that white America can be so evil?" she asked Sarah.

"Are you kidding? Of course I can! It's nothing new to me. Hal and I saw that evil when the Rosenbergs were executed. I still see it in dreams."

"I didn't understand then," Wendy said humbly.

"I'm glad you do now. With Hal gone, I need someone close to me to share my indignation. It's indignation that keeps me going."

Charlotte was indignant too, but not because of politics. Each year Marshall spent more of his time on his music, working toward a concert even though his music teacher urged him to give up the idea and simply enjoy his music like a talented amateur. He wasn't good enough. He would never be good enough. Most pianists begin as children. The only famous pianist who had begun later was Dame Myra Hess, and she had started at eighteen, not at forty-five. But Marshall was adamant. He believed that if he worked as hard at music as he had at business, he would be equally successful. It was all a matter of effort and of will.

He had rented a practice studio, was rarely home, and increasingly refused to attend social events. Charlotte told her friends in panic, "His teacher said that it would be perfectly acceptable to give a small concert in the recital hall but he wants Carnegie Hall! Can you imagine what that costs? It's absolutely ludicrous. The critics won't come, and he'll have to paper the house. And for what? An insane folly that will impoverish us! He's obsessed. I thought I was marrying a successful businessman, not a second rate musician. Oh, it's all turned out so badly."

"Things haven't exactly turned out perfectly for any of us," Sarah said irritably. "I hate being back home again. My father's on fairly good behavior because he doesn't want me to walk out. But it still hurts me to see how repressed my mother is."

"I know it's awful for you, but you do not have an immediate crisis on your hands. I do. I'm afraid that if Marshall keeps ignoring the agency it might fold. Sometimes he doesn't go in for days. I'd like you and Wendy to come for dinner Saturday night and try to talk him out of this nonsense."

"I'll listen, Charlotte, but I don't think Wendy and I should interfere in this. I'm sure you don't really have to worry. He's been successful for a long, long time. He wouldn't let his business go under. So why not just leave him alone? He's said many times that he'll go back to his usual patterns as soon as the concert is over. Life is so short. Think of Hal. Shouldn't each human being have the right to fulfill his dreams?"

"Not if he has to support a family. Mature people control their dreams and fulfill their responsibilities. Anyway, what about my dream? I'd like to paint."

"So why don't you do it?"

"You know why. Because I'm so snowed under with the details of running our lives. I'm the one who has to send off packages to Teddy, and now Marshall wants to take him out of that school, so it's my job to find another. One of the boys there sniffed Freon gas last week and died.

"And Kitty, too. I'm the one who has to take her to the Barclay dance classes at the Colony. When the chauffeur takes her she refuses to go inside. Sometimes I worry that she's as peculiar as Teddy. She's home with imaginery illnesses more than she's in school. You don't know how lucky you are that your kids never give you any trouble. That's why I can't find time for creative work."

"Excuses, excuses. If you wanted to paint you'd do it. I'm working on my doctorate even though I'm teaching. That's the only reason I'm staying with my folks. The minute I have that doctorate, I'm on my way. You could have been painting, but instead you've chosen to work for organizations. My advice to you is to leave Marshall alone and do your own thing. He's been a great husband, and he's entitled to reach for the stars."

"Oh, easy enough for you to say. I suppose it always boils down to whose ox is being gored."

Wendy found the situation amusing. "Music's a harmless enough obsession. Count your blessings. It might have been another woman."

"That would have been a lot cheaper and a lot more quiet. If I hear the 'Revolutionary Étude' one more time I'll puke. Do you think Robert will join us on Saturday night?"

"I doubt it, but I'll ask him."

Each year Wendy and Robert became more estranged from each other. He had married her for beauty and she had married him for strength and stability, but neither one of them seemed to need those qualities any longer. For the most part they led parallel lives, meeting mainly to attend some grand function, to be with Bobby, or to entertain. It was a much admired public life but an empty private one.

But Bobby made everything worthwhile. If they had to produce only one child, they both agreed, they'd produced a practically perfect one. Bobby was tall, handsome, well-made with Wendy's black hair and violet eyes. He was not much of a scholar, but he managed to get by in school and was well liked by his teachers and popular with his classmates. He had inherited Robert's athletic prowess, and the two of them did everything together: sailing, skiing, riding, racquet ball, tennis.

Her life flowed by serenely. It was well ordered, calm, comfortable. They traveled for two months each year, skiied winters at Gstaad, attended the best cultural events, the most prestigious benefits, the most glittering parties. They never quarreled and were unfailingly polite to each other, but there was no passion, no heat, no excitement, no surprises in the relationship. "I've been bored with Robert in the best hotels in the world," she laughed to her friends. "And he's probably been equally bored with me."

Whenever she became impossibly bored, she found a lover, but none of them engaged her imagination for very long. Sometimes she had the eerie feeling that she was asleep back on the island, dreaming her present existence.

Actually, she wasn't dissatisfied. That was the wrong word. Unchallenged, unstimulated, *underutilized* would probably describe her condition more precisely. What sustained her were Maurice's infrequent visits to New York. He brought her his vibrancy and a whiff of the real world, and she gave him peace. They had so little time together that they made every moment count. No matter what her plans were, she dropped them when he called.

And each time he left her to return to the civil-rights wars she worried that she might never see him again. Her life with Robert was a dream. Only this was real.

CHAPTER
Forty

In 1960, a few months before he turned eighteen, Teddy was thrown out of school for selling marijuana. He hitchhiked home one morning and appeared shortly after breakfast, dressed in ragged jeans and torn tennis shoes, shivering, filthy, disoriented, and stoned. The school had already called her to say that he had gone.

Charlotte looked at him with the old, familiar sorrow. "You smell absolutely foul. I hope you know that none of the tuition will be refunded to us. And if you were a year older, you would be in jail. Don't you dare get Kitty involved in drugs."

He looked at her angrily. "What a great welcome! But no different from what I expected. I live here, Stepmother. Remember? In fact, I lived here before you invaded and conquered. I lived here with my mother and grandmother, and we were all very happy until you polluted the atmosphere. And I'm not a bad influence on Kitty. You are."

Charlotte hurried to close the heavy, paneled door. She

was determined to stay calm, not to let him get to her. "The servants will hear you. Please go and take a shower. When your father comes home, we'll decide what to do with you."

"Shower!" he laughed bitterly. "Your solution for everything. Godliness is next to cleanliness. Right? I don't want anything done with me. I want to stay home where I belong. I'm going to live here and have my friends in and do just as I please. And I'm going to have a normal allowance just like other kids. Or else, I'll go right on dealing. Right from here."

She struggled for control. Sarah and Wendy always scolded her for rising to Teddy's bait, but they didn't have to put up with him. They really had no idea of how he upset her. She didn't want to let him make her cry.

He always knew how to turn the knife.

In his filthy clothes, Teddy sprawled out on her clean couch, lit a joint, and slowly drew on it.

She looked at him in horror. "Put that out! It's illegal."

"So is cruelty to children. No, maybe that isn't illegal. At least you've gotten away with it for years, Stepmother."

Suddenly, Charlotte was out of control. She flew across the room and smashed him across the face. "You ungrateful bastard." He was responsible for all of her problems, all of them.

He stood up, ground out his joint on the oriental carpet, and smashed her back across the face, knocking her to the ground.

"Just in case you haven't noticed," he said. "I'm bigger than you."

"I'm calling the police," she wept, pulling herself up and moving toward the phone. She felt violated, the way she'd always been by her mother.

He stood there beside the phone menacing her. "I don't think you want to do that," he said. "Publicity! Photographs!"

"Go to your room," she screamed, but when he didn't move, she hurried out herself, went to her bedroom, and called Marshall.

Then, on the verge of hysterics she called Sarah. "I can't have him here. He'll be a terrible influence on Kitty. They're already in league together against me. What should I do? Maybe I could send him to Israel."

"I don't know, Charlotte. You can't ship him off to Israel unless he wants to go. Try to calm down, and then when Marshall gets home you can both discuss it with his therapist. If you can get him to go, it would probably be good for him. But you'll have to present the idea calmly as if you're doing it for him, not for you. Try to be patient."

"He would try the patience of a saint. The point is, Sarah, that he's crazy, and you can't understand because your kids are so normal. I had to go into therapy because of him, and now I spend my expensive sessions talking to my therapist about nothing but him. But nothing does any good.

"It's been almost fifteen years of unrelieved misery. Isn't there some time when a parent gets off the hook? He's going to be eighteen years old, and I just don't want to be bothered with him any longer. Either he goes to Israel, or Marshall gets him his own apartment, or he goes to another school or a mental institution. But something has to be done.

"It's all so unfair. Wendy sails through life with perfect looks, a perfect husband, and a perfect child, and even though you lost Hal your children are wonderful. But things still seem to go wrong for me. It's kind of like that line from *Julius Caesar*. I don't know if the fault is in my stars or in myself."

"Probably a little bit of each," Sarah said honestly. "Don't blame yourself too much. Life is a big battle for each of us. At least you still have a wonderful, devoted husband. Wendy and Robert hardly communicate, and I'm miserable living at my folks' and sleeping in the same narrow bed I slept in when I was a kid. I wake up sweating in the middle of the night and thinking that nobody else in my entire life is ever going to make love to me."

"I never thought about that. You mean you miss sex?"

"Of course. How could I not? I miss sex and I miss love and I miss Hal. But I try not to think about it. Neither Wendy nor I have anything you should envy. And think of poor Arla. One of these days she'll finally leave Lenny, and then she'll have to go on welfare. So count your blessings and try to relax."

"If you have to count your blessings, they don't count."

Sarah laughed. "Yes, they do. Please tell Teddy I'll be over to see him on Saturday. I'll bring him a welcome-home present."

"A present. What for? People don't need rewards for screwing up. I'm the one who needs a present."

"I'll bring you one, too," Sarah laughed. Charlotte's saving grace was that she was always funny.

Sarah was anxious to see Teddy. Ever since she'd saved his life, she'd felt a special bond to him. When she got to the apartment the next day, Charlotte was pacing about indecisively. She had to leave for a meeting of the Adams Board of Trustees.

"I don't know what to do." She wrung her hands. "He won't come out and won't allow anyone in except Kitty. And Marshall has been absolutely useless in this situation. He keeps telling me to leave him alone and give him time to find himself. Find himself! There's nothing there to find. And even if there were, he couldn't see it beyond that fog of marijuana smoke. This apartment smells like an opium den. Stop laughing, Sarah. It's not funny.

"He has not been out of his room since his arrival yesterday. I tried to exert the pressure of not feeding him unless he came out for meals, but Kitty insists on bringing them to him in a misguided belief that she's helping. The two of them are in league against me. I will never cease to wonder at how one neurotic boy can disturb an entire household."

"Where's Marshall?"

"Where do you think? At his studio! Practicing! He said that Teddy is straightening out. Can you believe such blindness? What should I do?"

"I'll stay for a while." Charlotte kissed her gratefully, hurried on her way in a cloud of Joy, and Sarah knocked on Teddy's door. "Please open up. It's Aunt Sarah. I've brought you some books."

"Go away. I don't want to see you, and isn't it about time we stopped this Aunt Sarah, Aunt Wendy, Aunt Arla crap? You're not my aunts. You're not my anythings. You're her friends, and if you're her friends, you can't be mine. Like they say, if you're not part of the solution, you're part of the problem. So go away and don't come back unless it's with some grass."

"Not like they say, Teddy. As they say."

"Oh, great. Thanks for the English lesson. That's exactly what I need right now."

"Do you plan to come out of there soon?"

"I have no plans. Now leave me alone."

"I'll leave the books outside your door, Teddy. I'll drop by to see you again tomorrow."

Sick at heart she walked across the park, thinking for the first time that maybe Teddy was beyond help. For fifteen years they had been pouring money into him, and even so, he'd deteriorated. Maybe there was no help for childhood trauma. How ironic that she had saved him from the ledge ten years before, only to have him end up hiding in his bedroom with marijuana for comfort and company. It was hard to understand him. Even with all of her sadness about Hal, she'd never given up on life. None of them had. Not even Arla. And yet, that poor boy was so passive, so useless, so wasted. What could be more tragic then being finished by the age of eighteen?

CHAPTER
Forty-One

The moment Arla had her high-school diploma she was ready to escape. She got a job as a file clerk for a publishing company and found a two-bedroom walk-up apartment in Chelsea. One day, as soon as Lenny had gone to work, her friends and Wendy's chauffeur helped her and Peter to move. Stewart and Mark were no longer around. They had left home and were hitchhiking around the country.

Arla proudly led them up the four flights to her apartment for which she'd purchased two beds, a kitchen table and chairs, and a second-hand couch. It wasn't much of a place: bare floors, antique refrigerator, and a rusty shower. But to her it was paradise. When they had finished unpacking, they ate the picnic lunch and drank the champagne that Wendy had brought.

"Here's to the sorority," Arla said, tears of joy rolling down her face. "I'm a phoenix. You saved my life." She was no longer the bony, sallow, slattern they had known. But she was still afraid, so her phone was unlisted. "I don't think you have to worry," Sarah said. "You're not asking for anything."

"I am worried. He doesn't need a reason to be vindictive."

"You have to get a lawyer and sue for divorce," Charlotte told her. "When you start to ask for something for you and your children, an unlisted phone might be essential."

"I don't want anything. All I want is what I have right now. Peace and freedom."

"Romantic nonsense," Charlotte said. "Freedom is only fun with money."

Two weeks after her move, Wendy and Robert were just sitting down to dinner with Bobby when the hospital called. Arla had been mugged. "Will you come with me, Robert?" Wendy pleaded.

"Bobby and I have not finished our dinners, and I've had a very hard day. However, I'll be glad to call the hospital and check on her condition."

"Marshall will come," she snapped at him, surprised at her anger because he did work terribly hard, and it was draining to deal with death and dying year after year, but she wished it were different. Marshall always came with Charlotte. And Hal would have been there with Sarah. She threw on her sable coat and directed her chauffeur to pick up Sarah, to whom she talked about her anger. "But you and Robert have led separate lives for a long time," Sarah answered.

"I know. But this is an emergency, and he knows that I hate hospitals. Those long months with my mother, and then the hysterectomy."

"Well, I'm here. It's all so awful. After nine years we finally get her to move out, and she's immediately mugged."

"It's almost enough to make you believe in fate."

"Not for me," Sarah said stoutly. "This fate crap is a way

of subjugating the masses. If you believe in fate, you don't struggle, and the fat cats walk away with it all. This mugging has nothing at all to do with her moving out. Besides, to believe in fate, you have to believe in some kind of supernatural deity, and I don't and never will. We can always make a difference, but we have to work at it."

Wendy hugged her. "Don't ever change," she laughed affectionately. "You're so strong and wonderful."

"Only on the surface." Sarah answered.

On leave from her job, she steadily worked away on her doctorate, and despite her continuing grief for Hal, she projected a stable, wholesome face to her children and the world. But alone at night in her narrow bed, she still mourned her loss.

Her father was not quite as bad as in the past. Having grandchildren around had mellowed him somewhat. Still, it had not been easy for her to return to the status of a child, and he was cranky and opinionated and accustomed to subservience. But living there while she finished her degree was the only way to eventually gain her independence.

It was not hard to wait now. It had been five years of hard work, and the sacrifice of her freedom, but soon it would be over. In June she'd be thirty-eight, have her doctorate, and get a college teaching job. She'd be able to support her family alone.

She'd really stayed more for the children than for herself. She could not have provided them with a beautiful home in a safe neighborhood, braces, summer camps, riding lessons at Claremont Stables, and the private schools that her father gladly paid for. She hoped that he would be decent enough to still help them after she left.

When they reached the hospital, they found that Robert had already phoned, and Arla had been moved to a private room on the second floor. "How bad?" Sarah asked the nurse on duty.

"Arm broken, nose broken, they kicked in a couple of her ribs. You just can't live in New York anymore. They're getting so aggressive there's no stopping them. Thanks to Martin Luther King. He pays them to demonstrate and attack white people."

Wendy's eyes flashed with anger. "How do you know the mugger was black?"

"Oh, please." The nurse's voice was weary. "What else? We get the victims all day long."

"We should try to get her fired," Sarah whispered indignantly.

"She'd probably be replaced by a clone. This is the kind of awful slander Maurice always has to face."

Charlotte and Marshall met them in the hall, and they walked to the room together. Arla was sedated but awake. Her face was terribly battered.

"Are you in pain?" Sarah asked.

"I want to die."

"After the way we worked to clean up that apartment!" Charlotte joked.

"I want to die. I want to kill myself."

"But first tell us what happened," Charlotte said, trying to be funny, "so we didn't make the trip downtown for nothing. Where were you? In the subway?"

"No, in the hall, taking out the key to my apartment."

"Did you see the attacker?"

Tears slid down her battered face. "It was Lenny. He was waiting for me and threw me down the stairs. I don't know how he did it, but he found me right away. I'll never be free."

"That bastard. But you can't give up now," Sarah said.

Arla was inconsolable. "But I am giving up. You don't understand. None of you. You've never been beaten. Once you are, you never feel the same. It makes you hate yourself. And you're always afraid. Once it happens you're different, and you can never go back again. I'm always afraid." She lay there trembling. "And there's something else. Mark called me yesterday from California. Stewart's in jail for drugs."

"At least he had the good taste to be arrested far from home," Charlotte quipped. "I think Teddy's dealing in Central Park."

"We're not certain of that," Marshall reproved her gently.

Sarah cast about wildly for the right words. "Prisoners

recover from torture. My father used to beat my brother, and he even hit me a couple of times."

"But Hal erased the bad memories for you, didn't he? I watched you together. Envying you. He made everything all right. But I've been hit all my life with no one to heal the wounds. Lenny's no different from my pa or any of the men I've known."

"My mother would have shot him," Wendy said. "*There* was a woman with guts."

Then, restless because she couldn't smoke, she turned the television back on. All of them stared at it in shock.

"It's Lenny," Arla gasped. "Look! In handcuffs with the police. Do you think Peter turned him in? If he was arrested because of me he'll kill me."

"That would spare you from committing suicide." Charlotte was still trying to cheer her up with humor.

But that wasn't why he was under arrest. One of the multifamily houses that Lenny owned had burned down the night before, killing eight people; four adults and four children. About twenty people had escaped from the three-story wooden building. Although it was believed that the fire was sparked by a cigarette or ash in an easy chair in a third-floor apartment, he had been charged with three counts each of second-degree reckless endangerment and of violating a law requiring smoke detectors in dwellings—both misdemeanors.

The newscaster continued, "Although he claims that smoke detectors had been installed, police, survivors, and investigators have found no evidence of detectors. Bail has been set for him at $25,000."

"He'll be released in fifteen minutes," Arla said despondently. "He has friends in high places. But *I* know he never put those smoke detectors in."

"He didn't?" they chorused.

"He never does. He's such a miser. He cheats on all the building codes, and then just pays people off."

Marshall smiled at her. "You don't have to die, my dear. Your life is just beginning. I have the distinct sensation that your troubles have come to an end."

Wendy looked at Marshall. He sat beside Arla holding

her uninjured hand, his eyes radiating kindness, warmth, compassion. She liked the informal way he was dressed in a suede jacket and open-necked cashmere sweater that made him look younger, more relaxed, boyish somehow.

And attractive! Yes, attractive. How strange! She'd known him for fifteen years, and this was the first moment that she'd ever perceived him as an attractive male. He wore well.

She liked the way he always took charge, just the way he had with Maurice, never asking Robert's question, "Why do *I* have to get involved with my wife's friends?" Marshall always accepted his responsiblity to the outside world without hesitation. He probably would have preferred to be practicing the piano tonight, but here he was. He was a fine man, and it was a shame that Charlotte didn't just leave him alone with his music. He deserved to do whatever made him happy.

But Charlotte wasn't happy either. She'd only really been happy for the short time after Marshall proposed. Wendy thought of Charlotte's ecstatic letters to Mexico when she'd first started to see him. She'd thought she would live happily ever after, but as soon as she had him he had lost value for her. That was the way she was about most things. Always unsatisfied! She looked more beautiful and well dressed each year, but that was only cosmetic. Inside, she was still an emotional mess. Perhaps she would never really understand how fortunate she'd been in her choice of husband.

When Marshall had finished listening to Arla's story about the smoke detectors, he seemed pleased. "I'll go and have a talk with Lenny tomorrow morning. I don't want him as a client any longer, and I think I'll be able to make him see reason about a divorce. It seems to me that he has enough problems without antagonizing you and turning you into a witness for the city."

He permitted himself a little smile. "Yes, I'm sure he'll see that it's in his own best interest."

"But you're going to have to fight for yourself, too," Sarah said. "You're going to have to go into court and talk about how he treats you and get a decent divorce settlement.

Promise you won't let him walk all over you. What good is it to get a divorce if it leaves you impoverished?"

"I promise," she said weakly. She lay there exhausted, still frightened and not believing, but her three friends threw their arms around Marshall, exuberant with joy. After so many terrible years, Arla was finally free.

PART THREE

Coming Apart

CHAPTER
Forty-Two

In August of 1961, Sarah went with a group of other activists to Monroe, North Carolina, to picket the courthouse with the Freedom Riders. It was a nightmare. They were spat on and physically attacked, and she was afraid every moment that she was there.

White mobs, encouraged by the police, indiscriminately beat the picketers, all the while yelling, "Nigger go home!" "Nigger lover!" and "Kill the nigger!" Ed Bromberg, another Freedom Rider from New York, was struck by a pellet from a high-powered pump air gun while picketing. He fell and Sarah knelt to help him.

Suddenly she was surrounded by three menacing white men. "Bet she sleeps with a nigger," one said. She began to hyperventilate. They had to get Ed to a hospital. Then she saw Maurice.

"Hang on," he said, fiercely pushing aside one of the men. Delighted with this provocation, one of the others turned, raised his gun, and violently brought the butt down hard on Maurice's forehead. She stood there screaming as blood came gushing out like a volcano, running down his face and into his eyes. Instantly, the police stepped forward to arrest Maurice, pushing him into a squad car and speeding off to the police station. It was like the scene in Mexico, all over again.

As soon as the ambulance came for Ed, she and another man from New York grabbed a cab to the police station where they were also arrested. "Arrested?" Sarah said angrily. "We came here to look for a friend."

"Nobody invited you here to upset the town," the policeman answered.

There was no sign of Maurice. She frantically kept swiveling her head around, trying to catch sight of him, when she saw the local FBI man who had been making notes but not doing much more walk over to the police chief, look at her, and say a few words.

"You're free to leave," the police chief spat at her, "but I want you out of Monroe this afternoon. He says you're a judge's daughter. A judge's daughter, mixed up with this scum!"

"I insist on seeing the man whose head was just split open."

"You are not in a position to insist on anything. Show this nigger-lover out." Two policemen took her forcibly by the arms and dragged her outside the police station. She took the next bus home, filled with disgust for the human race, struggling against despair.

Claude and her father were waiting for her when she dragged herself into the apartment. Her father's voice was icy. "Just a minute. I want to talk to you. The children are asleep. Look at you. Dirty. Disheveled. A disgrace to this family."

"A disgrace! You should be proud of me. You know what those poor people down there want? They want a place to swim in to escape that rotten southern heat. That's what they want! They wanted to swim in the public pool. And for that they're getting their heads broken."

She burst into tears, thinking about Maurice.

"Kindly spare us the melodrama. I can't bear hysterical females. You have no right to endanger yourself this way. It's bad enough that your children have no father. And in addition, a mother who's an unwholesome influence on them! You're a terrible mother! More concerned about strangers than your own children!"

"That does it! I'm moving out! I'll find an apartment this week. I'll have my degree in June, and it's time to lead my own life."

"You're free to leave anytime you like. But you're not exposing my grandchildren to your way of life."

"They're my children. You have no rights. No rights at all."

"We'll just see about that. The discussion is ended."

"Can he do that, Claude?" Claude shrugged without answering, and she felt menaced as she remembered that her father was a powerful man with powerful friends.

After checking on the children, despite her exhaustion, she went to see Wendy. Charlotte was there too. Sarah explained the situation, and Wendy immediately telegraphed bail to Monroe for Maurice and members of the New York delegation. "What about bail for the others?" she asked.

"I don't think they'll come. When they dragged me out I heard the women yelling, 'No bail. Everybody on hunger strike.' They want to dramatize the issue."

Wendy was terribly worried about Maurice. "I should have been there. Next time I'll go with you."

"You know you won't go," Charlotte said. "There are no private bathrooms or maids. You don't have the right clothes for a picket line."

"Oh, very funny! You'll see. I want to do something more than give Maurice checks. I want to put my body on the line."

"That may be the one place it hasn't been," Charlotte teased.

Sarah's search for an apartment was interrupted by a seventieth birthday party and fund raiser for her father, held at the Plaza that Saturday night to benefit the Museum of the City of New York. Her father's colleagues, major dignitaries from the cultural world, and the most important officials in state and city government, joined together to honor him. Everybody who was part of the machinery of power was to be there. Sarah's friends had taken a table, and even Robert had come.

All of the judge's family were seated on the dais except for Maggie, who was only five years old. Jimmy, now fifteen, listened with rapt admiration and complete agreement to the wonderful things said about his grandfather in speech after speech. The way he looked and listened made Sarah even more anxious to move out.

She looked out at the assemblage, which included so many people she hated—Judge Kaufman and Irving Saypol because of the Rosenbergs, Roy Cohn and G. David Schine because of McCarthy. Who would guess that Judge Stern's daughter, seated up here in a magnificent dress from Martha's, was a penniless radical?

She felt concern about the children. How would they feel about moving? They had their schools, their friends, and their routines. And she had to admit that living with her parents wasn't destructive to them. It was only destructive to her.

When the ceremonies were over, among the crowd at the dais congratulating her father, she noticed a handsome, well-dressed dark-haired man who moved with the grace of a panther, automatically creating an air of self-confidence and success. Who was he? Well, what difference would it make? A man that attractive undoubtedly had a wife and children.

He said a few words to the judge, then looked at her. "Would you like to dance?" His smile dazzled her.

"Yes." Why had he asked her?

She stepped off the dais and moved into his arms. His skill at dancing was as polished as his appearance—sure, competent, completely in command. His name was Jerry Lasker, and he was in the investment business.

It had been a long time. She was ready for romance.

"Is there a Mr. Gordon?" he asked.

"I'm a widow."

His brown eyes looked into hers compassionately. "I'm a widower. That's why I've just moved here from L.A. Memories you know."

"Oh, yes, I know. Any children?"

He shook his head. "The tragedy of my life. I've always wanted children. Your son appears to be an exceptionally well-poised boy."

"He is. And much more than that. I have a little girl, too."

"Does she look like you?"

"Much prettier."

"That doesn't seem possible." Confused, she didn't answer. She never quite knew how to deal with people who said this kind of thing. Both she and Hal had lacked easy charm. In fact, they'd equated charm with lying. Their outlook on life required that they speak simply and sincerely and that they tell the truth.

Jerry tightened his arms around her, and despite her wariness, she felt aroused for the first time in years. "When can I see you again?" His lips brushed her ear.

"I don't know. You'll have to call me. I live with my folks."

"Then we'll go to my place." His voice was sure and sexy. "I just moved into the Dakota. I haven't had time to furnish it yet, but I do have a king-size bed."

"You'll have to call," she said, running to her friends for safety. He followed her, pulled up a chair, and joined them.

He sat with them for the rest of the evening, his arm around Sarah's chair. "Staking a claim," Charlotte whispered to Wendy.

Charlotte phoned her as soon as they got home. "What an attractive man," she said, looking apathetically at Marshall sleeping beside her. "Do you like him?"

"I don't know anything about him. He may not even call me."

"Please don't reject him just because he's well dressed," Charlotte teased her. "Even the Politburo wears suits nowadays."

"What did you think of him?" she asked Wendy, when she called.

"Sexy!"

"What else?"

"That's as far as I got. Robert says he's with a good firm, and according to the *Wall Street Journal*, he has a high rate of investment success."

"Then I'm not interested. He's probably a Republican."

Wendy laughed. "Then why not hold out for what you want?"

"Nobody else has asked me to dance in years."

"Then go with it and see what happens. It's all right to sleep with Republicans. Really, you can't tell the difference in bed. You don't have to marry him. Just have a little affair."

"I don't know. It's not easy living here. My mother still waits up."

"Be brave. Think of it like vitamin pills. It's essential for good hair and nails."

"He probably won't call, anyway."

"See him if he does. After all, you have nothing to lose. It will make you feel alive again."

CHAPTER
Forty-Three

Jerry called Sarah three times before she agreed to see him. But he was persistent. "Would you like to go to Lutèce?" he asked, when she finally agreed.

"Thank you, no. I don't believe in spending so much money on food with a world full of hungry people. But anyway, my friend Wendy is having a few people to dinner. You might enjoy that."

"Afraid to be alone with me?"

"Certainly not," she lied.

He chuckled as though he could see right through her, and they made arrangements for him to pick her up.

It was a charmed evening, with everyone on best behavior, but beneath the surface friendliness certain fires were burning. Charlotte agonized at the contrast between Marshall and Jerry. She gazed at Jerry and saw a young, handsome, successful, and dynamic romantic figure, beside whom Marshall looked old. How could Sarah, who didn't give a rap about appearance, attract someone like that? What did he see in her? She was dressed in some kind of impossible polyester dress, wore no makeup, only went to a beauty parlor when her hair needed cutting and the rest of the time simply washed it and let it dry naturally, and wore not one piece of jewelry. How was it possible?

Wendy was also concerned about him. He was just too good to be true. He reminded her of a maitre d' at her hotel who was also excessively suave and charming and accommodating. He'd turned out to be a wife murderer who'd escaped from a prison in Italy and made his way to the island. It made her worry. She watched him anxiously throughout the evening.

But she did not tell Sarah. It seemed illogical to be concerned because Jerry reminded her of a maitre d'. How could she spoil Sarah's fun? She had not seen her so happy since the early days with Hal.

During the weeks that followed, they were out every night at parties, concerts, benefits, nightclubs. He took her to the Rainbow Room and the Empire Room, to hear Lenny Bruce for the first time at Basin Street East, to the Gaslight on MacDougal Street to hear Mississippi John Hurt. He moved in a crowd of interesting and sophisticated people, other upwardly mobile hustlers who had followed the beacon of success to New York. One night, after they had been seeing each other for a few months, he took her home with him to the Dakota. "You're staying with me tonight," he said firmly.

Instantly, she became flustered. "I don't know if I should. The children. My parents. I'm afraid they'll worry."

"I don't think they're waiting up, and if they are, they shouldn't be. You're a big girl now."

As soon as they entered his apartment she became agitated. He handed her a drink.

"I don't drink."

"Maybe you should. Go ahead. Drink it down and then have another."

He saw that her hands were trembling. "Cigarette?" he asked.

"Maybe I should. I've stopped smoking but I'm very nervous."

"Why are you nervous?"

"It's been such a long time."

He knelt on the floor at her feet. "It's been a long time for me, too. I'm also nervous."

He'd said exactly the right thing. "I never thought of that," she said.

"Think of it," he said, taking off her shoes.

After that, it was easy. Suddenly they were comfortable with each other for the first time. He took her hand and led her through the empty, cavernous rooms to his bedroom, where they hurriedly threw off their clothes.

She was frantic to know again the wonder of making love. She would not let the happiness of the past destroy any present or future happiness. She could feel his tongue inside her mouth and the lovely texture of a mouth. She had never thought she could make love to anyone again, but now she reached for him, holding him, stroking him, and finally pulling him inside her with an urgency that was close to desperation. She felt as if she were drowning, as if she were exorcizing memory.

And later, when he fell into an exhausted sleep beside her, she lay there looking at him and feeling good. Hal would have wanted me to try again, she told herself. He would have wanted me to be happy.

The next morning Jerry asked her to marry him. "Think your folks would furnish this barn for a wedding present?" he joked.

"I don't see why not. I'd rather that they give it to me now than later."

After breakfast, they walked hand in hand along Central Park West to break the news to the judge. "Your grandchildren will only be three blocks away from you," Jerry told him. He was smart all right. It was the perfect thing to say.

Her parents were delighted. This would make up for the last time. "What would you like for a wedding present?" the judge asked, more expansive than she had ever seen him.

"Could you help us to furnish the apartment, sir?" Sarah looked at the two of them in amusement. Hal had never said "sir" to anyone in his life.

"Glad to do so. I want the best for my grandchildren. You two get busy and send the bills to me."

Charlotte rocked with laughter when Sarah told her about it. "Your father is going to be very surprised. He hasn't furnished an apartment for fifty years. Just wait until he finds that it now costs a minimum of ten thousand dollars a room."

"I don't think he cares. At last I've done him proud."

"So how is sex?"
"It's all right."
"As good as with Hal?"
"Of course not. But we were young."

Sarah's parents invited three hundred guests to the Pierre. It was a perfect wedding, from the flowers to the guests, and when Jerry finally smashed the glass under his heel, her mother sighed with relief.

"At last you did the right thing," she said, embracing her daughter. "You made me happy."

CHAPTER Forty-Four

Unable to dislodge Teddy from his bedroom, and concerned because of the long hours that Kitty spent in there with him, Charlotte decided to send her away to boarding school when she was fifteen. "Please don't make me go, Mommy," she begged. "I like being here with all of you. I'll miss Teddy."

"That's precisely the point. Don't even bother to argue. I wish somebody had sent me to an expensive boarding school when I was a girl."

Kitty started to sniffle, and Charlotte irritably averted her eyes to hide her dismay at Kitty's appearance. She had not turned out pretty. There just was no way to predict how genes would work together. In Kitty's case, they hadn't worked, they'd battled. All of Charlotte's and Marshall's worst features had been combined. Her thin hair was a nondescript brown, her skin was pasty white and invariably broken out, and her neck always looked dirty. She dressed only in jeans. She was a slob.

How could that be possible? Nobody could be more meticulous than Charlotte, and yet her daughter looked dirty. She'd also inherited Marshall's bad eyes, and she peered at Charlotte now through her thick glasses, looking like an unappealing fish. Much as she loved her, the sight upset her. Another example of her bad luck!

There was Sarah, barely average looking, and Hal who had been below average in that department, and they'd produced an adorable girl, a cheerful, happy, sparkling rosy-cheeked child who was popular and smart as well as pretty.

It was enough to make her feel like Job.

She had come to Manhattan with one dress and no money but had always looked fresh and neat and pressed. Under the worst circumstances she'd done her best.

But Kitty had the best of everything from the day she was born. Her bedroom had thick carpets, a mirrored private bathroom, recessed lighting, a color television and Fisher stereo, and a white-lace four-poster bed. It had been photographed in color for *House Beautiful* with the caption, "For a Fairy-Tale Princess." She'd had fine clothes, private lessons, travel, prestige, the best schools, and two magnificent homes. But none of it showed. Expression had a lot to do with it. How could Kitty look pretty if she sat there gnawing on a nail with a hang-dog expression? Why did she always look so unhappy?

She should be grateful, she supposed, that Kitty was so very obedient and hard-working and always did well at school. But any honest mother would admit that intelligence was not enough. Girls had to be pretty. That was another reason why she wanted her to go away to school. Perhaps she could come back "finished," wearing sparkling white gloves and a cheery stewardess smile. Perhaps she would straighten out once she was away from Teddy's pernicious influence. He was enough to depress anyone.

Kitty sat there dabbing at her face with a grimy tissue. Charlotte tried to encourage her. "This is a wonderful school. Every student comes from a good family. You'll be able to ride every day and improve your tennis and find your first boyfriend there. You'll love it there."

"Do I have a choice, Mommy?"

"No."

"All right. Then I'll go."

Wendy took all of them to the 21 Club for a farewell luncheon, and the sorority showered Kitty with gifts. She took the gifts politely and kissed each of the group good-bye, but her eyes lacked any enthusiasm for her future.

The initial reports Charlotte received from the school were satisfactory, and she was certain that she'd made the right decision until, in the spring of 1962, just after Kitty had turned sixteen, the school's director phoned. A serious problem had arisen. He had to speak to Kitty's parents, but Marshall had a full schedule that day. Arla was working, and Sarah was in Las Vegas with Jerry. She'd written that she hated it there, but Jerry liked to gamble. She'd already read ten books sitting at the hotel pool.

Wendy was glad to go with Charlotte. "That's what our sorority is all about." Her chauffeur picked Charlotte up, and they drove the hour and a half up the Taconic Parkway to investigate the problem. It was a magnificent spring day, the first green covering the rolling fields, and the first forsythia dotting the hills.

Charlotte was too filled with anxiety to appreciate nature. "At ten thousand dollars a year," she said, her stomach churning with worry, "wouldn't you think they'd be able to take care of problems without bothering the parents?"

When she reached the director's office, she found out why they couldn't. Kitty was pregnant. "Don't you watch over these kids?" she scolded, close to tears.

"We can't be in bed with them," the headmaster said mildly. "You'll have to take her home with you. She's waiting in her room."

Kitty was cowering on her bed when they entered, bedraggled and pathetic in ragged jeans and an old toggle coat. Her hair hung limp and lank to her waist, and her bony shoulders were hunched over. "Is this true?" Charlotte demanded.

Instead of answering, Kitty began to sob noisily. Charlotte also began to cry. "How could you? How could you do this to me? All your life I've given you the best, and now this is my reward."

"Let's not waste time with that," Wendy said. "That poor child feels bad enough already. Come outside for a minute. I have to talk to you."

She pulled Charlotte out of the room and closed Kitty's door behind them. All of her memories of Paula came flooding back, and she was determined to minimize this terrible experience for Kitty.

She put her arms around Charlotte. "Be gentle," she said. "She feels bad enough already. It could be worse. Let's just get out of here."

Her chauffeur loaded the car with Kitty's possessions and headed for New York. Wendy opened her bar and poured brandy for the three of them. "I'm afraid I'll throw up," Kitty said.

"You won't. Just try it."

They sipped the brandy and settled back. "Please forgive me, Mommy," Kitty pleaded.

Charlotte again burst into tears. Then she put her arm around her unfortunate, pathetic daughter, and they cried together.

After they had calmed down, Wendy told them the story of Paula. Before this, she had shared it only with Maurice and Sarah. But this was the time to do it in order to help Kitty.

"You don't have to worry, Aunt Wendy. I wouldn't do anything like your sister. I'd like to have the baby."

"You must be out of your mind," Charlotte said. "It's not like getting a puppy or a goldfish. What would we do with a baby?"

"I'd take it," Wendy said quickly.

"Oh, no," Kitty said. "You could visit and play with it, Aunt Wendy, but I want to keep it for myself. I'd keep it in my room."

"For God's sake," Charlotte snapped, "you have absolutely no conception of what it means to take care of a baby. And what about your education? And what about your future husband?"

"If he loved me, he'd have to love my baby."

"You are out of your mind. No man wants someone else's bastard." Kitty winced. "You will have to have an abortion."

"Where? It's illegal, Mommy. And I think it hurts."

"Nevertheless, people have them all the time. Wendy, you'll have to ask Robert to get her admitted somewhere for a D and C. I'm sure he'd certify that she's in no mental condition to have a baby."

"He's not that kind of doctor."

"Then ask him to get a favor from a psychiatrist friend."

"Is this what you want, Kitty?" Wendy asked.

"No. I told you that I want to keep it in my room. But if Mommy doesn't want me to, then I guess I can't."

It's strange, Wendy thought. She's like Marshall in her docility. The only person in that family with any strength is Charlotte, but it's the wrong kind of strength. The wrong kind of strength produces weak people. The right kind of strength, like Sarah's, produces winners.

She dropped them at their home, promising to phone that night with the information. Charlotte, determined to present her habitually confident surface, greeted the doorman with a smile.

"Home from school already, Miss Kitty?" he asked.

"Just for a little visit." Her smile was as cheery as Charlotte's.

But the moment they were out of the elevator, Kitty began to cry again. Immediately after entering the apartment she went scuttling to Teddy's room, and both of them came out a moment later, his arm around her. His hair was almost as long as Kitty's, and the sight of the two of them nauseated her.

"Why are you making her have an abortion?"

"This has nothing to do with you. Get back to your pigsty."

"Fuck off. I'm not leaving her alone with you."

Now the servants had appeared and were watching. "Go into the library, both of you," Charlotte ordered. They followed her inside, and she closed the heavy, soundproof door. They sat down on the beautiful, antique leather couch and lit a joint.

She looked at them and felt as if her heart were breaking. Why had she always been fated to live with enemies? First her mother and now her children! And where was Marshall now that she needed him? Why did she always have to face these things alone?

"Why are you making her have an abortion?" Teddy repeated.

"There is no other solution, unless of course, she wants

to marry the boy, although I don't know of anyone from a good family who gets married that young. Is he at least from a good family?"

"I'm not sure, Mommy, exactly who it is. And I wouldn't want to marry either of them. Marcus is a recovering autistic, and Kim is a kleptomaniac."

Charlotte looked at her in genuine bewilderment. "You mean that at the age of sixteen you slept with more than one? Why?"

"For fun, Mommy."

For fun? Again she had the feeling she had always had with Wendy and Sarah. They had found something in sex that she'd never known. And so had her daughter!

Just then Marshall came in, and Kitty ran to him. "Sorry I couldn't come with Mother to get you," he said, "but it's wonderful to see you, darling. Now why don't you tell me all about it?" He sat down, and Kitty flung herself on his lap, as if she were a child, wrapped her arms around his neck, and told him her story.

"I thought it would be nice to have the baby, Daddy, but Mommy wants me to have an abortion. What do you think?"

"Does the father want to marry you?"

"We've been through that," Charlotte snapped. "To begin with, sixteen-year-olds are not fit parents. In addition, she's made a specialty of sleeping with undesirables. I cannot let her ruin her life."

"What do you think, Daddy?"

"I think your mother is right. You wouldn't want to be saddled with a baby. When you go to college, you'll meet a fine young man to marry, and then you and he will have your own children. By then, you'll have forgotten completely about this experience."

Teddy snorted with laughter. "Oh, sure. Let's sweep everything under the rug as usual."

"I tell you what," Marshall said, trying to raise their spirits. "Why don't we all get dressed up and go out to the Auto Pub for dinner."

Teddy hooted again. "For God's sake, Dad, look at us. We're not children any longer."

"Very well. We can go anywhere you like. It's just that you used to enjoy that restaurant so much."

"I'm not going anywhere with him with that hair," Charlotte exclaimed.

"I'd like to go out, Teddy," Kitty said. "Could you pull it back into a ponytail? Or maybe let me trim it a little?"

"All right. I'll do it for you. I wouldn't do anything for her."

How sharper than a serpent's tooth is a thankless child, Charlotte told herself. Even if the child is a little bastard.

CHAPTER
Forty-Five

Robert located a gynecologist who performed abortions. His office was on Park and Sixty-ninth Street. "How do they get away with it?" Charlotte asked Wendy. "I wouldn't want a police raid in the middle of an operation."

"Robert says they're paying a fortune in kickbacks. He says you don't have to worry about a thing."

"Yes, I do. I have to worry about how much those kickbacks will cost us."

Because of Paula, Wendy spent as much time as possible with Kitty before the abortion and picked up the Bermans on the morning of the operation to give them emotional support.

Kitty clung to Teddy. "I want him with me."

"They'll think he's the husband," Charlotte said, "and I'm embarrassed enough already without that."

"Let him come," Wendy said, "if it makes her feel better. Who cares what he looks like in an abortionist's office."

Kitty and Teddy laughed uproariously at that. They always irritated Charlotte when she tried to deal logically with their drug-induced smirks and giggles. "They're stoned," she whispered to Wendy.

"Not a bad idea," Wendy whispered back.

They entered the doctor's office filled with apprehension

but were pleasantly surprised. Instead of the sleazy den they had expected, they found an elegant, well-lit room that was furnished in antiques. Charlotte examined the paintings. "Even great art," she noted. "Well why not, at these prices!"

The other patients were well dressed and seemed quite relaxed. Perhaps they were not all there for abortions. After all, he was a licensed gynecologist. The nurse also seemed quite proper.

"Will you step in here for a moment?" she asked Charlotte. "I'd like you to fill out some papers."

In the private office, she produced no papers but only held out her hand to Charlotte. Charlotte handed her an envelope with cash, and she proceeded to count the money as efficiently as a croupier. Then she said, "I'm afraid there's been some mistake. There's only eight hundred dollars here."

"That's the price I was quoted."

"I'm terribly sorry. The price has gone up three hundred dollars."

"In one day?"

The nurse waited patiently. A highwayman, Charlotte thought indignantly, but there was nothing she could do. She took out her wallet and emptied it. "I'm afraid I have only two hundred dollars. I never carry much cash. I could come back tomorrow, even this afternoon."

"We prefer that our patients do not return. We'll have to settle for this, but if you recommend a friend, do not tell them how much you paid."

She put the envelope into a drawer and locked it, then without embarrassment, she put the two hundred dollars into her pocket, not even bothering to conceal her actions.

I've been had, Charlotte realized. I should have said I had no cash at all with me. But she caught me off balance. This corrupt bloodsucker had counted on that. But I can't afford to make her angry. She might take it out on Kitty. "Will you use anesthesia?" she begged.

"Oh, yes! Certainly! We always do! Now don't you worry about a thing. Your daughter will have the best of care. Why don't you go back to the waiting room and just relax. Have some coffee and miniature Danish. They're excellent.

From Greenberg's. I think they make the best miniature Danish, don't you?"

"I usually can't afford them," Charlotte said pointedly, but the nurse ignored her.

Her face flushed with anger when she returned to the waiting room. "What was all of that about?" Wendy whispered.

"Tell you later."

Kitty was shaking. Charlotte put her arm around her and whispered, "The nurse promised me that you won't feel a thing."

"Oh, thank you, Mommy. But I'm still afraid."

They sat there for another hour. "This sucks," Teddy said. "Let's blow this joint. There must be others."

"Shuush!" Charlotte said. "Don't turn this into a problem. Either sit there and keep quiet or go home."

"Don't turn this into a problem?" Again, he and Kitty laughed uproariously and then proceeded to eat every last one of the pastries.

The nurse finally appeared and caroled, in that false, cheery stewardess manner, "Miss Berman. We're ready for you now." Kitty threw her arms around Teddy, then followed the nurse meekly, as a lamb to the slaughter.

Charlotte thought she'd go mad waiting. If only they wouldn't hurt her daughter. Half an hour later, the nurse led her out. "We're just fine," the nurse beamed. "Just take her home and put her to bed." Charlotte could have wept at how frail and damaged Kitty looked.

She tottered toward Teddy, and he put his arms around her. "Can you walk?" She nodded and they slowly inched out to Wendy's waiting car.

Teddy and the chauffeur handled her like fragile china. Once she was in the car, he asked, "Did they hurt you much?"

"Not much. Just a little." Charlotte held her hand and tried not to cry.

They found Sarah waiting for them at home. Teddy gently led Kitty to her bedroom, and the three friends sat down in the library to discuss what happened. Charlotte told them about the crooked nurse.

Wendy laughed. "What a scam!"

But Sarah was not amused. "They can get away with anything because abortions are illegal. What absolute nerve that the law should dictate what women do with their own bodies. Abortions should be legal. In Russia they are. In Sweden and Japan they are. The government has no right to control women's bodies. Some day soon it will be legal, and then these quacks won't be able to get rich on women's misery."

"I feel so awful," Charlotte said. "I insisted that she go away to school. What an abysmal record. One kid is mentally disturbed and the other is tarnished."

Her friends broke into healing laughter. "There's no such thing as tarnished anymore," Wendy said. "It's different from when we were girls. No man expects his wife to be a virgin. It's a whole new era."

"Well, it's not one I like."

"But it's one we all have to accept," Wendy said. "You'll survive. You always do."

CHAPTER
Forty-Six

Kitty did not want to go away to school again. In September she returned to Dalton, and whenever she was home, she remained closeted with Teddy in his room. Charlotte no longer felt comfortable in her home. It smelled like an opium den, and she always had the feeling that they were plotting against her behind her back. She was out at charity functions or with her friends as much as possible.

That December, shortly before the family was due to leave for Palm Beach, Marshall came into the study to speak to her. "I'm afraid you're in for a bit of bad news, my dear," he said hesitantly.

"Teddy?"

"It's not Teddy. I'm afraid it's me. That is, it's my business. I have to sue for bankruptcy."

"Bankruptcy? What are you talking about? I thought everything was going all right." Concerned about his agency, Marshall had recently begun to devote himself to it again with the old energy and singlemindedness that had made it so successful.

"I wasn't giving you false hopes. I did think I could easily repair the damages, but it's never wise to be an absentee landlord. My major account supervisors have gone elsewhere and taken my accounts with them. My personal and professional debts are staggering."

She felt numb. "It just doesn't seem possible. What are we going to do?"

"We'll all have to pull together and make some radical adjustments. Fortunately we own our homes, but the servants will have to go. It breaks my heart to do this to them. We've been together for twenty years."

"To them? What about me? How can I run our homes alone? They're too large for even one servant."

"Everybody will have to help. But we'll manage. Maybe Teddy could vacuum."

"Fat chance of that. The only way I've been able to keep his room livable is to have a team of workers go in there to fumigate once a week."

"He'll have to clean it himself now or it will stay dirty. I've canceled Palm Beach, and I'm afraid there will be no Christmas gifts this year, except to the building staff. And no further charitable contributions. I feel especially bad about that. And it's evident that I'll have to forget about the concert for the foreseeable future."

That's just about the only compensation, she thought ironically. "Didn't I warn you to pay more attention to your work and less to your music? How could you let this happen. You've failed your family! I will never forgive you for this, Marshall. Never!"

"There's nothing you can say to me, my dear, that's as bad as the things I've been saying to myself. But let's hang on and try to look on the bright side. This is only a temporary setback for us. I've always made lots of money, all my life. From the day I got out of college! And I will again. Just be a little patient, and we'll get through this dry period."

"Why didn't you tell me before? Did it just happen this morning?"

"No. Of course it didn't. But I wanted to spare you. If things had straightened out, you need never have known. I'm only telling you now because there's no further way to avoid it. For the moment, we're out of money. You cannot charge even a ten-dollar purchase on a credit card. But I promise to pull us out of this."

With a wail of despair, bumping into furniture, totally hysterical, she ran out of the room and slammed the door behind her. I don't want to think, she told herself. I simply cannot deal with it right now. Reaching into the medicine chest she took two sleeping pills to knock herself out and immediately sank into blessed oblivion.

She began to fall apart. For the next few months, refusing to see or even talk to her friends, she lay in bed brooding. Why should she see them? Their ordered lives and continuing affluence stabbed at her like banderillas to a bull. Sarah and Wendy had started life rich, and they still were rich. It wasn't fair.

Everything had turned out wrong. Marshall had been a lifeline to her when he proposed, but that line had frayed. She'd bet on the wrong horse. Now she understood that she'd never really had a chance. Everything in life was connected, predetermined, and it was her mother's fault that she'd had to marry the first man who asked her. How her mother would laugh now at the way her life had worked out. It wasn't fair! She had married a rich man, not a poor one. Why else would she have put up with Teddy?

She no longer cared about how the apartment looked or how she looked. She'd done enough housework as a girl. Her family tiptoed around her, and she did not answer when they spoke to her. Day after day she brooded over the disaster of her life. Life had mocked at all of her efforts! After seventeen years, she was almost back to square one. There was no point in trying.

Kitty spent her days at school, and Teddy roamed aimlessly around Central Park looking for drugs. Each morning Marshall cleaned up the kitchen, then went to look for a job. But all of the friends and acquaintances who had been so cordial when he was on top now fled from the contagion of failure. Each night when he returned he was more quiet. If he didn't get a job soon, they would have to begin to sell some of their precious art, the collection that she had painstakingly acquired with so much love, research, and energy. She couldn't even bear to think about that.

When the house phone rang one day, it took her a moment to remember that she had to answer it herself. Moving heavily, like an old woman, she walked into the kitchen. It couldn't be anything important. Nothing important happened to them any longer. Since she had stopped entertaining and resigned from all of those presidencies and committees that required large charitable contributions as the main requisite for leadership, all of the friends she'd made in that capacity had drifted away. And she'd stopped going to meetings of the Adams trustees, afraid of bumping into a sorority girl who might gloat at her downfall.

The phone buzzed insistently again, and indifferently she picked it up. The doorman announced: "A man here to see you, madam. From a detective agency."

Detective agency! Teddy! It figured, but she didn't give a damn. No point in worrying about public appearances any longer. There were no public appearances. And as usual Marshall was not here when she needed him, and all of the family problems were dumped on her shoulders. "Very well," she sighed. "Show him up."

She braced herself for the kind of hard, tough, sleazy private eye of a detective novel, but the man who was shown in was ordinary-looking and middle-aged, dressed in a navy blue suit. He carried a briefcase.

"Sterling Detective Agency," he said, holding out his card.

"My husband is out right now."

"It's not your husband we want to see. It's you! Was your maiden name Charlotte Lewin?"

She nodded, and her stomach tightened. So it wasn't Teddy for once. It was that other albatross, her mother. She'd finally tracked her down. Well one thing was certain. Whatever her mother wanted, she'd waited too long. Charlotte had nothing to give her.

"I'm sorry to report," the detective continued, "that your mother passed away last September. We've been looking for you ever since." He held out an envelope and a receipt for her to sign.

"This is a letter from her attorney. My part of the job's finished now. Good day, ma'am."

"Good day," she said. She turned the letter in her hands, for a moment feeling the old terror and fear. Then, forcing herself to be rational, she opened the letter with shaking hands, read it through, and phoned the attorney.

She listened to him, almost as shocked as she had been by Marshall's announcement of bankruptcy, as he told her about the will. Everything had been left to her. The house had been sold by the attorney, as her mother had requested before dying, and in addition, there was a life insurance policy. "It comes to quite a tidy sum," the lawyer said.

"Might I have some idea of how much?"

"Something around five hundred thousand dollars." She gasped audibly. "Of course, it will take a while to get it. The will must be probated."

"Can I get some of it now? We need money!"

"I'm afraid not. But you can easily borrow against it. I'm affiliated with the Greenpoint Saving Bank. I'll send you the name of someone there who can help. You shouldn't have any difficulty."

She'd been saved. As unbelievable as it was, this detective had come, and she'd been saved. She could feel life and energy flowing through her again. Dancing with joy, she hurried into the shower and washed her hair, standing under the healing rush of water for a long time and remembering the shower long ago in Wendy's apartment, when she'd shucked off her old skin. Maybe she wasn't so unlucky after all. She was a phoenix. Still bewildered by her sudden change of fortune, she scrubbed the kitchen floor and made herself a cheese sandwich and a cup of tea. After that she phoned Sarah.

Sarah was thrilled to hear from her. "Welcome back to the land of the living. We've missed you. Are you all right?"

"My mother died. She left me a lot of money."

"Oh, you poor thing. I'm so sorry. I'll come right over."

"No, please don't. This apartment is filthy. I don't want anyone to see it until I clean up. I have to call a cleaning service."

"You know I don't care about the apartment. I wanted to comfort you. I know how bad you must feel."

"No, you really don't. See you tomorrow."

She didn't feel bereaved. For years, she hadn't thought about her mother at all. She'd wept when Edita died, but she didn't shed one tear for her mother. Her mother had almost wrecked her life. The money was one way of making amends.

She phoned Wendy next, and Wendy was delighted for her. "Now," she said, "you'll be able to help Marshall till he gets on his feet again. I'm happy for all of you."

Help Marshall? Help Marshall how? Wendy's words made her uneasy. Marshall had gone through his fortune and mismanaged everything. She had no intention of letting him do it again. It was her money, not his.

What would she do if he said something like, "All through our marriage I've shared everything I had with you. Now you can do the same." He would find that he had quite a shock in store for him. She had no further interest in a penniless failure with a disturbed son. She would ask for a divorce, and he and Teddy could move out. She and Kitty would stay here.

At last she would be able to realize herself. She would go to art school for a few years and open a gallery. It was too late for her to become a great creative artist, and perhaps she had never been exceptionally talented. That dream was gone! But she did have a marvelous eye, and many people needed help with selecting good art. She knew with unshakable certainty that she could make a success of a gallery.

She was sitting with the opened bottle of champagne beside her when Marshall got home. He looked old, worn, and almost defeated. "Any luck?" she asked.

"Nothing definite, but some very encouraging leads." Then he noted with alarm the bottle of champagne. "I hope you're not going to begin to drink. I know how frustrating life is for you right now. You have too much time on your hands now that you're no longer active on your committees."

"I'm not turning into a lush. You should know that I don't drink. I'm celebrating. Have a glass of champagne."

He furrowed his brow in concern. Had she cracked? "What exactly are you celebrating?"

"A detective visited me today to tell me my mother had died." He looked at her with increased concern.

"Died? But you told me you were an orphan when we got married."

"Psychologically I was. I hated my mother. She was a vicious, evil monster. The worst person I've ever known. After I left home I was determined to put her completely out of my mind."

"But you could have told me. I would have helped you to deal with her."

"That's why I didn't tell you. I was afraid that with your usual misguided kindness you might insist that I see her."

He looked at her soberly. "I don't know if kindness is ever misguided. Everybody's fighting a battle, just to survive. You must feel very guilty. So many years without even a phone call!"

"I don't feel guilty. If I did, I wouldn't be celebrating with champagne. I feel jubilant, ecstatic, triumphant. I now possess half a million dollars. I'm rich."

He put his arms around her and kissed her. "That's absolutely wonderful. Now you'll be able to do some of the things you've always wanted to do."

She looked at him, taken aback. This was nothing like the scenario she had imagined. "What about you?" she asked. "Don't you want some of it?"

"Certainly not, so please don't press it on me. I know that I'd be called old-fashioned, but I've never yet taken money from a woman, and I don't intend to start. That's your money, for you, for the children if you like. But for me to take your money would be the last coffin nail. I'm not finished yet. I'll get a good job. You'll see."

She looked at him and suddenly remembered Greta. He was the best person she'd ever known since then, and all these years she hadn't really appreciated it. He didn't want to take anything from her. All he wanted to do was give.

"Marshall," she said, her voice trembling, "I love you."

Nobody's home right now. Let's do the kind of thing that Wendy always does. Let's get drunk and make love."

His face crinkled into a smile. "I've always thought money was good for your libido."

"Oh, it's not money," she said softly. "It's you."

That day, for the first time in all their years of marriage, Charlotte had an orgasm.

CHAPTER
Forty-Seven

In April of 1962, the four friends met at the Plaza for Wendy's birthday. Arla had taken Edita's empty seat. They toasted Wendy, then toasted Edita, "who gave us a lasting vision of beauty."

"Can you believe we're pushing forty?" Wendy's voice broke at the reminder of Edita.

"I don't mind," Sarah said. "This is one of the best times of my life. The kids are fine, my father's off my back, and I'm no longer slaving away at my doctorate, and Jerry and I get along fine. He wants to have a tremendous party in June to celebrate our first anniversary."

Arla looked at her in awe. "You're the first friend I've ever had with a doctorate."

"It's not such a big deal. You should see some of the idiots who have them. That was the way that I got through. I would look at someone dumb and tell myself, if he did it, so can I. I'll probably never use it now, but I like having it. It's like money in the bank."

Charlotte was helping to run a small gallery that specialized in the work of young artists. She had been successful, capable, and competent from the day she started, and gradually they were letting her sell, acquire, and work personally with important collectors. Enthusiasm bubbled out of her.

"They like me," she said in wonder. "They appreciate what I know, what I am. All my life I've been a round peg in a square hole. When I think of how much I wanted to belong to a sorority. I feel like the ugly duckling who turned into a swan."

Marshall was also employed. He had obtained an account-executive job on commission, but his small salary from that plus the dividends on Charlotte's money had enabled them to continue to manage, although in a somewhat simpler style than before.

She didn't care. At the moment, she had no interest in volunteer work or fund-raising events. All of her socializing was done in relation to her work. The gallery had given her an expense account, and she could be seen having lunch with new artists at major restaurants around the city. She was so happy and busy that she didn't even have time to envy her friends.

The children were now her biggest problem. Teddy disappeared for weeks on end, and Kitty continued to be morose. She was doing all right in school, but she had few friends, still was not pretty, and never looked cheerful. But Charlotte didn't have time to worry about them.

And Arla had blossomed, although money was a problem. Ever since Marshall's warning talk with Lenny about what she knew, he had let her alone. But he never sent the money he'd agreed to, and it was hard for her to manage on her salary at Blackstone Publishers. Pride prevented her from telling her friends just how hard it was, and she knew it was only temporary. "They're going to train me to be a proofreader," she said proudly. "And I'll get a salary increase."

It figures, Charlotte thought wryly, that somebody who used to read only junk is going to become a proofreader.

Arla's sons Stewart and Mark were living together in San Francisco's Haight-Ashbury district, and Peter, a freshman at N.Y.U., still lived with her. She did nothing but work and go home to him, but she was happy. She was even pleased that she'd put on forty pounds. It gave her strength and solidity that was like a suit of armor.

"What about romance?" Sarah asked.

"I've had enough of men to last for the rest of my life."

"What about sex?" Wendy asked.

"I'd rather read about it in romances than do it."

All three of them, Wendy thought, were growing more than she was. She took courses, rode each day in Central Park, attended the designers' collections in Paris and New York every fall, and was at theater and concerts and social events six or seven nights a week. And yet she felt bored.

Maurice was rarely around to lift her spirits. He phoned her from time to time, and she continued to send checks, but she had only seen him once since the terrible events of Monroe, and it had been a depressing visit. Again suffering from headaches from the blow he'd received trying to protect Sarah, he was tired and discouraged, and he increasingly questioned the slow pace of nonviolence.

"Malcolm X said that nonviolence is a fool's ploy, playing into the hands of the white man," he told her. "Maybe he's right. The more nonviolence there is, the more *I* get hurt."

"Sarah feels guilty about your getting hurt," she told him. "She said you saved her from some good old boys."

"I would have gotten hurt anyway. Tell her it's not her fault. You should have seen her, Wendy. The tiny little thing standing as tall as she could and trying not to cry."

"Next time I'll be with her. I promise. I want to do it for you. It hurts me that I can't share some of your pain, that I can't see more of you! Isn't it ridiculous! People think I can have anything, but we might just as well be back in the days of Romeo and Juliet. I can't be with you."

"I don't want you with me. I don't want my wife either. There's enough to worry about, and I don't want you hurt."

Sarah's voice interrupted her thoughts. "Jerry wants to rent this summer in Southampton or East Hampton and look around for a house to buy."

"Oh, please don't rent *this* summer," Wendy said. "Robert is taking Bobby on safari to Africa, and I'll be all alone in that big house. In fact, I'd even thought of not opening it. Please come."

"I'd love to. The children will be delighted."

Charlotte turned to Arla. "And we can go out weekends together after work." She loved the way that sounded. After work. Wendy had never worked, and Sarah had worked hard enough for a lifetime, but it was all wonderfully new to her. She could not imagine how she had existed without it.

After lunch, Arla and Charlotte went back to work, and Wendy walked home with Sarah to see the newest furnishings in the apartment. "It's strange," Wendy mused aloud, "that the two of them are so involved in their careers, and you and I are housewives. I'm beginning to think I should find some kind of career. My problem is that I can't seem to figure out what really interests me."

"Well, you have me to play with for awhile. I've never had lunch at Chauveron or Laurent or the Peacock Lounge, or even the Russian Tea Room. I love this new leisure. Hal used to feel a little bad about how poor we were, and he often asked me if I had regrets. I always told him that of course I didn't, and it was the truth, not just something to make him feel good. He was more important to me than money. But now that I'm married to a rich man, I have to admit that it's relaxing not to have money worries. It's easy to become corrupted. I wish Hal's life could have been easier."

"Still think about him?"

"Of course."

"But you're happy with Jerry?"

"It's different. With Hal I always felt that I knew everything about him. He was open and honest and easy to know. But with Jerry, I always feel there are things going on that I know nothing about. A whole hidden life inside him. He uses his charm as a mask."

"That's the way most men are. Afraid to let you get inside them! Each year Robert becomes more of a stranger to me. How's that for a paradox? And much of Maurice is hidden also. Maybe that's just the way men are. We can't know them the way we know women."

CHAPTER
Forty-Eight

The weather was perfect that summer. Robert and Bobby had returned from safari, and Bobby played happily on the beach with Maggie. Jimmy, a senior at Bronx High School of Science, studied much of the time. Wendy and Sarah went antiquing, took tennis lessons, and Wendy even persuaded Sarah to go horseback riding on the beach. They played game after game of Scrabble with Jimmy, who invariably won. On weekends they were joined by Arla, Peter, Marshall, and Charlotte. Everyone was sunburned, healthy, and reasonably content.

One morning in August, when Jerry was out of town on business, Sarah received a strange phone call from her father. "Did you charge a car to me?"

He must be getting senile, she thought sadly. "Of course not. I haven't budged from the beach, and you know I wouldn't do such a thing. Why do you ask?"

"I have here on the desk in front of me a coupon book for a loan on a new Lincoln. And it's signed with my name. Do you by any chance have a new Lincoln?"

"No! I'm driving the Ford LTD, and Jerry drives a Jaguar. Obviously there's been some kind of mistake."

"Let me talk to Jerry."

"He's out of town for the week, but I'm sure his secretary could give you the number."

"I tried that first, of course. The answering machine said his secretary is away on vacation."

"Then we'll have to wait till he gets back. Please don't worry. It must be a mistake." The conversation gnawed at her for the rest of the day, and she felt even more perturbed when Jerry failed to telephone her that night.

But she pushed the subject out of her mind because the next day they were all going to Washington, D.C. The previous June, President Kennedy had proposed a comprehensive civil rights bill and given the government's blessing to a march for black civil rights, which he described as "a peaceful assembly for the redress of grievances." It was the first time all of the sorority had joined together on a political issue.

Marshall and Charlotte came with Kitty. Teddy was off on one of his usual rambles, and they had not seen or heard from him for three days. Jerry was still out of town, but Sarah brought Jimmy and Maggie, who was a perky, bright, uninhibited, happy little first grader at Dalton. Wendy brought Bobby, and Arla brought Peter. Sarah looked at the expanded group with pleasure. The next generation!

Because they could not all fit in her Rolls, Wendy hired a minibus that was driven by her chauffeur. And she had arranged for the entire party to stay at the McLean, Virginia, estate of a cousin of Robert's, the senator from Pennsylvania, who was in Marbella for the month.

"Robert was furious on the phone last night," she told Sarah. "I have never heard him as angry about anything as my taking Bobby today. I assured him that nobody is expecting any violence, but he said that was not the only problem. He said he'd had quite enough of my exposing his son to the wrong kind of people."

"He thinks anybody who's not in the social register is the wrong kind. He's never really thought any of us were good enough for you."

"He never said that."

"He doesn't have to, Wendy. He avoids seeing us as much as possible. He's such a snob."

"I know. It reminds me of those sorority girls, getting their kicks from keeping people out. I think it's boring to only know one group of people, but up to now, it's never really been a problem. He has his world and I have mine and we meet in the middle for social functions. I'm certainly not going to ever ask his permission to take Bobby places. He made the safari arrangements without my permission, and I was terrified that Bobby might be exposed to bad water and mosquitoes. And he didn't ask me to join them."

"Oh, well. He'll get over this. Do you think we'll see Maurice?"

"He's supposed to be on the platform, but with a quarter of a million people expected, we may not be able to see much of anything."

They took off for Washington in a rosy haze of good fellowship, all petty worries and concerns set aside on this historic day.

Wendy had provided picnic baskets, and they dug into the chicken in aspic and endive salad the moment they left the city behind. Her friends drank beer and wine but Wendy sipped her brandy. Robert's unusual flare-up had upset her.

She looked over to where Marshall and Charlotte were sitting. His arm was around her shoulders. Charlotte had mellowed somewhat since receiving the legacy and getting her job, but the endurance of that marriage was a mystery to her. It was inconceivable that either Robert or Maurice would tolerate Charlotte's high-handedness, and yet Marshall's devotion had never wavered. It's funny, she thought. Charlotte's always been jealous of me and yet at this moment, I feel a little envious of her. It's his devotion I envy. Marshall is her friend, but I don't know if Robert is mine. He spends more time away from me than with me.

I'm nearly forty years old, Wendy mused, and have been married to a stranger for twelve years, and I don't know where my life has gone. On the outside, my life looks stable and glamorous, but inside, I'm still like the Flying Dutchman. Given the current statistics, I might live for another forty years. Impossible to continue this aimless existence. I must get a job.

All around her women were beginning to work. Even Dina Merrill, one of their Southampton friends, worked hard at acting and insisted on getting paid scale, regardless of the fact that she was one of the richest women in the world. But what kind of job could *I* get? Wendy wondered. She could not be confined all day like Arla or Charlotte, and she had no desire to teach, like Sarah. Besides, the very earliest she had ever been able to function in the morning was eleven o'clock. What jobs started then?

She could do volunteer work, but she'd never been attracted to it, and Margaret Mead had recently spoken out strongly against volunteerism, saying that women's lives could be improved if they were paid as professionals to do the work that they now did for nothing.

She continued to think about the problem, but her personal concerns were swept away the next morning by the glory and grandeur of the occasion. Half a million people completely covered the ground from the Lincoln Memorial to the Washington Monument in a joyous coalescence of men, women and children of every rank and color whose consciences had at last been awakened to the conviction that blacks could no longer be denied those rights that other Americans had always taken for granted.

Sarah's arms prickled with gooseflesh. "We're part of history," she told her children. "How I wish your father could have lived to see this." The group of friends pressed close to each other, holding hands as they and their children listened and wept at the poetic words of Martin Luther King. "I have a dream that one day this nation will rise up, live out the true meaning of its creed; 'We hold these truths to be self-evident, that all men are created equal.' I have a dream that one day on the red hills of Georgia sons of former slaves and the sons of former slave owners will be able to sit down together at the table of brotherhood. I have a dream that one day even the state of Mississippi, a state sweltering with the heat of injustice ... will be transformed into an oasis of freedom and justice. I have a dream that my four little children will one day live in a nation where they will not be judged by the color of their skin but by the content of their character." A half-million voices joined in singing "We Shall Overcome."

Afterward, euphoric, they strolled to where the chauffeur was waiting for them. And then, just as she was about to enter the bus, Wendy saw Maurice. He was standing with John Lewis, the leader of SNCC, an organization of younger black activists who were strongly opposed to King's nonviolence. Lewis's speech that day had been far tougher and less conciliatory than the others.

Then for the first time she saw Maurice's wife and son. His wife had her hand linked through Maurice's arm, with the unquestioned right of possession. Her body leaned against his, and her head rested lightly against his shoulder. She was very pretty, with honey-color skin and a flashing white smile. The thirteen-year-old boy, already tall and broad and strong looking, was a smaller version of Maurice. They were a proud, connected family, and the sight of them sent a shock through Wendy like the sudden chill of an exposed nerve.

How absolutely stupid she had been. Never until that moment had Maurice's wife had corporeal reality. Never before had she pictured him having breakfast with another woman, sleeping with another woman every night, confiding in another woman, sharing his life and his dreams with another woman.

Silently she watched and grieved. He's not mine. We don't belong together. He says he loves me and I'm sure he does, but what does such love mean? How much weight does that carry measured against the pattern of life with his wife and child? That's his real life standing there beside him. What am I? A sequinned Band-Aid? A diversion? I probably serve the same purpose for him as the summer week in the country given to ghetto children by the Fresh Air Fund.

Her heart was breaking. She had everything and she had nothing. She loved a man who was not part of her life, and the man who was part of her life was almost totally indifferent to her. She loved children, but all she had was one son who would soon be busy with his own world.

Still she gazed hungrily, but Maurice did not see her. He was completely involved with his group.

Sarah, standing beside her, followed her gaze and immediately understood the situation. "Come on, Wendy honey." She gently took Wendy's hand. "It's time for us to go."

All the way back to New York Wendy sipped her brandy and laughed and chatted, but her heart felt ripped apart with the old, familiar torment of loneliness.

CHAPTER
Forty-Nine

Wendy and Charlotte were going directly back to the Hamptons from Washington. They dropped off Arla and Peter, and then, almost on impulse, Sarah asked them to drop her at home. Jerry was due back from his trip that night, and she felt a sudden urgency to ask him about the matter her father had called about. The children could continue on with Wendy, and she and Jerry would drive out together the next day.

When she reached the Dakota, everything seemed much as usual. She greeted the guard in the little kiosk outside, took the elevator up to her apartment, unlocked the front door, and then stood there in shock.

They'd been burglarized. The entire apartment was empty. Every expensive piece of antique furniture had been removed, the priceless art collection was no longer on the walls, and the three cut-glass baccarat chandeliers had been taken down from the ceilings. The oriental rugs were gone, and all of the equipment had been removed from the kitchen and laundry rooms.

She knocked on the maid's door, then opened it. The furniture was still there but the maid's closet was empty. Was it possible that this maid had been part of a gang of thieves?

Sick with shock, she continued to explore. How had the thieves come in and how had they been able to take so much stuff out without the doorman's noticing? She'd heard of thieves using a moving van. Perhaps that was how they'd done it.

Dazed and numb, she moved through the apartment. Everything seemed intact in the children's rooms. Obviously the thieves had known what they were doing, for their sets of furniture were ordinary ones from department stores. She shivered before opening the door of her own master suite, then resolutely turned the knob and walked in. I've lived through the horror of losing Hal, she told herself. That mattered! This doesn't! I will not collapse over material possessions. They're only things, and I'm sure we're very well insured. Although she was drenched in perspiration, she steeled herself to remain calm until Jerry got home.

The master bedroom and sitting room were as empty as the front of the apartment, but her clothes closets were exactly the way she had left them. However, the cedar closet in which she'd stored her furs were empty. Back to no furs, she thought wryly. She opened Jerry's dressing room and found that all of *his* clothes had been taken. Why had the thieves taken his clothing and not hers?

The inspection over, she tried to switch on the light to call Jerry's office. Perhaps he had gone there first, before coming home. But the lights did not go on, and the telephone was dead.

Suddenly she was frightened, although she knew that no one was in the apartment. It had been plucked clean, and there was no reason for the criminals to linger further. Then waves of nausea at the violation swept over her, and she felt an overwhelming need to escape.

She ran downstairs to inform the doorman of what had happened. But before she could speak he said, "Sorry to be losing you, Mrs. Lasker. I had a long chat with your husband when he came with the movers yesterday. Do you think you'll enjoy living in Hawaii?"

Hawaii? "Please call me a cab," she said in a strangled voice. "I'll be back later."

Where should she go? Her parents were in Maine, and their apartment was closed, and Wendy and Charlotte were in the Hamptons. She would go to Arla. She gave the driver the address, praying that she and Peter had not gone out for dinner.

But Arla was there, and as soon as she saw her, Sarah said, "I think I'm going to faint."

"Put your head between your legs, and I'll get an ice bag."

She ran back in a moment with the ice bag and put it on the back of Sarah's neck. When she was able to sit up, Arla gave her some cognac. "Sip slowly, then tell me what's wrong."

Sarah quickly told her story. "I feel plundered," she cried.

"That no-good bastard," Arla exploded. "That's just the kind of thing Lenny would have done."

"But Jerry's not like him. In the year that we've been married he's never been anything but kind and courteous. For heaven's sake, Arla, he's never abused me."

"Apparently, he was saving it up," she said cynically. "Men! They've never brought me anything but grief."

"What do you think we should do, Arla?"

"Nothing tonight. I think you should take a few stiff drinks and go to sleep. We can call Marshall tomorrow."

"I think I'd better call Claude. He's with my folks in Maine, and they're rather frail. I wouldn't want them to hear anything about this suddenly. He can break it to them gently."

As Claude listened to her story he became increasingly agitated. "We're all in trouble! Do you know how much I've invested with that guy? Your friends have too! And Dad paid for all of those furnishings! I don't know what to say. First Hal, and now this bum! I'll fly down in the morning and expect you at the office at noon."

She was too weary to even fight back against his unfairness. To lump Hal and Jerry together! But she wept when she learned that Arla, as well as her other friends, had invested with him.

"How much."

"Two thousand. All I had. Please don't cry, Sarah, dear. Think of what you did for me. Remember when you told me I had nothing to lose but my chains. I didn't even know what you were talking about. I owe you."

"I'm ashamed. I've never been more ashamed."

"*You* shouldn't be ashamed. Why do women always do that? That's exactly how I used to feel. Ashamed! *I* felt ashamed because Lenny beat me. I once went to one dumb analyst who told me I really wanted him to. How's that for blaming the victim? He had the nerve to tell me that I specifically picked him because I was a masochist. Can you imagine paying for that kind of advice? I married him because he was nice to me, not because he wasn't."

She sat with Sarah, holding her hand, until Sarah finally fell asleep. Still, she sat there gazing fondly at her. How tiny she was! Asleep, her face ringed with curls, she still looked young and innocent. How could anybody be so cruel to a trusting, kind, vulnerable woman like Sarah? Then her lips curled wryly. She, too, had been vulnerable and trusting.

It was almost impossible now to understand the person she had been. It was as if she had been brainwashed. She'd accepted the myth that she had no rights and was lucky to get married. She'd cooked, cleaned, sewn, shopped, driven the children to school, picked them up, taken them to dentists, to scout meetings, and to therapists. Everything had been her responsibility. Her chores had lasted from day to night. But instead of gratitude or even appreciation, she'd been repeatedly raped, reviled, mocked, and beaten. Her mentality had been that of a slave. Don't make a fuss and maybe it will go away. Make a fuss and it will get worse.

You poor thing, she said to her old self. How very sad that you never expected anyone to say thank you. She would never again be involved with a man. It was too dangerous. They fucked you over and blamed you. Most men were abusers! She would not generalize that all were abusers. She had known too many fine men to say that: Hal, Marshall, Peter. But the men *she* had known romantically throughout her life *had* been abusers. It was as if she had some kind of special antennae sticking up in the air, antennae that emitted a frequency heard only by potential abusers. And they would find her.

If that were true, it would be even more reason for her to stay away. Men to her were like liquor to an alcoholic. She couldn't handle them, and they in turn diminished and degraded her. Therefore, like an alcoholic who is lost if he takes even one drink, her solution was not to start. Total abstinence was her prescription for her past, present, and future! And her new stocky body was one form of protection.

She thought about the sorority's relations with men. Jerry had fucked Sarah over for no good reason. And Wendy had two men, neither of whom did her much good. You didn't have to be a mind reader to see that she was bored. She needed love and warmth, and she certainly wasn't getting that from Robert or Maurice. Robert was a cold fish. She'd disliked him from that first evening at Charlotte's so long ago. He was a smug snob without an iota of sympathy or compassion. Maybe he was different with his patients, but that never showed in his personal life.

And Maurice just didn't have enough left over from his own life and struggles to fill Wendy's life. It was destructive for Wendy even to see him because she felt even more lonely and depressed after they'd been together.

Marshall was a good man, of course, but he was a weak man. Maybe being weak and more like a woman made him a better person.

Suddenly, like a jolt of electricity, a revelation hit her. Not one of the women in their little sorority trusted or needed men as much as they trusted and needed each other. Her entire body broke out in goose bumps. My God, she thought, suddenly I understand. Suddenly I know what I am. I'm a feminist!

The word was in the air nowadays, but this was the first moment that she had understood its relevance to her. She'd just read *The Feminine Mystique*, which told about housewives who felt empty, isolated, bored, and useless in their marriages, who did not know who or what they were, and who had finally retreated, as she had during her marriage, into passivity. And in common with her, all of them had paid an incalculable price for this passivity. Her two older children were still paying and would pay for it for the rest of their lives.

Arla had thought about it, but it wasn't until just this very moment that she made the connection. She was a feminist, by God, that's what she was, and she would never again be so alone.

The worst part of her life was over. She did not have to go through the charade of dating or looking for a man. I do not need a man. I do not want a man, and I will never hesitate to say so. She bent her head in silent gratitude. I know what I am. I am complete unto myself.

CHAPTER
Fifty

Peter and Arla were having breakfast when Sarah staggered into the kitchen the next morning. He jumped up to hold a chair for her. "Mom just told me what happened, Aunt Sarah. From the sublime to the ridiculous. Yesterday Martin Luther King, today Jerry Laskar. I wish I was finished with law school. I'd sue your husband for every penny he's worth."

"If you could find him," Arla said cynically.

"How far could he go with a big moving van, Mom?"

Sarah looked at him with affection. She'd always liked him. At eighteen, he was a fine young man, with brownish blonde hair, fair skin, and an open ingenuous smile. "The best of the litter," was how Arla often referred to him.

They were doing their best to make her feel better, but her soul felt sick. She'd been a dupe—an innocent, stupid, trusting fool. Had it only been a scam? Had he really fallen in love with her or had he married her because he'd seen her up on that dais and assumed that Judge Stern's daughter would be rich and have rich friends? She tried to remember the morning of their engagement. Had he asked her father to furnish the apartment or had her father volunteered? The memory was unclear. Either way it made her sick.

Why had they all been so gullible? Because he'd said the right things and dressed the right way and carried himself the right way nobody had ever checked his background, his family, his old life in Los Angeles. Undoubtedly, he'd counted on that. She'd been the perfect sitting duck because she never lied and was naive enough to think nobody else ever did. Yes, that's what she'd been. An innocent! A perfect sitting duck for a con man! Waves of nausea swept through her.

After Peter left for school, the two friends sat talking until it was time to leave for Claude's office. At the thought of this confrontation, Sarah ran into the bathroom and threw up her breakfast. Then she brushed her teeth, and they set out.

Arla was impressed when they were ushered into the inner sanctum where Claude sat behind the largest desk she'd ever seen. "Wow," she whispered to Sarah. Apart from several phones, the top of the desk was polished and shining and completely empty.

Sitting there in splendor in his custom-made suit, his bald pate shining, his eyes behind the glasses as cold and opaque as her father's, Sarah found it difficult to remember that this man was her brother. How she and Jimmy used to joke about his total lack of a sense of humor! Suddenly she felt nausea sweep over her again. She made a mad dash for the bathroom, threw up, cleaned herself up, and rejoined them.

Claude was drumming on his desk impatiently, probably annoyed at the thought that she'd messed up his pristine bathroom. He waited for her to sit back in the soft opulent chairs deliberately designed to make people look up at him. "Well, Sarah," he said, "you really loused up again. You never did have any sense. You used to bring home every stray dog, and when I think of how you tried to unionize Mattie."

"What does that have to do with anything?" Sarah gasped, stung by the injustice.

Arla indignantly rushed to her defense. "Don't scold her. Can't you tell how upset she already is? Just tell us exactly what's going on. What have you discovered?"

"It appears that your supposed husband has taken your possessions and gone into hiding to stay out of the hands of creditors. Among these are the Internal Revenue Service, Sotheby's, Christie's, Cartier's, Jensen's, Tiffany's, the Knoedler, and others too numerous to list. He never paid for the furniture with the money Dad gave him. He pocketed the money and took the furniture. In addition, he is being dunned for child support by his first wife and for alimony by his second wife from whom it appears he was not completely divorced at the time of your marriage.

"He has not paid the rent, phone, or electricity bills for

three months, has charged a new Lincoln to Dad, as you already may have guessed from Dad's phone call, and has completely cleaned out your joint account, which included all of the wedding-present money you received. We've already put detectives on his trail, but we have no idea when he'll be found. Therefore, Sarah, at this moment this is the situation. You have no money and no husband. You and the children will have to move back in with the folks. Your carelessness in this entire situation astounds me."

Ignoring his last sentence she asked, "Are you saying that I'm not legally married?"

"So it seems."

"You mean I've been living in sin?" At his nod, she began to laugh uncontrollably while tears flowed from her eyes.

"Please try to get hold of yourself. There are people in the waiting room." This made Sarah laugh even harder. Arla held her tightly in her arms until she regained control.

"Why are you laughing, Sarah? May I ask what's so funny?"

"What's so funny?" Her voice was uncharacteristically bitter. "You are. You and the family. You all think you know so much. None of you brilliant, perceptive people liked Hal," her voice broke on a sob at his name, "and you never doubted for one moment that you might be wrong. But he was the best man who ever lived. He wasn't good enough for you because he didn't care about fancy clothes and all the nonsense that possesses you. He'd never heard of Gucci or Tiffany's or the Knoedler. He always lived within his tiny income and died not owing a penny. You could have made his life better, easier, maybe made him live longer. Damn it, he never had a winter coat that was warm enough or a pair of snow boots that kept his feet dry!

"I'll never forget how you humiliated him that first night, just because he was poor. You claimed he wasn't good enough for me, but what you really meant was he wasn't good enough for *you*. He wasn't part of our crowd. But Jerry was! Everybody adored him! At last I had done the family proud. Mom danced with him at our wedding with her eyes closed in ecstasy. And what was the end result of all this perspicacious judgment?" She began to laugh again, "I married a con man and a crook, and he fleeced all of us. Surely even you can see the humor in that."

Claude looked at his watch. "I'm a busy man and I have a client waiting. My secretary will give you a check on your way out. Move back to the folks as soon as possible."

She shook her head. "Nothing doing. The children and I can stay with Wendy or Charlotte until I find a job. Thank God I finished that doctorate. I'll get a job somewhere teaching at a college, and we'll go wherever it is."

To her surprise he was hurt. "I don't know why you have always preferred your friends to your own family. If you don't want to go to the folks, I understand that. Dad gets more cranky and difficult every year. But you could stay with us. Ann would be perfectly willing to have you."

She walked around to his side of the desk and lightly kissed his cheek. "I really appreciate it, but we'll go to my friends. We've spent so many summers together that I feel comfortable with them, and the children do too."

"Very well. You're being foolish and headstrong as usual, but I can do nothing more. If you change your mind, my offer is still open, so think about it. I'll contact you as soon as I have some more information about Jerry. Perhaps we can get some of your money and possessions back."

"You can do whatever you like to get *your* money back," she said, "but please don't waste time, energy, and money looking for him on my account. I never want to see him again. I don't want to be involved in any court cases or prosecutions. He no longer exists. He's an unperson from now on. Thank God I'm not really married to him. That chapter of my life is locked shut as of this minute, and I never want to hear anything about it again. Thanks for the check and for all your efforts on my behalf. I really do appreciate it."

"Oh, well! It's family! I wish things had turned out better for you."

For the first time in her life Sarah felt a little affection for him. He hadn't even mentioned how much money he and her father had lost investing with Jerry. That was decent of him.

Coming Apart (317)

She maintained some semblance of control until they were out of his office and safely inside the ladies room down the hall. Then she was overcome again. "I want Hal," she wept. "I want my Hal." He hadn't died seven years ago. He'd died yesterday, and the pain of the reopened wound cut through her like a knife.

"Let's go to the movies, Sarah."

"The movies?"

"Let's go to one or two or three. That's how I got through the bad periods. We'll cash the check and go."

"You know something! That's a wonderful suggestion. A lot better than brandy."

She washed her face, and they walked to the bank to put Claude's check into traveler's checks. Sarah looked at it for the first time. Five thousand dollars! And he must have spent a lot to get all that information so quickly. Well, he may be a rotten reactionary, but he came through for me. I'm glad I kissed him and showed some gratitude, she told herself.

Sitting in the movies, Sarah gradually regained her balance. I guess I never was really cut out for money, she thought. It was always like playacting. The role of a rich, useless lady was never right for me. I always felt ashamed wearing furs or jewels or driving in an expensive car. Once we had to get off the West Side Highway to get gas, and we ended up in Harlem. I felt so ashamed. I wanted to get out and apologize to all those poor people. It was like Mexico where I couldn't eat because of those starving kids pressing their noses against the window to watch.

Regardless of what Arla says, I blame myself. From the moment Jerry started to woo me, I was selling out. I kept doing things that weren't me. Like standing at his shoulder while he gambled in Las Vegas. There I was, smiling and looking enthusiastic, and all the time I was thinking that gambling was disgusting. All I really wanted was to be in my room reading a good book.

The truth of the matter is that Jerry never really got inside my soul. I never felt connected to him. I didn't even miss him when he was away. Now I know why. He wasn't a real person. He was a phantom, a con man, the great imposter, the man of a thousand faces, host to thousands but friend to none. I haven't lost a relationship, because we never really had one.

I'm sorry that the children have to be dislocated again. They've moved around so much. But we have enough love and strength and good common sense to get us through. I'm certain I'll be able to get a college teaching job. I see dozens of ads each Sunday in the *New York Times*. It won't be a great job at a top-notch college because it will be my first job, and I've never published anything, but I'll get something.

"Give me some more popcorn," she said to Arla. "You know, in spite of everything, I feel lucky."

CHAPTER Fifty-One

In common with most other Americans, the four friends and their families were heartbroken about Kennedy's assassination. But after awhile, their lives continued undisturbed.

In December, Wendy and Robert took Bobby and went cruising the Caribbean on a friend's yacht. The only reason she had consented to go was that none of her old friends was available for the holiday season. Arla and Charlotte were too involved in their jobs to leave New York, and Sarah was working in some little town up the Hudson. So when Robert had proposed this trip, she'd agreed. After all, she had to get a sunburn somewhere.

One night, after Bobby was asleep, they played an old parlor game. Each of the passengers had to write an obituary notice for himself or herself and for their spouses. She had no problem in doing one for Robert. She listed his elite family, his schools, his clubs, his son, and his outstanding contributions to oncology. She quickly filled two pages about him and then came to the task of writing about herself. She wrote the names of her husband and son, the names of her parents, and data about the hotel. Then, disturbed because there was so little of importance, she added the words *good mother*, *good friend*, and *philanthropist* and looked down at the page in dismay. It wasn't enough. It just wasn't enough. She was even more disturbed when she listened to what Robert had written about her: heiress, beautiful face, beautiful figure, likes to sleep late. This is my epitaph, she thought. How shallow! She was ashamed. Stuck on that yacht for the month, she began to write down her thoughts, feelings, and problems every day in a leather-bound notebook. Somehow it gave her comfort.

When they returned to New York in January, her little sorority was still not available for the usual support of the past. Charlotte was increasingly successful. She seemed to have the intangible gift of discovering artists of significance before they were priced out of the market. In addition, she was taking art history classes in preparation for opening her own gallery. Arla adored her work at Blackstone Publishers, and she worked overtime every day and even weekends if she were needed. And Sarah was seventy miles upstate.

It wasn't just her three friends who were otherwise engaged. Nobody was around anymore during the day. All around her women were trying to escape the feminine mystique that had thwarted women's needs by telling them they never had to grow up, that had encouraged them to ignore and even flee from the question of who they were and what they wanted to do with their lives.

It was no longer enough simply to "be." Now it was necessary to "do." The roles of wife and mother had become as insufficient for women as the roles of father and husband had always been for men. People at parties had begun to ask women as well as men "What do you do?" All over America women were trying to find themselves, and she was one of them.

Several times she met Arla and Charlotte for lunch, but they were always looking at their watches, too worried about getting back on time to relax for one of their old three-martini, gossipy lunches.

She had also offered to visit Sarah, and although Sarah was as loving and welcoming as in the past, she was concerned that Wendy might have to wait around most of the day because of her classes and faculty meetings. "I'm insanely busy," she had said, but her ebullient voice showed clearly that she loved every second of the pressure.

And Bobby, too, was also increasingly busy now, with school, riding lessons, French lessons, tennis lessons, swimming lessons, and ballroom dancing lessons at the Barclay School. He loved Wendy just as much as she loved him. "I have the most beautiful mommy of all the guys." But with his school and friends and lessons there just wasn't that much time they could be together each day. His nanny still served him dinner in the nursery at six and took him to school in the mornings before Wendy was up, so they rarely dined together.

More and more she spent her free time reading and writing. Each week she assiduously poured through the pages of the *New York Times Book Review*, phoned her order for the new novels that interested her to the Strand Bookstore in the Village, and immediately received the books by messenger. Often, she found herself thinking, I could do this. I could write this well. But these thoughts did not lead to action.

Nevertheless, for lack of something better to do, she continued to write and study, and after a while, imperceptibly, her work habits acquired some structure. Each morning, after her exercise man had gone, she would work without interruption until lunch was served. She began to consciously imitate many of the writers she read, especially those in the *New Yorker*, trying to learn by imitation. Why shouldn't that be a good method for writers? Many times she'd seen artists in the Metropolitan or the Louvre, copying the work of the great masters.

Gradually she began to view her daily journal entries with a kind of timid respect. They had become more than mere self-expressions. They had become writing, and some of them, she thought with pleasure, were not bad. She didn't talk about her writing. People were accustomed to viewing her as a dilettante, and she felt a mother's need to protect her burgeoning talent from amusement or contempt. She planned to take a writing course at the New School for Social Research when she felt a little more confident.

For the first time in twenty years, despite her continuing concern about his safety, Maurice was not the center of her universe. She saw his name from time to time in news reports of the worsening southern violence. He had been beside James Meredith, been beaten by Bull Connor, and had wept at the funeral of the four teen-age girls who had been murdered by a dynamite explosion in a Birmingham church. She loved him, and she worried about him, but things had changed. He no longer filled her mind. Her work did that now.

The next time he called, she found that she no longer felt the old, wild excitement. It was not only her work that had come between them. Now that she had seen his wife and son, she felt less comfortable about her role in the triangle. The emergent philosophy of sisterhood implied not taking other women's men.

She was not sipping brandy on a chaise in the garden when he arrived that day. She was working at her desk. As soon as he held her in his arms, he knew that something had changed. "Someone else?" he asked.

"No," she said, surprisingly shy. "I have a lifework now, just the way you do."

"You? You're joking. What kind of lifework? Growing orchids?"

"No. Writing."

He dismissed her work. "That's a luxury."

She was surprised at how hurt she felt. "It's more than that to me. And there's something else. I saw you with your wife and son in Washington."

"So?"

"It bothered me."

"I don't have time or energy for jealousy, Wendy. I'm going to Mississippi, and it's like being sent to the front."

Instantly she was contrite and guilty. "I'm sorry. Are you afraid?"

"I'm always afraid. I wish I didn't have to go. I'm tired of the struggle. I wish I could hibernate right here with you in front of this fire. I always wanted a house with a fireplace. And time to rest and look at it."

Oh, Maurice! She wanted to weep for his terrible life.

The thought of his battered body would always torment her. She wished that she could write about him, tell the world how broad and strong and beautiful he could have been—an African king—if it had let him alone. But he had never been able to stop running. He had never been free of the furies of prejudice.

It was true that he was no longer the center of her life, but he would always be part of it. He had made her less selfish, and she would always love him. She folded her arms around him. "The fire is glowing. Stay with me tonight. The way it used to be in Mexico, when so many things seemed possible. We've had so little time with each other these past few years. Stay with me. Stop running tonight."

"Here? What about your husband?"

"He's in Washington. Consulting about some congressman's wife. Stay with me tonight. Let the struggle wait!"

"That's probably the single best invitation of my life."

"You will?" He nodded, and her eyes shone again like the girl he first knew. She picked up the house phone to say good-night to Bobby. "I love you, darling," she said. "Sleep well. I'd like to have dinner with you tomorrow night."

"I can't, Mommy. There's a birthday party for my friend Jeff at Tavern on the Green."

"Very well, darling. Call me when you get home."

She turned again to Maurice. "Nothing will interrupt us now. We're all alone in the world."

Her butler wheeled dinner in and opened two bottles of Richebourg burgundy. "Thank you," she said. "I'll leave the table outside when we're through."

"Very good, ma'am."

He closed the door behind him, and she locked it although there was absolutely no possibility of anyone's disturbing them. Then they sat there together eating butter-soft filet mignon, drinking, and reminiscing like any old married couple. When he reached for the television to hear the eleven o'clock news she stopped his hand. "No outside world tonight."

"It's forgotten," he said pulling her down on the white fur rug in front of the fireplace. Lying there on the rug, the flames licking at their faces, they made love slowly, with no lessening of the passion of the past, but with a new desperate intensity born of fear and separation. She kept wanting to cry.

This must be the way women have always felt when their men go off to war. But she would not spoil their time together by showing sadness or fear. "Not bad," she teased him afterward. "Kinsey said men your age are way past their prime, but he certainly missed you."

"Men like me," he said, also pretending the old braggadocio, "are too busy making love to be in a lab talking to creepy old scientists about how many times a week."

Her hands moved lovingly over his body. "I would attest to that."

"But I always did want to make love in front of an open fire like you rich folks, and now I have. That might interest Kinsey."

"Wow! What a perversity!" They lay there joking in each other's arms until the fire died.

"Will you do one thing for me?" she begged. "If you're hurt or in trouble, have someone let me know. Will you do that?"

He always understood her so well. "You mean if I die?" She shivered at his words. "I'm going to do my damnedest not to die, but if I do, I promise that someone will call you. But I wouldn't want you at my funeral. I wouldn't want my wife to see you."

"You mean she knows about us? All these years?"

"Not who you are. She knows there's someone white I love. I told her that before we got married. But if she saw you she'd know and I don't want her upset. It's the worst possible time for this to have happened, but she's pregnant!"

"Pregnant. Again?" She wanted to weep.

"I don't want you to feel bad. I know how you feel about children." When she didn't answer he said, "It doesn't have anything to do with us."

"Yes, it does," she said, trying to shut out of her mind the picture of him making love to his wife. But she couldn't.

Their mood had changed, and now sadness fogged the room. He fell into an exhausted sleep, but she lay awake beside him that night trying to memorize every line of his face and body, feeling with some kind of terrible precognition that they would never meet again.

CHAPTER
Fifty-Two

It was over and she had her work. But even so, Wendy could not shake her feeling of loss. And so she agreed, when Sarah asked her, to go to Selma, Alabama, on October 7, 1963, for Freedom Day. She felt that she was bearing witness for Maurice.

They stood in the blistering Selma heat, watching blacks waiting to register to vote. All day the blacks stood in the sun without food or water, without being able to go to the bathroom, because state troopers warned them they could not leave the line and return. "Sadistic bastards," Sarah muttered.

"It's the first time I've been this hot since Mexico," Wendy said, thinking that some people are this hot all the time.

Also watching were the menacing, helmeted members of Sheriff Clarke's vicious police, armed with clubs and guns. Newsmen stood there waiting for violence, and FBI agents and Justice Department lawyers also stood watching, doing nothing to help the frightened blacks. Finally, in exasperation, Sarah and Wendy walked over to a Justice Department lawyer and demanded that he tell state troopers that the blacks had a right to get some water. With newsmen's cameras clicking away, he told them, "I think they do have that right. But I won't do it."

Finally, at two in the afternoon, two young black men stepped forward toward the line with their arms filled with food. It gave the police what they had been waiting for. In a flash, they jubilantly moved forward, all of them converging on the two black youths, beating them, kicking them, and jabbing them with electric cattle prods. My God,

Wendy thought, this can't be happening. It's even worse than those Mexican policemen. And then, involuntarily, hearing the thwack, thwack, thwack of the clubs and seeing Maurice in every beaten black men, she ran forward screaming, "Stop that. Stop that at once," as they dragged the two bloodied men away and threw them into a green arrest truck. And the cameras clicked away. The two women stood there sobbing in each other's arms, and unable to do anything more, they flew home that night.

When she finally awakened at noon the next day, Robert was sitting on her Queen Anne armchair looking at her. She sat up holding the sheet against her and then thought, isn't it silly to be modest in front of my husband. But still she held it. Then she looked at his face. It was white with anger as he held out the morning paper to her. Beneath a picture of her screaming at the police was the headline, "Noted Socialite Goes to Selma." He then held out a picture of her and Maurice in bed and grimaced in distaste.

"I was willing to close my eyes to your on-going affair with this person," he said, "as long as you kept it discreet. But your political activities are indeed another matter."

Struggling to control her shaking hands, she lit a cigarette and took a few gulps of coffee. Then with studied insolence that took her back to when she'd been kicked out of school she asked, "How on earth did you get this picture of us? From my balcony?"

"From your balcony."

"I can't believe that you went creeping around outside in the middle of the night."

"Not I. There are people who do this sort of thing."

She looked at the picture carefully. "Do you have others?"

"Why do you ask?"

"If you do, I'd like to keep this one. I've never had a nude picture of Maurice."

"When we got married, you promised not to screw around. Have you ever kept that promise?"

She shrugged disdainfully. "I can't remember."

Struggling to control his anger he held out to her the picture of her clutching her dress at the Copa while Maurice struggled in the background.

"Is this the same man?"

"Yes, it is."

"I thought so. You've been seeing him for all these years. It's inconceivable. You had me and you had Bobby, and yet you saw him? Why? Is it some kind of kinkiness? Some perversity? A sickness?"

For the first time she laughed, and her laughter gave her strength. "Don't be silly, Robert. I love him. He's the healthy part of me."

"You can't love a man like that. Did you do it to hurt me?"

"Hurt you? Of course not. I've never wanted to hurt anybody. This has nothing to do with you."

"Oh, yes it does. We happen to be married, and your dirt can quite easily taint Bobby and me. Are you aware that this man is on the FBI's list of dangerous subversives? Are you aware that your friend Sarah is too? Are you aware that subversives organized that Selma Freedom Day?"

"I suppose you got that information from your cousin." One of Robert's first cousins was Hoover's assistant. "Maurice is not a subversive. Neither is Sarah. That's all absolute nonsense."

"You've been a dupe and a fool, Wendy. Don't you know that they have a record of the large sums you've contributed to Martin Luther King?"

"So what? It's my money and my private business."

"Yours and the FBI's! I cannot understand why you would be so foolish and endanger yourself and your family. Did you do it just for that man?"

"Of course not. I don't like to see anybody pushed around."

He looked at her in perplexity. "Did you love me when you married me?"

"Not the way I loved him, but I've always been very fond of you. We've had a satisfactory working relationship."

"It's not satisfactory any longer, and it's not working either. I want a divorce, Wendy, and I'm taking Bobby with me."

Suddenly she was terrified. "Bobby? You're out of your mind. You'll never get Bobby. If you want a divorce you can go. But he's my son and judges always give children to their mothers."

"Not a mother like you. Not with your history! With these pictures of you in bed with a black subversive, the Copa story, and now your little exploit in Selma, there's not the slightest chance you'd get him, even if I didn't have my family connections."

She was increasingly frightened, but she forced herself to sound calm. "Children have to stay with their mothers. That's all there is to it."

"Oh, he'll have a mother."

That brought her up short. "You mean that you've been seeing someone?"

"Of course. Otherwise why would I have brought this to a head?"

"You hypocrite. It's not political at all. You're just using that. Well, if you bring up my affairs in court I'll bring up yours. It's no different for you than it is for me."

"Oh, yes it is. The woman I want to marry is social register, impeccable family, impeccable politics, a DAR, a debutante. In fact, she's the current director of the Junior League in New York. I don't know of a single judge in the city who won't think that's a better atmosphere for a young, impressionable boy than a den of black militants. I have a feeling that most judges would find you an unfit mother."

She fought to control her rising hysteria. "You would give him to a stepmother? Like Charlotte? Never."

"Not all stepmothers are like Charlotte. And not all men are wimps like your friend Marshall. Do you think that I would ever stand by like him and permit my child to be mistreated?"

"You don't know. People change when they remarry."

"But I won't. My son will have the best of everything and will grow up to be a productive, powerful member of his class. Please don't fight this, Wendy. Give up now and don't waste time, energy, and money on legal fees. Don't expose Bobby to a scandal. You don't need Bobby or me. You've never needed anybody except for that man and your ridiculous little band of women. You'll still have them, this house is yours, and you're rich and still beautiful. I'm certain you'll be able to buy as many black boys as you need to service you."

She looked at him with contempt. "Get out of my house today," she said. "But you cannot take Bobby. I'll fight you every inch of the way for him in court."

"You'll lose," he said as he walked out. "I guarantee you that. You'll lose."

CHAPTER
Fifty-Three

By 1964, Arla had become assistant to the president of Blackstone Publishers. Nobody had ever worked harder than she for the company. She arrived first in the morning, usually left last, rarely took a lunch hour, and was always willing to work overtime. Being Mr. Blackstone's assistant would not have been a plum to most people, but it rapidly became evident to all concerned that the company was her life. Her salary was low, she still was asked to serve coffee at meetings, and she had no real authority. She was a jack of all trades who could be asked to do anything at a moment's notice. Several times she had to take his cleaning to be done when his wife was out of town, and once she had to go all the way out to the eastern tip of Long Island to Montauk to deliver eye drops to his wife. But she bided her time. She had discovered herself at this company, and it was only a matter of time before she would be promoted to a position of real significance.

That moment came when he turned to her one day showing a gloominess that was usually hidden behind the corporate facade of optimism. "Things don't look good, do they?"

The stocky, forceful woman who answered bore absolutely no resemblance to the wretched emaciated shadow of a person that she had been before her divorce. Her hair was a subdued blonde, and she wore it in a neat, formal, businesslike French twist. She'd studied the Alexander Technique to carry herself erect instead of hunched over in fear, and had taken speech lessons to erase all remnants of her despised southern accent. She walked, talked, dressed, and moved like a professional.

She was determined to conform to her mental picture of a career woman, and even though all three of her friends now wore slacks more than dresses, she wore only suits. If corporate men could wear uniforms, why not corporate women?

So she dressed conservatively in well-tailored suits and silk blouses with stock ties. Her clothes were always clean and pressed, and the high-heeled leather pumps that completed her image were buffed and polished each day to a high sheen. Her increased weight, her firm manner, and the way she dressed gave her authority, made her a presence in the firm even before she had any authority. People automatically deferred to her and assumed that she knew what she was talking about. At the age of forty-one, she had come into her own.

She had not seen Lenny since the divorce. He had managed to be exonerated from all the blame for the building that had burned, in the way he had always gotten away with everything—cheating, lying, paying people off. It made her sick even to think about him.

Although Peter despised him, he had dinner with him from time to time because Lenny was paying for his education. Peter told her that Lenny had gone out to Haight-Ashbury to look for Stewart and Mark, both of whom had apparently joined some kind of strange new commune and had not been heard from since. She forced herself not to worry about them. She had never been able to protect them when she was married, and she could not do it now. But she wanted to do her best for Peter, to give him a mother he could be proud of instead of a beaten wretch, and the only way to do that would be to become well-paid and successful in her career. She would allow nothing to get in her way.

Her only concern was the situation in Vietnam. Strange as it seemed to her, the North Vietnamese had apparently attacked two U.S. destroyers in the Gulf of Tonkin, President Johnson had sent U.S. planes to bomb North Vietnam, and now America was really in it. But Peter had vowed never to go to Vietnam. He warned her that he would rather go to jail or leave the country than to kill people who presented absolutely no danger at all to the United States.

Her boss's voice brought her back to the present. "I just said that things don't look too good, and you still haven't answered."

"Sorry," she said. "I was thinking. I'm not surprised that we're doing poorly. I would never read the kinds of books we publish if I didn't work here."

Instantly he became defensive. "I've always thought we had a fine list."

"Oh, we do. I just wouldn't read them. The kinds of books we publish are the kind read in college classrooms, but I never went to college, I'll bet nobody would read our books unless they were assigned. I like to read about rich, successful, happy, beautiful people. About winners! But our novels have dwarfs and giants and bag ladies and alcoholics and junkies and southern ladies with one leg and people in mental institutions and sharecropper cabins and boring couples who are busy destroying each other. I don't like to read about people with all kinds of frustrations and what's that word you use? Oh yes, angst! Angst is boring! Angst turns me off.

"I don't want to read about bad plumbing or the Nazis. I like romantic books that turn out well in the end. And I like to read movie magazines and gossip columns because I want to know what it's like to be those people. They're different from ordinary people, larger than life.

"But you're not publishing books for people like me. You're publishing pretentious books for a few professors to bore their students with."

They sat there talking for hours. "If you were to do the kind of book that interests you," he asked finally, "whose life would you choose?"

"Oh, that's easy. Ava Gardner. Because she comes from the South, the way I do. She was one of six children and had an unhappy, loveless childhood like mine. And just look at the people she's been married to—Mickey Rooney, Artie

Shaw, Frank Sinatra. Isn't that amazing? But she hasn't been married since 1957. Why? Why is a beautiful woman like that alone? She hasn't made a good movie since *On the Beach* in 1959, and she looked awful in that. Why? People say she drinks. Does she? Those are the kinds of things that interest me, Mr. Blackstone. You probably think all of that's dumb and low-class.

"I know that my friends do. But they think it's perfectly acceptable to gossip about high-class people like the Kennedys or Mrs. Woodward or Maria Callas. They think that makes it different, but it's really just the same thing. I wish you'd also do a book about Marilyn Monroe. With lots of pictures. People cared about her. She was a poor girl like me, and she made something of herself.

"My friend Sarah lent me a book called *The Day of the Locust*, which she said is 'an accurate representation of Hollywood.' Of course, she's never been there! Neither have I. So how does she know? I hated that book. It's a depressing put-down of fans, and it makes them evil and ugly. Maybe some of them are, but not all of them. This whole country is a country of fans. I don't want to put them down. I'm one of them. And I want to give us books that tell them what they want to know. And that's mainly who slept with whom."

Mr. Blackstone winced. "All right," he said. "Go ahead and try it. Make an appointment with Ava Gardner or anybody else you'd like to snag. See if there's a book in her. I'm willing to try anything once. Frankly, I don't think it will work. A whole book about a movie star? I doubt it. But I'll give you your chance. Fly out to the Beverly Hills Hotel. Meet with someone in the Polo Lounge. Do the whole Hollywood bit and see what happens. But remember that it probably won't work. Nobody will ever be that interested in full-length books about movie stars."

CHAPTER
Fifty-Four

The month after their confrontation, Robert had gone skiing in Switzerland with his girlfriend, intending to sue for divorce immediately upon his return. But one beautiful winter day while skiing they were caught in a sudden, violent avalanche. The girlfriend died, smothered by the snow, and Robert's injuries kept him in and out of Swiss hospitals for the next year. By the time he was well enough to return to work, his skiing days were over. He was a lonely man, and a bitter man who wanted his son. And finally, the day Wendy had dreaded for so long came to pass. The papers were served.

She phoned Sarah. "Should I hire Claude?"

"I don't know. He's very successful, but you know how difficult and irascible he is. I'll talk to him first about it."

When Sarah described the situation to Claude, she was both amused and indignant at his response. "I don't know how you and your girlfriends always manage to get into these stupid scrapes. One more incident like Selma and you may very well find yourself out of a job. Neither one of you knows how to follow the rules. You have no sense of self-preservation. You're stupid and she's equally stupid. And that also applies to the rest of your little group."

"Stupid? I've just been promoted to associate professor, two of the books Arla acquired are on the best-seller list, Charlotte's about to open her own art gallery, and Wendy only made the mistake of falling in love."

"Falling in love with the wrong person is stupid. I'm sorry for her, but she picked the wrong guy for an affair. A backlash is going on, in case you don't know. Nobody likes black people anymore after what they did in Watts. No matter how much money she has she's going to lose the kid."

"There must be something we can do. She's a wonderful mother."

"I believe you. But nobody else will. Try to look at it objectively, the way a judge and jury would. On one hand you have this promiscuous slut who's hot for blacks, and on the other hand you have a society doctor from one of the country's most prestigious families. He'll limp into court with his gray hair and blue eyes and fair skin, and you can bet your bottom dollar that the judge knows at least one person who's come to Kingman for medical help. He'll come off smelling like Mr. Clean. So there's no way she can win. I feel for her, but there's no way I would take this case. I'd rather be on his side. Advise her to make some kind of settlement so that at least she gets to see the kid. If she doesn't, she'll end up waiting seven years until he's eighteen."

Wendy refused to listen to Claude's advice. All her life people had looked at her beautiful face and beamed. The same thing would happen now. "I'll go into court and take my chances."

"Wendy's still living in never-never land," Charlotte warned Sarah. "She's not a beautiful young thing any longer. She's not going to get her way on the basis of her face."

Wendy could not have predicted that the old magic wouldn't work. And she also could never have predicted that this would become a media event. The headlines screamed, "Black Leader Named in Socialite Divorce," and the old *Daily News* picture of Wendy clutching at her dress was juxtaposed in the tabloids with a shot of her at Selma. Claude had been right. There was no way that she could win. But she refused to settle.

On a terrible day, the second most terrible day of her life, her friends stood beside her to hear the judge's decision. Bobby had been given to Robert, and she was forbidden all visitation rights. She gasped and swayed against Marshall. But she refused to crumble. Pride was all she had left. Outwardly maintaining her savoir faire, surrounded by her friends, and leaning on Marshall's arm, head erect, she walked calmly from the courtroom ignoring the popping of flash bulbs and the shouted queries of reporters.

Her servants served lunch to her friends, and she carried on the way Edita had after each loss. It almost seemed as if nothing had changed, but of course everything had. She was alone again. Her home was no longer a sanctuary, no longer the island of peace that Maurice had found so comforting. She had received so much hate mail and so many obscene calls that she had changed her phone number twice and automatically threw out all unfamiliar-looking mail without opening it.

Her friends suffered with her. "Don't despair," Sarah begged. "We'll think of something. We'll get Bobby back."

"Don't give her false hope," Charlotte said realistically. "She brought this on herself. I warned her about flaunting Maurice on the night they were at the Copa."

"Isn't that a little unfair, dear?" Marshall reprimanded gently. "Things happen whether the victim causes them or not. Look at what happened to my wife and Teddy."

"I wish that after all this time you'd refer to her as your first wife," Charlotte sighed.

Sarah looked at her friends and thought about the strangeness and unpredictability of life. Four friends. Two of them divorced, one widowed, and only one of them still married. Charlotte. Why had that marriage endured? It certainly hadn't been easy.

She had never been able to figure out if Marshall were saintly or foolish. How was it possible for him to have such clear perceptions about others and be so blind to the decline of his own life? Teddy was a heroin junkie, who at the moment was at Synanon in Santa Monica trying to kick the habit, and Marshall was again unemployed. Apart from Kitty, he seemed to get little pleasure out of life. And yet he acted serene and optimistic. And he stayed.

How had Marshall, that most successful of men, turned into Willie Loman? He no longer dreamed of a concert, and his passion for the piano had been reduced to little more than a hobby. Marshall was a tragedy, but at least he'd had some good years. Teddy had had none.

Every time Sarah asked Marshall how Teddy was doing, he always said brightly that his son was on his way to recovery, despite his obvious difficulty in conquering his addiction. She thought of her own wonderful children and shuddered. You can hide everything in life except your children. What a bitter fate for Marshall! What could be a greater torment than to have a son who was a junkie?

Charlotte looked at her gold Rolex. She had an appointment with an architect to discuss the design for a building she had bought in an area called Soho, which everyone was predicting would be the important art center of the future. "I have to go, Wendy. You won't commit suicide, will you? My father committed suicide, as you know. I'd never speak to you again."

She'd made Wendy smile. "Of course I won't. I saw one suicide in my life and that was enough. I couldn't leave that kind of legacy to Bobby. I won't kill myself. I won't give that satisfaction to Robert."

"I always thought Robert was a stuck-up stick," Sarah said, "but I still can't believe he'd be so cruel about Bobby."

"I'm not surprised at what he's done," Arla said. "That's the way men are. But there's a way you can get even. Tell your side of the story. Write all about Maurice and make Robert sweat. And after that write more novels. Think of all the wonderful, glamorous things you can write about. The people who used to come to your hotel and the people you and Robert have always mingled with. Write about being on Onassis's yacht, about the Crespis, about the Patiños and Rothschilds. Write about the Paris Ritz and all those places with the fancy French names: St. Tropez, Cap Ferrat, Monte Carlo. Help all the ordinary people like me live your kind of life."

"I don't know if it's really all that interesting."

"Then make things up. Say that Robert liked to screw goats. The more outrageous the better. Write a novel about you and Maurice before somebody else writes about you. I don't think there's been a good sexy interracial novel since Han Suyin's. For years you've been saying that you want to write. Here's a perfect opportunity."

"I'll have to think about it," Wendy said. "Right now I'm too worn out to think of anything."

"I have to leave," Charlotte said again, worried.

"I wish I didn't have to," Sarah said, "especially with all of those crazy letters you've been getting."

"I'll be all right. Maggie needs you at home."

"You stay with her, Marshall," Charlotte ordered. "You have nothing better to do."

Her resentment that he had been unemployed for three months was almost uncontrollable. His major function now was the carrying and delivering of paintings. Who could ever have predicted that she'd end up supporting him?

"My servants are here," Wendy said to Marshall. "I won't be alone. Please don't put yourself out for me."

"It would be my pleasure," he said with his usual gallantry.

After the others had gone, she and Marshall sat quietly together in her elegant living room with its famed collection of paintings, priceless jade carvings, and oriental rugs, sipping brandy and listening to music. She was glad that he had stayed. He had always been a comforting presence for all of them from the very first time he'd saved Maurice from jail. For the thousandth time she found herself wondering how he could be so strong and reliable for everybody else and so blind for himself? Didn't he see how contemptuously Charlotte now treated him?

Wendy knew that he had never talked about his feelings, having been brought up at a time and in a tradition that did not encourage it, but she tried anyway. "Why do you take Charlotte's abuse? Why do you permit her to diminish you? It hurts me to watch."

At first she thought he wouldn't answer. But then he sighed and began to talk, blaming only himself, another aspect of his code of gentlemanly behavior. "Because I *am* diminished. I am unemployed, and it's she who has the responsibility for Kitty's tuition and for Teddy's rehabilitation."

"For heaven's sake, that's sexist nonsense. That doesn't diminish you. Didn't you support her completely for all these years? You gave her whatever you had when *she* brought in nothing. So why is the reverse situation so unthinkable? *I* don't think you're diminished because you're not head of a big company any longer. You're still the same person. Your problem is that you're too damned polite. Remember that movie in which James Cagney pushes a grapefruit into Mae Murray's face. I always wished that you would do that to Charlotte, just once. I just don't understand why you've stayed married for twenty-one years."

"If you asked a random five hundred men why they've stayed married, they couldn't tell you," he answered. "At the beginning, apart from Teddy, everything seemed fine. I was in love. Kitty came along. My work continued to prosper. As for Teddy, I was prepared for things *not* to go smoothly. How could there not be psychological results of his terrible experience? And Charlotte was very young, so I made excuses. She would mature. He would get better.

"I suppose the question in both business and personal life is where to draw the line between what is acceptable and what is unacceptable. What should be overlooked and what is unforgivable. It's a juggling act. You move together, you draw apart. You quarrel and you reconcile. You call something unforgivable and then your wife does something so lovely that you instantly forgive. You say that after all, nobody's perfect. Day by day by day you sell yourself out. That's how it happens. And after awhile it's too late to change.

"But it isn't just my way. I've watched your little sorority for a long, long time, and the situation is very much the same. You quarrel and you make up. I've heard Charlotte say dreadful things to you, call you a nymphomaniac, and yet she's there when you need her."

She looked at him in astonishment. "You're absolutely right. I've never seen the similarity before. Sometimes I've wanted to strangle her."

"So there it is. People put up with a lot because one never can be quite sure of the correct moment at which to take a stand. Very few marriages are completely satisfactory, so those people who want to stay married survive as I have done. Through extracurricular activities."

"You, Marshall? Women? I'm surprised. Really surprised."

He almost blushed. "No. Of course not. Not women.

Music. Music has been my source of comfort as Maurice has been yours."

"I love music too. But it's hardly as satisfying as a warm body in bed."

"Perhaps it's even more satisfying."

"Then show me. Play for me. I've never heard you play a complete piece through. Charlotte always interrupted before you could finish. Now you can do it. All these years you've wanted to give that concert. Give it to me now. You can pretend that we're at Carnegie Hall. Do you need music?"

"Certainly not. I have several concerts memorized."

"Then do it please, for me. To make me forget how awful and plundered I feel. Go out of the room, then make your entrance and bow, and I'll applaud, and then you can begin."

When he hesitated she said, "If you don't play for me I'll get really drunk."

His eyes twinkled. "Well then, if it's medicinal."

He walked outside, closing the heavy oak doors behind him, then opened them again, walked to the Steinway concert grand, faced her, and bowed. She stood up, cheering and clapping wildly, as he gravely bowed again, acknowledging his enthusiastic audience. Then he sat down, waited for silence, and began to play.

He played for three hours without intermission. The Schumann *Carneval*, the Bach *Chromatique Fantasie and Fugue*, Beethoven's *Waldstein*, the Chopin *Sonata in C* with its wonderful funeral march, Cesar Franck's *Prelude, Fugue and Variations*, and Ravel's *Sonatine*.

While he played, he was a man transformed, as romantic as Franz Liszt, with that special aura of sexiness that attends great performers or athletes who transcend the normal boundaries of what man can do and who heighten the viewer's sense of life. Again she had that flash of feeling she'd had in the hospital. He was majestic when he believed in himself as he did at the keyboard. Music transformed him into Apollo, roaming proudly over a world that belonged to him.

It was dusk when he finished. He looked at her and saw that her face was wet with tears. She crossed to where he still sat at the piano lost in beauty, bent her head to his and gently brushed her lips against his. "Magic," she whispered. "Thank you. You've taken one of the worst days of my life and made it beautiful."

He looked at her and his eyes were also wet. And then he put his arms around her, pulled her close to him, and kissed her with all of the romantic passion unleashed by the magnificent music.

"Oh, my," she said, when she finally pulled away. "I don't think this was quite what Charlotte had in mind when she asked you to stay with me."

He laughed like a boy. "I don't either." He reached for her again and felt himself joyously drowning in the beauty of her eyes, her lips, her fragrant hair that gently fell against his cheek.

There was a knock on the door and they both jumped. "Dinner is served madam," said the butler.

"We'll be right there," she answered.

He crooked his elbow and held it out to her. "May I escort you to dinner?"

"You can escort me anywhere," she answered.

CHAPTER
Fifty-Five

They sat across from each other toying with their food. "We have to talk," he said.

"I'm listening."

"I think I've always loved you. From the day that Teddy first climbed on your lap and said he wanted you for his mother. I looked at you, and at that very moment something I would never acknowledge began in my heart."

"You never said anything."

"What was there to say? You were in love with Maurice, and I was married, and that was that.

"That night after the Copa, when I brought him home, and you held out those lovely arms to him, I wished they were for me. And when you came to us after Edita died, and we sat talking on the terrace, all I wanted to do was take you in my arms and soothe your hurt and get you to stop drinking and keep you safe forever."

"You encouraged me to marry Robert."

"How could I have done otherwise? I was married with a wife and two children, and you had never shown the slightest indication that you saw me as anything more than Charlotte's husband. That's true, isn't it?"

She nodded.

"One night," she said, "it was different. I didn't look at you as Charlotte's husband. I felt attracted. It was when you came to the hospital to help Arla. You were dressed informally and you looked so boyish, and you took charge of the situation so well. But I did what you've always done. Pushed it away."

They sipped espresso in the living room after dinner. She had never seen him so gay. "You've always wanted me to play the piano for you," he said, "and I just did. There's something I've always wanted from you. I want you to dance with me. I want you to dance with me the way you used to dance with Maurice. I want you to look at me with your lips slightly parted, the way you used to look at him."

She put on the phonograph and held out her arms to him. They danced to all of the romantic songs that were so popular that year. "The Shadow of Your Smile," "I Will Wait for You," "What Now, My Love?" and then that most haunting of melodies from *Doctor Zhivago*, "Somewhere my Love." When the music ended, they stood holding each other with soaring passion.

"This is a dream," he murmured. "I can't believe it."

Her loins were moist with passion, and excitement made her exotic voice husky. "Let's go upstairs to bed."

At those words, he shook his head like a man trying to see in a fog, and he moved away from her. "No. We have to talk."

"We can talk in bed."

"In bed I won't remember what we have to talk about."

"Then it can't be very important."

"But it is. We have to talk about Charlotte. How do you propose to deal with her?"

"We won't tell her, of course."

He looked at her in surprise. "I couldn't do that. I don't want to come sneaking around here for a few stolen minutes in bed. I don't want to be your substitute for Maurice. I don't want to be just another man. I want to marry you."

"You mean you'd divorce Charlotte?"

"I can see no other way."

"It would rip the four of us apart. The sorority would be destroyed. Charlotte would never forgive me. It would be a mess, and I've just finished with one such mess. I haven't the strength to go through another. Not even with you at my side."

"Then what do you propose?"

"I don't know. It's been a long, terrible day, Marshall. One of the worst of my life, and I'm suddenly completely exhausted. I just want to go to bed and find oblivion. I can't think of anything more right now."

Then suddenly with startling clarity, she knew what she had to do. "I'm going away. I need time to lick my wounds and let this awful publicity die down. I want to become anonymous again. I'm tired of all the hate mail and the obscene phone calls and the photographers. I want to live in London. Edita and I always had such happy times there. I'll go to London, buy a house, and try to write a book. Arla was right. Writing is the best revenge.

"And there's something more. If you want to end your marriage end it, but not because of me. I'd be happy to be your reward, but not your reason for doing it. I don't want to be blamed. I don't want to be your crutch.

"If you want to get out, then get out without mentioning me. After you're free, we can find out what we can be to each other. I'll wait for you in London. You can come to me in London. Charlotte would still be angry, once she learned of it. There would be no avoiding it, I guess. But not the way she would if you spoke to her tomorrow. I guess I'd prefer to be on a different continent."

"I'll do anything you say if you promise to wait for me."

"Of course I will." She put her arms around him and

held him close but now in friendship rather than passion. "I need you as much as you need me."

And they left it at that.

CHAPTER
Fifty-Six

Nineteen hundred sixty-eight was the best year of Charlotte's life. It was a time of exploding interest in modern art, and her gallery was an immediate success. Everyone agreed that she had the best new young artists. Overnight, her gallery was ranked with that of the four most influential modern-art dealers: Leo Castelli, Andre Emmerich, John Weber, and Ileana Sonnabend. Her first show was sold out before it opened, and then she was ready to change the rest of her life.

It was Teddy who provided her with the final reason to end her marriage. He had disappeared again for six months, and they'd been unable to find him until the phone rang one night from a jail in Miami Beach. Marshall went down there, got him out of jail, and returned to the apartment with him in the middle of an elegant dinner party that Charlotte was holding for some of New York's most prestigious critics. She blanched in horror at his filthy, strung-out appearance, but she continued with the dinner party as if nothing had happened. As soon as the guests had gone, she summoned Marshall.

"I want a divorce," she said without preliminaries. "How dare Teddy come in here stinking like that. He's too disgusting to be even pathetic."

"You always have been noted for your compassion." He sat there looking at her with a wry, sardonic little smile instead of being devastated and pleading with her, as she had assumed he would be.

"Teddy is now your responsibility," she said. "Kitty will stay with me when she's home on vacation." Kitty was a senior in college.

"Are you sure that this is what you want?"

"Absolutely."

"Very well then. It's your decision. We've been together twenty-three years. A long time!"

"Long enough! Time for a change!"

He flew back to Florida with Teddy for his trial, and Charlotte phoned Arla with her news. "Listen, I have a good idea." Arla said. "I have to go to London. Why don't you come with me? I'd love the companionship, and the change will do you good. I'm sure we can stay with Wendy."

"That's a wonderful idea. I want to talk to Francis Bacon and Julien Freud and see what's happening on the art scene." They left New York before Marshall and Teddy returned.

It was Arla's first trip to England, and she was hoping to sign John Gielgud, Deborah Kerr, and Laurence Olivier. Mr. Blackstone had promised that if she did, she would receive the title of publisher. "I still can't believe it," she burbled to Charlotte above the noise of the plane. "That I should be meeting with people like them. I'm glad I took speech lessons."

I can't believe it either, Charlotte thought gloomily. There's no accounting for luck!

Arla's lap was filled with guidebooks. "I want to see Madame Tussaud's and Piccadilly Circus," she said. "I don't want this to be just the same old business trip."

Hah, Charlotte thought. A few years ago she couldn't even spell business trip. Suddenly she felt depressed and abandoned. Why am I feeling so bitchy, she wondered. I'm getting everything I ever wanted. I'm dumping that wimp, I have my own gallery, and I don't have to worry about money. I guess I'm upset because he didn't fight me. All this time it never occurred to me that he might be as sick of me as I was of him.

She couldn't stop talking about the impending divorce. His easy acceptance had turned her victory into ashes.

"Your situation is not unique," Arla told her. "We're doing a book right now on the increasing frequency of divorce among older couples. In the past, older women clung on to their marriages because they had no way to survive without them. Everything's different today. They have career options and personal options. A lot of older women are taking up with younger men. One of the women in our office threw out all of her high heels, left her husband and children, put on jeans, and hitchhiked to a commune in Arizona on her fiftieth birthday."

Charlotte listened to her and became increasingly depressed. Why exactly had she dumped Marshall? It would have been better to have had Teddy incarcerated in some mental institution. Marshall would have agreed to that. Suddenly she remembered all the thousands of times he had been kind, the way they'd made love after she'd learned of her inheritance, and she knew that she'd been a fool. She'd made a terrible mistake. I'll phone him from London the moment I get there and make it all up. He'll agree, of course. He's always forgiven me for anything I've done. We'll deal with the problem of Teddy together.

Arla noticed her gloom. "Don't feel bad about your decision. I've been able to live very well without a husband. Better, in fact. I'm glad that you're moving toward conscious feminism. Sarah's still not there. I asked her about it, and she said the class struggle cuts across sex and race. She said she feels solidarity with the wretched of the earth, regardless of gender. And Wendy probably never will be a feminist. Even after everything that Robert has done, she still likes men and sex. She wrote to me that she has a new young lover. A Lord somebody or other."

"I haven't received a letter. Why did she write to you?"

"She needed some advice about the book she's working on."

"Did she say if she'd heard from Maurice?"

"She wrote to him after Martin Luther King's assassination, but he didn't answer. She thinks he may have been too heartbroken."

"What about Bobby?"

"Nothing. That ex-husband of hers is a real stinker. He's sticking to the letter of the law. Bobby just entered Deerfield, by the way."

Wendy and her chauffeur were waiting for them at the airport, and Charlotte thought Wendy was a little cool to her but perhaps that was her imagination. Wendy seemed to have completely recovered from that terrible trial over Bobby. She was as glowing and beautiful as ever. She must have had everything lifted, Charlotte thought. She took them to the Connaught for dinner, and while they were eating superb salmon in fresh dill Charlotte told her about what had happened with Marshall. "What do you think? Should I try again with him?"

Wendy looked strangely disconcerted. "I would," she said hesitantly. "He's a wonderful man."

"The funny thing about it is that he was not more upset."

"Perhaps he didn't think you really meant it."

Suddenly Charlotte was happy again. "Yes," she said, "that probably explains his attitude. I'm sure that everything will be exactly the same as in the past when I get home. What do you think, Wendy?"

"I honestly don't know. You'll just have to wait and see."

It was a wonderful week. Wendy took them to the Tate, to the National Gallery, down the Thames to Windsor Castle, to a play at Stratford-upon-Avon, and to a party given by Lord Summerfield, Wendy's current lover, at his stately home. My God, Charlotte thought. He's not more than twenty-five, and he looks like a drowned rat, like a scurvy British seaman in an old Errol Flynn movie. How can a lord look grubby?

The home was magnificent, but Charlotte continued to watch the peculiar guests in amazement. The girls were dressed in crazy Mary Quant clothing, and some of the men with prestigious titles had cigarettes permanently dangling out of the corners of their mouth and actually looked as if they were dirty under their Savile Row suits. One reeked of perspiration.

Arla, watching Wendy laughing, dancing, and flirting, was suddenly filled with a certain discontent. She looks ten years younger than I do, she thought. Maybe I ought to take off some of this weight when I get home. I'm safe and successful. I don't have to be afraid of men. I don't have to look like a Mack truck to fend them off. I like to dance, and here I stand like a fat old woman. It's too soon for that. It's a lot better to be whirling there in the middle of the action like Wendy than to be standing on the sidelines like Charlotte and me.

At the end of the week, just before they left, Wendy shyly presented her with a manuscript. "I don't know if it's any good," she said, "but you told me to try so I did."

Arla was thrilled. "I can't wait. I'll read it on the plane going home and phone you as soon as I've finished."

CHAPTER
Fifty-Seven

The day after they returned from London, Arla and Charlotte met Sarah for lunch at Lutèce. They both looked smashing in new black mink coats, but Sarah wore the same cloth coat she'd had for a few years, cheap snow boots, and fake gold earrings. She didn't seem aware of the differences. Charlotte told her all about England and about the quarrel with Marshall. "I was afraid he might have moved out while I was away," she said, "but he and Teddy are still there. So I guess it's business as usual."

Sarah hurried to share her exciting news. Her father was sending Maggie to junior high school at Oakwood, a private school across the Hudson River in Poughkeepsie, where she would get a much better education than in the local public school. And even more wonderful than that, he was going to pay Jimmy's tuition at med school.

"I could almost forgive him everything for his treatment of Jimmy," she glowed. "Jimmy really loves him. He doesn't see him as the monstrously reactionary Judge Stern. He sees him as his grandpa, his link to tradition. They're in Israel right now. My father's being honored for endowing the Judge Stern Chair of Jurisprudence at Jerusalem University."

"I read about it in the *Times*," Charlotte said.

"I wish that I could go myself," Sarah said. "I've always wanted to see Israel, but I just can't get away from classes right now. Some day I'll go back with Jimmy."

She absolutely adored her son. He had worked on Allard

Lowenstein's Dump Johnson campaign and had gone to Washington with a group of friends for the Democratic Convention. She and Maggie had clung together and wept in horror as they watched the televised coverage of the police viciously and indiscriminantly beating the defenseless kids who were bravely chanting, "The whole world is watching, the whole world is watching," while the billy clubs came down smack, smack, smack on their heads.

Jimmy had come home without injuries, but for weeks afterward Sarah's old nightmares about her brother returned to haunt her, and she'd almost regretted having passed on to him a political philosophy that could place him in so much danger.

"He's a fine boy," Arla said, "and so is Peter. But I have news for you about my other two. Mark has been drafted and Stewart's back in New York. And guess what he's doing? He's living and working with Lenny. Isn't that the strangest thing? Can you imagine voluntarily going back to live with someone who abused you so badly? The therapist I saw after my divorce said that abused children often cling to the parents who abuse them, but he's not a child any longer. I worry that I set him a terrible example by staying there myself all those years while I was being beaten.

"I'm a lot more concerned, really, about Mark. His last letter said something about a Tet New Year's Festival. He was worried. Why would he worry about a festival? I wish this damned war would end. Peter said if they draft him he won't go."

"Nobody should go," Sarah said. "Jimmy won't go either."

Her friends had to get back to work, and she had to get home. She took the 4:30 bus at the Port Authority, picked up her car at the station, grabbed a pizza for dinner at Chez Joey, then headed up the mountain to her little house.

When she saw Claude's Cadillac in the driveway she began to tremble. Gooseflesh broke out on her arms, and alarm bells jangled in her ears. Something must have happened to one of her parents. Well, Claude was probably right again. He'd warned them that the trip to Israel might prove too arduous. Jimmy must have called him.

As soon as she opened the door Maggie ran to her screaming, "Mommy, Mommy, Mommy, something's happened to Jimmy. Something bad happened to Jimmy."

Her heart stopped beating. She shook so badly that she could hardly talk. "Is he hurt?" she whispered.

Claude bent his head and cried. "I'm sorry Sarah. He's dead. Jimmy's dead."

He had been walking along the beach taking snapshots of birds, when the invaders pulled up on shore in rubber boats and instantly shot him in the stomach and chest. He had apparently heard the sounds, turned, smiled, and raised his unsuspecting hand to wave. They emptied five rounds of ammunition into him. He died still smiling in surprise, murdered on a beach in Israel as the Six-Day War began.

* * *

Wendy flew in from England the next day, and she and Marshall stayed at Sarah's house with her until the period of mourning ended. Charlotte and Arla came as often as possible. Sarah, who had never been religious, insisted on sitting shivah, not bathing, rending her clothing, and sitting on a wooden crate. Maggie, who was as bright and as mature as Jimmy had been, kept constant watch over her mother. "Oh, God," Sarah wept to them. "How much is anybody expected to bear?"

The week passed in a dream. Wendy offered her Valium and liquor but she accepted neither. She would not be anesthetized out of her grief. She wanted all of her faculties clear so that she could sit and remember her wonderful son. Gradually, during the week, she started to pull herself together. She had to be strong and sensible and honorable for Maggie's sake. That was all there was now. Her life was over. It no longer mattered. She would live it now for Maggie and anyone else she could help.

She tried to comfort herself with the thought that she was not the only one who had been so bereft. Tens of thousands of boys had died in Vietnam, so many had died in Israel, so many had disappeared in Argentina. She would force herself not to be egocentric, to think of the world. And she kept going, taking an odd kind of pride in the fact that she never collapsed and was never unconscious, not even for a day. She behaved according to her conception of a mensch. By the end of the week of shivah, she was ready to return to work. She had a responsibility to her students, and she had been elected president of the local faculty union. She would keep busy and try to live through her pain.

Before leaving, Wendy and Marshall told her about their feelings for each other. He and Teddy were going to join Wendy in London. He would tell Charlotte when they went back to the city and ask her to get the divorce she had asked for. He had hoped that Wendy need not be involved, but Charlotte had to know where he was going.

"I'm sorry about Charlotte," Sarah said. "I think she really does love you, Marshall. In her own way." She threw her arms around them, and they cried together. "But I'm glad that you'll be happy. Someone should be happy."

Marshall nerved himself to tell Charlotte about Wendy the day after Wendy left for England again. "All this time? You mean even when I visited that traitorous bitch in London you and she were already connected? I've never looked at another man. How could you do this behind my back?"

For once Marshall was firm. "Teddy and I are going to London, and I would appreciate it if you would get the divorce, the way you said you were going to do when you kicked me out."

She burst into tears. "But I changed my mind. I told you that. Please don't do this to me. Please don't leave me. I don't want to be another divorced woman floating around the city. I don't want to be alone. Please don't leave me. You know I can't cope alone." She sank down on her knees and threw her arms around his waist. "Please. I'm begging you."

He gently disengaged her arms. "This isn't easy for me. I'll always be there if you need me."

"Bullshit. I need you now. Wendy doesn't need you. She has dozens of men. All I've ever had is you."

She was plunged back to the misery of her childhood. What good was all of her success? Nobody loved her. Nobody cared about her and nobody ever would. She drove up to Sarah's for comfort, and was angry to find that Sarah already knew.

"You can't be friends with both of us," she wept. "It will be just like college again with those sorority girls talking about me and sneering."

"You know we would never do that. We could never be cruel. Maybe this is for the best. You and Marshall have evidently used each other up. But he isn't the only man in the world. You should feel good about yourself. You're a howling success! You've revolutionized the world of art! You're constantly in the news! You're invited to wonderful parties! You know important people! You lecture, travel! You have jewels and magnificent clothing! You've beaten every sorority girl who ever snubbed you! So what more do you want?"

"Nobody loves me!"

"Kitty loves you."

"No, she doesn't. I hardly see her anymore. She's totally involved in some crazy political organization called the SDS."

"I love you."

"No, you don't. Not enough anyway. If you really loved me, my enemies would be your enemies."

"They're not your enemies. After the initial hurt passes, we'll all be friends again."

Sarah looked at her with compassion. Charlotte was the least happy of them all. The others were made unhappy by external events, by things that happened to them. But Charlotte's unhappiness was worse. She was unhappy with what she was.

"Stay for dinner tonight," she urged. "Don't rush back to the city."

"I wish I could. I really need some human warmth. But I'd better go. I always have this knot of depression in my stomach anyway, and since Marshall told me, it's even worse than before. I have to keep running all the time because the moment I stop, I start to sink. Besides, there's a party tonight I should attend. Lee Radziwill will be there. She came in yesterday and said she'd be back tomorrow. I can't miss an important sale like that."

"It's up to you. But I'd like you to stay."

"I'm too nervous to stay. Only work deadens my anxiety."

"Why don't you get some more therapy?"

"Because I think it's all a total fraud. I may be difficult, but I'm not stupid. I've had Freudian therapy and Maslow therapy and primal scream and Jungian therapy, and none of it's made a difference. It's all a waste of time. The only purpose therapy serves is to make shrinks rich. It's like religion. Faith based on nothing visible. Teddy's a living example of that, if you call it living. Besides, the therapists I've encountered are so screwed up themselves you wonder how they could possibly help anybody. I'm more interested in the art on their walls (usually pretty bad), than in their canned, clichéd advice." Sarah laughed for the first time since Jimmy's death.

"All right," Charlotte decided. "I guess I will stay for dinner. But I'm not going to do a thing about getting the divorce. If they want it, they can do the work."

Sitting at dinner with Sarah and Maggie, Charlotte found it almost impossible to believe that Jimmy had died so recently. They ate pizza and ice cream, talked and gossiped and laughed. Without hesitation, Maggie joined in whenever she liked and whenever she said anything, Sarah looked at her with delight, as if she were the most marvelous, brilliant creature in the world. They kept each other brave and strong. Charlotte sighed for her lack of rapport with Kitty.

"I think I saw Maurice on television the other day," she suddenly remembered. "He was leading a group called the Black Panthers, at San Francisco State. Have you heard of them?"

"Of course I've heard of them. So that's where he is now. It's logical! That's what he was always like. A black panther! Or maybe a wounded lion. I'll never forget how brave he was for me. If he's with them, I'm worried."

"He's survived everything else thus far. He'll probably survive this, too."

But Sarah *was* worried. At San Francisco State, black students had led a campus-wide strike that had already been going on for four months and had led to hundreds of arrests, hundreds of injuries, a dozen fire bombings, and the presence of hundreds of policemen on the campus. It was dangerous to be a Black Panther. The FBI had joined with local police departments around the country in attacking Panther groups, raiding thirty-one Panther headquarters during the past year, arresting hundreds of them on spurious charges, demanding high bails, and disrupting party operations through spies and agent provocateurs.

"I hope it wasn't Maurice," Sarah said. "I don't know how much more beating he can stand."

"Have you ever heard anything about Jerry?" Charlotte asked.

"Not a word! Claude thinks maybe he's in Costa Rica or else that the mob did him in for gambling debts." She shrugged. "He'll probably come to no good end."

Charlotte laughed. "I don't know. It seems to me that con men like that always triumph."

"I liked him," Maggie said. "I kind of hoped he'd read about Jimmy and call. But he hasn't. I'm sorry he turned out to be such a rat."

"He was a likable rat," Charlotte answered. "Incidentally, I've hired an assistant, Terence Hall, who has that same kind of easy charm. He has one of the best eyes for authenticity I've ever come across."

"Romance?" Sarah asked.

"Absolutely not. He's thirty-five and gay."

"Really? I've never known a gay man personally. Or if I did, I didn't know it. What's he like?"

"Like anybody else. He's handsome and charming and witty, and he escorts me to functions when I need someone. Our relationship is only that of employer and employee, but I like it that way. I have an impressive escort without any emotional turmoil."

Listening to her, Sarah thought, yes, that's really what she's always needed. An escort she didn't have to love.

After Charlotte had gone, Sarah and Maggie sat together playing Scrabble. "Aunt Charlotte is so beautifully dressed," Maggie said timidly, wanting to be tactful. "She's just as old as you but she hasn't let her hair go grey. Why don't you dye your hair?"

"Oh, darling! What difference does it make now?"

"I want you to look nice. Jimmy would want you to look nice."

Sarah took her in her arms. "I have neither the time nor money nor inclination. I don't want to be a slave to anything except you." Maggie laughed, then gently kissed her mother's sad, worn face. "Mom, would you rather be her than you?"

"Certainly not."

"How come?"

"Because then I wouldn't have you."

"Oh, Mom. I just can't have a serious conversation with you."

CHAPTER Fifty-Eight

Wendy's chauffeur would have gone to Heathrow alone to meet Marshall and Teddy, but Wendy could not bear to wait one minute longer to see them than she had to. She was so anxious that she arrived an hour early. Leaving her chauffeur outside, she waited impatiently at the rail outside of customs, a tall, thin, beautifully turned-out woman whose raven hair and queenly carriage caused people to keep glancing at her with the little surreptitious looks given covertly to beautiful women and celebrities. She wore high black-leather boots, a butter-soft black leather cape and matching skirt from Loewe, and a violet cashmere turtleneck sweater the color of her eyes. The diamond studs glittered in her ears, and on her wrist was the old diamond bracelet from Mexico, which normally she would not wear during the day but which somehow seemed like a talisman to her today. On her finger glittered a large sapphire-and-diamond ring that had belonged to Marshall's first wife and which he had been saving for Kitty.

"I want you to have it," he'd said, when he'd given it to her on the night before she'd returned to London. "Kitty's fiancé will buy her her own."

"Or I'll give her one of Edita's. I have so much to pass on to a daughter."

Passengers from the New York plane began to disembark, and one by one, as they drifted out, every head turned to look at her as they passed. She didn't mind the stares. Today, nothing could bother her. She was so content, so full of happiness that she wanted to smile back at them, to embrace the world.

She couldn't wait to tell Marshall the good news. Arla was going to publish her book.

Despite the agony of Bobby's loss, she had prevailed, and now so many good things had coalesced: love, health, creativity. After she'd lost Bobby, she'd thought that she would never be happy again. And yet at this moment she was. And somehow she'd get him back.

She'd written continuously to him, letter after letter pouring out her love, but he'd never answered. Probably he hadn't received the letters. She wouldn't be surprised if Robert had done that. But once she was married to Marshall, with him at her side, they'd fight for visitation rights, at the very least.

She waited and waited, craning her neck like an eager child, each minute thinking I see them, I see them. But when the last passenger had come through and the next batch were speaking German, she broke out in perspiration and clung to the railing suddenly faint. Now hold on to yourself, she warned sternly. They had to be on the plane, or they would have wired you.

Unable to bear the tension for another moment, she ducked under the railing and dashed past the Indian guard on duty. "You can't go in there, madam," he called after her. But ignoring him, she ran to where she could see the expanse of customs. Thank God! They were there! Marshall was pleading with a customs official.

But then her heart sank. She looked at Teddy in dismay. She would not have recognized him had he not stood beside Marshall. Oh, that poor, pathetic boy. He was twenty-six now, Marshall's height, about five feet ten, but he couldn't weigh more than a hundred and ten pounds. His thinness was painful, as if he were wasting away from cancer! His hair was down to his shoulders, and he was dressed in torn jeans, worn sneakers, and a plaid shirt held together with safety pins.

The customs officials were meticulously searching through Teddy's suitcase. Suddenly he exploded. He began to scream and jump up and down like Rumpelstiltskin, "You're messing up my personal possessions, you assholes. What the fuck are you looking for? Why the fuck would I bring drugs into England when they're legal here?"

"Restrain your son," one of the officials warned Marshall, "or we'll have to call the police."

"It's all right," said the other. "I think we're finished here."

Marshall and Teddy reloaded their bags on the dollies provided by the airport and began to wheel them toward the exit where Wendy stood waiting. "Marshall, Marshall," she called, waving her hand at him. He waved back, anxious not to spoil this moment by showing how troubled he was by Teddy's appearance and behavior.

But when he reached her and looked at her loveliness, breathed her wonderful Cabochard, and saw the naked joy in her eyes, all sadness was immediately forgotten as he swept her against him and just held her close.

"My heart is beating so fast," she said.

"And mine," he echoed. "The bridegroom cometh."

"Welcome, bridegroom," she said, kissing him.

Then she turned to Teddy. Up close he was slack-jawed and slovenly. His eyes were glazed, and he was petulant. "Welcome to London," she said.

"Some welcome! Did you see what those assholes did to my luggage? That's the way these fascist pigs treat anybody who has long hair." Marshall sighed.

"Forget about it, Teddy," she said forcing herself to kiss his unwashed cheek. "You're finally here, and I've planned a marvelous week of activities before we go home. Say you're glad to be here." He shrugged as her chauffeur took their bags, and they set off for her house.

Wendy prattled along cheerfully to lighten Marshall's mood. "I've made dinner reservations at the Connaught for tomorrow night and for La Gavroche and the Dorchester and tea at Claridge's. And tomorrow I thought you might like to go sightseeing. Perhaps the Tower of London. What would you like, Teddy?"

"Most of all, I'd like you to leave me alone. But if I have to do the tourist bit, I'd like to see Stonehenge. Could we go there?"

"Anything you like. I want this to be a wonderful vacation for all of us. I want you to be happy. I know lots of young people and if you like, I'll have a big party before you go. But you'll have to look a little better than this. Do you have any nice clothes?"

"No."

"Then tomorrow we'll go shopping. We'll go to Savile Row and then to Harrod's. You won't believe the food halls. I want to fatten you up, too."

Marshall kissed her hand gratefully. Perhaps together they could finally straighten Teddy out.

When they reached her house, she said, "You should both go to sleep now for a few hours. These night flights always knock me out."

Jarvis, her houseman, led Teddy to his room while she showed Marshall how she'd restored the house. "How absolutely beautiful," he said, looking at the collection of late seventeenth- and early eighteenth-century blue-and-white porcelains, the geometrically patterned marble floor, the high arched windows, and the carved mahogany doors separating the main rooms. Two pairs of Tuscan columns divided the living room, and a curved niche in the hallway held a Giacometti sculpture.

The dining-room table was eighteenth-century English, and a Picasso oil hung on the dining-room wall across from the fireplace with its classical marble mantel. And she'd rented a Bösendorfer piano for him to practice on. Trying to repress his emotion, he took off his glasses and polished them.

"A Bösendorfer? One of my lifetime dreams."

Delighted, he sat down and began the Chopin Scherzo in C minor. Then he stopped, looked at her, and stood up again. "There will be plenty of time for music," he said, taking her in his arms.

She took his hand and led him to the bedroom adjoining her own. It was decorated in all modern colors, pink and beige and white and black, with paintings by Julien Freud, high ceilings, and large high triple-glazed windows that let in shafts of light but kept the city noises out. Her houseman stood waiting there.

She introduced them. "This is Jarvis. He'll help you unpack and draw your bath, and then I'll be in. I think we should have lunch served right here."

He put his arms around her. "I'm not hungry. Are you?" She shook her head. "Come back without the food," he murmured softly.

When he came out of his steaming bath, wrapped in the enormous, thick terry-cloth robe that had been placed on the towel warmer for him, she was sitting in an easy chair, wearing a white cotton nightgown that made her look like Alice in Wonderland. Her legs were curled under her, and her dark thick hair was tied back in a violet ribbon. Trembling, he buried his face against her hair, breathing her fragrance. "I still can't believe my luck. I still can't understand what you see in me."

"Oh, darling. I've tried to reassure you so many times. I trust you. I've had my fill of studs and athletes and pretty boys and egomaniacs. I've had my fill of isolated, alienated, selfish men. I'm forty-five years old, and I want solidity and stability. The only thing I ever envied about Sarah was the way that she and Hal used to talk nonstop. They never ran out of conversation. He was her friend. And I want you to be mine. A friend who is always beside me."

"It still bothers me that it's you who has the money."

"Be glad I do. We couldn't make it if I didn't. I used to feel guilty about it. That was why I gave so much to Maurice. But I don't any longer. It will never be a problem between us. It will be ours, and we'll spend it together. We can do anything we like; travel, hire Albert Hall for your concert, or lead a good, quiet life. You can practice the piano and I'll work on books, and we'll never be lonely. And you can't be sure that you won't be bringing in money again. You can start another business if you like. But what I was hoping you might do was to work with me as my adviser and business consultant. I'd like to start a foundation to give away some money. So please don't let it come between us."

"Suppose you get tired of me?"

"Suppose you get tired of *me*? There are no guarantees."

"I'm nervous as hell about going to bed with you, Wendy."

"Don't be nervous. I love you." She dropped her gown to the floor.

Passion shot through him, and he pulled her down to the bed beside her. "Oh, my God," he groaned. "After all these years."

Slowly, with reverence and disbelief, he ran his hands over her beautiful soft body, her high breasts with their firm nipples, her long legs and firm thighs, and then, transported to ecstasy, he bent and kissed her everywhere: her nipples, her small round belly, and the inside of her loins. Softly, with his hands behind her narrow hips, he ran his tongue over the clitoris, slowly, slowly, then faster and faster, wanting only to give, only to please her and make her his, wanting only to make her come and come. And unlike Charlotte, Wendy responded to the gift. She was all loveliness and warmth, laughter and quicksilver movements. As she tensed and tightened and moved and finally let the orgasm come with a wonderful "Oh," he rose erect and began to believe again in his manhood.

And afterward, all of the tension and strangeness between them was gone. In that calm, quiet, shuttered room in the center of London they held tightly to each other as they slept, hoping that at last they had come home.

CHAPTER
Fifty-Nine

Sarah met Stephen Farrell, a professor of Irish literature, at a retirement dinner for a colleague. It was held at Chez Vincent, a seedy local restaurant favored for some obscure reason for such events, a place of dim lights, red lamp shades, black shiny Naugahyde banquettes, and a standard menu of inferior steaks and chops, salads drowned in Russian dressing, cardboard-tasting apple pie, and bad house wine.

She had forced herself to go. Retirement dinners depressed her. It was like being alone in an empty theater after the curtain had gone down. But the honoree had been in her department and had been a good union member, and so she felt that it was her duty to attend. Kathryn, another member of the department, picked her up.

She was always reluctant to leave Maggie alone. "Please don't worry, Mom," Maggie said when Sarah kissed her good night. "You don't want to turn into an overprotective mother, do you? You have to go out. Maybe tonight you'll meet the man of your dreams."

"Maggie, darling. I'm forty-five years old, and I'm not looking. That part of life is behind me. You'll have to bring the next male into this family."

When Kathryn honked, she ran out into the crisp winter night, marveling that she could say such things without dissolving into tears. But the air felt good, and a million stars filled the sky. She popped into the car, greeted Kathryn, and said, "I hope we won't have to stay late."

"I'm with you. I hate these boring events. Let's split immediately after the speeches."

They stepped from the crystal-clear, star-filled winter night into a hot, smoky, noisy room, checked their coats, and made for the bar. The price for these dinners always included one glass of wine and a gift for the retiree. All other drinks were "Dutch treat," according to the invitation.

Kathryn ordered a Bloody Mary, and Sarah, unaware that someone was standing close behind her, ordered a glass of the house Soave and then heard a man's voice say, "I'll pay for that."

Surprised, she turned and looked at the man who had spoken. She'd never seen him before, but that wasn't surprising. Perhaps he was from the Department of Liberal Arts. She rarely got out of the ghetto of the Education building, and most of the people in Liberal Arts looked down on those in Education.

He was young and damned attractive with blue eyes, dark curly hair, firm, cleft chin, and horn-rimmed glasses. An intellectual from central casting. A Clark Kent type!

"Really, that wasn't necessary," she protested.

"I only do things if they're not. I can't be compelled to

do anything." What a beautiful voice. Perhaps he'd been an actor at one time. He was certainly good-looking enough. He cradled his drink and smiled at her, a radiant, confident, open smile as if they were old friends.

"But you've just compelled me to let you pay for my drink," she teased him.

His eyes were warm and sexy. "I didn't say I played by the rules." She looked down at her drink, thinking, I never did know how to make repartee.

Frantically she searched for conversation and then came up with, "I have a friend who's an active feminist. She says it's sexist for men to automatically pick up checks."

He moved closer to her, so close that she could feel the heat of his body. "Are you saying, Dr. Gordon, that I bought you a drink because I'm sexist?"

"Are you?" This delightful young man was flirting with her, but so what? It felt good! It made her feel alive.

"Sexy," he said, "not sexist."

Off balance again, she hurried to change the subject. "You know my name. Have we met before?"

"No, but I've seen you scolding the faculty at union meetings. What was your slogan that made everybody so angry?"

Now she laughed as she repeated the slogan. "If your friend doesn't belong to the union, he or she isn't your friend."

"I'm Steve Farrell," he said. "Irish Lit."

Then suddenly she placed the name. "Oh, yes. Steve Farrell. I've heard about your wonderful articles. Wasn't your wife one of my students?"

She could not remember the woman's face exactly, but she remembered that she was married to someone in the English Department who was viewed as a star. He moved his face so close to hers that their lips almost touched. The heat of his body scorched her.

"Ex-wife," he said, "and I'm available."

Oh my! That was a conversation stopper if she'd ever heard one.

Even as a girl she'd lacked the ability to banter with a

man, and now she was no better. He was flirting with her, but why? Surely he was at least ten years younger than she.

He put his hand across her shoulder and pinned her to the bar, reminding her of an unself-conscious child who will perch on any friendly knee without fear of rejection. She could feel his breath on her neck.

"You have to sit with me at dinner or I'll die of boredom. Will you? Please?" he begged.

"I'm supposed to sit with my friend Kathryn. I came with her."

"So ask her to join us. Please." His charm made her uneasy, but she fought against her discomfort. Jerry had left her permanently nervous about charm, but it would be foolish to assume that all charm was synthetic.

He turned to get them fresh drinks, and she studied herself in the mirror above the bar. Was it possible that he found her attractive? She'd looked like a ghost since Jimmy's death. But her figure was still thin and erect, thank goodness, and she took a certain pride in the erectness of her breasts. After a certain age, she'd found to her delight, it was better to have small breasts. But she wore no makeup, which was foolish. She remembered Maggie's suggestion about coloring her hair after Charlotte's visit. Maybe she should consider it.

When dinner was announced, he put his arm around her with a careless gesture of ownership and led her to a table where he introduced her to Hugh Powell, a young professor with whom he had shared a rented house since his divorce. Hugh looked so terribly young, about twenty-five, that it made her feel self-conscious about Stephen draping his arm across her shoulders. But she did not quite know what to do without seeming rude.

What could she say? "Take your arm off my shoulders because your roommate is so young." "Take your arm off my shoulder because I hardly know you." Either statement sounded terribly stiff, and she didn't want to come across as rigid or uptight. In her generation, touching people meant something, but this generation seemed much more demonstrative. She had often observed students openly soul kissing in public.

He confided in her as easily as he touched her. She

learned that he had two children: Adam, twelve and Debby, seventeen. Debby was the daughter from the first marriage of his ex-wife, who was five years older than Steve. "The bitch got my house," he said gloomily. "The house, the kids, everything. I'd like to ask some of the goddamned women's libbers about that. Why does the woman automatically get everything?"

"Hey," she reprimanded him. "Now you *are* being sexist. Most women end up poor!"

He also told her about his professional problems. He'd received great praise for his articles, but of course he made no money from them. He hated the college and hated his students and couldn't wait to split. But that took money, and besides, there were no jobs available in Irish Lit. His dream was to write a best-seller. "But it's damned difficult. There are forty thousand books published a year. Talent is meaningless without connections."

"Did you ever hear the name Arla Wine? She's a friend of mine who recently became publisher of Blackstone Books. And she's publishing a novel by another one of my friends."

"Really? I'd like to meet her some time. Could you arrange for that?"

"She never has enough time to come up here."

He leaned close to her. "Perhaps we could go down to the city one day. Take in a show."

"Perhaps."

When he asked about her marital history, she left Jerry out, telling him only that her husband had died thirteen years ago. "My daughter never knew him."

"Do you have anyone now?" She shook her head. "I don't either." His voice was low and lovely with a faint Irish lilt. "I'm looking for commitment." She was getting uncomfortable. How had their conversation become intimate so quickly? "I divorced my wife because she took a lover."

She said nothing. What can anybody say in response to a statement like that? He quickly filled the conversation gap.

"I hope you won't mind if I express my condolences about your son. When he died, I thought of lines from Shakespeare's *King John*. Do you know them?"

"I don't think so. Say them for me."

Yes, he must have been an actor, she thought, as he said the lines in his beautiful voice.

> "'Grief fills the room up of my absent child,
> Lies in his bed, walks up and down with me,
> Puts on his pretty looks, repeats his words,
> Remembers me of all his gracious parts,
> Stuffs out his vacant garments with his form.'"

Her eyes were moist when he had finished. "That's the way it is. 'Grief fills up the room of my absent child.'"

"I saw you the month after he died, up there on the platform scolding everyone about the union. And I thought to myself, that's one zesty, gutsy lady. I wanted to meet you and tell you how much I admired you."

"Thank you," she sighed, totally disarmed. She'd had an unexpectedly pleasant evening because of this man.

Then he leaned still closer to her, brushing her ear with his lips. "I came with Hugh," he whispered, "so you'll have to drive me home tomorrow morning to change before class."

Her mood instantly shifted. The nerve of such assumptions. "I hardly know you," she said. "And besides, my daughter is at home."

"So?"

"I just don't do things like this."

"Like what?"

"Like spending the night with strangers. I'm just not casual about these things."

He instantly got sulky. "Suit yourself." Without another word he walked away from her and immediately became involved in conversation with another woman. She sat there trying not to feel hurt.

She asked Kathryn about him on the way home. "Is that the way things go nowadays? 'Hello, my name is Steve, do you want to fuck?'"

"You can't take him seriously. He's such a self-indulgent child. I think he's had an affair with every unattached woman on this campus. I heard that's why his wife dumped him."

Maggie was asleep by the time she got home. She tiptoed

in to look at her, then took a hot bath to comfort herself. Damn it! He'd turned her on, and she was feeling horny and frustrated and hopeless. Maybe she should have gone to bed with him. Viewed him as a kind of campus service. No. She could not make love to a stranger with her teenage daughter in the house. It just didn't feel right to her.

Hungry as she was, a fast fuck was not the answer. But as she lay there tossing and turning for the rest of the night, she found herself wishing that she had never met him. It was far less upsetting to remain in a permanent state of hibernation than to get so excited needlessly. She had almost begun to enjoy feeling dead.

The entire incident left her depressed and unsettled. The world seemed out of joint, and she was cranky, critical, dissatisfied, and unlike her usually optimistic self. Her students didn't study and turned in hand-written, misspelled term papers on uneven sheets torn out of spiral notebooks. Everything annoyed her.

I'm not a machine, she protested angrily to herself. But like an old workhorse, she continued to do what she should. She picketed, lobbied, and fought, but so many faculty members refused to participate in the union that the salary and tenure gains achieved by the few were minimal. Why, she asked herself at times, should I continue to kill myself for others who do nothing? Teaching on a college campus no longer seemed to her like a great, wonderful achievement. I'm unhappy, she finally admitted. I want a husband! I want romance! I want love! I'm not a machine.

On the rare occasions that she caught sight of Stephen, he was with a young woman, and she always felt slightly embarrassed about it, sheepish, and at a disadvantage. I could kick myself, she thought, for letting him get under my skin.

When Maggie, in exasperation, finally asked, "What's going on with you, Mom? You're turning into the wicked witch of the west," Sarah told her about meeting Stephen at the dinner.

Maggie burst into laughter and hugged her. "Honestly, Mom. Sometimes you're such a child. Face it! You liked the guy."

"I don't know about that. It was just that it's been a long,

long time since I've had that kind of teasing, sexy conversation with anybody. But 'liked' is too strong a word for one meeting."

"Please, Mom. Let's not turn this into an English lesson. The guy turned you on. So what's wrong with that?"

"Kathryn says he sleeps with every available woman on campus."

"So what?" Maggie giggled. "Either he really is a great stud or else he gets great p.r. What do you care?"

"I vowed that after Jerry nobody else would ever make me feel foolish again."

"How could anybody ever make you feel foolish?" Maggie said lovingly, "when you never are."

They hugged each other. Sarah put Stephen from her mind and returned to normal. She had Maggie. She was lucky!

CHAPTER
Sixty

Charlotte sat with her bookkeeper and accountant for one week going over her accounts. Something wasn't right. By the end of the weekend, there was no way to escape the terrible facts that confronted her. Terence was stealing from her. There was no other way to explain the discrepancy.

Dreading what she had to do, she sent for him. Her insides were in such painful turmoil that she thought she might be getting an ulcer. As soon as he saw her face he understood, so he impudently sat down, put his feet up on her desk, lit a joint, and slowly inhaled. Marshall would have thrown this bum out by the seat of his pants but she couldn't. Women aren't trained to be tough this way in business. "How could you do such a thing?" she asked.

"I needed cash."

"We all need cash, but stealing happens to be against the law. Don't you know that you could go to jail for this? I pay you a good salary."

"To begin with, Charlotte, my love, you don't pay me

enough to live on. And in addition, I've developed a big cocaine habit."

She shuddered in distaste. "I pay you as much as you'd get at any other gallery."

"None of them pay enough."

"I take you to dinners and parties and the theater."

"You do that for *you*, not for me. And that's not cold cash."

She felt defiled just talking to him. I ought to sell out and retire, she thought, knowing she would never do it. I hate unpleasantness and confrontation. And damn it, I hate betrayal. For a moment she thought of Wendy and Marshall, and her chest filled with grief.

She struggled to sound calm. "Well, you're not going to get away with this. I'm phoning the police."

"Oh, I wouldn't do that if I were you."

She reached for the phone. "Before you make that call," he said, "there's something I'd like to tell you. Remember those two Dufys you sold to the Hunts last month?"

"Of course I do. What about them?"

"They're not genuine."

"But you said they were."

"A little bit of insurance. Nobody forced you to believe me. I was expressing my opinion, and you accepted it without sufficient scrutiny on your own."

"But I always believed you before. And you were always right."

"I was right this time, too. I knew that they were fakes. Like I said, a little insurance. I knew I might need it. So why don't we just call it quits, Charlotte, for the moment. Of course, I might get in touch with you again when I need a little money."

"I thought you were my friend."

"How can my boss be my friend? I've had a job with you, that's all. Your friend? I don't even like you. I think I should have been recompensed far better for squiring around an old bag like you. Ciao."

She shuddered, sullied by the shame of betrayal. Why were people so mysterious and awful? She had been good to him, really good. And this was the way he'd paid her back. He was a languid, lying, son of a bitch. Oh, it was just one more nail in her coffin. She was all alone confronting a repulsive thief, and Marshall, Wendy, and Teddy were together in London laughing at her. She had not heard from Kitty recently. Probably they were also poisoning Kitty against her.

She had never felt more alone. She socialized with great art collectors, but did anybody in that world really like her? Would they see her if not for her work?

Now that she had crossed Wendy off her list, Sarah and Arla were her remaining friends, and she really did think that Sarah loved her, but what would Sarah do when Marshall and Wendy came back to New York? Arla's first loyalty would be to Wendy because Wendy was writing for her, and she'd always been grateful to Marshall for helping her with the divorce. There was nobody with whom she really came first.

Kitty was another big disappointment. She was enthralled with a boy she'd met at college—Danny, a Maoist, whatever that meant in the context of being an American. They belonged to a revolutionary organization called the SDS, lived in a collective, went out of their way to look like unwashed vagrants with their long hair, work shirts, and scruffy blue jeans, and they were humorless and intolerant. They thought promiscuity was wonderful and neatness a crime.

They made no secret, of course, of the fact that they were sleeping together. Sexual freedom they called it, although she personally would regard it as sexual punishment to have to sleep with that repulsive, unsanitary young man.

She shuddered at the memory of his recent visit with Kitty. He'd baited and criticized and waited to pounce on her, rudely describing the profits that gallery owners made as the worst possible kinds of capitalist exploitation of the creative artist. "Art should belong to the people," he ranted.

"Why?" she'd asked, and he and Kitty had gone into those awful, silly, stoned giggles the way Kitty and Teddy used to laugh when she talked to them.

Many of the things he had said actually seemed insane to her, as if he'd destroyed his brain cells with drugs. He was opposed to monogamy, even among married couples, and he regarded romantic love, privacy, and even heterosexuality as extremely middle class. He had said that people like her were worse than Spiro Agnew. "Give me an outright reactionary any time, instead of a phony liberal. With a real reactionary, at least you know where you stand."

Kitty had sat there listening with such uncritical adoration that Charlotte had wanted to shake her. And she'd been afraid for her daughter. They were planning to return with the members of their commune to Chicago for a rematch with Mayor Daley's police on the opening day of the Chicago Eight conspiracy trial, which was connected somehow to that awful Black Panther party that Maurice was now so active with.

They were obsessed with what had happened to their friends at Kent State. "Those murderers have sent us a message," Danny had said. "We're going to have to be ready to die for what we believe."

He had the slightly nutsy stare of a fanatic, shouting to her as if he were up on the barricades instead of sitting across from her in a living room. And she'd been afraid for Kitty but powerless to interfere.

They'd snickered at her fears. The major attitude displayed toward her that night had been contempt. All the things she'd worked so hard to achieve—her independence, her gallery, her appearance—were irrelevant to them.

Now, remembering the humiliation of that night, and her scene today with Terence, she was too depressed to get up out of her chair. I hate life, she thought. No matter what I accomplish, it becomes meaningless sooner or later. As she sat there and brooded, she began to feel physically sick. She called her internist and made an appointment for him to take a look at her at five o'clock that day.

CHAPTER
Sixty-One

Wendy knew that something was wrong the moment Marshall got off the phone. His hand was shaking.

"That was Charlotte," he said.

Kitty was in the hospital. She was one of six Weathermen who had been hit with buckshot on the Day of Rage in Chicago. Marshall was distraught. "They're at war with our kids. That's just what it is. War! All my life I've believed in our system but not now. Those bastards are killing and maiming our kids because they don't want war. And, damn it, they're right. I don't know what we're doing in Vietnam."

Kitty's boyfriend was also in the hospital, having been clubbed to the ground by the police. "These kid are heroes," his voice broke, "they don't have to do this. They're putting their lives on the line because of this goddamned demented war."

He poured himself some brandy with shaking hands, trying to calm himself. "And that's not all. Charlotte has breast cancer. She has to have a mastectomy. She sounds to me as if she's having a nervous breakdown. She kept talking about someone at her gallery who's robbing her. She can't take care of Kitty. She can barely take care of herself. Oh, Wendy darling. It's such rotten luck, but I'm afraid I'll have to go home. I can't see any other way."

"It's all right," she comforted him. "We'll go back. London will still be here. I'll take you to the earliest possible flight and follow in a few days. I feel so sorry for Charlotte. My mother went through hell."

"This kind of cancer's not as bad."

"Any kind of cancer is bad. I learned that listening to Robert."

"You're generous to let me go."

"I'd feel too guilty if you didn't."

When it was time to go to the airport, they couldn't find Teddy. Marshall paced back and forth in frustration.

Finally she said, "Just go and don't worry. I'll bring him home with me."

"You don't mind being stuck with him?"

"It will only be a day or two. Jarvis is packing for me right now."

He held her against him and breathed her fragrance. "I'm so afraid of losing you."

"Please don't worry about that. I'll see you at the end of the week."

* * *

Teddy was skulking around when she returned from the airport, and she scolded him because Marshall had been forced to leave without him. "You really should be more considerate." His eyes were glittering, and he was in a highly agitated state. It was evident that he was high, but she had no idea what to do.

"Hey, man," he answered. "You're beginning to sound like Charlotte."

She ignored that. "I'll be ready to leave in a few days, but you can go home tomorrow."

"I don't want to go home. I want to stay here."

"You can't stay here. I'm closing the house. The servants will come home with me."

"Then I'll stay somewhere else in London."

"Your father would be terribly upset if you didn't come home. You're in no condition to stay here alone. And you should be at home with Kitty and Charlotte."

"Why? I hate Charlotte, and there's nothing I can do for Kitty. I don't want to go. Please give me money to live on so I can stay in London for awhile." He was close to tears.

"I won't give you the money, and I don't want to discuss it any further. You should have been on that plane today. Charlotte has cancer and Kitty has been shot and I won't let you stay here and fritter away your life on drugs."

"It's not your business," he shouted.

"Oh, yes it is! Now go to your room and start packing. I'll make a reservation for you on tomorrow morning's plane."

Coming Apart

He ran from the room, violently kicking a two-hundred year-old chair. She could hear him banging around upstairs for a while, and then he ran out, slamming the front door behind him. He had not returned by dinner time, and when Jarvis came to her at midnight, asking what to do, she told him to close up. Teddy could ring whenever he decided to come home.

At three that morning she was awakened by the sound of someone opening her bedroom door. Startled, she switched on the light beside her bed and saw Teddy entering her room. He was flanked on either side by two skinheads, teenage hoods with shaved heads who were carrying knives. She reached for the buzzer beside her bed, but Teddy quickly said, "Don't bother. It's cut."

"Teddy! How could you?" She had never been more frightened in her life, so terrified that she could not control the shuddering of her body. Instinctively she knew she had to play for time. Forcing her voice not to tremble, she asked, "How did you get in?"

"Marshall left his key on the dresser. I took it today."

"I see. What do you want?"

He seemed on the verge of crying. "You know what I want. Money. This is your fault, Wendy. I told you I needed it. You should have given me the money this afternoon without forcing me to bring my friends."

Some friends! They looked like time bombs waiting to explode.

"Stop wasting time," one of them snarled as he emptied her purse and took the cash.

"Now open the safe," the other ordered.

When she got out of bed, in her transparent lace nightgown, and walked to the closet where the safe was hidden, one of the boys let out a low whistle. "This really your stepmum? She's gorgeous."

She opened the safe and stood back while they took out the cash, her diamond bracelet from Mexico, and the engagement ring Marshall had given her. She watched the bracelet, her talisman for so many years, and Marshall's ring, her new talisman for the future, disappear into a pocket. Keep cool, she warned herself, don't set them off.

"Where's the rest of the jewelry?" Teddy asked.

"In the bank vault."

The other friend finished counting the money, and in a sudden gust of anger drove his knife into her easy chair. "Two hundred bloody pounds. You told us she kept thousands here, you stupid bloody bastard. You fucking wasted our night."

"It's better than nothing," Teddy said nervously. "Let's get out of here."

"Nothing doing. I kind of fancy your step-mum."

One of the boys advanced toward Wendy, and Teddy became so agitated that his entire body shook and he started to stammer. "D-don't you touch her. You c-can't touch her. That wasn't part of the deal."

"Who cares about you and your bloody deal, you fucking pansy. Get out of my way."

Teddy stepped in front of her and stood there shaking. "No," he said.

One of the boys stepped forward in a sudden, quick, casual movement and drove his knife into Teddy. Teddy grunted, a low, gutteral, animal sound and stood there for a moment dazed. Blood began to spurt from his chest as he crumpled heavily to the floor like a murdered bull in the ring. A pool of blood began to form around him on the oriental carpet, and then she heard her own scream rise higher and higher like the wail of an advancing siren.

"Shut up, you bloody cow." The one who'd knifed Teddy advanced toward her with the blood-stained knife. She backed up toward the fireplace, grabbed a fire iron and brandished it before her. "I'll kill you if you come any closer!"

"That's all right, Mrs. Kingman," she heard Jarvis's blessed voice. "You can put it down. I have my gun trained right on them."

The iron fell out of her bloodless hand, and she ran to the telephone. She called the ambulance and the police, then sank to the carpet beside the unconscious young man. His friends stood there twitching like cornered rats, obviously needing a fix.

Teddy was still unconscious when they carried him out on the stretcher. "Will he be all right?" she asked the driver.

"No way of telling," he answered.

After the hoods had been taken away, she sat in her library with Jarvis in attendance while the police tried to piece together her story.

"Have you any idea of how they got in?"

"No, I don't. Perhaps through the garden."

"They said the young man let them in."

"That's absolutely not true. He tried to save me."

"Can you tell us why he was dressed in street clothes in the middle of the night?"

"He's slovenly. He sleeps in his street clothes and rarely washes or brushes his teeth."

"Would you say that he's on drugs, madam?"

"He used to be, but no longer."

She turned to Jarvis after they had gone and noted his disapproving expression. "I know what you're thinking," she said, "but he did try to save me. There's some good there. If he lives, I want to give him another chance. Will you help me to do it?"

His face was impassive again. "Whatever you say, madam."

She did not want to disturb her chauffeur. "I'll get dressed. Please call a taxi for me."

"Very good, ma'am. I'll have the blood cleaned up while you're gone." She grabbed a bottle of brandy and a book and went to the hospital. They were already operating. She was still too shocked to read. She filled a cup from the water cooler with brandy and bummed a cigarette from a nurse. She wanted to stop smoking, but it would have to wait.

She found herself remembering one of Sarah's speeches back in school. "I am she who didn't die in a concentration camp. Only an accident of geography saved me. But I believe I have been saved to make a difference. I believe I have been saved to bear witness."

I could have been knifed instead of Teddy. I believe I have been saved to make a difference. I believe I have been saved to save him. She knelt beside the bench and prayed. "Please, God. Save him." And then she could do nothing but wait.

She awakened two hours later to find a doctor gently touching her shoulder. "He's a most fortunate young man.

The knife missed his heart by inches. He'll have to be with us for a time, of course, but he's going to be all right."

How wonderfully polite and understated the British could be. "I'll send a contribution," she said, "in your name."

Jarvis was waiting for her outside. "I was concerned about the availability of taxis. You should not be out alone this late at night. How is the young man?"

"He's going to be all right."

"A questionable gain for the world."

"Please don't think that way. We should rejoice. It would have destroyed his father."

"I've moved you into the gray room for tonight. Your carpet is still wet."

"Thank you. Please bring my breakfast please at nine."

"That early? But, madam, you need sleep!"

"I'll sleep in the afternoon. I'm anxious to get to the hospital."

"Will you want to put in a call to Mr. Berman?"

"Yes. We'll have to figure out the time difference. But I won't tell him about Teddy. He has enough to cope with at the moment. I'll have to think of some good reason for delaying our return."

"Very good, madam."

He will always disapprove of my saving Teddy, she thought before falling asleep. But I'm going to prove him wrong.

At ten the next morning she was sitting beside Teddy's bed when he opened his eyes.

"How do you feel?" He turned his face away from her.

"Am I going to jail?"

"Of course not." She held up the paper to him. "'Heiress Saved from Intruders.' You're a hero, Teddy."

"You told them that? Why?"

"You were so brave. To put your body in front of mine. Do you know what that means?"

"What?"

"It means that you're capable of choice and morality and loyalty. It means that if we could get you off drugs and get you functioning in a career, you can live a good life. Oh, Teddy. When I saw you bleeding on the floor all I could think of was the first time we met. You were so adorable. I held you on my lap."

"Charlotte threw it up to me for the rest of my life. She said that I began to humiliate her from the moment I saw you. I said that you were prettier and I wanted you for my mother."

"That's right. You did. And what you did last night was what a son would do for his mother."

He smiled for the first time. "Not for Charlotte, I wouldn't. What will you tell my dad?"

"Just what the paper says. That you're a hero and that I'll remain here with you until you're discharged."

"And then?"

"And then I have a plan. I'd like to send you to the Menninger Clinic. Get you straightened out once and for all."

"Yeah! Dad always talked about it, but it was something like fifty thousand dollars a year."

"Don't worry about the money."

"Will you ever tell him the truth?"

"I don't think so. Maybe some day you will want to. Or maybe it will never seem necessary."

"Thank you." His voice cracked. "I'm real sorry."

"I know."

She was at his side every day, reading to him, talking to him, and reading some of her novel to him. "It's like Romeo and Juliet. Your heroine really loved that black guy, didn't she?"

"Yes, she did."

"There are interracial couples all over London. Nobody really cares about that anymore. Was that what kept them apart?"

"First it was that and then it was the times. I don't know. I guess it just wasn't meant to be."

One afternoon, she was sitting with him and watching television when a special BBC news announcement came on. In the United States, police in southern California had attacked the Black Panther offices, leaving two men dead, wounding many others, and carting bystanders off to jail. She had a sudden chilling premonition even before they showed the pictures of the two who had been killed. She forced herself to look at the screen. One of them was Maurice.

She doubled up in a paroxysm of pain, bent her head and wept, while Teddy lay immobile, cowed before a grief that was so monumental. "Is there anything that I can say?"

"No! Just hold my hand. Just hold me." He held her hand, and she wept until she had no more tears.

"It's terrible to love someone so much," he said.

"It's terrible and it's wonderful. But without it you only live life on the surface."

When he was released from the hospital, he came back to her house, and they recuperated together. Each day they would walk a little farther, pouring out their hearts and healing each other with companionship.

The following month he was well enough to leave England. Jarvis was taking him to the clinic in Kansas and would join her later in New York. She was flying directly to Kennedy.

"I'll miss you, Wendy," Teddy said. "In my whole life, this time with you has been the best."

"This is just the beginning, Teddy. The best lies ahead."

"I'm sorry," he said. "Sorry about everything. Sorry about what I did. Sorry about that man you loved."

She put her arms around him. "You helped me get through that, Teddy. I'm counting on you now to take your life in your hands."

"I'll try. Honest, I'll try."

Choked with tears, she hugged him and hurried to the plane to New York. During the trip home, she neither ate nor slept, but only gazed out of her window at nothingness, trying to imprint forever on her memory the image of Maurice. She mourned his life. She mourned because he'd never had a vacation, because he'd always been pursued and beaten and humiliated, because he was a man of peace who had always been at war.

Good-bye Maurice, she whispered to the air. The sixties were over!

PART FOUR

The Survivors

CHAPTER
Sixty-Two

THE SEVENTIES

Wendy returned to New York in triumph. Her novel reached the best-seller list and was immediately optioned for a movie, with the proviso that Wendy be one of the screenwriters. "No reason why your career can't expand in that direction," Arla advised. As an author, Wendy's past notoriety seemed to be an asset rather than a liability. Everybody was intrigued with the story of the beautiful heiress and the black militant, thinly disguised as fiction. The book tours, interviews, and her work in Hollywood, all prevented her from seeing much of Marshall.

"Robert must be dying at the publicity," Sarah said gleefully. "So how does it feel to be a big success?"

"You should know. You're the only one of us with a doctorate."

"My mother still doesn't believe it. She was visiting last week when one of my students called and asked for Dr. Gordon. My mother said she had the wrong number."

Marshall was as busy as Wendy. He had round-the-clock nurses to take care of Charlotte and Kitty because he was needed to supervise the gallery. Charlotte lay in bed recovering, alternating between anger and depression. Every time she touched the scar where her breast had been, she felt nauseated with self-disgust. And that was worse than the pain.

It was strange having Marshall home again, not divorced but certainly not the same as before. Would they still be sharing a bedroom, she wondered, if she were not ill? Then she reminded herself that she was being silly. He was only there because she was ill, but he was so gentle and considerate that she wanted to weep at the thought that as soon as she and Kitty were well, she would soon have to give him up for good. Kitty lay in her room also alternating between the same two moods; depression because the cops who shot her could get away with it, and anger because she could not take revenge.

Charlotte was consumed with another strong emotion. Hatred of Wendy! She had lost a breast and a husband, and there was Wendy, as beautiful as ever, her body still pliant and graceful, talking away with charm and poise on television shows. So damned sure of herself. She had stolen Marshall, alienated Teddy from the time he was a little boy, and been able to turn her experiences into a best-selling book from which she was making vast sums of money she didn't need. The unfairness of things ate at her.

Sarah tried to reason with her, to remind her that *she* had originally dumped Marshall and that she should appreciate Wendy's kindness in letting him take care of her, but she was totally illogical on the subject.

"She's had a wonderful life," she sobbed. "Everything works out perfectly for her."

"How can you say that? She lost her mother, she lost Maurice, she lost her son, and she had a hysterectomy. She's had her share."

"No matter what you say, she's had a better life than I. Just look at the television screen. That's all the proof I need."

* * *

Sarah returned from teaching one day to find Arla asleep on her living-room couch. She instantly knew that something was wrong. Arla never took a day off from work, and she hated to drive. And yet now, in the middle of the week, she'd driven the seventy miles to New Paltz.

Maggie came tiptoing out and threw her arms around

Sarah. "Mom," she cried, "Mark was killed in the Tet offensive."

"Oh, poor Arla." They cried together. Sarah felt as if she were losing Jimmy all over again. She knew that never-ending pain.

"This damned useless, pointless war!"

"She said she crept up here for comfort because..."

"Because we lost Jimmy."

"Yes! That's what she said before she fell asleep. It makes me so proud, Mom. That your friends always know they can find comfort with you."

"We find comfort with each other. And I, most of all with you, darling."

When Arla awoke she sat there looking at them, unable to move. "I feel so guilty. He was a middle child. I never gave him enough attention. Apart from Peter, I haven't even really thought much about anything but work in recent years."

"You did the best you could. You had to survive. It's not you. It's this terrible, useless war. Remember during World War II, how different we felt about the war? That feeling back then, Maggie, was indescribable. There was something wonderful, heady, euphoric about being alive and being an American."

"You're kidding, Mom. How could any war be wonderful?"

"It wasn't the war. It was the feeling of unity in the country. It was the feeling of being proud because we were Americans and we were fighting on the right side. It was a righteous war. Just like the Spanish civil war. In this war, we're opposed to the government. Imagine how wonderful it is to feel that you and your government are one, not that the government has needlessly killed your son."

"Yes," Arla echoed in a ghostly voice. "Needlessly. I'll never let Peter be drafted. One son killed in a pointless war is too much. I keep thinking of all the things that were wasted, you know, silly things like teeth braces and baseball gloves and learning to ride a bicycle. Everything you put into a child dies with him."

"Oh, don't I know," Sarah wept, and the two friends and Maggie wept together.

"Is it all right if I stay for a few days? I can't seem to pull myself together."

"Of course. You can have my bed. I'll sleep in the living room so I don't disturb you in the morning."

Each morning Arla said, "I must be getting back to work," but she could not seem to throw off the depression that was paralyzing her. Sarah would leave for the college and Maggie for school, but Arla would remain behind, watching soap operas.

"We're reading a play in drama club," Maggie told her one day, "called *The Sea Gull*. In it, one of the characters says, 'I'm in mourning for my life.' That's what you're doing, Aunt Arla, if you don't mind my saying so. You know Mom sat shivah for a week then went back to work."

"There's no fixed period for grief. I'm just not ready to go back yet."

"You know what you should do, Mom?" Maggie suggested. "Have a party. I can't stand the morose atmosphere around here any longer. It's damned depressing."

"But wouldn't it seem somehow sacrilegious?"

"Maybe! But it might also cheer us all up. Why don't you invite the stud? I'll help you cook."

"Well, why not," she suddenly agreed, feeling as she said it a surge of energy and a sudden rebirth of zest. And, best of all, Arla agreed to get dressed and also to help.

CHAPTER Sixty-Three

Sarah was a nervous wreck on the day of the party, but she did her best to keep things under control. It was ridiculous, wasn't it, for a middle-aged woman to be so gauche? What's the point of all this living, she asked herself, if you never feel poised and confident about men? Having Stephen to a party had been a good idea, so why agonize over it? It would give her the opportunity to watch him interact with Maggie, Arla, and her friends, and it would help her view him objectively. He might no longer appeal to her, and become just another taken-for-granted colleague.

She'd planned cocktails and hors d'oeuvres at seven and dinner at eight, but he was still not there at nine. Everybody was hungry. The hot foods were drying out and the cold foods were wilting.

"That does it," she told Maggie. "We're going to eat. The one thing I can't tolerate is lateness."

"Don't be so uptight, Mom. Only teachers are always on time."

"That's obviously not true. He's a teacher, too."

"Well, anyway, I think he's here. Look out the window. Is that his car?" The car he was stepping out of could have been a prop for *The Grapes of Wrath*. It was peeling, dented, rusty, caked with mud, and the license plate was hanging from one corner. Somehow the sight of its imperfections aroused her sympathies and slightly lessened her annoyance about the spoiled dinner.

Maggie ran to open the door. "Well hel-lo," he said to her in that magnificent, intimate voice with the accent placed seductively on the second syllable as if to indicate wonder at the marvelous fact of her existence.

Maggie wrinkled her pretty little nose at him. What a phony creep! "Hello yourself," she answered in her composed no-nonsense, direct manner. "I'm Maggie. My mom said you had a sexy voice. I bet it drives the girls in your classes wild."

"Would it drive you wild?"

"Not a chance. I'm into political guys right now, like Abbie Hoffman or Jerry Rubin. Besides, you're too old."

He turned his back to her, and walked over to Sarah, grabbing her by the shoulders and brushing her lips with his. "Well hel-lo," he repeated seductively, with the same intonation. "I've been thinking about you."

"Apparently not enough to get you here on time. Let me introduce you quickly so we can start dinner."

"Uh-oh. I hear my parochial-school teacher talking."

"Don't be unfair. The food is getting cold."

"I didn't come for food. I came for you."

"Oh, please! I haven't budged from this campus since the night we met. Where have you been all that time?"

"I thought of calling you a hundred times but you scared me. I was afraid you thought I was a forward jerk."

"Not a jerk. Just forward. But let's forget all about that and eat. I'd like you to sit next to my friend Arla. She's the publisher I told you about. Here's your chance to tell her about your writing. You're in luck tonight."

"You make me feel lucky." His voice made her shiver. He pressed her hand to his lips. "Later," he sighed.

After meeting Arla, he remained at her side for the rest of the evening, and for the first time since Mark's death, Sarah heard Arla laugh.

Stephen held Arla's hand, sandwiched between both of his, gazed into her eyes, and said, "I see in you the gypsy soul that Yeats saw in Maude Gonne."

"Who are they?" Arla asked.

"He was a great Irish poet who knew how to appreciate women."

"I never heard of him," she said. "I don't read foreign books."

After the guests had gone and Maggie went to bed, Sarah and Arla sat with Stephen in front of her little fireplace drinking and talking. Arla found Stephen captivating. He was young and vibrant, and it was hard to resist the admiration with which he gazed at her. It was still almost inconceivable to her that would-be writers like him, with fancy degrees, should defer to her.

It was fun being with him. He seemed to say anything that came into his head without the self-censorship that was part of her armor, and he had a way of asking direct, personal questions that made her talk easily about herself. That was good for her, too.

When he asked about her marriage, something she had never discussed with anyone outside of the sorority, she answered him at length, flattered that someone would be so interested in the litany of sordid facts.

"Your ex-husband sounds like a sociopath."

"No. A real, honest, out-and-out psychopath."

That broke the three of them up, and they sat there laughing. They were all feeling mellow.

"My daddy wasn't much better," Arla added.

He took her hand in his. "But I promise you that not all men are alike. I know what the feminists are saying, but lots of times they're really off base. They claim the man is always the heavy, but I wasn't. I was an abused *husband*. My wife divorced me as a direct result of belonging to a consciousness-raising group. First she decided to ration sex and then she took a lover."

"She did?" both women exclaimed together. To Sarah, the disloyalty of having a lover while married was still unthinkable, and to Arla, the danger and risk of cuckolding Lenny were equally unthinkable. Besides, sex was bad enough with one person! Why look for more?

"She sure did. Up until then we were very happy. At least I thought we were. I tried to hold on. I bent every way I could for her. I never yelled at her. I told her I didn't care if she fucked him three times a week as long as I got equal time. Do you think that was unfair?"

"It would have been too much for me," Arla murmured.

Sarah winced. "It's one of those monumental problems I've never thought about."

Her irony escaped him. "And this was another problem. How much of the food budget each week should be spent on pot?"

"Are you joking?" Sarah asked.

"No! I'm serious. How much?"

"How much of the food budget? None."

"That's what I told her, but she kept talking about being free to be you and me." He put his hand under Arla's chin and gently tilted her face up. Then he studied it carefully. "I can't believe that anyone would beat a woman like you. No matter what my wife did, I never laid a finger on her. Do you hate your ex?"

"That's putting it mildly."

"I hate mine too. She ended up with everything, the house, the kids, child support, but even so she's still so angry that she won't even talk to me on the phone. I've tried to be civil because we have joint custody of my son, but she hangs up every time I call. Instead, she sends me note after note about what a lousy father and husband I was, am, and always will be. Her lifework is the chronicling of my failings!"

Arla's sympathies were aroused. "My ex-husband was like that, too. He even blamed the changes in weather on me."

Stephen stayed until the fire died. Before leaving, he arranged to mail his manuscript to Arla and meet with her in the city when she was ready to discuss it. When Sarah walked him to the door he pressed her hand to his lips. "My good angel. I'm indebted to you. Come to my house for dinner next week. I'm a very good cook."

Then he bent down and gently kissed her. "And you'll spend the night?" She felt her body yearn for his, but still she resisted. "I don't know. It's not easy for me. I've never done something like that. So casually!"

"Then it's about time you did. If not now, when? Kierkegaard said that if a man does not look up from his path he can live out his life with a certain dull security. Is that what you want? Dull security? The same old path?"

He bent and kissed her neck, and delectable little flashes of excitement raced through her. "I don't know what I want."

"Then let me tell you. You want me."

"I'm not sure."

"For heaven's sake, Sarah. Gather your rosebuds..."

She finally capitulated. "All right. All right. I will."

"When. I want a definite night right now."

"Maggie is spending next weekend in the city with my brother's family. How about Saturday night?"

"Fine. Either Friday or Saturday. It's up to you. I'm having some people to dinner Friday whom you might find interesting."

"Probably Saturday. I'll call if anything changes."

"You won't disappoint me, will you?"

"No. I promise not to. I'll be there. I never break a promise."

He looked down into her eyes. "'Journeys end in lovers' meeting.' I'll be waiting."

She was glad that Arla and Maggie had gone to bed. She

didn't want to discuss Stephen until after she took the plunge. And she still wasn't sure she would go through with it. She'd never felt comfortable with the idea of running with the herd.

CHAPTER
Sixty-Four

After Arla left the next morning, Sarah was again racked with ambivalence about Stephen. She was sorry she'd made the date. I want to get married again, she thought, so why should I waste my time with someone who's obviously not marriage material? He may have a doctorate in literature, but he's still coarse and vulgar and perhaps even a little stupid.

Life has become too different from the past and too complicated for me. I don't want to be a swinger at my age. I don't want to make out or screw or hump or ball. I don't like the modern world. I liked the world I knew with Hal, the world of romance and commitment where if you wanted to sleep with someone, you got married.

All week long she was on a seesaw of indecision. Each time she would reach for the phone to tell him that the date was off, a small warning voice inside her would say, this may be your very last chance, so use him. You don't have to marry him. Let him make you, fuck you, do you, plow you, satisfy you. Love and commitment are out of date. This is the modern world!

She could not deny her need. She had read a novel about some women in Vermont who were achieving total satisfaction with vibrators, but the very idea of that made her shudder. It seemed evil and ugly to her that with a precious daughter under the same roof one could huddle in a bedroom using a vibrator. How lonely and unsavory.

And yet! And yet! As far as she could tell, nobody on campus had ever looked at her as anything but a union leader. And now that somebody finally had, she was going through the ridiculous virginal decision agonies of teenagers. This present generation seemingly no longer went through that kind of self-flagellation. Everything was permitted. The pill had changed that. So if kids could do it so casually, what would be so wrong about going to bed with Stephen? Maybe she would love it. Maybe she would hate it. But how would she ever know if she didn't try?

She'd have to check the union records. She couldn't possibly go to bed with one of those nonjoining finks she'd been inveighing against since becoming president. But if he were a paid-up member, she'd do it. However, something else forced her to decide. That night she was awakened at three by an obscene phone call, the first one she had ever received. "Dr. Gordon?" a man's voice asked.

"Yes," she said, instantly awake, her pulse racing with fear about her aged parents. "What is it?"

"Sarah Gordon?"

"Yes. I just told you that. What is it?"

Then he spoke again in a disarming, ordinary, all-American voice. "Dr. Gordon! Sarah! Can I fuck you?"

She dropped the phone as if it had turned into a snake, but for the rest of the night, the ice-water shock of the experience kept her awake. It was always a shock to find out how many crazy people were floating around. And she and Maggie were so alone up here. So vulnerable!

Kathryn was casual about it. "Oh, those dumb calls go in rashes. Just ignore it. They usually start around Halloween. If he keeps bothering you, change your number."

The second night he called at one, three, and five o'clock. She slammed the phone down each time. The third night he called at four. This time she held the receiver in her hand, shaking as if a rapist were in the room, determined to tell him she had informed the police. But before she could speak, he chided her. "I don't like the way you keep hanging up on me. I'm only trying to do you a favor. I know that widows get horny. Hey, you know the origin of that word? Horn means erect penis. And that's what I have for you. The biggest erect penis you've ever seen. Just tell me when to bring it over."

She slammed down the receiver, ran to Maggie's room, and dashed into her bed.

"Hey, Mom," Maggie said sleepily. "What's shaking?"

"I was lonely."

Maggie threw her arms around her and sleepily said, "There, there, baby. Now go to sleep."

"What was going on with you last night?" Maggie asked the next morning.

Sarah was reluctant to alarm her needlessly. Perhaps the calls would stop. "I was lonely. I don't know what it is, really. Lately I've been feeling like a nervous wreck."

Maggie hugged her. "Most mothers are nervous wrecks. You can come and sleep with me, anytime. Don't worry, Mom. You and I are still a nation of two."

Kathryn also tried to reassure her. "Those callers never *do* anything. They're just playing with themselves when they call. Change your number." Sarah blushed in embarrassment, decided to call the telephone company about a change, but then began to get angry. How dare anybody harass her this way! The next time he called she wouldn't hang up. She would try to find out why he was calling her and who he was, and then she would report him to the police.

He called at three AM again. "I'm getting a little miffed at you." His voice was evil and slimy. "If you hang up on me this time, Sarah, I'm going to come over there and talk to you personally. Are you going to hang up on me?"

She clenched her teeth to keep them from chattering. "Who are you and what do you want?"

"Don't tell me you don't remember me, Sarah. I was in your Monday class last year, and you kept putting me down."

"That class was very large. What's your name?"

"Listen you cunt, I'm not stupid. But you thought I was. You failed me, and I'm unemployed today because of you. Now the time has come for me to fuck you over. But I'm going to let you dangle a while first."

"You can't do this to me. I'm going to call the police."

"Ooh, ooh, ooh, you really scare me. The police! Don't make me laugh. There's not a thing they can do. This town has four, maybe five cops. Nighty night, sleep tight, don't let the bedbugs bite. One of these days I'll be over."

She threw on her bathrobe and ran around locking doors and windows. They had always left the house unlocked. She would have to explain things to Maggie tomorrow and warn her. I have never been so afraid, she thought, since that day Maurice saved me from those rednecks. But somehow that was different. I've seen terrible things. I've known death. And I've seen a lot of social and political evil. But never before this kind of personal malignity.

She went into the kitchen to make herself a cup of Earl Grey tea, and as she reached for the overhead light she suddenly froze. Better not! Suppose he's looking in. She put on only the stove light, made the tea, and shaking with fear, she carried it up to her bedroom.

When she was a little girl, her grandmother had lived with them, and many nights they had all been shocked awake by a thin, wailing, terrifying scream as her sweet kind grandmother dreamed of long ago when the cossacks slit the throat of her gentle, scholarly father. Fifty years had passed since that murder but still her grandmother wailed in her sleep like a terrified little girl. And that was how Sarah felt at that moment. Like a terrified little girl in the body of a middle-aged woman, living in a world of menacing shadows.

There was nobody around to help. Her friends all lived seventy miles south in New York City, and she wasn't on sufficiently intimate terms with anyone up here to disturb them in the middle of the night. She had many colleagues and acquaintances, but they weren't friends. She shivered with loneliness.

She had told Stephen that she would see him on Saturday, thinking she would use Friday night to catch up on her grading. But with Maggie going directly into the city on the Trailways bus after school on Friday, she would now be left alone for the night, waiting in terror for the phone to ring.

Suddenly she felt very lucky that Stephen existed, that there was a man in her life who could help to protect her.

The next morning she called him. "Maggie's going into

the city today after school. I could come tonight if you like."

"Fine! Tonight! Tomorrow! Whenever you like. I told you that I'm having some other people for dinner. Will you stay the night?"

She took a deep breath and said, "Yes. If that's all right with you."

"All right with me?" he laughed. "I thought that you would never ask."

CHAPTER
Sixty-Five

Sarah phoned Charlotte to find out how she was feeling, and Kitty picked up the phone. She was crying. "Everything's in a real mess here. I'm feeling better and we let the nurse go, but Mom's at the doctor's right now. Dad took her. They think the other breast must come off."

"Oh, no. I'll be down to see her tomorrow."

"Better wait, Aunt Sarah. I think next weekend would be better. She doesn't want to see anybody right now."

"Whatever you say. Give her my love and call me whenever you want me. I can always find someone to cover a class. What's happening with the gallery?"

"Dad's been running it and doing a marvelous job. He really enjoys it. It's opened up a whole new world to him. I'm going to start work there today."

"No more politics?"

"I wouldn't exactly put it that way, Aunt Sarah, but I'm still recuperating. It's just that once you get shot, you get scared. It's not fun and games any longer. I still can't believe it happened. We gave them flowers and they shot us. Our own people shot us. Soldiers our own age shot me and my friends. So I'm scared. I'm not leaving the struggle. I just need some more time to recover. I'll always be interested and involved in politics. I couldn't live unless I felt I was making some kind of contribution to the world. You couldn't either! Could you?"

"No! I feel the same way. I get fed up at times with the apathy to the union, but I go on."

"I know we really do it for ourselves, Aunt Sarah, not for anyone else. But sometimes it's hard. When I saw that *Newsweek* poll, I asked myself, what are we killing ourselves for? This country's crazy."

A special *Newsweek* public opinion poll taken after the Kent State slayings indicated that 58 percent of the respondents blamed the students for the shootings and only 11 percent felt the National Guard was at fault. One person said, "The National Guard made only one mistake—they should have fired sooner and longer. The score is four, and next time more."

"I find myself thinking," Kitty continued, "that if this country's full of ungrateful assholes, it's dumb to lay down my life for them. I'm shot up at my end and my mother has cancer at the other end, and I say to myself that it's time I started to just think about in between. I'm twenty-five years old, and I want to get married and have children and not worry for a while about being beaten or reviled or shot. That doesn't mean I haven't kept the faith, Aunt Sarah. But I'm tired. I need R and R just the way our troops do. Does that make you think less of me?"

"Of course not darling. You've done more than most people."

"I'm not giving up," she repeated. "I still believe that the individual can make a difference. I mean, look at what Daniel Ellsberg accomplished."

"My favorite contemporary hero," Sarah agreed. "If only I could find a man like that."

"That's what I want, too," Kitty said.

"What happened to your boyfriend?"

"Unbelievable as it sounds, he went to work for the *National Enquirer*."

"How very odd. Did he say why?"

"It's no mystery. He wanted to make some money and he got tired of being beaten. There's just so much time that you can live on top of a volcano. Everyone's entitled to a little R and R, I guess. Do you have another minute to talk, Aunt Sarah?"

"Of course."

"I'm worried about Mom. I don't know how she can manage without Dad. I wish she and Dad could get back together. She needs him and Wendy doesn't. Wendy could get anyone. For her, Dad's just frosting on the cake. Could you talk to her?"

"Kitty, darling, you know that I can't interfere. Your parents are adults, and your father has gone far beyond the line of duty. Your mother asked for a divorce before she knew anything at all about Wendy."

"But she's so pathetic now."

"I can't interfere," Sarah repeated. "They'll just have to work things out by themselves. Wendy's alone too. You can be a star and still be alone. In fact, all of us are alone. I'll be down to visit next week."

She spent all of Friday morning at the beauty parlor having her hair cut and dyed and blown back into a fashionable style. The night before, Maggie had shown her how to use makeup. She allowed herself two hours to get ready for the evening.

Following Maggie's instructions, she used astringent and moisturizer. She put it all over her neck too because her skin was getting so dry, then rubbed the remainder into her cuticles. She put coverup under her eyes, and then liquid foundation over her face and neck. She brushed translucent powder over that, then brushed on delicate gray eye shadow, eyeliner, and mascara. She looked at the false eyelashes then pushed them away. She couldn't get them to stay on. And how did you keep them on while making love?

When she'd finished with the makeup, she sprayed herself all over with toilet water, Madame Rochas, which Maggie had given her for her last birthday. All the while she worked she felt irritated at being a party to such nonsense, at having to put on a mask to appeal to a man she was not even sure she wanted.

In a small bag she packed her toiletries, a nightgown, and a skirt and blouse for the next day. I really should have a new nightgown, she thought. It's just that I haven't thought about such things in a long time. And although there was little probability that she was going to conceive, she packed her old diaphragm. How long do these things stay workable, she wondered.

She put on an old blue silk dress from her days with Jerry, and put a bottle of wine next to her purse. She decided to leave her bag in the car in case she changed her mind.

She didn't really want to go. I am betraying myself, she thought. I'm betraying myself out of loneliness and fear. And yet when she thought of the alternative, of phoning him to cancel the evening and then waiting for the obscene caller to ring, a cold chill of loneliness froze her heart and made her shiver with depression.

Oh, for God's sake, she silently wailed, go to bed with him and be done with it. It's no shame to be lonely. Squaring her shoulders, she took her purse, the wine, and her tiny suitcase and walked out to her car.

CHAPTER
Sixty-Six

Wendy's book tour was an unqualified success. In Brentwood, California, her name was up on the local bank in revolving lights, like those of the old *New York Times* building. "Welcome Wendy da Gama." *Publishers' Weekly* wrote about her as one of the major new novelists. Strangers wrote to her in care of the publisher to thank her for the book.

It was an intoxicating experience to be functioning at full capacity, meeting new people in every city, speaking, lecturing, giving interviews. There was a certain relaxation in having her entire schedule programmed for her, not having to do anything but smile and sign. It continued to astonish her that people would buy her book and then line up to get it autographed. She could not imagine herself waiting on a line for anyone. She didn't understand it, but she loved it. For the first time in her life she felt like a complete person, not just a rich, beautiful woman, but a creative artist who had made a contribution to the world. She especially enjoyed being on television interview shows. She was fast, witty, and able.

But she was also often lonely when the applause died, and she returned to an empty hotel room, no matter how lavish it was. She phoned Marshall every night to recount the day's triumphs. "I wish you could be here with me."

"I do, too."

He cried when he told her about Charlotte's second mastectomy. She too was upset. It made increasingly clear to her the fact that he was still emotionally involved with his old life.

She phoned him when the tour was ending. "I'll be home tomorrow night," she said. "Will you be waiting for me?"

"I wish I could but we're holding an important reception at the gallery. I'll be over the next morning."

Filled with anger, she went down to the hotel bar, selected the man whose appearance pleased her the most, and took him back upstairs to bed. Afterward, she got rid of him as fast as she could and had a good night's sleep.

When she got home the next day, Jarvis, waiting at the door, took her bag and said, "You have a visitor, madam."

It must be Marshall after all, she thought. She hurried into the library where a tall young man sat reading a magazine. He looked up at the sound. She began to tremble. Tears rolled down her cheeks. "Bobby?" her voice shook. "Bobby. Is that you? Is that really you?"

He stood up politely, and they stood there regarding each other. At sixteen, he looked like her. He was six feet tall, well-built, with the same white skin, dark hair, and fringed eyes. He was a knockout. One of the most handsome young men she had ever seen.

"Oh, darling!" Weeping, she ran to him and folded him in her arms. "Oh, Bobby, Bobby, Bobby. I didn't think I could see you for another two years. You don't know how much I've missed you."

His eyes also filled with tears. "I wanted to see you, too, Mom," he said in his well-bred prep-school voice. "But you know how he is. He always said that it was strictly forbidden by law."

"That's true," she said. "But I wrote to you. So many times. I thought perhaps you didn't get my letters. That he'd instructed the schools not to deliver them."

"You're right. I didn't. But I read about you. All the time! And I read the book. Whew! Sexy!"

"Were you embarrassed?"

"Hell no! I was proud! I just kept wishing you could visit so I could introduce you to the guys."

"Does your father know you're here now?"

"He sent me here. He kicked me out."

"Really? How wonderful!" It was one of the happiest moments of her life. "Why?"

"I've been expelled from school."

"Why?" she repeated. "Not that I care. I was thrown out of college. I am absolutely thrilled about anything you did that would bring you back to me."

"Mainly it was my grades, although there were also a few other little things. But mainly it was my grades."

"I didn't do well in school either. I was always on probation. It never interested me."

"It was the same with me. I want to be an actor, Mom. I'm good. I can sing and dance and I have the looks for it. I want to go to Professional Children's School and be near the theater scene in New York. I've been away at school for ten years. It's enough. It's more than enough."

She put her arms around him again and drew him close. "Of all the things I've wished for in my life, this is the thing I've wanted the most." She kissed his cheeks, then rang for Jarvis. "Come on, let's put your luggage away."

They took the elevator to his old floor, and he stepped out, stopped in amazement, and looked about him. "It's exactly the way I remember it. I don't think you've moved one teddy bear."

He walked around touching things. "My desk, my electric trains, my rocking horse."

"You're right, darling. I didn't. I've always been waiting for you to come back."

"You didn't really want to get rid of me so you could be with that black guy?"

"Oh, Bobby darling. I wouldn't have let you go for the

world. Nothing was ever more important to me than you, and now you'll see that. We'll have a wonderful life together. You can start to make any changes you like in this room tomorrow; the best color television and a stereo and telescope. Anything you want! Jarvis will work with you and take these old toys away to the Children's Hospital."

"I don't want to make changes. Not yet, anyway. I used to dream about my room and my sitting room and over there where my nanny slept. Right?"

"Right!"

All through dinner she kept touching him, taking his hand, loving his presence there. He made her feel complete.

They talked late into the night, filling each other in on all the years between, and when he finally went to sleep, she tiptoed in and looked at his head on the pillow. It was like looking at her sister Paula all over again. She sat there for a while, watching and listening to him breathe.

Finally she tiptoed out and went up to her own floor, thinking, this house is too big. I don't want to be separated from him by a floor. And if Marshall is not going to come to live with me — then she stopped and thought to herself, when did that happen? When did I begin to know that he was going back to Charlotte? And when did I begin not to care?

She could not date it from Bobby's appearance that day. No, she must have subconsciously known it for some time but been unwilling to face it. But now she could. It would be nice to have a husband, but she no longer needed one. Jarvis, her secretary, her agents, her accountants, and her lawyers had been far more essential during this period than Marshall. Sex was always somewhere around for the taking. She had become strong enough to stand on her own.

I don't need someone to take care of me, she thought. I can take care of myself. Not only that, I can take care of Bobby. Oh, my son, my son. You've come back to me, and I'm going to show you the world. I'll reopen the London house and we'll buy a house in Bel-Air. If you want to be an actor, that's what you will be. I can buy you the world. You're down there right now, my darling, down there in your old bedroom, where you belong. God's in his heaven, all's right with the world. My son has come home and I'm completely happy. I have everything I want.

It was a moment of epiphany!

The next morning she phoned Marshall, then walked over to his apartment. They kissed each other hello and went into the library to talk. "How's Charlotte feeling?"

"She's a tough fighter. She's begun to conduct her business from bed, and she's ordering me around again. That should tell you that she's on the road to recovery. She should be up and around in about a week. Tell me about Bobby."

"He was kicked out of school for poor grades."

"Anything else?"

"I don't think so and I don't care. All that matters is that he's home again. But there's something we have to talk about. We have to be honest with ourselves." Holding his hand she gently said, "Marshall, darling, we have to face facts. You don't really want to be married to me, and I no longer need to be married to you. I think I realized that you didn't belong to me in the middle of last night. I wanted to phone you to tell you that Bobby was back, and I couldn't because I was afraid of disturbing Charlotte. The thing is, Marshall darling, that I'm not alone any longer. You don't have to worry about me. Charlotte needs you more than I do."

"What about my needs?"

"I think that you need to be needed. I think you need your old life here. If you didn't need it, you wouldn't be here. Other men who break up with their wives don't go back if the wives get sick. I'm not criticizing and I'm not complaining. I'm just pointing it out. You've picked up the threads of your old life, and I think it's what you really want."

His kind, honest face furrowed in confusion. He took off his glasses and wiped them. "I don't understand myself. Do you know how many times I've wanted to strangle her?"

"Countless! I have too! But I don't think that has anything to do with the connection between you. You two are connected in a thousand invisible, mysterious ways that mean family. And you can't just shuck it off. But if I may make a suggestion, don't throw away your advantage. Don't let

The Survivors

her feel too secure. Bullies always need something held over their heads. You're in the driver's seat. Don't blow it again."

"Oh, Wendy. I wish I understood myself."

"None of us are that wise."

He held her against him for the last time and breathed the lovely fragrance of her hair. "I may be sorry about this for the rest of my life."

"But you aren't sure you will be. That tells you something."

"I'll never be sure about any of this. But you're right about one thing. I'm needed here, and I can't turn my back on my responsibilities."

"She would not have done it for you."

"She is what she is. I am what I am. And we play out our destinies."

They kissed for one last time, but the passion was gone for them both. Then she followed him to Charlotte's door where she lay propped up in bed talking on the phone. Tears came to Wendy's eyes. She had never seen Charlotte's hair undyed. Why, Charlotte's hair is white. That beautiful mass of red is white. How did we get so old?

When Charlotte saw her, she let out a scream. "How dare you come here. Did you come to gloat? I don't want you in my house, you nymphomaniac. I don't want you in this room, you husband stealer."

"That's quite enough of that," Marshall said firmly. "Put down the phone, keep quiet, and listen."

Wendy swiftly crossed the room and sat down on the chair beside the bed. "I don't want you here, you ungrateful traitor," Charlotte wept.

"Oh, yes you do," Wendy answered, and she took Charlotte's hand in her own. "Marshall is staying with you. He doesn't love me. He loves you."

"Is that true?" she asked timidly. "Are you staying with me?"

"I suppose so. But you have to be courteous to me."

The two old friends sat there looking at each other and wept.

"Hurry up and get well," Wendy said through her tears. "I'm planning a big welcome-home party for Bobby."

CHAPTER
Sixty-Seven

Stephen's son opened the door for Sarah, and for a moment they stood there soberly regarding each other. "I'm Adam," he said, "and you're the new one." Instantly, she wanted to flee. What did he mean, you're the new one. New what? Surely Stephen couldn't have discussed meeting her with this twelve-year-old child. Could he? Why? And thus far, what was there to discuss anyway?

She was equally surprised at the boy's appearance. With a jaded, dissolute quality about him, he was so pale, white, and thin, that he reminded her of the strung-out drug addicts, ex-students, leftovers from the sixties who still haunted the town's Main Street. But of course he couldn't be on drugs at twelve, *could he*? No. He probably just needed a little sun.

"Steve's in the kitchen cooking."

She hated this custom of kids calling parents by first names, another sign to herself that she was "over the hill." What was the purpose of having kids use their parents' first names? Nothing in the English language sounded more beautiful to her than mother and father, mama and papa, mom and dad. His son called him Steve. She supposed she should too.

She followed the boy through the entrance hall and into a haze of thick enveloping marijuana smoke. The living room, through which they had to walk to reach the kitchen, reeked from it. She had to thread her way carefully to avoid stepping on something or somebody. In this gigantic wastepaper basket of a room a dozen people lay about on the carpet smoking pot. What an environment for a kid!

The place was an absolute pigsty. Piles of old newspapers, magazines, and books made an obstacle course for her high heels. Large ashtrays on the floor were spilling over, and the stuffing was coming out of a gash in the faded maroon satin couch. She recognized nobody except for Hugh, who was stretched out on the floor with a young girl, eating buttered popcorn from an enormous bowl and watching television. Everybody else seemed to be equally young. Hugh waved but did not stand to greet her.

"Hi," Hugh called. "This is Ella. She works in the dining hall." The girl was round and giggling and dressed in a blue velvet dress that looked like the Thirties clothes that thrift shops were now selling. Under normal circumstances Sarah would never have met her. There was almost no social mixing between faculty and staff. Adam introduced her to Seth, a boy of about his own age who was Ella's son, and without another word they dashed upstairs.

Sarah stood there holding her coat but since nobody made a move to take it, she reluctantly dropped it on a pile of other coats on the floor, bothered because it was her best coat. She was too dressed up and felt out of place. I can always leave, she kept reminding herself.

The kitchen was as chaotic as the living room, with fossilized food particles on chairs and walls and even the ceiling, and dirty dishes covered all of the counter space. A totally stoned girl, with wild, dusty, dishevelled black hair sat on a high bar stool eating ice cream out of a dripping half-gallon container.

Steve stood at the stove stirring something that smelled delicious. He wore cut-off jeans, no shirt, and his smooth muscular back was firm as marble. He seemed like a high-school boy standing there, as young as his guests.

"Hello," Sarah said shyly.

"Sarah," he bellowed, waving a greeting with the dripping spoon, "Sarah, baby, you're here. And you look gorgeous. I'm almost finished. Just hang out and talk to me. There's some wine breathing in the dining room. Be a good girl and bring two glasses for us in here."

"Thanks, love," he said when she handed him his glass. "Set it down on any clear space." She looked about for a place to sit, and he pointed to a chair that was covered with crumbs. "Brush them on the floor. Next week the cleaning service comes. We do that every few months when we can't stand it any longer."

She sank down and quickly began to drink, hoping it would relax her, but suddenly he bellowed again at the girl, and Sarah jerked up in shock, spilling some wine on her best dress. "Betsy, will you fucking put that ice cream away? It's for dessert, you asshole."

Lazily the girl extricated her legs from the stool, walked over to him, showed him the inside of the carton and giggled, "Too late."

"Oh, fuck. You drive me absolutely bananas. Go to Carvel's and get an ice cream cake."

"I don't have any money."

"That figures. How much do you think one costs?"

She giggled again, her arm still clinging affectionately to his naked shoulders. "Maybe five dollars. I don't know."

"You asshole. I don't have five dollars either. Sarah, would you give her five dollars? I'll write you a check after I clean up. This is Betsy, by the way."

She reached into her purse and took out the money. "That's all right. Please consider it as a contribution to the evening."

"Pay attention, you asshole," he bellowed again to Betsy. "That's the way a lady behaves."

"Since when do you like ladies?" Giggling idiotically, she snatched the bill from Sarah's hand and skipped out.

"One of my students," he explained. "A little crazy but a real good kid."

One of his students? My God! She invited her students home for a Christmas party each semester at which she served tea and finger sandwiches and cookies. They always maintained a respectful distance. And so did she. She felt like Alice in Wonderland.

He dipped the large spoon into his pot, tasted from it, added some spices, tasted again, and said, "Superb. OK, love. Come on upstairs while I clean up and change." She followed him up the stairs to where Adam and Seth, smoking pot, were glued to his bedroom television. "Out," Steve ordered. "Wash up and meet me downstairs for dinner."

"OK, Steve," they answered. Did she imagine that his son winked at them?

"Did you notice that those boys were smoking marijuana?"

He instantly grew defensive.

"Sure. If that's what they want to do, that's what they should do. I believe in complete freedom of the individual. If they want to smoke, it's their right. I want them to see me as their friend, not as an authority figure like traditional parents."

"But they're only twelve."

"Forget about them!" He smiled at her with such dazzling warmth and intimacy that everything else fell away. "God, I'm glad you came. I can't wait until I hold you in my arms. Just give me two minutes to shower."

She looked about pondering where to sit. Even when she and Hal had been at their poorest, they'd never lived in such disorder. Every chair was stacked with piles of student papers to be graded, magazines, newspapers, books, a repetition of the decor of the living room. He noticed her dismay.

"Terrible! I know! I'm ashamed to invite someone as classy as you to this house. It's all the fault of that bitch. I need bookcases desperately but would you believe it? She wouldn't even give me one. Depriving me of the tools of my trade! I'm lucky she gave me my books. Sit on the bed. I'll be out of the shower in a jif."

The bed, which looked as if the grimy sheets had not been changed for weeks, was a double mattress right on the floor. Since that was the only uncluttered spot she sank down on it in an awkward position, her leg stuck straight out in front of her like a marionette in repose. If only she'd worn jeans. This was impossibly uncomfortable! Unwilling to put her shoes on his bed, an inhibition probably not shared by any other guest, she kicked them off and curled her feet under her.

He returned in a few minutes and stood in front of her totally naked, shaking water from his curly head, like an excited puppy, rubbing the towel so vigorously across his back that his balls bounced around. Embarrassed, she averted her eyes.

He tossed the towel to the floor, then, still naked, he

dropped to the mattress beside her, pulled her against him, and kissed her. She could feel the wonderful hardness of his erection burning through her dress, and passion surged violently through her like water bursting through a dam. Oh, how she'd missed this, missed this wonderful male warmth and sweetness, missed wanting and being wanted.

Suddenly nothing mattered. Not the mess or the dirt or the people or the pot. She didn't care if he was a phony. She didn't care if he'd slept with everyone on campus. She didn't care if she were to feel used and foolish and ridiculous afterward. All she knew at this moment was *need*. For the first time since Jimmy's death she felt alive again.

Just then Adam called from outside the door. "Come on, Steve. Everybody's starving."

"Later," he whispered to her, throwing on his clothes.

She found dinner both amusing and disconcerting. The other dinner guests, all of whom were in their twenties, were an off-beat group she would not normally meet in her daily life in this town: Hugh and his girl, one couple that specialized in taking groups white-water rafting, the owners of a local herb farm, and the local karate teacher and his girl. Odd professions! So different from what young people went into when she was married.

All of the couples lived together but were not married. How things had changed since Wendy had been thrown out of college. Nobody indicated disapproval or surprise at the unusual combination of Steve with a woman so much older than he. Even though they mouthed that cliché about not trusting anybody over thirty, they obviously didn't care. She was the only person who seemed to feel uncomfortable. The old ways had broken down.

They also seemed to have broken down in the way that dinner was served. Stephen put the cooking pots right on the table, without pads or trivets under them, and the guests helped themselves with their own utensils. There were no serving pieces and there were no napkins. A big roll of paper towels stood upright in the center of the table, and the guests tore off pieces as needed.

All of the others drank beer, but she and Stephen drank wine, a good Margaux. When he noticed her looking at the label he said with amusement, "I do have some of the accoutrements of a gentleman. I know good wine." She colored, embarrassed that he seemed to know what she was thinking.

She listened to their conversation with interest. Ecology, nutrition, fallout, pollution. They grumbled and groaned about the mess the world was in, but their major defense against it was to buy health foods, take vitamins, meditate, and experiment with drugs.

"I've stopped reading newspapers," one of them said. "I don't vote either. That's my protest."

"Sheer laziness," Sarah shot back. "The world goes on even if *you* don't vote or read newspapers. Don't you know how precious the vote is? The Freedom Riders of the sixties risked their lives to give people in the south the vote. It's wrong to just throw it away. Do you know that in 1960, 63.8 percent of the eligible electorate went to the polls but that this year, it fell to 55.7 percent. And people like you who don't vote are part of the problem."

Betsy clapped her hands. "How can you remember so many numbers? I guess that's why you're a professor."

Stephen's reply was equally irrational. "You can use statistics to prove anything. What good is the vote if the candidates are Tweedledum and Tweedledee? You knock yourself out with the union, spinning wheels, but exactly what have you accomplished? Personally, I think whenever you see an activist, you see someone who's not getting fucked enough. People like you aren't active for *me*. You do it for yourself! To fill your time and make you feel important. Not that I'm criticizing. I accept it. That's the way of the world. Everybody's in business for himself, and it's phony to pretend otherwise. And face it, Sarah, baby. Despite all of your union efforts, our salaries are still abysmally low. I show my protest by nonparticipation."

"Nonsense. That's just a lazy abdication of responsibility." She'd forgotten to check out his membership in her agitation on the obscene calls.

"Right on. I don't want anybody to be responsible for me, and I don't want to be responsible for anybody or anything. If everybody let everybody else alone, maybe the world would start to be a decent place. Until then, let's screw and get stoned."

She looked at him in astonishment, and then a big, broad smile spread over his face. Maybe he was only joking. But even so, it left her disconcerted. She didn't understand him and his friends. What did they stand for? There were no good guys and bad guys as there had been in her youth. They thought everybody was bad. They were anti-America and anti-Russia and anti-China, antilabor, anticapital, antireligion, antipsychiatry, and anticommitment. They took it for granted that anybody who went into politics was no good. George Wallace had only gotten what he deserved, the American people had reelected that war criminal Nixon because they were stupid, and the recent arrest of five burglars inside the Democratic National Committee was just a big fuss over nothing. Everybody knew that in politics dirty tricks were part of the game. Look at what they'd done to poor Ed Muskie.

She was amazed. How could young people be so jaded? If Jimmy had lived on he'd be twenty-six, about the same age as some of these kids. She had to believe that he would have been different, that he would have kept the faith, would have remained committed to the betterment of mankind. Of course he would!

Their favorite literary works seemed to be books she'd never heard of. *The Prophet* by someone called Kahlil Gibran, the writings of a guru called Carlos Casteneda, who believed that men could turn themselves into cars and dogs, Robert Heinlein's *Stranger in a Strange Land*, and something called *Dune*. The names of the rock musicians and songs they liked were also unfamiliar to her. She was increasingly bored and uncomfortable.

After dinner, Hugh brought a tray to the table with cigarette papers and a large brown dried leaf of marijuana. It looked just like a leaf of tobacco. Stephen started to pound some up, and then, feeling her gaze, looked up, smiled and confided, "This is the best you can buy." She smiled back weakly. Oh, wonderful!

Surely they weren't going to smoke marijuana with Adam and Seth at the table. But apparently they were! They automatically passed the joint to the boys, but when they passed it to her, she shook her head, feeling as compulsively hygienic as Charlotte. Apart from the fact that she'd never smoked pot before, she was repelled at the idea of putting into her mouth what had touched the insides of so many other mouths.

She stood up. "Good night, everybody. I really must be going." She would just have to cope with the obscene phone calls. She would notify the police tomorrow.

He followed her out of the room. "What the fuck is wrong with you?"

"I don't smoke pot. I don't believe in smoking pot in front of children, either."

"I don't get it. You don't smoke pot so you don't think anybody else should either?"

"That's not it. I don't care what you and your playmates do, but I don't want to be part of it."

"You've been critical and judgmental all evening. You look down on me and my friends."

"I didn't at first. But there's not one social conscience among the lot of you. All you do is contemplate your own navels and sneer at people who want to make the world a better place."

"If you were getting laid you'd be less intense about the world."

"That's really dumb! Equating the search for social justice with sexual frustration. Anyway, I thought you hotshots had replaced Freud with Gibran. I'm going." She started to go through the pile of coats on the floor.

Suddenly, with a reversal of mood that took her off balance, he threw his arms around her and flashed his dazzlingly sensuous smile. "Please don't go, Sarah baby. Why do you want to make me unhappy? I thought you and I were really beginning to reach each other. Please don't go."

He seized her and kissed her passionately and in spite of herself she began to feel her body responding again. And she thought of the obscene phone caller.

He felt the hesitation in her body. "Come on upstairs with me. Let's talk about this. I'll apologize for anything that bothers you. Pleeease! I'll make it right."

He bent down and kissed her neck. Shivers spread through her. Then he put his arm around her and drew her up the stairs. "Relax, baby," he crooned. "Just try to relax."

Inside his bedroom, he motioned toward the mattress on the floor, then took a joint from his desk and lit it. "Time for you to try, Professor. You need it! Don't worry. You're not going to turn into Mr. Hyde or a werewolf. I've been stoned for months on end. Right through my orals as a matter of fact. All of us were at Woodstock. How do you think we got through that? How do you think I got through my divorce? How do you think I get through the boredom of living in this dull town? Nicotine is a lot worse for people than pot. And a lot more addicting. Don't you know that the campaign against pot is paid for by the tobacco lobby? Don't you want to feel good? How do you deal with all that pain you're carrying around inside of you? You can't tell me that your union work does that for you. What do you do for Sarah?"

Her eyes grew wet with the tears that were always so close to the surface since Jimmy's death. "What makes you think I'm in pain?"

"Don't snow me. You're dripping blood. You're an open wound. You can't kid me. It's obvious. You're not happy."

"Apart from Jimmy, I'm not unhappy. I do my best."

"You're lying and you know it. Come on! Take a chance! Relax! Surrender! Find yourself by losing yourself. Why not try? You're here with me. I'll take care of you. I'm offering you a little joy in this lousy, fucked-up world, and you look at me like a fucking nun."

Still, she hesitated. "Ah, please," he murmured, burying his lips in her neck, "be with me just this one time. Don't close your mind and body to new experiences. Don't you know that's really the beginning of death and old age?"

He certainly had a knack for finding her exposed nerves. Well, why not? Why shouldn't she! Everybody else seemed to do it and she was curious. Gingerly, she took the joint from him, held it the way that he had, inhaled and held the smoke the way he had, then passed it back to him. "I don't feel a thing," she said.

He grinned. "Just keep smoking. Relax. You hold it as if it's a snake."

"Still nothing," she said after the next toke, nestling against his arm. How pleasant this was! When the first joint was finished, he lit another. And then she felt as she had before dinner: free, young, sensuous, relaxed. And in a dream, almost without volition, she dropped her clothes and found herself naked in bed beside him and everything seemed so easy and so warm. She rubbed her cheek against his shoulder. "It's not just sex," she murmured. "It's having someone's legs against yours."

"Dr. Gordon," he teased, "you are high."

"Absolutely not. I don't feel a thing."

"Oh, yes you do. And you're going to feel a lot more." He moved on top of her and she could feel her hips yearning toward his as the door burst open. It was Betsy!

"I have a lift home now, Steve," she giggled. "I'll come and help you with the dishes tomorrow. See you at the college, Dr. Gordon. Maybe some day I'll take one of your courses."

An alarm bell clanged in Sarah's head. She struggled up with a cry of embarrassment. "How dare you come in that way," she scolded angrily. "Don't you believe in knocking?"

"Not around here," the girl giggled. "He doesn't even shut the bathroom door. Like he always says, 'If you can suck someone's cock, why should going to the bathroom be private?'"

Sarah gasped, struggled up, and began to dress. She had never felt more mortified. He grabbed her wrist, and she averted her eyes from his erection. "Hey! What the fuck are you doing?"

"Leaving! This is just not my 'scene.' I can't have students see me turning on. I can't have students see me in bed with someone. I can't do anything to jeopardize my career. I have myself and Maggie to support."

"You're fucking out of your mind. Betsy's so stoned she won't even remember this by tomorrow morning. Grow up! This is the postprivacy age. The human body is beautiful. Sex is beautiful. It isn't the dirty secret it used to be."

"Sorry. I don't believe in socializing with students, and

I don't feel comfortable about your son and his friend being part of this scene."

Now he was angry. "Let me tell you something about my relationship with my son. He's not going to be screwed up about sex like you when he grows up. He's walked in one me several times while I was in bed with somebody, once with two somebodies, and he's cool about it. He's not going to grow up like you, thinking sex is something dirty you have to hide."

When she remembered making love with Hal, with only the two of them alone and brave against a hostile world, she wanted to wail aloud. She struggled to keep her lips from trembling. "You don't know anything about what I think. I don't think it's dirty. I think it's private. I can't make love in Grand Central Station. When making love is right, I think it's beautiful."

"It's not dirty and it's not beautiful, it's just something great to do. It makes you feel good. It's for recreation."

"Recreational sex? Sorry! Not for me!"

"Face it, Sarah. You need it."

"You're absolutely right. But sometimes we have to do without the things we need."

"You're in no condition to drive."

"Oh, yes I am. That marijuana didn't affect me at all. No more than a glass of wine. Good night. Thank for you for dinner."

"It *has* affected you."

"Good-bye."

As she drove away she was crying so hard that at first she didn't notice the strange behavior of the car. It was off the ground. The wheels had stopped turning, and the car was flying effortlessly through great colored sunbursts of gold and orange, exploding like Fourth-of-July fireworks. She looked at them with wonder, dimly realizing that this couldn't be happening.

When suddenly, without warning, another car shot out of a driveway she actually expected not to hit it because her car was flying so high above it. And then she heard the crash!

CHAPTER Sixty-Eight

Arla looked at Steve, stretched out in a chair in front of her desk. God he was good-looking and sexy and so openly opportunistic that it amused her. But he also made her stomach flutter. He'd come to discuss his manuscript with her, but the first thing she asked him about was Sarah's accident.

"I don't understand it," she said. "Sarah's always been such a cautious driver. I remember how carefully she always drove in East Hampton. And she doesn't drink. Do you know what happened?"

"It was her first experience with pot, and she wasn't prepared to handle it. I warned her not to drive. She's lucky to be alive. The car was totalled, but her daughter told me that her leg should be out of the cast next week."

"Sarah? Pot? Did you have to hold her down?"

He laughed. "Practically. She's such a sober, serious woman."

"She used to be merry and gay when she was married to Hal. What a marriage that was! Everybody marveled at it. We all loved him. Have you seen her since the accident?"

"I've tried, but she doesn't want to see me. I think she blames me. I don't know why, but if it makes her feel better, I can handle it. I sent her flowers but that didn't help. Maggie said her grandmother spent a few days with them and brought one of the old family servants who's been with them since Sarah was a girl."

"Our friends Wendy and Charlotte have visited her," Arla said guiltily, "but I just haven't had the time."

"Someone as important as you are probably has other priorities. I hope you don't mind me saying this, but it's unusual to find someone as lovely and feminine as you who's head of a big company. I thought so when I met you at Sarah's. And I wanted to know you better."

"Let me tell you something, Steve. You met me when I

was really down, but now I'm back to normal. I've been a successful businesswoman for twelve years, and one of the ways I got here was by recognizing bullshit. And I'm an active feminist. So please don't flatter me."

"Maybe you've become too hardened to recognize sincerity. I thought you were marvelously attractive that night and I still do. Nobody would ever dream that you had grown sons. I thought you were about my age."

"Would you think I was attractive if you didn't want a book published?"

He stood up indignantly, his eyes flashing fire. "I don't have to stay here to be insulted. You don't know anything at all about me. I'm being honest about my feelings, and you're biting my head off."

"All right, all right. Please sit down. I didn't mean to insult you." His lips still quivering, he sat down again but in a rigid, angry pose, not the relaxed slouch of before.

She did feel sorry. Why should she be so suspicious? Maybe he really did find her attractive. She certainly looked better than ever before in her life. She'd become slim again and had a regular masseuse who came to her office during lunch hours. Once a week she had a facial at Georgette Klinger, she'd had a face lift, an eye lift, and a tummy tuck. Since her surgery, people often expressed surprise when they learned that she had grown sons. There were little secretaries in her office who were probably about the same age as Steve but who looked lousy because they had no money to take care of themselves. People reached their prime at different ages, and this was the time of her full glory.

Maybe it was also time for a change of attitude. She thought she'd given up men forever, equating femininity with being weak. And after that she had equated feminist with being anti-men. But now she was strong enough and rich enough and famous enough not to be afraid. She could be a feminist who was in command, looked attractive, and had a little masculine attention. And here was someone making overtures to her, and she was shooting him down before he got off the ground.

"May I take you to lunch?" she asked.

He was as delighted as a kid. "Sure. Where?"

"Do you like sushi?"

"I've never tried it."

"You're in for a treat. I love it. But if you don't like it, you can always order something cooked, like chicken teriyaki. I first tasted sushi about five years ago, and ever since I've been an addict. Besides, it isn't fattening. I've heard that before World War II there were only two Japanese restaurants in New York: Miyako on Forty-sixth Street and Aki up at Columbia. Now there are a few on every block around here."

"It makes you wonder who won World War II!"

"Or any war. Did you know my son died in Vietnam? It still hurts. It's such a waste. Such a terrible waste. I used to be kind of religious, but now I can't believe in God. Are you religious?"

"Hell no. I went to parochial school. That's enough to turn anybody off religion." She laughed. He certainly was easy to be with.

In the restaurant they sat across from each other on tatami, Japanese style. Occasionally she would feel his toe against hers, and she would withdraw her foot quickly. But by the second carafe of saki she let it stay. How warm and comforting even a toe could be. Steve attracted her more than anyone in years, but she was still not sure he wasn't conning her to get a book published. And what about Sarah? She'd been at his house smoking pot with him just before the accident. That seemed fairly intimate to her.

She looked at him, and for the first time felt the thrill of power that successful men must feel all the time toward much younger women. She could own this young man. She had something he wanted. And why shouldn't she? Older men and younger women never caused comment, not even when the men were fifty years older, like Oona O'Neill and Charlie Chaplin. It was sexist to deny the same kinds of relationships to women. So what if he were younger than she? She didn't owe anything to anybody. She was successful enough to reach out for exactly what she wanted. And she was beginning to think that he would fill the bill.

It would be fun to do a reverse version of *Pygmalion*. He was, of course, not as backward as she had been when she married Lenny. After all, he had a doctorate in Irish literature. But he was too poor to have the range of experiences that were now offered to her in connection with her work, and that denied him a certain level of sophistication.

She took pleasure watching his delight at the artistic arrangement of the sushi; the yellowfish wrapped in seaweed and sprinkled with sesame seeds, the rich red of the tuna, the sweet egg wrapped in seaweed, the tekkamaki rolls of rice, cucumber and tuna, the shrimp, crab, and mounds of ginger and mustard. Again, she had that feeling a powerful man might have. It would be fun to spoil him.

When at last they sat back, sipping plum wine, the soles of their feet firmly touching, she began to talk to him about his book. "I've tried never to be discouraging to anybody who wants to write because I remember my husband's telling me I couldn't do anything. And if you tell that to a person often enough, she starts to believe it. I believed it for many years, and it almost destroyed me. So I would never take away anybody else's hope. But on the other hand, I have to be honest with you about what the readers said. I had two people read the manuscript because I took a personal interest in you.

"They both said that the articles you submitted on Irish literature showed that you had fine control of your subject area. But fiction is another matter again. You can write even the most outrageous things, if readers believe in your characters. The readers both said they couldn't believe in them."

"But it's based on my own life. Those are real characters."

"Saying it doesn't mean anything. You have to make the readers feel it."

"Didn't you read it?"

"No. I never read manuscripts."

"But you're publisher and editor in chief. How do you edit if you don't read?"

"Everything is farmed out to experts. Perhaps Sarah told you that I never graduated from high school. I'm really in awe of someone like you or Sarah who can get a doctorate. But the point is that I don't know anything about good literature, and I assume that's what you were aiming for in your book, so I use readers who are as educated as you. I'm really only interested in biographies and autobiographies of the movie stars."

"How on earth did you get so far?"

"I've always understood the common woman. I'm the mother of the celebrity bio. I understand their dreams and what they want to read. What's the most popular TV program right now?"

Without hesitation he replied, "*All in the Family*."

"Yes. And it's about the common man. That's what people want to see and read. The readers of your manuscript said that you write fiction for a learned journal. That's not what readers want. They want to have fun, to laugh, to cry, to forget themselves for a few hours."

"My God." His face sagged, and he moved his foot away from hers. "Maybe you didn't want to discourage me, but that's exactly what you've done."

"Don't be discouraged. When one door closes another opens. Tell me something. Exactly what is the nature of your relationship with Sarah? Are you two lovers?"

"No. I told you that she won't even let me visit. I don't think she likes or approves of me at all. But why do you ask?"

"I want to make sure you're not her property. Nobody in the world has ever done more for me than she has. She was the first one of my friends to care about me. She noticed that I was being bullied and abused, and she began to raise my consciousness about it. She said she was like somebody called Marlowe, in Joseph Conrad's books, who couldn't avert his face from the sufferings of others. Of course I've never read his work. Have you?"

Despite his chagrin, he smiled. "Yes, I have."

"So what about Sarah?"

"We're just casual acquaintances."

She thought about his answer for a while then decided to accept it. It would be dumb to lie. He knew she could check it with Sarah. Then she asked, "Tell me some more about you."

"There's not much to tell. My parents were killed in a

car crash, and I was brought up in a foster home. My marriage didn't work out. I'm looking for something."

She smiled. "Very well then. Let's talk business. What is your salary?"

Embarrassed, he mumbled, "Sixteen thousand."

"My secretary gets that. Why don't you come to work for me?"

"As what?"

"I'm willing to bet that there are many jobs in publishing you could do. Editing, for example. I have an intuitive feeling that you'd be a lot better at that than at fiction. Would you miss teaching?"

"Hell no. Would I have my own secretary?"

"Perhaps."

"Would I have an expense account?"

"Within reason."

"Really? I've always wanted an expense account. But if I took you up on your offer, there would be another problem. How could I afford to live in New York?"

"I'll ask you, Steve, for the last time. Are you sure you're not romantically involved with Sarah?"

"I swear I'm not."

"Then I think I've just solved your housing problem. I'm taking you home with me."

CHAPTER
Sixty-Nine

In 1974, Wendy held a joint fiftieth birthday party for the members of the sorority. It was also a farewell party to her beautiful home. The house had been sold to a developer, and she had bought a house in Bel-Air and a small apartment on Fifth Avenue and Seventy-second Street. Now that she was as successful at screenwriting as at novels, she had become bi-coastal.

Each of the women was fifty years old, and for the past year each had known a period of comparative peace. Arla, improbably married to Steve, seemed to have a good working relationship with him. Charlotte's cancer was in remission, and she was back at the gallery, working side by side with Marshall and Kitty, a cooperation that had made the gallery even more successful than before.

And Sarah, on temporary leave from teaching, was state head of her union, jetting all over New York, proud to be using all of her energies to work for labor. Maggie, at eighteen, was about to enter Sarah Lawrence where Bobby, at nineteen, was already the star of every school play. Peter was a successful lawyer, and Stewart still worked with his father.

And Teddy, after four years at the Menninger Clinic, was finally coming home. He would be there in time for the party. Charlotte phoned Sarah in a panic at the idea of seeing him. "He's as impossible as ever," she complained. "Marshall and I have been fighting all week about his coming home. I wanted him to go to a hotel to avoid conflict, and Marshall kept browbeating me about his coming home. But then he called and said he didn't even want to stay with us. Typical of the kinds of fusses he's always caused!"

"Where is he staying?"

"He's staying at Wendy's apartment until he gets his own place. Then he's going out to California to work for her."

"Really? In what capacity?"

"Well, you know that Da Gama Fund she set up to give money away? He's going to work with that. He's been studying accounting and law this past year while living in a kind of halfway house out there. I can't believe that she would entrust him with anything, but apparently she does. Well, why not? If she loses a million dollars here or there she wouldn't even miss it. It would probably be a useful tax deduction. I just hope he's really off drugs."

"I don't think you have to worry. He's thirty-one now, and I read someplace that if these junkies just get past their twenties, they start to taper off. You know, like William Burroughs."

"I don't know about Burroughs tapering off. Didn't he kill his wife? Like William Tell? Find me a better example."

"Please don't worry, Charlotte. It will be a wonderful party. Everybody's happy at last."

Maggie and Sarah were also staying at Wendy's that night, for the last time. "I'll miss that gorgeous house, Mom."

"We all will. But it's really far too big. They're turning it into ten apartments."

Maggie drove them to the city. She'd done most of the long-distance driving since Sarah's accident. Funny, Sarah thought, that obscene caller had never called again. Perhaps he'd given up during the time she was in the hospital.

Sarah looked at Maggie's profile lovingly. In the same way that people had been awed by Sarah's special relationship with Hal, they admired the special feeling between her and Maggie. "You're so lucky to have a child like Maggie," Charlotte had said wistfully on several occasions. "I still can't get through to Kitty. We relate well at work, but there's no communication on the personal level. I know she sees friends, but she doesn't bring them home. It really hurts to admit that she doesn't seem to like me at all."

"She loves you." Sarah tried to comfort her.

Sarah had not seen Steve since the night of her accident. Maggie, seeing her gaze pensively out of the car window, asked, "Do you feel funny about seeing that Steve, Mom?"

"I suppose a little. But it's illogical. The only thing we had in common was geography, and now we don't even have that."

"Are you sure you won't feel bad?"

"I think so. Logic tells me not to feel rejected that he immediately transferred his attentions to Arla, but...."

"But not even you can be logical all the time. And as usual, Mom, you're being kind. I don't think he transferred his so-called affections to Aunt Arla. The only person he has affection for is himself. It was simply a case of this stud for hire, and she outbid you. Frankly, I think that you were lucky that he didn't snare you. It would be just like Jerry all over again. Even so, I will never understand why you weren't angry at them."

"Why should I be angry? I didn't want him. I don't want to be like the Russians with the Jews. They don't want them, and yet they won't let them go. I didn't want him. So how could I object to his going? She called me about him, and I told her I wasn't interested. Why shouldn't she try to find a little happiness?"

"She may have become a successful publisher, Mom, but her taste in men certainly hasn't improved much."

"What makes you such an authority on taste?"

"Because I'm in love with the perfect man. I'm in love with Bobby. I can't believe I'm going to be at school with him all next year. I'm going to tell him I love him tonight, because I'd die if he even looked at someone else. I'll zap anyone who even looks at him. If he asked, Mom, I'd marry him tomorrow."

Sarah looked at her with concern. She was aiming high. Bobby was described in the society columns as one of the most eligible young men in New York. He was very rich, his father was in the social register, his mother was a famous writer, and he was as handsome as Wendy had been beautiful. People had already begun to stare at him as they'd stared at her.

"What kind of political ideas does he have?"

"None, my darling mother. But he's for me, not for you. He has absolutely no social conscience."

"Then why do you want him?"

"Any girl would want that hunk."

"That wasn't what I wanted. When I was a girl, I wanted a working-class hero."

"Working-class men today are like Archie Bunker. They're not heroes. Besides, you couldn't stand their grammar, Mom."

"I don't want you to get hurt, darling."

"Don't worry, Mom. I'm sure Bobby loves me too." She seemed so confident that Sarah pushed away her concerns.

Never had Wendy's house looked more elegant and festive than that night. She was determined to have a memorable farewell party. Although she was sad to leave, the house had become a burden to her in the past few years, and its sale had made her millions.

She was still magnificently beautiful in an off-one shoulder Balenciaga, Fracas perfume, and diamonds glittering in her hair. She and Bobby stood together joyously greeting her guests, a fascinating array of New York's socialites and literati. And as always, there was a number of adoring young men standing about from which she selected escorts when she needed them and with whom she might spend an hour in bed from time to time. Two of them now stood behind her, hovering about protectively.

At her side, as spectacular looking as she and dressed in a perfectly tailored dinner jacket, stood Bobby. He was, as Maggie had said, the handsomest man in New York, godlike, unmistakably Wendy's offspring, but with the broad strong shoulders and narrow waist of a weight lifter. As a budding actor, his major interest was in his body, and he spent long hours every day at the gym and at dance classes.

Although he was only nineteen, he had already had the kind of experiences that most people only dream of or begin to achieve after a lifetime of working. He had been on safari in Africa, rafting on the Colorado River, skiing all over Switzerland and Austria, and he crewed annually in the Bermuda race. He had his own plane and pilot's license, and his newest dangerous sport was hang gliding. Sarah's heart sank. It did not seem conceivable that he would marry Maggie.

From time to time, Wendy would glance at him with pride. Having him back these past three years had given her a contentment she hadn't known since childhood.

Wendy threw her arms around Sarah and asked, "Can you believe we're fifty?"

"I think we're both still eighteen," Sarah answered.

Marshall and Charlotte arrived soon after with Kitty. Charlotte was clearly agitated at the thought of seeing Teddy again. "Is he here yet?" she asked anxiously.

"He's upstairs getting changed. Just wait till you see him," Wendy said with pride. "You won't believe it. You're going to be thrilled at the difference."

Kitty clapped her hands. "I can't wait to see him."

"Nor I," Marshall echoed.

It seemed to Wendy that Charlotte had shrunk. After her mastectomies she had become almost as thin as Sarah, the one advantage, she said, of all this agony. She carried herself with a kind of brittle hauteur, as if most of her energy were based on mental determination rather than physical strength.

Marshall too seemed thinner and smaller with each passing year. It was almost impossible for Wendy to remember feeling passion for him. But they were still good friends.

"Thank you for bringing Teddy back," he whispered.

Maggie was holding their suitcase. "Come on, Maggie," Bobby said. "I'll take your luggage up. Jarvis is busy."

Maggie threw Sarah a triumphant glance that said, this is a great opportunity to be alone with him for a moment.

"You don't have to come now, Mom," she said. "I'll take care of everything with Bobby."

"What was that all about?" Wendy asked.

"She's in love with Bobby," Sarah sighed. "Poor thing."

"Why poor thing?"

"Your son looks like a god. I'm sure he has to fight women off."

"He fights them off so well that I've never met a one. She probably has a very good chance. Thus far, it seems to me that he is more interested in sports than in sex. Sometimes I can hardly believe that he's my son. Robert must have fed him on white bread only. Maggie might not even be interested if she got past the surface. He's a dear boy, but he's certainly no intellectual. But if your darling child wants him, she certainly has my blessing. Can you imagine us as mothers-in-law?"

"I want to imagine us as grandmothers."

Maggie followed Bobby to her favorite guest suite, the one with drawings by Hödler, Miro, and Modigliani, painted walls, and the early modern 1895 furniture by the Viennese designer Leopold Bauer. "I'm going to miss this house," she sighed.

"I won't. I like the one we bought in Bel-Air much better. It's all modern, looks like Frank Lloyd Wright. I hate all this old antique junk. And we're going to buy a weekend house in Malibu. I'm transferring to U.S.C. I found a trainer in L.A. who's much better than anyone here. And I'll be able to run on the beach all year round."

"You can't do that," she wailed. "I'm only going to Sarah Lawrence because you're there."

He looked at her in surprise. "You are? I didn't know that. Hey, listen. You can transfer too. Come out to the coast. It's where all of the action is now."

"I couldn't be that far from my mother. She'd be too lonely."

"She'd manage. Sometimes I think those four don't need anybody but each other."

"Please don't transfer, Bobby. When would I see you?"

"We have our new apartment here. And we'll be back and forth a lot."

"You don't understand. That wouldn't be enough." She stood on tiptoe and threw her arms around his neck. Then she pressed her lips against his and said, "I love you, Bobby. I love you! I'll die if you move away."

"Oh, God!" He gently disengaged her arms and led her to the couch. "We have to talk."

She covered her ears with her hands. "No! I don't want to hear. You're going to tell me there's another woman."

He gently pulled her hands away from her ears. "No, there isn't. Please stop crying, Maggie, and listen to me. There isn't another woman. If I ever picked a woman it would be you. But don't you understand, Maggie?"

"Understand what?"

"For God's sake. Don't be dumb. I'm gay."

"Gay? You mean like in homosexual? I don't believe it. You're only telling me that to get rid of me."

"I love you, Maggie. You're my friend. But you have to believe me. I'm gay."

"You can't be gay. You're so handsome, so masculine, so athletic. It's just not possible. How do you know you're gay? What makes you gay? Have you ever slept with a woman?"

"Yes."

"And you didn't like it?"

"Not especially."

"And," she shuddered. "You've also slept with men?"

"Yes."

"And you liked that better."

"Yes, I did."

Beads of perspiration covered his forehead, and his lovely

eyes, so much like Wendy's, were troubled. She held him tightly.

"Do you want to be gay?"

"I don't know, Maggie. I'm confused."

"Maybe you're not gay. I love you, Bobby. I feel as if I'm dying of love for you. Make love to me here. Right now! Maybe it will be different for you. I love you so much I'll make it different."

His beautiful eyes looked at her in confusion. Again she begged, "Please try, Bobby. I promise that if you don't like it, I'll never bother you again."

"I love you, too, Maggie. I've always loved you, since we were little kids on the beach. Maybe you *can* make it right."

In a moment they'd dropped the clothes from their lithe young bodies. She clung to him, whispering, "I love you, I love you," afraid he might turn away from her, not wanting to spoil things by telling him she was a virgin. And when he entered her she hid her pain, wanting him to lose himself in pleasure so that she would not lose him.

Afterward, he rolled off and lay beside her and lit a joint. "You dope," he said. "You didn't tell me you were a virgin."

"I didn't want to be a virgin anymore."

"You didn't come either, did you?"

"No. But I don't care. I was concentrating on you. Do you think you still like men?"

He held the joint against her lips. "Please don't get me wrong, Maggie. I like being with you. I love being with you, but it's just not the same. You'll just have to face facts. I'm gay and that's all there is to it."

"It doesn't have to be, Bobby, darling. You can change. You can have therapy. I heard a program on TV about some group called Aesthetic Realism that reclaims homosexuals. Will you please try to do something, Bobby?"

She began to cry as if her heart were breaking.

"Let me think about it, Maggie. Right now I'm feeling real confused. Will you still be my friend?"

"Yes, of course I will. I love you. But that's not what I want. Does your mother know?"

"No. She'd be real upset. All these years she's talked to

me about how she didn't have any family left and how I should have six kids so we'd never be alone and would carry on her family line. I don't have the guts to tell her."

"Besides, maybe you'll change."

"Don't expect anything, Maggie. Let's just see what happens."

They lay on the bed together, finishing a joint, both of them equally sad and depressed.

Downstairs Wendy looked at Sarah and smiled. "Are you thinking what I'm thinking? It's been over an hour."

"They could be watching TV. But yes, I'm afraid that I am thinking the same thing."

"Oh, Sarah. Remember us in Mexico? The night we met our men?"

Sarah's eyes filled with tears. "Don't make me cry."

"I don't want to get old," Wendy said.

"I know," Sarah agreed. "But somehow those kids make it all right."

CHAPTER
Seventy

Maggie watched Bobby dress, and his beauty tore at her heart. She hid her physical discomfort because he was so sad. "I'm sorry Maggie. Please say that you forgive me."

She forced herself to be cheerful. "I'm not giving up this easily," she answered. Pasting radiant, carefree smiles on their faces, they rejoined the party. Bobby went back to Wendy's side, and Maggie went to speak to Kitty, forcing herself to do what Sarah always had done, talk about politics as a way of coping with personal misery. "I'm so proud of you for getting shot. Wish I'd been there."

"Wish I hadn't. You just don't know. My body now can predict weather changes. I've had more than enough violence for my twenty-eight years. I feel a hundred. Have you seen Teddy?" Maggie shook her head. "I'm dying to see him. Wendy says we're in for a surprise."

"Well here I am." A stranger stood beside them.

"Teddy?" Kitty shrieked in disbelief. "Is that you?"

"It sure is," he said with shy pride. She threw her arms around him. At thirty-one, he bore no resemblance at all to the strung-out skeleton Marshall had taken to London. Now that he was off drugs, his color was ruddy and normal. He was neatly dressed in clothes that Wendy had purchased for him—a navy suit, white shirt and Countess Mara tie—and he had a short, thick dark Mark Spitz mustache and a shag haircut like Warren Beatty's. Skid Row had been exchanged for Savile Row.

"Hey, sis, don't cry. You'll make *me* cry."

She looked at him gravely for a moment, then said in delight, "You're not angry any longer." She'd spent years in therapy examining her guilt about Teddy because she'd wanted so much to help him while he was growing up and couldn't. "Charlotte would cut us each a piece of pie," she'd told the therapist, "and she'd give me a piece that was too big to eat and give Teddy a little sliver. If he asked for more, she'd accuse him of being greedy. If he dropped a crumb on the table, she'd send him to eat in the kitchen. She never let him breathe. If not for me, she might have treated him better."

Intellectually, she understood that she was not to blame, but emotionally she'd always felt guilty. And now, the sight of him—well dressed, confident, and restored to health—lifted a lifetime burden from her shoulders. With his arm around her shoulders, they went to find their parents. Teddy moved toward them confidently.

Marshall could not conceal his delight at Teddy's demeanor. "I don't care if you're too old for this," he said, kissing him. "I'm going to kiss you anyway."

It was the first time he'd seen him since leaving England. The clinic had informed him that Teddy didn't want to see any family members and that it was essential for his recovery to respect his wishes. "How's the piano, Dad?"

"Oh, I hardly play anymore. The gallery keeps me running. But there's a marvelous woman pianist, Alicia Delarrocha, I'll take you to hear. A lot of wonderful new pianists around. Young ones."

"Hello, Teddy. So they actually cleaned you up."

"Hi, Charlotte." Wow! She looked terrible. He had once thought she was six-feet tall, strong as a hurricane, dangerous as a land mine. This woman who could not be more than five-feet-four looked brittle enough to break. Why, he could blow her away with a breath! And she'd have to watch for the possibility of cancer for the rest of her life. A life sentence! No need for him to retaliate any longer.

"I just want to tell you a few things, Teddy," she snapped, "I think it was outrageous of you not to let any of us visit. And what a slap in the face for you to be staying here with Wendy. But I'm not surprised."

Teddy looked at Kitty and the two of them collapsed into gales of laughter, hooting and howling while tears ran down their cheeks. Kitty, shaking with amusement stammered out, "Some things never change," and they were off again.

"I don't have to stand here to be insulted," Charlotte said indignantly.

"Nobody's insulting you," Marshall said firmly. "We're all together again, and we're going to be a happy family."

"I don't want to fight," Teddy said. "The past is over."

Maggie watched the scene sadly. Charlotte was a little nutsy and Marshall was weak, but they were a family. There were four of them. All she had was her mother, and now it looked as though she would never have Bobby. The enormity of her loss suddenly hit her so hard that she wanted to wail. Bobby was lost to her forever. Her plan to be close to him at college for the next three years had been shot down, and she felt rootless, purposeless, and terribly alone.

Her grandmother had left her enough money to go anywhere to college, to study anything that interested her. But ever since childhood, Bobby had been the only thing that really interested her. He had been her beacon, and she'd crashed on rocks following that false light. Now what should she do? She could follow him to California, but what would be the purpose of that? Wouldn't it be dumb to stand around watching him make out with some guy, hoping he'd change? And she couldn't leave Sarah all alone. The memory of that terrible automobile accident, when she and Claude had driven up to Vassar Hospital in the middle of the night, still made her shake.

She knew that it was sensible, even essential, for all women to have a means of supporting themselves. But what she had always wanted most was not a career, but to have a husband and children and to re-constitute her family. She never talked much about those feelings, but she'd seen how empty and lonely even the best career could be without a man to love. She'd wanted Bobby first, and everything else could follow after.

She was proud as could be of her mother, but she didn't want a life like hers. She didn't have that kind of nervous energy.

Ever since Sarah had been elected statewide president of the union she was busier than ever; lobbying, speaking, cajoling, exhorting, convincing, arguing, begging, battling, working herself into exhaustion and coming home to an empty bed and her electric blanket. Aunt Arla would die if she ever heard Maggie express such anti-feminist sentiments, but she often wondered what good it was to be applauded during the day, if you slept alone every night. Not that Sarah ever complained. That wasn't her way. Her career appeared to satisfy completely her emotional needs.

But it wasn't what Maggie needed. She wanted a husband, six kids filling the house with lots of friends, three horses, two dogs, and one cat. She wanted a big old house that was never, never empty. And for as long as she could remember, Bobby had been the man in that house.

Her vagina was aching, and she needed to be alone. Unable to remain with the celebrants, she hurried into the library, sat on the Regency sofa under an enormous full-length portrait of Bobby, looked at it in despair, and burst into tears.

"Hey there, little girl," she heard a man's voice say. "Why are you crying? This is supposed to be a party."

For a moment she thought she was dreaming. The man made her think of Mephistopheles with his penetrating black eyes, as cold and hard as marbles, a pointed black beard, and long fingernails that made her shiver. He was about thirty-four or thirty-five and expensively dressed. "W-who are you?" she asked.

"I guess you were too little to remember me. But I remember you. You're Maggie and you've turned into quite a dish. And I'm Stewart!"

"Now I recognize you," she said. "I saw your picture in *People* magazine when you opened that disco, Valley High."

"Have you been there?"

"No. I'm stuck upstate. I only get into the city to see my mom's friends or relatives. Some of my friends wanted to go down, but we were afraid we might make the trip and not get in."

"Now you can get in whenever you like. My name is Open Sesame! Impress your friends! Bring them along."

"Really? That would be great!"

"Now tell my why you were crying." At first she wanted to tell him to mind his own business, but then when she caught sight again of Bobby's magnificent portrait, she felt a need to talk. "Bobby," she said.

"What about him? The guy's gay. Everybody knows that."

"No, he's not. Don't you dare say that. I'm in love with him."

"He's a baby. You need a man."

"How would you know what I need?"

"I know everything there is to know about little girls like you. They need men. Not boys." He reached into his pocket and pulled out a paper of cocaine. He snorted a line, then held it out to her.

Well, why not! Everybody else at school seemed to have tried it when they went home on vacations. But this was the first time it had been offered to her. Maybe it would make her feel better. She'd take anything that would do that.

She took a hit, handed it back to him, and started to feel wonderful. "Want to come home with me now?" he asked.

"Of course not. I just told you that I'm in love. Besides, this is the last party in this house. Kind of an historic occasion. Wendy moves out and the demolishers move in. And I want to be here when the four of them cut the cake.

Did you see it? It's gorgeous! Four tiers! Wendy had it made at Dumas."

"OK. I'll give you a rain check. Come to the disco without any friends and stay over with me. I have a jazzy art deco duplex right on top of the disco."

"Stop pushing, Stewart. You're sixteen years older than I am. And aren't you married to some model?"

"That relationship ended about one hour ago so I'm free, white, and thirty-four. So what if I'm sixteen years older than you. If Arla can make a fool of herself with that asshole Steve, why can't I?"

She looked at his brocade jacket, matching tie, and silk pleated shirt. He was dressed like a dissolute, Edwardian dandy. "My mother would never approve. You have a bad reputation with the sorority for being a roué, a gambler, and God only knows what else. And they don't even know about the coke."

"Fuck the sorority. Teddy and I always were the sacrificial lambs. And my father too. Everybody else was so pure and fine and noble, but the three of us were no good. They needed us to dump on."

"You're out of your mind, Stewart. I've heard the stories. Your father was a sadistic bastard who almost destroyed you, and you should be proud of your mother. Look what she's made of herself."

"You've got to be kidding! Arla's still stupid. The only way she got to be a publisher is that she gave the soap opera crowd something to do in-between the afternoon soaps and the evening sitcoms. And that husband of hers makes me want to retch. Can you believe the stupid nerve of that guy. He showed up at Valley High one night with some little broad in tow and expected me to let them in. The guy is fucking ungrateful. He's been a bust at every assignment she's given him, and now they pay him *not* to come in. Whatever she says about my father, and frankly I think she exaggerates because it takes two to make an abused wife, at least she wasn't supporting *him*. And he didn't screw around."

The library door opened and somebody called, "Come

into the dining room, everybody. They're going to cut the cake."

Stewart quickly crossed the room, knelt at Maggie's feet, and slid his hand up between her thighs. "Come and spend a night with me," he said.

"Get your hand out of there." She gave him a push, and he sprawled back on the carpet. She wanted to cry again. She'd rather have a gay Bobby than this hetero creep.

"You love it. You know you do. I'll call you here tomorrow morning."

"Don't waste your time," she hurled at him before running out. "I don't like you, and I don't like your attitude toward the sorority, and Bobby isn't gay."

In the dining room, Sarah stood waiting to cut the cake. Suddenly she felt a kiss dropped on the back of her neck. She whirled in surprise to find Steve. "How dare you," she snapped.

"If you add the words 'you cad,'" he grinned at her, "we'll really be back in the Victorian era. Don't be angry, Sarah baby. Frowning causes lines! I hear that you're a union bigshot now. I certainly have a knack for romances with successful women."

"You never had a romance with me, Steve." She turned her back and walked to where Peter, a chunky, blonde young man, who had just been appointed to the Manhattan district attorney's office was standing. She had always especially liked him from the time he'd been so sympathetic after Jerry's defection.

"Aunt Sarah," he said. "Just the person I want to see." He took her hand and led her into an empty hallway.

"I wish you'd talk to my mother. Stewart's getting himself in trouble, and she just won't listen to me about it."

"What sort of trouble?"

"To begin with, he and his partner are skimming money off the top of that disco. Sooner or later the IRS is going to catch up with them."

"How do you know?"

"Everybody knows. He brags about it openly. But that's not all. The second problem is that the money he's siphoning off is going into the pornography business. He's become a major distributor of pornographic films, books, and magazines, and he's also operating peep shows in Times Square. He's transporting obscene videotapes across state lines for distribution in Canada, and worse than all of that, he's beginning to deal in child pornography. There's no way he won't get caught, and when he does the shit will really hit the fan. My career will be threatened, and my mother's name will be blackened. He can't do much damage to my father."

"If your parents won't interfere and if you can't control him, Peter, why tell me?"

"You've always been so sober and sensible. I thought maybe you could do something with my mother."

"I'll talk to her, but I don't blame her for not wanting to get involved. His behavior is past my comprehension. If he weren't part of us, I'd cheerfully see him in jail. But anyway, since he's changed his name to Winters, would they be able to trace him to you?"

"You know the scandal sheets! And *Time* magazine always writes a.k.a. and gives the original name. My major concern is that all of this might come up while I'm in the D.A.'s office."

"I'll talk to your mother about this tomorrow, but I wish I didn't have to. Now we'd better get back for the cake cutting."

How very strange life was, she thought. Here in one family, you had one child pornographer and one straight arrow. She thought of Jimmy and immediately was assailed with the familiar agony. He would have made such a contribution to society, and he had died. And someone as depraved and antisocial as Stewart continued to pollute the world.

CHAPTER
Seventy-One

For the past two months, Sarah thought, Maggie had been acting very strange. What had happened to her happy-go-lucky, open daughter? The clear mountain stream had become opaque. It often seemed to her as if Maggie had been crying, and she was spending too much time with her friends in the city at Stewart's disco. That worried her. She didn't want Maggie to be anywhere near him. Of course his disco was exactly the kind of place that appealed to kids today, but nothing Stewart was involved in could be wholesome. Then one night Maggie announced to Sarah that she was going in alone because none of her friends could come, and she might have to spend the night in the city. "Absolutely not! I don't want you going there alone. And you certainly can't spend the night with him. That man is a menace to society."

"Relax, Mom. I'm eighteen years old and I can go anywhere I like. If I were at college you wouldn't even know the difference. And it so happens that I have no intention at all of sleeping with him."

"It's not *your* intentions I'm concerned about."

"What have you got against Stewart?"

"He's a depraved character, Maggie, and you know it. I have nothing but contempt for that whole twilight demimonde he runs around with. They're all involved in drugs. You know that. And Peter says Stewart is now involved in pornography."

"I have to do something, Mom. Being there takes my mind off my problems. In a way it's really funny. History certainly has a way of repeating itself. You always told me with great indignation about how your parents tried to control your seeing my father, and now you're doing the same thing all over again."

"Yes. But the difference is that I'm right."

At her words, the two of them burst into laughter, and then, abruptly, Maggie began to weep. Sarah threw her arms around her beloved daughter. "Maggie. Maggie darling, what's wrong? What happened with Bobby? You've been unhappy since that night. What is it? I don't want you to be unhappy. If it means that much to you to go to the disco, then go. I love you, darling. I don't want to see you so unhappy. Maybe Stewart isn't as wicked as I think."

"Yes, he is! Every bit as wicked. But that's not the problem. He's just an interesting kind of diversion. The problem is I'm pregnant."

"Pregnant?" Sarah's heart flip-flopped. "By Stewart?"

"Of course not. He's a scum-bag. Not Stewart. Bobby."

"Bobby? Thank goodness. You're too young to have a baby but that's a little better. Does he know? Do you want to marry him?"

Then, weeping, Maggie told her the entire story. When she had finished, Sarah rocked her in her arms and asked, "What do you want to do, darling? Do you want an abortion?"

"Absolutely not. I want the baby."

"Then you will have to be married, whether Bobby wants it or not. I have to talk to Wendy."

"Mom, you don't understand."

"Oh, yes I do. Whether he likes girls or not, he has to have a legal responsibility for your baby. I'm not going to have you live a life of poverty the way your father and I did. It's a different time, and I want the best for you and your baby."

She called Wendy in California to tell her about the baby, but she didn't have the heart to tell her that Bobby was gay. He would have to tell her himself. Wendy was absolutely thrilled. "A baby! How marvelous. I'll call you back, Sarah, darling. Tell Maggie there's nothing to be upset about. In fact, tell her that I'm ecstatic. You know how I feel about children."

Bobby was playing with the pro on their court. She sat there watching him until he had finished the set and came bounding up to her. "Hi, Mom," he said. "How did I look?"

"Gorgeous as usual and you know it, you egocentric creature. Sit down, I want to talk to you."

"I have to shower, Mom. I have a date."

"Sit down." Jarvis came out with iced tea for them, and she waited until he had gone.

"What's up, Mom?"

"Wonderful news, you sly thing. You are going to be a father."

"Are you crazy? What are you talking about?"

"Maggie!"

"Maggie?"

"She's pregnant, and she says you're the father. Are you?"

"I guess so if that's what she says."

"You had no idea?"

"None at all."

"But you did sleep with her?"

"I didn't sleep with her. We screwed once for about ten minutes."

"That's it? And nothing since then?"

"That's right! Nothing!"

"Don't you like her?"

"Of course, I do. I love her. Next to you, I love her best of all."

"I don't understand this, Bobby. You love her, but you haven't seen her or called her or spoken to her or attempted to make love again. When I fell in love with Maurice, it was painful to be apart for an hour."

"I don't like girls."

"What does that mean?"

"Just what I said. I'm gay."

"Gay?"

"Homosexual."

"I know what gay means! That's not the point. I just don't believe it. You're a jock. Women worship you. I've never known anybody more normal than you."

"But it's true. That's the other reason I was kicked out of school, but you were so happy to see me that I didn't have the heart to tell you."

"You're certainly making up for that right now. You mean, even when you were that young?"

"Always."

She burst into tears. "I'm sorry, Mom. You know that I would never want to hurt you. But that's the way it is."

"Maybe you'll change."

"Don't even hope. Maggie was trying to change me. That's why this happened."

She covered her face with her hands and wept. The Lord giveth and the Lord taketh away. Tears were running down his face too, arousing her compassion for him. "Do you still love me, Mom?"

"Of course. I could never stop loving you."

"I'm sorry."

"Stop saying that. It does absolutely no good." She blinked away the tears and straightened her shoulders. "I'm absolutely devastated, Bobby. Devastated! It is absolutely unbelievable that someone as indisputably heterosexual as I should end up with a gay son. It's not because you hate me, is it?"

"Don't be dumb, Mom. It has nothing to do with you. It's just the way I am. What should we do about the baby?"

"I want the baby. I want a grandchild. So does Sarah. I want you to marry Maggie and give it to me. It's the first thing I've ever asked of you. Marry Maggie and after that, you can do whatever you like, disgusting as I find it. Will you do it?"

"If that's what you want. I love Maggie and I love Sarah. I like the idea of having a kid myself. But after that, no strings. All right?"

"If that's what we have to settle for, that's what we'll do. It's better than nothing."

"And no big wedding, Mom. Just the sorority and Dad if he wants to come. I'll call him and see if he does."

Moving heavily, as if she'd been dealt a mortal blow, she walked into her study to phone Sarah. Teddy was there pouring over her papers. He looked up with concern. "What's up?"

"Did you know that Bobby was gay?"

"Yeah! He talked to me."

"Thank you very much. Why was I the last to know."

"He didn't want to hurt you."

She burst into tears again, and he came around the desk and took her in his arms. "There, there," he soothed her, and she was surprised to hear how like his father he sounded.

CHAPTER
Seventy-Two

Robert was furious about the match. He yelled at Wendy, "It's your pernicious influence that has him getting married at nineteen to an insignificant little Jewish girl from upstate. I had such plans for him. He could have married anyone. I'm surprised you're not marrying him off to one of your blacks. I won't come. You don't need me. You have your sorority."

"You're right," she snapped back. "I don't need you."

In August 1974, Sarah and Maggie flew out to Los Angeles. Wendy had sent them first class tickets, and Sarah enjoyed the unfamiliar luxury, but Maggie was too nauseated to eat. "I was nauseated with Jimmy," Sarah said, "but not with you. The first time is the hardest."

"I'm nervous about seeing Bobby. Suppose he changes his mind about getting married."

"He won't. He's as honorable as Wendy. The real question, Maggie, is what happens after the wedding. Do you want to come back to New York with me, move in with Wendy? Would Bobby let you move into the gatehouse with him?"

"I'd like to stay with Bobby, but he probably won't let me. So I guess I'll stay with Wendy if you wouldn't mind. I can go to U.S.C. with Bobby during the fall semester, maybe even finish the semester. And after the baby comes, I don't know. Maybe he'll change once he sees the baby. Could you manage, Mom?"

"Of course I can. Please don't worry. I'll come out at the end of the semester. In spite of everything, I'm thrilled about a grandchild. Wendy is too. What a lucky child that will be. No child will ever be more loved."

Wendy, Bobby, and Jarvis were waiting for them at the baggage area. "Oh, Mom, how beautiful they are." Maggie's hand trembled in Sarah's.

Bobby, dressed in jeans, a T-shirt, and running shoes was so magnificently impressive, towering above the crowd like a sun god, that people stood peering at him and wondering, "Who is he? Who *is* he? He must be an actor!" It was the way people had always looked at Wendy, Sarah thought, as if history were repeating itself.

And Wendy, still beautiful but undeniably older, was elegant looking in matching silk slacks and shirt from Eleanor Keesham with half a dozen gold chains around her neck. Mother and son stood on their own little island, guarded by Jarvis and protected by the armor of indifference they'd cultivated over the years. But when they sighted Sarah and Maggie, they ignored the people watchers and waved with excitement. Maggie dashed over to Bobby and spontaneously threw her arms around him while Wendy and Sarah hugged each other.

"Oh, Bobby," Maggie pleaded, "I've been so very nervous. And I'm too nauseous to live. Please don't scold me or say I've entrapped you or anything like that."

He hugged her back reassuringly. "Of course I won't. I think it's kind of wonderful that I'm having a kid. But promise you'll let me go when I want to go."

"I promise. I promise anything you like."

"Hello, Aunt Wendy," Maggie said, hugging her.

"Welcome, my lovely daughter-in-law," Wendy said in her husky voice. "I couldn't be happier."

The chauffeur carried their luggage to Wendy's new Rolls. "Wow," Maggie said. "A white Rolls."

"It's nothing out here," Wendy said. "Everybody has beautiful cars. That's the number one status symbol."

"Do you have a Rolls too?" Maggie asked Bobby.

"No. I have a Porsche. We'll get you one, too. I'll let you try mine out first."

Sarah felt the tension drain from her body. They were such children. Maybe everything was going to be all right.

As soon as they were seated, Wendy reached into the car's bar and took out a bottle of champagne. "I couldn't wait until we reached home to toast the next generation."

"That's a good excuse for drinking, Mom," Bobby teased. Solemnly they lifted their fluted glasses and toasted each other.

"I've already picked out names," Wendy said. "I'd like a girl to be named for either my mother or sister, and I thought you might like to name a boy after Hal or Jimmy."

"I don't think so," Maggie giggled. "I don't want this baby to be laden with any of the sadness of the past. I want this to be a happy baby. I want it to have a fun California name like Troy or Brad or Dawn."

"You can name the girl," Bobby said, "but if it's a boy he has to have my names. Robert da Gama Kingman V."

"You're out of your mind. Jewish people don't name babies after living people."

"Don't give me that crap, Maggie. You have as little interest in religion as I do."

"It's my baby."

"It's our baby and you'd just better remember that."

Wendy and Sarah looked at each other and smiled. "We'll decide," Wendy said. "You two just give us the baby and go off and do your thing."

This ability to be relaxed about religion was one of the better changes in the world, Sarah thought. When she was a girl, Hitler made religion everything. Millions of people died because of it. Now it meant nothing to these kids. Their big problems were ones that would affect anybody regardless of religion; nuclear war, pollution, birth defects, finding meaning in life.

So Maggie was marrying an Episcopalian! Thank goodness Sarah wouldn't have to explain that to her father. After her mother's death, he'd sold their apartment and gone to spend his final years in Israel to be close to the grave of his beloved grandson. He'd never forgiven himself for taking Jimmy to where he'd met his death and was too old to travel back for the wedding.

Yes, everything was different now. Nobody cared if Jews married gentiles or if blacks married whites. All of the great taboos of her girlhood had weakened or withered away. Couples like Wendy and Maurice were accepted and even admired. And yet, despite all of the gains, it was not better for her child. She thought of making love in Fortin, of the years beside Hal's body, of the warmth and companionship they had shared, and she could have wept for what her beloved daughter would miss.

"Well, here we are folks," Bobby said as they pulled into the estate off of Stone Canyon Road in Bel-Air, so carefully concealed from the road that only people who had received explicit directions would ever find it.

Bobby asked to be dropped at his own house first. "I have some things to do," he said. "I'll be up for dinner."

Wendy noticed the expression on Maggie's face. Poor thing. She obviously was still hoping. She quickly said, "Teddy's waiting at the house to say hello, and we have a tremendous amount to do in the next two weeks. I was wondering if you'd like to wear my wedding dress. My dressmaker could make it fit quite easily."

"Oh, I'd love that, Aunt Wendy. Anything you own must be beautiful."

"That dress really is." Sarah tried to sound cheerful. "It's covered with seed pearls." It had cost over five thousand dollars twenty-one years ago, just about Hal's yearly salary. "You'll look beautiful in it."

"And you can pass it down to *your* daughter," Wendy added.

Teddy was waiting outside the house for them. "Welcome, little sister," he said, hugging Maggie. She burst into tears. "You're not allowed to cry in sunny Cal," he said lightly. "Hurry up and change. Let's all take a swim. It's L.A. chicken soup."

Sarah looked at him. "He's more like Marshall every day. Maybe if he could change, Wendy, Bobby can too."

"We have to hope," Wendy answered soberly.

"How absolutely gorgeous," Sarah said, looking at the house. Far less formal than any of Wendy's previous homes, the modern glass and redwood house was nestled among bougainvillea, hibiscus, cypress, and cacti. A crew of gardeners was bustling about calling to each other in Spanish.

Jarvis carried up the guests' luggage, and Wendy showed them the rest of the house: the vaulted redwood living room, beyond it a terracotta terrace, an Olympic-size swimming pool, and a hot tub that was ringed with cypress trees. Two men were cleaning the pool, and another man was rolling the tennis court.

"You can't be unhappy in this setting," Teddy said to Maggie. "It's a great place to bring up children."

Her mood shifted mercurially, and she was her usual perky self again for a moment. "I'll go up and change," she said, "and I bet I can beat you."

"There are new bathing suits in the cabana," Wendy said. "In every size. The maid will unpack for you."

"Nothing like money!" Maggie dashed into a cabana and was out in a few minutes. "You can't catch me," she called as she and Teddy raced across the pool.

Wendy sipped a diet Coke, watching them with an ironic expression on her face. "Given Charlotte, he's the one who should have been gay," she said. "Instead, he's a dyed-in-the-wool hetero, busy making up for lost time. Out every night with a different starlet."

"Isn't life impossible," Sarah sighed. Wendy nodded in agreement.

"I feel so awful, Sarah. I still can't believe it. We always knew and talked about Oscar Wilde and André Gide and E.M. Forster and Jean Genet and Gertrude Stein when we were at school. And it never bothered me one way or the other. But those people were abstractions, not my son. Not my own beautiful son—good, sweet, kind, making love to other men. I can't bear to think about it.

"Know what they call them out here? 'Fudgepackers.' Can you imagine anything more graphically horrible?" She shuddered. "It breaks my heart. He has everything. He should have been the patriarch of a large family. Instead, he'll be alone all his life. Just the way I've always been."

"You've never been alone. You've always had us. And he won't be alone. You love him. I love him, and Maggie always will too. And he'll have a child. We'll have a grandchild. We've always managed to survive everything, haven't we? Try to think of it this way. I'd rather have Jimmy gay than dead. Arla would feel that way, too, about Mark. So try to count your blessings! We have two children, we'll have a grandchild, and you're living in paradise. I'm worried about how to pay for a new cesspool and a new roof and new snow tires. At least you don't have those kinds of worries.

"I suffer for Maggie," she continued. "My poor darling child is in love with a man who can never love her the way Hal loved me or Maurice loved you. It's funny, Wendy, when we were girls there were lots of problems, but homosexuality wasn't one of them. It was just one of those things we never thought about. Well, I suppose it's not easy for him either. So you and I have to be strong. We've survived everything else. Somehow we'll get through this, too. Remember that awful song we used to sing at school?"

Suddenly silly, the two of them sang together, "Violate me in the violet time in the vilest way that you know. Desecrate, savage me, utterly ravage me, and to me no mercy show. To the best things in life I am utterly oblivious, so give me a man who is lewd and lascivious. Violate me in the violet time in the vilest way that you know." They laughed until they cried together.

"Do you think they're drunk?" Teddy asked.

"Not my mother. They're just being silly together."

Wendy took Sarah's hand. "Please move out here, Sarah. Bobby is leaving after the wedding, and Maggie will be alone in the gatehouse. She'll need you. And I need you. Your grandchild will need you. Why should you be isolated up there in the wilderness with those awful winters? Retire! If you don't have enough in your pension, I'll give you whatever you need."

"I don't know. Let me think about it." The two old friends sat there talking about the children, life's joys and disappointments, the past and the future. Looking at Sarah's sweet worn face Wendy remembered a George Eliot quotation she'd used in one of her books. "Friendship is the comfort, the inexpressible comfort of feeling safe with a person."

"Come out here, Sarah," she begged again. "Whatever we have to face will be easier if we face it together."

CHAPTER
Seventy-Three

Unable to sleep, Maggie awakened early the next morning and strolled down to the gate house. As she approached, she saw a young man, as handsome as Bobby, come out of the house and drive away. She walked up to the door and banged the brass knocker.

Bobby looked at her in surprise. "You're up early. Been here long?"

"Not long. Just before your friend drove away."

"He's not just my friend." Bobby spoke gently, not wanting to be cruel. "He's the man I love. He's wonderful. His name is Kurt Miller, and I want you to meet him some day."

"I don't want to meet him."

"You'll have to. He's going to be my best man at the wedding. I'll stay here until the wedding, Maggie. Then I'm going to leave and live with him. I can leave now, if you like."

She struggled against tears. "Maybe it will be different after you see the baby."

"I intend to see the baby all the time. But I won't live with you, Maggie. You just have to face that fact. You'll have to stay at Mom's until I go." She burst into tears, and he put his arms around her. "Oh, Bobby. Isn't this ridiculous. You're comforting me because I'm crying over you."

"I wish it could be different. I never wanted to hurt anyone. Have you had breakfast?" She shook her head. "Come on inside and I'll cook for you. I don't have any servants. Wendy sends one down each day to clean up for me, and I'm never home for dinner. But once you're here you'll have full-time help. A cook and a maid. There's plenty of room for a nursery. It's a great little cottage."

"Some cottage," Maggie laughed.

Every room in the house had stereo speakers. He put on the Stones and began to work. First he ground coffee and put it in the automatic drip, then he squeezed fresh orange juice, set out a dish of perfect raspberries, some milk, and a box of Life cereal. When everything was ready, he put it all on a tea cart that already held six bottles of assorted vitamins and wheeled it outside to the terrace. "You have to start to take a lot of vitamins. We want this kid to be Olympic material."

The mention of the baby set her off again. "Oh, Bobby," she looked at him in supplication, "if only things were different."

"But they're not. And they never will be. But I'll always take good care of you, and I'm really glad about the baby. Since I've been out here I've been meeting a lot of rootless older gay guys, and all of them would have liked to have kids."

"How will we explain things to our child?"

"I don't know. We'll worry about that when the time comes. Hey, want to go to Disneyland?"

"I'd love to. I'm the only person I know who's never been there. I've always wanted to go."

"Then let's just go and be friends again together the way we used to be. Let's pretend for today. I'm not gay and you're not pregnant and we're off to have some fun."

"You're on."

"We'll have to call them before we leave."

He handed her the phone. "You'd better talk."

"Coward!" He grinned at her.

"Good morning, Wendy. I'm at Bobby's. We're going to Disneyland."

"But darling, you can't. Not today. You have to be fitted for the gown. And my hairdresser is coming to see what to do with your hair. And the makeup man. I made a reservation for tonight at L'Ermitage. And you two need a license. And it can't be good for the baby to go on those awful rides. Please put my son on the phone."

"Mom," he said, looking like a big, overgrown kid about to be scolded. "We want to go and play."

She turned to Sarah. "They want to go to Disneyland. Honestly, they're so immature."

"Let them go. They'll have plenty of time to be mature."

"All right," she said in mock exasperation. "But be careful with that baby. Will you be back for dinner?"

"I don't think so. Don't fence us in. Maggie's never been there before, so we don't want to rush."

"No speeding. Remember the baby."

"For God's sake, Wendy. Stop acting like a Jewish mother. You're supposed to be sophisticated."

"I'm both, you little brat. And don't call me Wendy."

That day, Maggie was happy again. Disneyland enchanted her. They went on everything, from the Peter Pan ride to the Jungle Cruise and then back three times to the Pirates of the Deep. They went back twice to the Haunted House and sat through the Saloon Show twice, drinking Pepsi-Cola and eating potato chips. All day long they ate junk food; ice cream, candy, frankfurters, hamburgers, fried chicken, tamales. "This is your last fling," he said. "After this only good food. I don't want my kid to be born with rotten teeth."

"Kids aren't born with teeth, dopey."

And wherever they went Maggie could see the way women looked at him—young women, old women, waitresses and cashiers—and then looked at her in wonder, trying to figure out how she had snared such a god. They should only know the truth, she thought ironically, but she could not deny the feeling of pride she had in being on his arm.

That night they watched the parade down Main Street and then danced under the stars. She leaned her head against his chest, loving him so hard she felt as if her heart would break. And she prayed to some god, please let him love me and stay with me. Please don't let me lose him.

When they finally strolled to the car, hand in hand, it was hard to believe that the day's magic was at an end. "Could I stay with you tonight, Bobby?"

"Not tonight," he said. "Not any night. I told you that."

"Please," she begged.

"For God's sake, Maggie, don't torture me." They drove home without talking, the day's closeness lost. As they entered the gate, another car followed close behind and pulled off at Bobby's house. It was the car and driver she had seen leaving that morning.

CHAPTER
Seventy-Four

Charlotte was filled with rage after she heard about Maggie's wedding. She snapped at her employees, almost lost control with an important client, and yelled at Marshall and Kitty right through dinner.

"For heaven's sake," Kitty scolded back. "These are two of your best friends. Your sorority. Aren't you happy for them?"

"Yes and no! I would be happier for them if I were happier for myself. I've known them now for thirty-two years, and in all those years, I've been the only unlucky one. I was the first to stop smoking and I was the only one to get cancer."

"But not lung cancer, Mom."

"Shut up, Kitty, and let me finish."

"She's just trying to help," Marshall said.

"You shut up too. If I may continue, I was the only one to get cancer, and I was the only one with a junkie for a son, and now Teddy is living at Wendy's, and Sarah's strictly ordinary daughter is marrying the richest boy in the world, and where are you, Kitty? Apart from that lunatic yippee who was responsible for your being filled with buckshot, you haven't had a date for years."

"I have friends."

"Nobody we ever see. If you were seeing someone decent you wouldn't be afraid to bring him home. Every day the gallery is filled with rich and interesting men. Your problem is that you don't even try."

"Oh, Mom. Either they're gay or over fifty. Besides, what do you want me to do? Trip them?"

"Very funny. You might at least smile at them. And you might at least fix yourself up so you don't look like a leftover flower child. You're twenty-eight years old and you might as well be forty. Wear makeup! You're not living in that

445

commune any longer. Makeup is not one of the ten deadly sins. Makeup is not capitulation to the bourgeoisie. Find a man and get married. Give me the pleasure of a grandchild."

"Will you please face reality, Mom. I'm not very pretty."

"You don't try. Every girl who tries nowadays can be pretty. If Teddy could be made over, so can you. I want you to look pretty at the wedding. I pay you a good salary, and I don't charge you rent the way some parents would. But you put every penny in the bank. It's not necessary. Take some of it and buy yourself a decent dress. Get your hair fixed and go some place like the Makeup Center to learn how to use makeup. I lost two breasts, but you never see me without makeup. Your father was attracted to me because I looked so nice, and all I had was one dress. There will be two eligible men at the wedding. Stewart and Peter. Set your cap for one of them."

"Peter's a nerd and Stewart's sick."

"They're better than nothing. And Arla has never spent a nickel on them. She looks great because she spends so much money on herself. That's how she managed to snare Steve."

"Do you think she loves him?"

"Don't change the subject. I'm talking about you."

"All right, all right. We'll get back to that. But do you think she does."

"I suppose so. I think she loves owning him."

"Do you think he loves her?"

"I think he loves being supported. But let's get back to you. I just can't get over Maggie and Bobby. It's rags to riches. The way that Rockefeller boy married their Swedish maid."

Marshall threw down his paper. "I can't listen to any more of this," he said. "How can you be so illogical? Kitty couldn't have married Bobby. He's nine years younger than she is."

"Maybe she'd meet someone if she had her own apartment. She should be off on her own."

"Do you want your own apartment?" Marshall asked.

"If you would buy me one. I want to save my money."

"Out of the question," Charlotte said. "I'm doing quite

enough by having you on the payroll. I will not buy a twenty-eight-year-old girl an apartment. I left home with nothing and made my way in the world."

Kitty pushed back her unfinished dinner. "I'm going out."

"Where?"

"Just out."

"Do you want me to go with you?" Marshall asked. "I'd like to take a walk."

"Don't go with her. She should go to a singles' bar. Maybe that Maxwell's Plum."

"I hate singles' bars. I don't like to drink, I can't stand the smoke, and I can't stand making conversation with assholes."

"That's part of your problem, Kitty. You think you're smarter than anyone else. How do you know they're assholes if you don't talk to them." Grabbing her purse, Kitty stalked out. Charlotte was surely the most impossible woman in the world.

She headed west through the park. She knew that it was dangerous, but tonight under a golden August moon, it was filled with walkers, joggers, young lovers, old couples walking sedately together. I can't stand my mother, she thought. And I don't know what to do about Steve.

When she reached Central Park West, she walked three blocks downtown to Sixth-third Street, entered the lobby of the Mayflower Hotel, asked for Steve Smith's room, and took the elevator upstairs. He always used a phony name even though he said that Arla was too busy to check up on him and probably would never suspect anything anyway. He claimed that he didn't give a damn if she did suspect. He was fed up with the way she always put her work ahead of him, and he would never forgive her for letting Mr. Blackstone fire him. He was just biding his time. But he still used a phony name.

When Kitty knocked on the door, she found him in a towering rage. "I've been waiting for you half an hour. Where the fuck have you been?"

She tossed her coat on a chair and sat down on the side of the bed. "Oh, you know. The usual problems with my impossible mother."

"Well, hurry up." He reached for the buttons on her blouse. "I have to pick Arla up after her meeting tonight."

"I don't want to fuck, Steve. I want to talk to you."

"We can talk in bed."

"No. I always lose my sense with you in bed. We have to talk about marriage. I'm going crazy living at home. My mother never stops nagging about marriage. I've waited and waited. We have to tell Arla."

"You're out of your mind. We've been through all this a hundred times. I don't have money or a job. I cannot get a college teaching job, and there's nothing else I'm fit for. It was easy to get a job in the sixties, but everything's changed. There are approximately nine hundred applicants nowadays for every college English position, and I have nothing to give me an edge. I haven't written anything since those Irish lit articles, and that was a long, long time ago. I have no name or reputation."

"But, Steve, if we're together we don't need much money. Money isn't everything. The happiest days of my life were spent living in a commune. We didn't need things. We cared about the world and politics and each other. You and Arla have money and you're not happy. My folks have money and they're miserable together. Wendy is super rich but she mourns for Maurice. The only one of the four who's usually contented is Sarah who's the poorest."

He lit a joint. The mention of Sarah always made him uncomfortable. "I've been poor and I won't go back. I won't drive a broken down car again. I won't freeze all winter because I can't afford oil. I won't keep my books piled on the floor because I don't have bookcases. And I'm still paying that damned child support."

She cast about for other arguments. "You don't have to teach. We could open our own gallery somewhere. Maybe in L.A. Wendy said there's a lot of money there and not much good taste."

"How much money have you saved?"

"About ten thousand dollars."

He shrugged. "There's your answer. We simply have to wait until you have some more. Arla has plenty, but she doles it out to me."

He looked at his watch. "Be patient a little while longer. You have to trust me! You know I want to get out of this marriage. I want us to have kids, just as much as you do. I never see my son any more. My ex has turned him against me completely even though I've never missed one month's child support. Trust me! Be patient just a little longer. Before we fell in love, Kitty, I felt like Hamlet. 'How weary, stale, flat, and unprofitable / Seem to me all the uses of this world.' You've changed all of that. Let's go to bed. You know I love you."

She brightened. "You really mean it? You really love me?"

"Of course I do. Just put everything on hold until after Maggie's wedding. I promise you I'll act right after that."

"You really promise?"

"Yes, damn it. Now hurry up. You've wasted most of our time together. I have exactly one-half hour left."

They made love for ten minutes, he showered for ten, dressed for ten, and was out the door. "Leave the key on the dresser. I told them we wouldn't be staying the night. Don't forget that I love you."

"I'll try."

After he had gone she lay in bed trying to figure out a solution to the problem. Teddy! She would ask him if Wendy's foundation might stake her to a gallery on Rodeo Drive. She knew almost as much as Charlotte by now about buying and selling. She'd stock it with paintings and sculptures by established artists like Garcia, Rauschenberg, Stella, and Jasper Johns and new popular young ones like Robert Longo, Cindy Sherman, David Salle, and Julian Schnabel. Maybe Wendy would like to get rid of some of her paintings. She had enough in storage to start a gallery herself.

She grew increasingly optimistic as she stood under the shower, letting the water stream over her for a long time, feeling reborn, optimistic, and cleansed of the past. The more she thought about approaching Wendy, the more logical it seemed. There was just no purpose in her keeping all of those paintings in storage for so long. I'm going to escape, she exulted. I'm going to escape. I can't wait to see Steve at the wedding and tell him that at last I've found a way for us to be together.

And then suddenly her mood changed, and she was filled with the guilt that tormented her each time she left him. This was not some stranger's man she was taking away. It was Arla's, her Aunt Arla. But really, it wasn't her fault. Steve had been dissatisfied for a long time. If he hadn't found Kitty, he would have found someone else. The marriage was destroying him. It had sapped his energy and his initiative.

Charlotte was right about that. His position was that of a lapdog, and it was hurting him. But married to Kitty, to a wife he really loved, who looked up to him, he could build a family, begin a new career, and regain a feeling of pride and independence. And with his easy charm, he'd do very well in a gallery.

She could do that for him. She could dedicate her life to that. He would be her cause. When the time came, she'd go to Aunt Arla and beg for her forgiveness and her blessing. "You've had your life, Aunt Arla," she'd say. "You've had your children. Please let him go so that I can have my husband and children. Please let him go so that I can have my life."

How would Arla react? Maybe she'd be hurt at first but sooner or later she'd realize that it was for the best. After all, what point is there in holding onto a man who doesn't want you? Everything would work out all right. Arla would let him go, and they would live happily ever after. Feeling optimistic and renewed, Kitty left the hotel and walked home.

CHAPTER
Seventy-Five

"Wake up, my darling." Sarah bent and kissed her sleeping child. "Today's your wedding day, and the exercise man is here."

Sarah was already in her leotards. Maggie groaned sleepily. "I cannot believe that Wendy wants me to do exercises on the day of my wedding."

"She asked me to tell you that she has a very special surprise for you at breakfast. Now, please come."

Maggie looked up at her mother and grinned. "Hey. Looking good! I always thought you were an intellectual commie, but all this time what you really were was a jock. From picket line to body line in one generation."

Sarah laughed sheepishly. "I know it's kind of silly to be doing all this stretching and huffing and puffing. But Wendy says it staves off osteoporosis, and my poor mother had a bad enough hump at the end of her life to permanently scare me. And maybe if I keep my body in readiness, one of these days I'll meet Allard Lowenstein."

"He's a little young for you, isn't he?"

"Only about four years and happily married, but that's the kind of man I'd like. A fit successor to your father." Sarah's face clouded up. She was giving the bride away tonight, but Hal should have been there to do it.

"Please don't start, Mom. We both have to fight against depression today. I'll get out of bed only if you promise me not to be sad for even one minute. I wish Dad and Jimmy could be here just as much as you. No father, no brother, no grandparents, no relatives. As a matter of fact, not even a real husband."

Claude had sent a large check, but he was in Europe with his family and didn't feel like interrupting his vacation. "At least we have the sorority," Maggie said. "Do Charlotte and Arla know the truth about the wedding?"

"Not yet. That's why Wendy put them up at the Bel-Air instead of here. She didn't want to do any explaining."

"Especially if Bobby kisses the best man instead of me."

"Will you get up?"

The phone rang. Wendy was buzzing from the exercise room. "We're coming," Sarah said, and they ran to join her.

"Good morning, darling," Wendy said. She was warming up at the bar while waiting for them.

"If you start now," Sarah joked, "you'll look like Wendy when you're her age."

"Only Bobby looks like Wendy. Another month and I won't even look like me. I'm glad nothing shows yet."

"Good morning little bride," caroled Linwood, Wendy's trainer. Maggie rolled her eyes.

"To work, to work," he said, turning the stereo to a deafening level. "Now remember. Don't overeat tonight and easy on the champagne. Ready ladies? Stretch."

In a way, Sarah thought, I kind of like this. I've never had time for exercise. While I'm doing it it's torture. But afterward, I do feel good.

After an hour of sweating, the three of them dove into the pool, then into the Jacuzzi, and then, wrapped in thick bathrobes, they sat together on the terrace eating breakfast. "Take your vitamins," Wendy said.

"Honestly," Maggie laughed, loving her. "Strip away all those jet-set layers, that convent education, all those layers of money and sophistication, and what do we have? A Jewish mother with, oy vey, an Episcopal son."

"Stop talking. Take them."

"All right, you slave driver," Maggie teased. "What's the surprise?"

Wendy handed her a small gift box that had been sitting on the telephone table. "Something old," she said.

Maggie opened it. "A diamond bracelet. You're lending me this?"

"I'm giving it to you, darling."

"I'm eighteen years old. I'm still a kid. I can't wear a diamond bracelet. I'll lose it."

Now Sarah was all misty eyed, remembering the past. "She was not much older when she 'liberated' it and almost landed us in jail. And everything lay before us like a land of dreams."

"And all things seemed possible," Wendy added.

"This is *the* bracelet?"

Wendy nodded, as close to crying as Sarah.

"Honestly," Maggie said. "You two are really soppy. Get all of the crying out of your systems now because if I see you crying at the wedding I'll cry too and ruin that expensive makeup job you're forcing on me this afternoon."

Wendy wiped her eyes. "I always thought I'd have a daughter to give the bracelet to. Now you're my daughter."

"When the marriage breaks up, I'll give it back to you."

"Of course you won't. You'll pass it on to your daughter or daughter-in-law. Half of it really belongs to your mother, anyway."

"OK. Your Mexican adventure will become a family legend."

Bobby, with his friend Kurt in tow, came walking up while they were having breakfast. Wendy, like Maggie, had determined to make the best of the situation. She smiled graciously.

"I didn't want to wait until tonight to meet all of you," Kurt said shyly. "Bobby says you're really wonderful. I hope you'll let me be an uncle to the baby."

"An uncle," Maggie's voice cracked, "that's a euphemism if I ever heard one. But what else can I do? We love Bobby and Bobby loves you. So I guess we're all going to be one large happy family. But no spoiling the kid with presents. Hear? I don't want a rich, spoiled Bel-Air kid. My kid is going to be one of the proletariat, out of respect for my parents."

All of them rocked with good, healthy laughter. "You're quite a girl," Kurt said, admiration in his voice.

"I wish I didn't have to be," she answered quietly. "But I'm my mother's daughter."

Sarah looked at the four of them and instantly made her decision. Why am I going home, she asked herself? My work isn't enough. This is where I belong now. I want to watch over my darling child, be here when my grandchild is born.

"Wendy gave you the bracelet, darling," she said. "I'm giving you me. I'll move out here within the month."

"This calls for champagne," Wendy exulted.

"Not this early in the morning," Sarah groaned.

"Champagne," Maggie echoed, kissing her mother.

CHAPTER
Seventy-Six

Charlotte had her face lifted before Maggie's wedding. She had never looked better. She wore a royal blue Halston gown, new gold jewelry designed by Paloma Picasso, and not one red hair was out of place. There were no signs at all of her operations, and just before the wedding her doctor had given her a complete bill of health.

And for once, Kitty had listened to her and also looked nice. She was wearing her contact lenses, instead of her awful thick glasses, and she'd gone to Charlotte's hairdresser and to the Makeup Center. She'd even let Charlotte shop with her for a dress.

"You look wonderful," Charlotte told her with pride.

"I think my whole life is going to change after this wedding," Kitty said.

Charlotte put her arm around her, grateful that at last Kitty was acting normal. It helped to lessen her terrible jealousy of Maggie.

"You look gorgeous, sis," Teddy said, sitting down beside them. "So do you, Mom. Nobody would ever guess that you'd been sick."

Teddy also was making her happy. He sat there beside Kitty, improbably dressed in a magnificent white dinner jacket and a pleated silk shirt, as well groomed and careful of his appearance now as he had been drugged and slovenly before, looking more like Marshall each year. Wendy was completely satisfied with the way he handled her foundation. He traveled often between Los Angeles and New York, moving easily among millionaires whom she only knew as clients.

Marshall sat beside her looking trim in his dinner jacket, and she slipped her hand through his arm, grateful he had come back to her from Wendy. How would she ever have managed without him? He was indispensable at home and at the gallery. It was hard to believe that he was sixty-five years old.

Wendy, with all of her beauty and money and social acclaim had lost him to her and was still without a husband. But if she minded losing Marshall, she certainly had never given any evidence of it. She still had that nutty obsession with black men. Her escort for the wedding was that low-class black rock star Hudson Henry, who may have sold a million records but was totally unattractive. He certainly lacked Maurice's dignity, and she didn't even like his raucous music.

Charlotte had come to the wedding thinking that she would suffer throughout from jealousy, but instead, looking at her little family, she felt an unfamiliar sense of gratitude and pride. Kitty kept turning and looking around the room. "What are you looking for?" Charlotte asked.

"I wonder where Aunt Arla is. I asked at the desk. They still haven't checked in."

"They'll be here," Charlotte said. "We've always been together for big occasions." She looked at Kitty curiously. Perhaps she had changed her mind about Stewart or Peter. Peter, of course, would be the better choice. But either one was better than no one. And if Teddy could straighten out, maybe Stewart could also.

Then Kitty saw Arla, Stewart, and Peter enter the room. Arla looked elegant in a long blue silk dress and magnificent pearls. But somehow even at this distance Kitty could see that she was moving strangely, leaning on the arms of her sons. What could be wrong? And where was Steve?

Waves of nausea swept through Kitty, and she began to perspire profusely. Something awful must have happened to Steve. Maybe he'd had a heart attack on the plane? Maybe he hadn't even come to California. But that could not be possible. She'd spoken to him just before leaving, and he assured her that everything was all right.

He must be in a hospital somewhere, badly injured or dead. But he couldn't be dead, could he? Arla wouldn't show up if he had died. Perhaps he was only injured. Something minor. She tried to send him a telepathic message, wherever he was. Don't worry, Steve darling, I'll take care of you. I'll nurse you back to health. I'll take care of you for the rest of your life even if you've been crippled. She took three Valiums from her purse and managed to force them down without water.

And then the procession began. It was an all-white wedding. The groom and best man wore white, and Wendy and Sarah wore white. The magnificent floral lily centerpieces on the tables were white.

The first person down the aisle was Bobby's best man. He was almost as handsome as Bobby. Then after a dramatic pause, Wendy came down the aisle with Bobby. Charlotte carefully examined Wendy's face. Not a line on it. She must have had a lift too, but she never mentioned it. And her lift is even better than mine, she thought.

How lovely little Maggie looked. It was a perfect, fairy-tale wedding. The first girl of the second generation to get married. Wendy and Sarah cried, and Charlotte cried watching them. Kitty, too, sat there crying.

Poor Kitty! She was ten years older than Maggie. She should have been the first married. Marshall reached across Charlotte to pat Kitty's hand. "Your turn is next. We'll make you a beautiful wedding, too." Kitty gave him a strained smile, then popped another Valium into her mouth. This must be very hard for her, Charlotte realized for the first time.

Kitty felt as if she were going out of her mind. What had happened to Steve? The wedding seemed interminable. As soon as it had ended, she pushed her way through the guests who were slowly filing out, and raced to where Arla was standing with Stewart and Peter.

"Hi, Kitty," Stewart said. "You're turning into quite a dish. I've never seen you look so gorgeous."

She had to be subtle. "How's the disco going?"

"Ahh. You know the Feds. IRS is always trying to pin something on us. But we're doing good."

Peter was leading Arla out of the room. "What's wrong with your mother?"

"She's drunk as a skunk."

"Arla drunk? I've never seen her drunk before."

"The son-of-a-bitch has flown the coop."

"What are you talking about?"

"Steve. That bastard's gone."

Joy shot through her, and she stood up straight and proud. So he had finally made the break. Now they would be together for always.

"Gone?" She hid her emotion.

"Ran off with another woman."

The room turned black and she struggled not to faint. Hang on, she told herself, Hang on. "Another woman?"

"Yeah. Mr. Blackstone's daughter. You know. Arla's boss. He's on the gravy train this time. Apparently that relationship has been going on for some time right under Arla's nose, but she hoped it would blow over if she didn't rein him in. She really liked the bastard, but in my opinion she's a thousand times better off without him."

Kitty slumped against Stewart, "Hey, Kitty. Are you all right?"

She struggled for control.

"Bad stomach cramps. Listen, Stewart, could you tell my folks that I've gone upstairs to lie down for a while?"

She fled before he could answer. When she got to her room, she locked the front door and unlocked the connecting door to Teddy's room. She had asked him to stay at the hotel so that she could discuss the art gallery plan with him. What a joke! How humiliating. What a fool she'd been to let Steve lead her on that way. She shook with disgust.

She ran around the room frantically trying to figure out how to kill herself. Not by hanging! The lighting fixtures were built in and the closet racks were too low. Too bad she hadn't asked Stewart for drugs. Even if she took her entire supply of Valiums that wouldn't do it. But she had to hurry.

She quickly called room service and ordered a bottle of

scotch. That would be the best because she hated the taste. While she was waiting for it to come, she downed her entire vial of Valium. After the scotch was delivered, she also downed that, glass after glass, while watching television. Fighting in Beirut and Angola, New York City going broke, and a U.S. evacuation flight of Vietnamese orphans had crashed on takeoff in Saigon, killing 155 aboard. What a world! She wouldn't be leaving much.

Struggling to control her nausea, she finished off the scotch, took a plastic bag off a blouse in her suitcase, put it over her head, and with her last strength fastened it tightly around her neck with a belt. In a minute, she began to vomit. She fell to the floor still vomiting.

"Kitty said to tell you she was going upstairs to lie down for a few minutes," Stewart said, after making his way to Charlotte. "Nothing serious. Stomach cramps. She'll be back soon."

"Come on, Charlotte," Wendy said. "We're going to get a picture of the four of us. Semper fidelis."

Despite everything, she was happy. The wedding was beautiful, the weather was good, and she would not let herself be depressed about a future that might never happen. Paula had died because of a baby. This baby and its mother and father would live and thrive, either together or apart. That was all that mattered. To live!

"Perhaps I should go and see how Kitty is?" Charlotte said to Marshall.

"Will you leave that girl alone! She's twenty-eight years old and if she wants to lie down for a few minutes, that's her right. She's an adult. Perhaps she's upset because she isn't married. Leave her alone."

"All right," Charlotte said. There really was nothing to worry about. Kitty had looked better than ever tonight. She was turning into a normal young woman. She hurried to join her friends for the group portrait.

CHAPTER
Seventy-Seven

Before dinner was served, Maggie came over to Sarah leading a man by the hand. He was tall, reedlike, about sixty-five, but still handsome with a shock of silky white hair and a warm boyish smile. "This is my wonderful mother," she told him. "Mom, meet my favorite professor. Win Allgood."

"How do you do," he said in that unmistakable, famous radio voice that she instantly remembered. "Congratulations. They're two fine kids."

Sarah looked at him with awe. "Win Allgood! I just can't believe it. You were always one of my heroes. My husband's too."

His fame, as the father of radio documentary, had been legendary. All during World War II, right through the blitz, with bombs exploding over his head, he had continued to broadcast from London, bringing news, hope, and inspiration to his listeners. She had not even known that he was still alive.

But she remembered listening to his broadcasts. They had unfailingly expressed the liberal ideals of the New Deal and single-handedly elected Roosevelt to a third term. He was universally admired, not only as a great writer and speaker, but as a man who employed his skills to fight for freedom and political justice. And the marvelous voice that had reached across the airwaves in World War II to inspire the allies was unchanged. Meeting an icon made her feel humble.

"I thought you two old lefties would have a lot in common," Maggie laughed.

"Hold still for a moment," Sarah said, putting her arms around her. "Let me look at you. Are you all right?"

"I'm fine, Mother, darling. There's nothing like champagne."

With a kiss, Maggie danced off, and Sarah turned to Win. They were immediately at ease with each other. His wife had recently died from Alzheimer's disease, and it had almost destroyed him, too. "But I never stopped writing and teaching, that's how I got through."

Meeting him was like coming home. For the first time that night her smiles were genuine, for during the ceremony she had hidden her sadness—sadness that it could not have been a true fairy tale for Maggie; sadness that Hal, Jimmy, and her mother could not be there; and sadness and concern for Maggie's future life without a husband.

But for the moment, she was spellbound, losing herself in memories as he spoke about the past, about the Hollywood Blacklist, about all of the good people he'd known: the Rosenbergs, Alger Hiss, John Howard Lawson, Dalton Trumbo, Lillian Hellman, Dorothy Parker, Clifford Odets. He spoke about the radio broadcasts of Paul Robeson and of friends like Jim Lardner, who had died in Spain with the Lincoln Brigade. His heroes were her heroes. He reminded her that one had to look at every moment in relation to history, and that the personal was always played out against the panorama of the world.

He brought back her era, her time, the frame of reference within which she and Hal had lived, but he brought it back with laughter, not sorrow. He reminded her of when the House Un-American Activities Committee came to Hollywood and dubbed Shirley Temple a Communist. Later, it also accused Helen Keller of the same thing. Sarah was the perfect audience for his anecdotes. Names, words, memories bubbled up. She again had found a friend with whom to discuss politics.

Before dessert was served, they took a walk outside under the velvet, moonlit night. And she, who was usually so reticent, told him about Maggie and Bobby. It was the first time since Hal had died that she'd found a man to whom she could talk as easily as to her women friends.

"I feel so bad that things haven't gone right for Maggie. As if there were something more that I should have done."

His voice was gentle and sympathetic. "You don't control the universe. You can't make everything right. Nobody can!

It seems to me that you're doing as much as anyone could do. You've given up your job to be with her. That's quite a sacrifice."

"At first I was afraid it would be. I was terrified at the very thought of retirement, as if I'd lose my identity. I've always worked, and whenever people asked me, What do you do? I felt proud that I could tell them I'm a professor, I'm a union worker, I'm a union president. What I did was what I was. I wondered, until the moment I actually handed in my resignation, how I could go from all of that professional pride to answering the question with the statement, I'm a person, I'm a mother, and I'm a grandmother.

"And then all of a sudden I began to feel good about it. For the first time, a tremendous burden of responsibility had been lifted from my shoulders. And I began to think, I am what I am. There's nothing wrong with that! I don't have to impress anyone with what I do. And then I got all excited about a new beginning. I suddenly realized that this would be a whole new life, and I was thrilled about it.

"Remember that line from Auntie Mame? 'Life's a banquet and most poor sons of bitches are starving to death!' In a way, that's the way it's been with me. Life hasn't been a banquet for me. It's been meat and potatoes without the frills. Now, after a lifetime of meat and potatoes, I'm ready for the banquet.

"I'm fifty-five years old," she continued, "and all I know of the world is what I've learned from books. The only foreign country I've ever visited was Mexico, and that was thirty-five years ago. I want to go to Spain where my husband fought and my brother died. I want to go to Israel to see my son's grave."

"I've seen a lot," he said, "but never enough. I've never seen the Great Wall of China, or the Taj Mahal by moonlight, or the castles of the Rhone Valley."

"I need a traveling companion," she said taking his hand.

They stopped in the moonlight, and he looked down at her. "I need a life companion," he said.

They stood there looking at each other. You don't find a friend, she thought. You recognize one.

CHAPTER
Seventy-Eight

Teddy looked at his watch. Kitty was missing dinner and all of the dancing. He'd better go and check on her. He walked along the path to the one-story two-bedroom bungalow they were sharing and knocked on her door. When she didn't answer, he opened his door and walked over to the connecting one. It was unlocked.

In disbelief and horror, he looked inside. Kitty's body lay sprawled on the floor, her head still in the plastic bag, her features obscured by a foam of vomit. A violent earthquake rocked his body, and he fell to his knees, frantically ripping the bag apart despite his certainty that it was too late. "Oh, Kitty," he wept. "Oh, Kitty."

Once he'd seen a friend o.d. on drugs and been unable to do anything to deal with the pain except to take a fix. But that was in another life, and now he had to be strong. He had to be strong for her. For all of them! And he had to hurry so that nobody would know what had happened. She'd left no note, and he didn't know why she'd done this, but he wouldn't have her mocked and reviled in death. He wanted accidental death, not suicide, and he wouldn't want his parents to blame themselves.

Shaking violently, he forced himself into action. He gently bathed her head, her face, her neck. Then he lifted her poor body and placed it on the bed and scrubbed the carpet. It took over an hour before all traces of the vomit had been removed. Then he took the empty Valium vial and scotch bottle and put them in the basket with the plastic bag. No! That wouldn't do. There would be a record of the delivery of the scotch. They'd look for the bottle. He took it out of the bag and tossed it beside the bed, trying to make it look as if it had fallen from her hand. They would do an autopsy, of course. But all they would find would be a combination of alcohol and Valium. Everyone would testify that she'd looked happier and prettier tonight than ever before. The ruling would be that death was accidental. That would be his final gift to her.

He left the room to dispose of the evidence, then returned to mourn again. "Oh, Kitty! Why did you do it? Everything was going so well. Why didn't you tell me about it instead?"

The only two people he had ever really loved were Kitty and Wendy. He needed Wendy now, but he held back from getting her. Imperfect as the wedding was, it still was a celebration of sorts. He would not spoil this evening for her.

He sat there grieving and remembering. Oh, Kitty, my beloved sister. All through his terrible childhood she had been his one friend, always standing up for him against Charlotte, always loyal, always fighting against her favored status. That was how she'd developed her fierce insistence on justice. By standing at his side.

She'd fought, yelled, protested, been beaten and shot, and all to no avail. Kitty, the fighter who'd survived being filled with buckshot while protesting against the Vietnam War, had died so uselessly and so ignominiously that it almost made a mockery of her life. And he'd never know why.

He made a final check, then nerved himself to go outside and act as if all were normal. He had to be strong for his family. Covering Kitty's body with a blanket, he locked the door between their rooms. He could hold off the discovery until the next morning. Give his parents one more night of peace!

He returned to the ballroom and told Marshall, "Kitty's gone to sleep. I'm going to split, too. I'll stay at Wendy's tonight instead of staying at the hotel. I have some work to finish. I'll be here in the morning to have breakfast with you." He could not have sounded more matter of fact.

Like an automaton, he drove to Wendy's house and went upstairs to the guest room he used when he was there. He waited until he heard them all come in, heard Sarah and Maggie say good night, heard Wendy go to her room. Immediately after, he knocked softly on her door, and the maid, who was helping her undress, opened it.

His agitation was evident. "What is it?" she asked in alarm.

"I have to speak to you alone."

She motioned the maid to go. "What is it?" she repeated.

He locked the door, turned to speak, and fainted, collapsing to the floor. A few seconds later he felt Wendy lifting his head and holding a glass of brandy to his lips. He sat up, buried his head in his hands, and wept.

"What is it, Teddy?" she asked, shaking in alarm. "Are you in trouble? Are you on drugs again?"

"That would be better," he sobbed, stammering out his story.

"Kitty dead?" Her horror matched his own. "Oh, my God. Your poor parents." They threw their arms around each other and wept together.

"Why?" she asked.

"We'll never know. Maybe seeing Maggie married at eighteen depressed her. Maybe she thought that she would never be a bride. Maybe she thought that she was looking at perfection that she could never match."

"What a terrible irony that would be, if she killed herself over the wedding." My God, she thought. Pretty little Maggie going to bed alone on her wedding night and Kitty killing herself. . . .

He began to weep again with shuddering sobs that convulsed his body.

"Come," she said, "you shouldn't be alone. You can stay with me for awhile. Just try to fall asleep."

She lay beside him, holding him in her arms, comforting him with her presence, until he fell asleep. Who could know better than she, the horror of a sibling's suicide? At least she'd had the cold comfort of knowing why.

And sometime in the night, deep in a dream, desperate for solace, they turned to each other and became lovers.

* * *

Charlotte was plunged into a nightmare of guilt. "Is it possible, do you think, Marshall, that Kitty committed suicide? My father committed suicide," she wept. "My mother drove him to it. Was this really an accident or did she take the Valium and scotch together because I kept nagging about her marriage?"

Marshall held her in his arms, and they grieved together. "Of course not, dear. It had nothing to do with you. She looked so pretty, so happy, so optimistic sitting beside you at the wedding. I'd never seen her look better. Try to find some comfort in that. She was feeling happy. It was an accident."

After the funeral, Marshall and Charlotte returned to New York and threw themselves into work to forget, but their hearts were broken. They would never be the same. The apartment was haunted by memories of Kitty. The gallery was haunted by memories of Kitty. New York was haunted by memories of Kitty. Finally, they gave up, sold everything, and opened a smaller gallery in Los Angeles.

During the following months, Wendy's house became the center for them all, much as Charlotte's house had been in East Hampton. They spent weekends there together, swimming, playing tennis, playing Scrabble: Sarah, Maggie and Win; Charlotte and Marshall; and Teddy. Arla stayed there on her frequent business trips.

"It's the first time," Charlotte said to Sarah, "that Wendy's ever been without a man. And yet she seems perfectly happy. I suppose she's had enough men to last a lifetime. And she's all involved with Maggie. Did you ever see such a layette? I guess she's due any day now."

Sarah opened her mouth, wanting to be honest about Teddy and Wendy, but reluctant to disturb her fragile state. But she would have to know soon. With Wendy's gift for publicity, it was only a matter of time before everyone knew. Sarah didn't want to keep the truth from Charlotte but this was up to Wendy and Teddy. She could not say anything until they did.

"Why is Maggie living alone?" Charlotte asked Sarah one day. "Bobby comes and goes with that best man of his, and they all seem to be on good terms, but he's living away. Do you know why?"

Sarah told her. That secret was hers to tell. Charlotte was

shocked. "Gay! You could never tell from looking at him. That poor girl. How can she act so happy?"

"She is happy. She's accepted the situation, and she looks on the best side of it. She's surrounded by people who love her and will love the baby. She'll always have plenty of money. And after the baby she intends to go back to school. When she's ready, she'll find another husband. I'm not concerned."

When Charlotte told Marshall, he was as surprised as she. "There seem to be a lot of gay men surfacing nowadays," he mused. "When I was young, I never knew a one. Perhaps they were all in hiding."

"Thank God Teddy's normal."

"Yes," he said. "Thank God." Teddy was unfailingly solicitous to them, taking them out to dinner, including them in parties, playing chess and tennis with Marshall, and relating to Charlotte without hostility.

On the night that Maggie delivered twins they were all at the hospital. Driving home afterward, Charlotte clung to Teddy's arm and wept. "I'm happy for them, of course, but I want the same for us. I hope that you'll get married soon. Our family is so small. We need grandchildren."

He looked at them in perplexity, not wanting to upset them but knowing they had to know sometime, so he might as well get it over with. Why let them go on hoping in vain?

Besides, Wendy would soon be going out on a new book tour, and she wanted him at her side and wanted to be able to say freely that he was her lover if she were asked.

"I'll probably never give you grandchildren."

"Why not? You're only thirty-two."

It had to be said. "Because I'm living with Wendy."

"What does that have to do with anything? You could still work for her if you were married. It's like having an office there, isn't it?"

"No, it isn't."

Charlotte looked at him in confusion. It couldn't be possible. "Do you mean what I think you mean?"

"Yes."

"My God! Everyone has lied to me. Even Sarah! All this time that we've been sitting there together, and I've been wondering why she didn't have a man, you and she were. ... It's awful! How long has it been going on?"

"Ever since Kitty died."

"And why didn't anybody tell me?"

"Because they knew how you'd behave. Nobody wanted to set you off."

"That does it," she screamed, with a flash of her old fire. "After everything that I've been through it's just too much. That slut stole my husband and my son, and now because of her I'll never have grandchildren. She has two grandchildren, but she's depriving me of mine. I don't want to see either one of you ever again."

Marshall took her by the shoulders and shook her. "That's quite enough," he exploded. "I won't let you drive Teddy away. Are you crazy? He's all we have. For God's sake, hasn't everybody suffered enough? Hasn't he? Look at him! He's happy and healthy and successful. Don't you try to take that away from him. Damn it, wish him well. Rejoice for him! Let him have whatever joy and pleasure he can find in life. God knows it's in short enough supply."

Teddy disengaged Marshall's hands. "Calm down, Dad. It's all right."

Marshall put his shaking arms around his son's sturdy shoulders. "It better be. I want you to be happy. I want us all to be happy. Nothing else matters. I never want to hear another word about this, Charlotte. The hell with propriety. The hell with jealousy. We all need love. And all of us need each other. I won't let you drive him away."

Teddy turned and looked at Charlotte. Then he held out his arms and moved forward to her in kindness and compassion.

Maggie named the twins Paula and Edita. "I decided that I really didn't like the names like Dawn or Fawn," she told Wendy.

Wendy kissed her tenderly. "Thank you. It's as if my mother and sister didn't die. They were waiting to be reborn in your babies."

"Wow!" Maggie teased her. "Heavy! I thought you were the ultimate sophisticate. Don't tell me you believe in reincarnation."

"Let her alone," Sarah scolded. "As you get older you have to start to believe in something more than yourself and more than the moment."

CHAPTER
Seventy-Nine

Arla was speaking at the Frankfurt Book Fair. She was proud, knowledgeable, confident, filled with the elixir of life. Wearing a red wool suit by Adolpho and makeup that skillfully accentuated her angular cheekbones and regal nose, she had never looked better. Her speech dealt primarily with Russia's refusal to pay royalties.

How wonderful it was to be a successful career woman. It seemed to her that even if she'd been happily married, it never would have been enough for her. This was all she needed now and for the rest of her life. Power! Respect! Admiration! There was none of the anguish or stickiness of personal relationships. No orgasm had ever given her the joy that this wave of applause did. She was perfectly happy until she walked off the platform. An usher was waiting to tell her that Peter was on the phone. She hurried to pick it up.

"Better come home right away, Mom. The shit's finally hit the fan. Stewart's been indicted, and they've set bail at two hundred and fifty thousand dollars."

Her first reaction, which she quickly suppressed, was one of annoyance. This was intruding on her work. "For income tax evasion?"

"Yes. But that's not all. They've got him for child pornography."

"Child pornography? I don't understand. What exactly is his involvement?"

"Publishing magazines with explicit pictures of adults having sex with children."

"How sick! Did you call your father?"

"Yes, I did. I called him first. After all, he's in New

York. He screamed at me. 'It's not my problem. Stewart doesn't work with me any more. Since your mother's such a howling success, let her handle it.'"

"I suppose it's just as well. He can't do Stewart any good. You have my power of attorney. Sell any stocks necessary to make bail. I'll get the first plane out."

Oh, damn! She didn't want to leave. It was really incredible. When the children were little, everything to do with them had been her responsibility and in that regard, nothing had changed. It made her furious. She wanted to be off the hook.

She reached New York in time for the shock of the late evening headlines: "Noted Disco Owner Indicted for Pornography" and "Publisher's Son Indicted for Pornography."

The mayor was quoted as saying: "We'll throw the book at him. This kind of scum should be put away for a hundred years."

She wept in the cab. This was her son they were writing about, her poor abused son who had almost been killed by a car when he was little, had been beaten for years by her sadistic husband, and was now being pilloried in the press. He had never been an upright citizen like Peter, and his cultivation of that demonic appearance was a bit theatrical, but she'd never thought he would hurt anyone.

But child pornography? How could he do something so awful? How serious a crime *was* pornography? Every newsstand in the city had racks of pornographic magazines. It was a billion-dollar industry. So how could it be illegal? And what was the punishment? They'd put Ralph Ginzburg in jail for a year for his magazine *Eros*. She'd read his pathetic letters from jail. Could they do that to Stewart? She had the normal middle-class horror of jail. When she thought about it, she visualized something on the order of Piñero's play *Short Eyes*: poor, weak, effete Stewart being gang-raped in the shower room.

Everything was so damned unpredictable. Just when life seemed to be going along fine, something came at you out of left field. Like Steve! Everything had been going fine when he took off without even the courtesy of a conversation. She hadn't even known where he was until Mr.

Blackstone had called to give her the bad news. At first she'd been shocked; she'd felt abandoned. But afterward, she'd realized that it had been for the best. Like most men, he was more trouble than he was worth.

Steve had called her just before this present trip and begged her to take him back. His affair with Amy Blackstone was over. "That's the problem with these kids," he'd complained. "No sense of commitment." She'd laughed. He'd always made her laugh. He was so outrageous, had no shame.

"So can I come back?"

"Of course not, Steve."

"Why not? I just needed a break. I promise that I'll never look at another woman."

"It's a matter of total indifference to me if you do. You come under the heading, Steve, of Nonessential Nonsense. I don't have time for anything nonessential, and I certainly don't have time for nonsense."

"Don't you need an escort any longer?"

"No."

"Can we still be friends?"

"No."

"Will you at least send me a check? I'm unemployed."

She hung up on him. To send any communication would perpetuate involvement. She had sworn to herself after her divorce from Lenny to remain uninvolved with men, but she'd forgotten her resolve and suffered because of it. She would not let it happen again.

Stewart was waiting at her apartment, twisting his sensual lips in annoyance. "Why did I have to come here? I'm due at the disco."

What an ungrateful little bastard. "I paid your bail. I want to know the facts. Are you really involved in such evil?"

"Evil!" He let out a snort of laughter. "You've got to be kidding. The whole world is evil."

"Just what do you mean by that?"

"Just what I said. The whole Vietnam War is evil. Did you see the pictures of children being napalmed, or gooks being tossed out of helicopters? Our government wasted an entire peasant country, and the majority of Americans supported that war. That's evil! They killed kids at Kent State, and nice ordinary church-going people were glad. That's evil. The whole fucking world is evil. So what's evil about what I do? Nobody ever got killed. Nobody ever got hurt. A few kids posed for a few pictures, and they were well paid for that. So what's so evil?"

"You exploited children for money."

"Everybody exploits children. They sell them crap to rot their teeth, teach them nothing in school, encourage them to smoke, and buy records and pet rocks."

She sat there stony-faced. "Your arguments are ridiculous. Pornography is abnormal. People involved in pornography are abnormal."

"Pornography isn't abnormal. Pornography is normal. Censorship is abnormal. Repression is abnormal. Don't tell me that you and your boy-husband never tried anything but the missionary position. Most married couples are bored to death with fucking each other. That's one of the biggest markets for pornography. You'd be surprised at all the nice, 'normal' people who need porno to turn on to their boring mates. People need kinky sex to save themselves from boredom.

"Picking on pornography is just a conspiracy by the establishment to distract us from the fact that they keep building missiles to blow up the world and are causing an epidemic of cancer that's like the bubonic plague.

"*That's* evil. And you're having a shit fit because a few little girls are showing their hairless twats? If I weren't producing it, someone else would. I'm going to plead the first amendment, and I'm going to get off, and I'm going to go right on doing what I've been doing. This is supposed to be a free society. I'm not ashamed, and I have certain rights."

"You don't see that what you've done is wrong?"

"Why is it any more wrong than your publishing books about actresses who have been poked by everything in pants in Hollywood? The only difference between us is that you're a hypocrite."

She stood up and felt so tired that she could feel her jaw

sagging. "I'm going to say good-bye to you, Stewart. I'll try to help you financially as much as possible, but I don't want to see you any more. I don't like what you stand for. Maybe the world is evil, but my son doesn't have to be. I may not be political like Sarah, but I do have certain beliefs, and one of them is that we have some responsibility to uphold the dignity of human life. If every individual refused to let evil loose in society, evil would end. And there can never be any excuse for perverting innocent children. I have nothing more to say to you until you understand that you have done wrong."

She turned her back to him, went into her bedroom, and closed the door. She did not attend his trial or hear the judge sentence him to one year in prison. Later his sentence was overturned on appeal.

CHAPTER
Eighty

Sarah and Win were getting married at Wendy's home. It was a beautiful day, heady with the fragrance of freshly cut grass. Everyone was there. Wendy and Teddy, Marshall and Charlotte, Maggie and the one-year-old twins Bobby and Kurt, Arla, Peter, and his new wife, Katy. Servants circulated with caviar and champagne while they waited for the ceremony to begin.

Wonderful fragrances drifted through the air: eucalyptus, pikake, plumeria, and expensive perfume. Well-dressed, healthy people laughed and talked and waited for the ceremony.

In the background, Peter Duchin's band played the songs of their youth, romantic music that they had danced to at the Temple Emanu-El USO; "Skylark," "Tangerine," "Sleepy Lagoon," "Moonlight Serenade."

The four old friends sat in Wendy's room sipping champagne, waiting to begin the ceremony. They were all dressed in chiffon dresses with large hats. Sarah's in light blue, and the others in soft pink. "We look perfect for a lawn wedding," Wendy said.

"I'm happy for you," Charlotte said, meaning it.

Sarah looked at her friends with love. The things they'd lived through. The things they'd known. So many, many deaths. The normal ones of their parents and then the others. Her brother, husband, son. Arla's son. Charlotte's brother and daughter. Wendy's sister and Maurice.

Here they were, four middle-class women, living in the most secure country in the world, none of them ever knowing real poverty or hunger, and even so it seemed as if they had not escaped any of the plagues of living: cancer, homosexuality, suicide, terrorism, drug addiction, wife abuse, pornography, political injustice, and the execution of the Rosenbergs.

They'd lived through so many wars, from the Spanish Civil War through World War II, the Korean War and the war in Vietnam. Israel had lived through four wars, and one of them had killed her Jimmy.

Ah, the things they'd seen and felt and wept over. And yet, they'd held on. To life and to each other. So many times in their lives they could have moved away from each other, but they held on. That was really all there ever was at the end. Holding on!

And what a valiant group they were. Arla had risen from abused wife to respected publisher. Wendy had escaped from the apathy of too much money and sadness and loss to become a world-famous novelist. Charlotte had survived cancer and single-handedly created a market for new modern art. And Sarah and Win, hand in hand, were fighting the good fight to ban the bomb, and for their honeymoon they were going to Israel and Spain.

Just four normal, middle-class Americans. Four women who had found each other and formed a sorority. Most sororities are based on a need to belong, Sarah thought. But we were a band of outsiders, and our sorority was based on love.

Sarah looked at her friends, and they seemed ringed in light. How beautiful they were! Her friends! Erect, strong, unbowed. In this room, suffused with sunlight and the smell of gardenias and plumeria, she could feel her soul expand and her senses soar, and she wanted to hold them all against her and tell them how she loved them. We are all survivors, she thought. We are all victorious. They'd held on, they'd come through, and she was proud to be one of them.

She held aloft her glass. "To our sorority," she said. "And to tomorrow."

Maggie, who was giving the bride away, knocked at the door and asked, "Ready, Mom?"

"Ready, darling."

And then, leaning on her daughter's arm, surrounded by her friends, all of them most improbable survivors, Sarah walked forward to a new beginning. And her friends walked beside her.